Keeping You

KEEPING YOU

by
Mollie Blake

Live For Now Publishing

© Mollie Blake 2014

Keeping You, by Mollie Blake

Published 2014
Live For Now Publishing
c/o SRA Books
Minerva Mill Innovation Centre
Station Road
Alcester
Warwickshire
B49 5ET
United Kingdom

All rights reserved. Apart from limited use for private study, teaching, research, criticism or review, no part of this publication may be reproduced, stored or transmitted without the prior permission in writing of the copyright owner and publisher of this book.

ISBN 978-0-9927200-2-5

Printed in the UK by TJ International Ltd, Padstow, Cornwall

Acknowledgements

I would like to thank Bob and Diane for all their help and encouragement during the writing of this book. Your support carried me through the whole exciting, fun process.

Thanks also to the Super Six – Caroline, Debs, Diane, Jill, Marie and Una – you guys gave me the confidence to complete *Keeping You*.

Importantly, thanks to all my family and friends who put up with my obsession with my characters, my plot and my desire to make people feel good while losing themselves in my book.

Thanks also to Sarah Williams, Sue Richardson and Katie Read for sharing my enthusiasm, supporting my dream to write a book to be read by lovers of erotic romance with a bit of thriller thrown in, and keeping my feet on the ground.

Of course, my love of fast cars, motorbikes, beautiful clothes and perfumes wouldn't be possible without Jaguar, BMW, Triumph, Belstaff, Armani, Hugo Boss, Karl Lagerfeld, Chanel and Versace; or Lawrence's love of music and singing, without Duffy and Stephen Booker, Paul Weller, Andy Williams, Simply Red, Emeli Sandé, Amy Winehouse and James Morrison.

NOTE: No men were harmed during the writing of this book, and no whores' meat was consumed.

Prologue – Three Years Earlier

"Let me go! I'm going to fucking kill him."

Lewis held his arms around Lawrence, barely managing to restrain him, desperately trying to calm him down. The scene was chaotic and violent, with Josh Black being held down by three of Lewis's security guards.

"Leave it, Lawrence," Lewis shouted above the obscenities pouring from Black's mouth. "The police are on their way. Let them deal with it. He's not worth it."

Lewis felt his friend's body sag, and slowly released his grip on him.

Lawrence hung his head for a moment, his eyes closed, fighting back the nausea that swept through him. Now was not the time to throw up. He stood up straight and walked to the other side of the room, to the woman crouched on the floor.

He knelt beside her and tenderly put his arm around her shoulder. He looked down at the towel around her arm, the blood beginning to seep through.

"Come on, Christine," and he steadily drew her to her feet, carefully lifting her and cradling her in his arms.

"Lawrence, the police will need to speak to her."

Christine nestled her head into Lawrence's chest and remained silent.

"I'm taking her to the hospital, and then I'm going to get her out of this hell." His face was grim and determined. Lewis knew there was no point arguing with him now.

The woman in the faux-fur coat stepped out of the shadows.

"Lawrence…" Her voice was quiet and controlled, with just a hint of wishful thinking. "Why don't you come back home to the apartment. I—"

He cut her dead. "You must be fucking joking! I left all that crap behind when I walked out, Miranda; and it was never *home*. Just look at her, for God's sake! And where the fuck's Jimmy?"

He glared at the man on the floor and pulled Christine closer to his body, to protect, warm and comfort her. He turned back to Miranda. "Think about how you can live with yourself. It's over."

Black's energy was spent and he remained pinned to the floor, silent.

Lawrence carried Christine out of the building, passing the police in the street.

"You'll find us at the Royal London Hospital." And he left.

Chapter 1

Suzy Harper closed her laptop and put it on her bedside table. She stretched over to turn the lamp off and tried to go to sleep, despite the fact she was still thinking about the next chapter in her book where her handsome hero, Lawrence, was going to discover he had a young son. This story was the latest in a long list of books she had written since the age of twelve. Nothing had ever been published, and many had never even been read by anyone else; not since her parents had been killed in a road accident. Her mother had been her biggest fan. In everything, not just her writing.

But right now she needed to get to sleep – she had work in the morning and it was already midnight.

The next minute she found herself staring at her alarm clock in the vain hope that she had misread it and that it was only 5.30 a.m., leaving her another hour to doze in bed. She wasn't quite ready to get up, savouring the memory of another delicious night of romantic antics with Lawrence. His sexual magnetism was transfixing, pressing her down into the bed. She could feel his caresses on her breasts, his tongue doing magical things and stimulating her body in that way only he could...

"Damn," she said. It was 6.30 and now she had to get up. And she really did have to try to stop dreaming about that bloody man – for goodness' sake, he wasn't even real!

She dragged herself out of bed and went into the bathroom for a quick shower. Hair was washed yesterday, so it'd do for today; quick rub down with her towel and then she squeezed into her skinny soft blue jeans and navy sweatshirt and yanked her socks on. Hair tied back and light touch of make-up applied; the reflection in the mirror told her she would do for another day working in the bookshop.

"Dominic, are you up yet and do you want breakfast?" she shouted along the landing as she made her way downstairs. She then heard, "Yes and yes," and put the kettle on and put bread in the toaster. She grabbed the butter, marmalade, fresh orange juice and two glasses, mugs, side plates and knives, and placed them on the table.

"Thanks for staying over last night," Suzy said as Dominic appeared in the kitchen, looking slightly dishevelled with his white shirt hanging out of his dark grey trousers, the top buttons undone and his dark brown hair damp from his shower. He walked over and leaned down to her five foot three inches and planted a kiss on her cheek.

"You're welcome, and good morning to you," he said in his oh-so-polite Cheshire accent. "But, Suzy, you've been in England over a year now and I think you need to start loosening up with the people around you. How long are you going to stay stuck in this fantasy life you've created for yourself?"

Suzy turned to face him and frowned.

"Look, I'm not going to start lecturing at this time in the morning, but we do need to talk, honey."

"I know what you want to say, but you're right, I don't need this now. I'm working at the bookshop today and then I'm going to review my advertising literature for the translation work. Can you come back tonight? I would really appreciate your input. I'll make dinner and we can talk."

Dominic smiled, picked up a piece of toast and said, "How can I resist such an offer? Richard isn't due back till Friday so I can stay another couple of nights if you like."

"I would like that," Suzy said, almost shyly. She was still bewitched by his handsome dark features and tall, slim physique. *Mmm, very nice, with his "nearly ready for work" look. Just remember he's your cousin!*

"Have you had many responses to your advert so far?" Dominic was referring to a flyer Suzy had written to try to get some French translation work. She was fluent in the language, having spent most of her life in Cameroon; now she was keen to see if she could make a career using her translation skills. She still wasn't sure whether to try it alone, work with a translation company or go into teaching. Teaching would mean further studies, but she would get to know a lot more people around her own age.

And that was Suzy's problem – getting to know people and letting them get to know her. Especially members of the opposite sex! She had lived in Cameroon from the age of three, where her English mother had worked as an aid coordinator and her American father with the American Embassy in Yaoundé. She was just seventeen when they died, and as Cameroon was the only real home she knew, she stayed there, living from one day to the next, continuing her studies of business with French, not really thinking about her future.

Last year Suzy's aunt, Dominic's mother, had died and left her a generous inheritance. It didn't take much for her to decide to sample life in the UK again; after all, there was nothing and no one to make her stay in Cameroon. She had a few friends, but there had never been anyone special. The death of her parents had cut her off from the other students. Some were unsure how to communicate with her any more and simply kept their distance; others tried to engage her in the usual student extra-curricular activities, but most gave up as they realised Suzy Harper was never going to be the life and soul of the party. She had a few genuine friends, who would allow her to be sad, with them or by herself, go on walks and bike rides, which she had always loved, and occasionally go sailing, which she had done with her parents. But she never let anyone get close to her, and after a while boys who showed any initial interest got the message and left her alone.

So she booked a flight and arranged to rent a small cottage on the outskirts of Nantwich, where her aunt had lived. She met her cousin, Dominic, for the first time at Manchester Airport, and couldn't fail to notice his good looks and friendly welcoming manner.

However, Suzy soon realised the same pattern was happening here in England. She knew very few people and still avoided anyone getting close, apart from her cousin. In fact, her evasion skills had stepped up a gear and whenever anyone threatened to ask her out she would mention Dominic's name. "I'm already seeing someone," was her constant response and that would put an end to any further pursuits. She preferred it that way.

But she was now twenty-three, still a virgin and wondering if, actually, she was gay. Had she any urges to seek out female companionship in any way other than as good friends? No, she hadn't. Anyway, she had the hots for Dominic, even if he was her cousin. She could appreciate a good-looking man along with the rest of them. And it wasn't hard to pretend she was on a date with him when she needed to.

She just hadn't met the right guy yet, and right now she didn't have time to even think about it. It was time to go to work.

They finished their breakfast and headed into the hallway together. "I'm going to the gym after work so I'll be home about 7.30. But just let yourself in and I'll see you later." She grabbed her gym bag, coat and shoulder bag and went out into the cool November air.

The bookshop was just a ten-minute drive from the cottage. One of the first things she had done when she arrived in Cheshire was learn to drive, and she was now the proud owner of a three-year-old Mazda MX-5 – her pride and joy. It was her turn to buy cakes today, so, after she'd parked, she walked to the deli and bought three skinny blueberry muffins before going into the bookshop. The shop was situated on Doctor Street and had a good reputation for specialising in non-fiction, mainly sport, travel, self-help and religion. As Suzy walked in she was greeted by Alison, her friend, gym buddy and boss in the bookshop. Alison was twenty-five and the two girls had become good friends, with Alison being sympathetic to Suzy's unwillingness to get involved with other people, especially men. Suzy knew she could trust her implicitly.

"Hi, Alison. I've brought cakes – are you OK for the gym tonight?" Suzy approached the counter towards the back of the shop and placed her bags on the worktop. Alison was checking the till and preparing to open for the day.

"Yeah, I've brought my kit. Have you seen Mike yet? I thought he would be here by now." At that moment a tall, thin guy appeared. He was wearing cycling shorts and shoes and a weatherproof jacket, and carrying his Giro vented cycling helmet.

"Sorry I'm late, guys," he shouted as he removed his rucksack and headed to the back of the shop to change into his tracksuit bottoms and sweatshirt. Mike was forty and owned the bookshop, having taken it over ten years ago from his parents when they had retired. With Alison's help, he had managed to increase the turnover and profits of the business, embracing mail order, access to sales over the internet via Amazon and the like, and improving the specialist areas, building up a regular clientele, both locally and nationally. The south Cheshire market town of Nantwich attracted historians, theologians, food and wine lovers (with its annual food and drink festivals), gardeners, canal folk and many other visitors to the area. Alison ran the shop for Mike and he was quite happy to do what she told him. He was more of a "go out and ride up a mountain" type of guy than a manager of a bookshop, and her local knowledge enabled them to react to the needs of customers. She was bubbly, knowledgeable and had a great relationship with customers. Mike was confident in her abilities, and trusted her business acumen, very rarely disagreeing with any decisions she made, although he had drawn the line at refurbishing the top floor of the store to accommodate a coffee shop. His main concern had been safe access, as there was a tight winding staircase to the second floor, and the cost and knock-on effect of replacing this had been the final factor in deciding not to pursue Alison's idea. He had, however, compromised and installed a drinks and snacks vending machine with a few comfy seats on the first floor. This had led to browsers becoming "paying guests" in this area and it usually led to at least one purchase; certainly the in-store turnover had increased and the vending machines were more than paying their way.

Alison had been keen to take Suzy on when she applied for the part-time shop assistant's job. She had good credentials from her school in Cameroon and references from friends of her family when she had returned to the UK. And Mike had known Dominic from their college days in the cycling club. He also knew Dominic could not be her boyfriend and was always at a loss to know why such a pretty girl should pretend he was. Suzy's French was a bonus, particularly during festival periods in the town when many foreign visitors came into the shop, and her African connections made her interesting to talk to. Although she never seemed relaxed chatting with a group of people her own age, she was very eloquent and confident when talking to customers and members of the public. It was almost as though she put up a protective barrier stopping anyone getting too close. And neither Mike nor Alison minded her promoting her translation work in the shop – she was a bright young woman and deserved a break.

Mike walked back into the shop and joined the girls at the tills. "Nice cakes, Suzy. So when do we get to eat them?" Built like a beanpole, Mike could eat for England.

"Not till later. All good things come to those who wait!" Suzy popped the bag under the counter, adding, "I'll just go through the delivery and put the new books out."

Alison opened the shop and they each went about their tasks for the day.

The morning progressed unremarkably: cakes eaten with coffee, odd details of each other's weekends shared, and comments from Mike and Alison on Suzy's flyers:

French Translation Services
Smart translation capturing feeling, humour and style
Specialising in French to English
No job too big or small!
For more information call Suzy Harper on
01234 516798 or email shtranslates@anymail.co.uk

"Have you had any enquiries yet, Suzy?" Alison asked.

"No. I'm going to go through the advert with Dominic tonight and see if I can improve it. Luckily, I haven't made too many copies of this version. I need a website too if I'm going to do it properly."

"How is Dominic? You guys must come over for dinner soon. I'll text you some dates and we'll get something in the diary."

Alison and Mike both knew Suzy publicly portrayed Dominic as more than her cousin; rather, he was her boyfriend from the moment other guys started to ask her out, and, bless

Dominic, he had agreed to go on a few "dates" with her when she was compelled to be seen with her "boyfriend" when socialising with the small number of friends she had made since returning to the UK. The fact that he was gay and his long-term partner, Richard, lived in Manchester never seemed to come up in conversation. And as Richard was often away on business, it was never too much of an inconvenience to go out with Suzy. Besides, Dominic really enjoyed her company and couldn't help feeling protective towards his young cousin. At least Richard could trust him and there was no need to be jealous or suspicious!

Suzy started to load some more new books onto a trolley, ready to distribute them around the shop, when the door opened and a man walked in. As she turned to give the prospective customer a polite smile, her face drained of colour and she dropped the books. She stared and then panicked as she realised the books had fallen to the floor, and immediately got down on her knees. The man who had just come in was the spitting image of Lawrence, the guy from her stories and dreams. It was too weird to take in: she could have conjured him straight out of her imagination – her Prince Charming (or maybe Casanova!). She knelt before him and couldn't resist looking up into his face.

Mike hurried over to help Suzy, and Alison shifted her gaze from Suzy on the floor to the drop-dead gorgeous man standing in front of her. He was looking straight down at Suzy with a look of such intensity that Alison hesitated to speak for fear of interrupting his thoughts. She was concerned at her friend's pallor and simply wanted to deal with this guy quickly and then attend to Suzy. Did she know him? In a nervous voice she hardly recognised as her own, Alison piped up, "Can I help you?"

The stranger was wearing dark blue chinos and a £4,000 Belstaff leather jacket with studs. Suzy found herself staring at his highly polished brown brogues. His voice was rich, mellow and sexy, without any trace of an accent, and his manner was one of confidence, control and wealth.

Without taking his eyes off Suzy, he responded, "I'm looking for a copy of *Inspired*, by Sir Steve Redgrave." And he finally looked towards Alison.

He was breathtakingly handsome, with searching green eyes, high cheekbones, and well-groomed sideburns fading into a trace of designer stubble, indicating a normally clean-shaven, firm jaw. His lips were set straight in a "don't mess with me" kind of expression, but it was softened by silky golden-brown hair, short at the back and yet floating, unruly, across his forehead and creating the perfect frame to his perfect face.

Suzy stood up and helped Mike rearrange the books on the trolley. "Are you OK? You look really pale, Suzy. I think you'd better go and get a drink. I'll finish putting these out," he offered.

Suzy was thankful to have a means of escape, and she hurried upstairs and took some water from the machine, trying to calm her breathing and stop herself from shaking as she sank into one of the large soft leather chairs.

The sports section was on the ground floor and Alison pointed the stranger in its direction and then ran upstairs to check on Suzy. The customer took the book from the shelf and walked over to the counter.

Up to me to serve, then, Mike thought to himself and went over to deal with the sale. It did not escape his notice that the guy took one of Suzy's flyers and put it in his pocket.

"I like your sports selection. I'll have a good look around next time I come."

Mike smiled in response and the stranger handed over his credit card. "Thank you," he said as Mike processed the payment and handed him the book and, with that, the stranger walked out onto the street.

His white Jaguar XKR-S was parked just around the corner. He took the leaflet out of his pocket and looked at the name Suzy Harper, the corners of his mouth almost, but not quite, forming a smile. As he got into the car he pulled out his iPhone and tapped into his email account.

Subject: French translation
Dear Ms Harper,
I require a translation of a purchase agreement. Please call me to arrange a meeting to discuss the matter. Yours sincerely, Lawrence Bane.

He pressed Send.

What are you doing? This is dangerous ground, Los; why have you let her get into your head? You only went to get a book. Go home and read it. Forget about the rest!

He hit the accelerator and headed towards home.

Meanwhile, Suzy had gone back downstairs, to face inquisitive looks from both Mike and Alison. "Are you sure you're OK, Suzy? At least you've got some colour in your cheeks now. You looked like you'd seen a ghost earlier. Was it the guy who came into the shop?"

Alison was just shutting the drawer in the till and getting ready to finish for the day, having just closed the shop.

"Yeah, I'd guess you ladies would call him something of a looker. Smarmy git, if you ask me. But good choice of book. And you can often judge a lover by his book." Alison and Suzy looked at each other with raised eyebrows. This was one of Mike's favourite sayings, and he could never understand why nobody laughed at his little joke.

"Well, I thought he was rude, staring at you, Suzy, when you were obviously flustered about dropping the books. He seemed to give you a bit of a weird look; it unnerved me and I nearly stuttered when I asked him if I could help! Anyway, I doubt we'll see him again. He didn't look the sort to be out buying his own, or anyone else's, books."

"I wouldn't be so sure. He said he looked forward to having a good look around next time he comes. And he took one of your leaflets, Suzy!"

"He did?" Alison and Suzy both blurted out in surprise.

"That's really weird," said Alison. "If he rings you, Suzy, you need to be careful. Tell him you won't be able to help. I wouldn't trust him – and you never know what weirdos are out there. I said I didn't think it was a good idea putting your mobile number on."

"Well, he hasn't rung me yet and I doubt he ever will." Suzy emphasised the word "he", still not over the shock of seeing her Lawrence in the flesh. He was very good-looking, beautifully dressed, well spoken – well, from the few words she heard anyway. Oh, how was she going to get him out of her head now? Dominic was right. She needed to stop living in this fantasy world and give herself at least half a chance of meeting a nice guy to settle down with. She didn't want to end up like Bridget Jones! Or any other singleton, for that matter.

"Anyway, I'm sorry for being a bit clumsy earlier; glad I didn't damage any of the books. Is it OK if I make up the downtime next time I'm in – I think it's Friday?" She looked towards Alison.

"Don't worry about it, Suzy, it wasn't long, and you're always putting in extra time when we need it. Just take it easy driving, and remember what I said about Mr Weirdo. Have a good couple of days and I'll look forward to seeing you on Friday. My turn for cakes."

"Yeah, take care, Suzy." Mike turned to Alison as Suzy left the shop. "What do you think about it, Alison? That guy will know that's Suzy because he will have heard me call her name out, and the leaflet has got her name on it. He didn't ask me anything about it – just put it straight in his pocket."

"I don't know. He looked classy, but that doesn't really mean anything."

Secretly, Alison always hoped Suzy would meet her Mr Nice Guy before too long, as she was worried she was saving herself for someone who didn't exist. Alison had no idea how this chance meeting would change Suzy's life.

Chapter 2

As soon as Suzy was outside the shop she went to check her phone for any messages. Damn, she had left it at home! She got into her car and drove to the gym. She'd forgotten to remind Alison she would see her there, but no doubt they would meet up in a bit. She wasn't really in the mood for a workout, but this was her routine, and hopefully it would help her to focus her mind and concentrate this evening. She needed to clear her head.

She saw Alison in the changing rooms. They met up with other members for an aerobics exercise class, chat soon moved to the latest film release, and Suzy forgot about the handsome stranger and French translations. For a while, at least.

As she was driving home, she tried to decide whether or not to mention her "Lawrence" lookalike to Dominic. He'd probably think she was bonkers – even she thought she was. Alison had left her, saying, "Let me know if that weirdo gets in touch and see what Dominic thinks about it." Maybe she would get his opinion, if indeed the weirdo ever did get in touch.

Once at home, she went into the kitchen in search of her phone, shouting "hi" to Dominic who was already in the house, flicking through the TV channels, catching up on the day's news.

"How's your day been?" he asked.

"Oh, OK. Nothing very exciting." (Who was she kidding? She had seen the man of her dreams and there was a slight chance he might contact her, even if only to do some work. That would be exciting, in her book, and she was beginning to realise that that was exactly what she wanted – excitement, anticipation, some passion, even.)

"Actually, someone picked up one of my leaflets from the shop – maybe I'll get some work out of it." Where was her damn phone?

Dominic walked into the kitchen. "Well, fingers crossed." He watched her frantically searching for something. "Suzy, what are you looking for?" And he opened the fridge and took out a bottle of Sauvignon Blanc.

"My phone," she said, somewhat distracted. "Just a minute, I'll check upstairs."

A moment later she came running back down, phone in hand.

She stared at the screen and gasped aloud on seeing the name Lawrence. *I can't believe it, this is really weird!* Not only does he resemble the image Suzy had for the fictional character from her stories, he even has the same Christian name! Hastily she opened the message. *He wants a meeting to discuss a piece of work...*

"So, what are you cooking for us?" Dominic put a brake on her thoughts, which were running wild, and handed her a glass of wine.

"Oh, thanks." She was obviously distracted. "Sorry, just got an email from the guy who took the leaflet – he wants to arrange a meeting to discuss a purchase agreement. I just need to send a reply." Her mind was racing. The mail was timed at 4.30 p.m.; he must have sent it as soon as he left the shop. Was he desperate for the translation, some deadline maybe? Or did he want to meet her?

"What's his name, do you know him?" Again Dominic's voice interrupted.

"Er – Lawrence Bane. I don't know him."

"Think I've heard that name before. Yeah, we've got a private tax client at work called Lawrence Bane. Rich guy, if it's the same one. Not sure he would be the sort to respond to a leaflet, though."

"Well, I may as well find out what it's about – could be my first assignment."

"Still, it seems a bit odd. Maybe arrange to meet at the house and I could work from here; be your guardian angel and all that. I'd just need to check my diary."

"I'm sure it'll be fine. I don't need a chaperon."

"You've changed your tune. You've wanted me as your date for the last twelve months!"

"That's different. I didn't want anyone thinking I was available. I'm just not ready to get involved with anyone, that's all. But this is professional. It could help me get started in business. Anyway, from what you've said, if it is your guy, sounds like he's way out of my league and probably nothing will come of it."

But deep down she hoped both these points were wrong. Was she now starting to feel ready for some romantic connection, and did she hope something would come out of it – professional or otherwise?

She replied:

Dear Mr Bane,
Thank you for your email. I would be pleased to consider translating your agreement. Perhaps you could email the document over to me and I could confirm that I am able to carry out the assignment and provide a quote. I look forward to hearing from you. With kind regards, Suzy Harper

Her hand hovered over the Send button. This way she would be doing herself out of the opportunity of seeing him again. But surely this was all that was necessary. She could do the job, or not, and he would accept the price or not. And Alison would be proud of her!

She pressed Send.

"OK." She turned her attention to Dominic. "Let me get on with dinner. Hot smoked salmon with brown rice and salad sound good?" and she started to move around her kitchen as Dominic nodded.

Her cousin powered up her laptop and started to look at what she had done so far for her advertising campaign.

"So what do you think?" she asked. "I think I need to give some examples of the type of work I could do and make it clear that I can work remotely with email. And I should set up a website."

After their meal, they talked and sipped wine for the next hour, with Dominic showing her examples of advertising literature and browsing several translation company websites. There were also plenty of companies offering website building services. Suzy prepared a plan of action, with a view to working on the points they had discussed over the next couple of days before she was back in the bookshop on Friday.

Then her phone showed an incoming mail.

> A meeting will be necessary as the document is confidential and I will need you to sign a confidentiality agreement. We can also discuss a few technical points. I suggest you come over to my house tomorrow at 11 a.m. Then I can go through my requirements in more detail and you can decide whether or not to accept the assignment. Please confirm that this is acceptable to you. I look forward to seeing you in the morning.
> Kind regards
> Lawrence Bane

Suzy's mind went into overdrive. His words were so direct, taking her acceptance as read.

He wants to see me/it's to sign a confidentiality agreement.

He wants to start tomorrow/the document is probably urgent.

He's put kind regards – less formal than his first email/still a bit formal – anyway, I put the same, as do most people!

> OK, see you tomorrow.
> Suzy.

She pressed Send.

Damn – she had forgotten to ask where he lived!

> Good. Address: The Sway, Willowford BB4 4YY

That was that, then. She was going to go. Armed with her laptop, dictionary, notepad and qualification papers.

* * *

Suzy cleared the breakfast dishes and wiped down the kitchen worktop. Dominic had left for work, and she went upstairs to search through her wardrobe for inspiration. She was going as a businesswoman, but, oh, she wanted to look good: attractive, sexy. Surprisingly, her sleep had been peaceful and dreamless, but now she couldn't stop seeing the image of Lawrence Bane looking down at her at the bookshop, his rich brown hair just sweeping above his eyebrows and those intense green eyes.

His own clothes had exuded luxury and expense. She wanted to look good, feel confident and do a good job. She was on a mission to impress! She chose smart black trousers and an open-necked white shirt with a grey V-necked sweater and black court shoes. Her reflection in the mirror filled her with confidence. It was a mild November morning, but she put her black coat in the car, just in case. She entered the postcode into her sat-nav and started the engine. A song by Keane was playing on the radio as she slipped the car into gear and pulled away, she tried to keep calm.

Having easily found the place, she turned in at the gatehouse and followed the long driveway as it swept through mature woodland. The Sway came into view. It was a huge, imposing building. The porch cast a dark shadow over the front entrance, leaving any visitor intimidated. Suzy was beginning to think this was a bad idea. There was a sense of isolation about this place, a feeling of cutting oneself off from society. She wasn't sure why she felt that way, but it was making her very uncomfortable and hot. If anyone had seen her car arrive, it would seem really odd if she were to simply drive away. She took some deep breaths and reached for her case as she got out of the car. *Come on, where's your sense of adventure? What could possibly happen? You've come here to consider some work; forget about the guy and concentrate on assessing the translation.*

She went up the steps, used the brass knocker and waited, with no idea whether anyone on the other side of the door would have heard her knock. It was only a few seconds before she heard bolts being pulled back. It was like something out of the Addams Family!

"Miss Harper, I'm glad you made it." Lawrence Bane smiled, and moved aside to welcome her in.

Chapter 3

The entrance hall was as large as Suzy's living room. The darkness was alleviated by a gleaming chandelier hanging over a grand sweeping staircase leading off to the right. Directly in front was a large oak-panelled door. There was a smaller door adjacent to the staircase, and Lawrence headed for this. He wore dark jogging bottoms with a pale blue T-shirt. Suzy couldn't help noticing his leopard-print slippers as he walked silently across the highly polished parquet floor.

"I've got the paperwork ready through here. I trust you had no problem finding the place?" He spoke steadily, using his words sparingly, almost cautiously, as though not wanting to say the wrong thing.

"Er, no. It was fine." Suzy watched his graceful movements as she plonked across the floor in her court shoes. Should she have offered to take them off? As she entered the well-lit room she glanced around at the light-coloured contemporary office furniture, and the large cream sofa underneath one of the windows. The ambience was softened by a deep-pile, mushroom-coloured carpet. At least there would be no sound of her plonking in here! There were several TV screens on one wall, showing news and money market information, with no sound. Lawrence went over to the desk and picked up some papers. He took them over to the coffee table in front of the sofa and waved his arm. "Take a seat and I'll get some coffee while you have a look through this confidentiality agreement. Or would you prefer tea, or a cold drink?" Suzy looked over at him, having barely moved inside the room. He looked very relaxed and extremely handsome. She felt as though she was shaking like a leaf – she hoped it didn't show.

"Coffee would be great. No sugar and just a bit of milk, thanks." She moved over to the sofa and placed her case on the floor beside her as she sat down. Once he had left the room she focused on regaining her composure and concentrating on the work she had come to do. Sign the agreement, look at the document to make sure there were no major issues with translation, and then take it home to work on. She started to read the agreement, assuming she would have to sign before continuing any further. Presumably he was going to explain the situation and the need for this.

Meanwhile, Lawrence had gone through to the kitchen to make the coffee. *I hope you know what you're doing,* he mused. *It's been a long time, but there is something about this girl. I want to get to know her, and can't stop thinking about her. Well, it's going to go one way or the other.*

As he walked back into the office Suzy stood up and put out two of the coasters which were on the coffee table.

"Thanks," he said and his eyes seemed to soften as they made contact with hers. He continued to look at her. "I guess I owe you a bit of an explanation about this document I need translating. I'm hoping to invest in a venture distributing some product into Africa. It's what I do – invest in companies, that is. It's early days and we need to keep a lid on it until I commit to the deal. A lot of the paperwork is in French. If you're happy to sign that, then we can go through the purchase agreement."

He sat next to her and she could smell him – fresh, woody, spicy and sensual. She tried to concentrate and glued her eyes to the document on the table.

She turned the pages and signed.

"I understand," she said, handing it to him. She tried to resist the urge to look at his face, but weakened, and their gaze connected again. This time there was no smile, just an intensity, as though he was burning into her, trying to read the very inside of her mind. Stillness seemed to hang in the air.

He took the document from her and broke the tension.

"Coffee." He handed her the cup. It seemed to be a relief for both of them.

They sipped their drinks. "I need to go out for a short while," he said. "Look at the file and then have some lunch with me."

Suzy hadn't expected this. And it sounded like an order rather than a request. "Oh, I thought you could email it to me, and I'll go through it at home and confirm a quote – make sure you're happy with me doing the work!"

"Then I wouldn't be able to see you. The quote will be fine, trust me." The intense look was back. Suzy was taken aback by his directness; she uncrossed her legs and smoothed her trousers down towards her knees.

He stood up, saying, "I'm sorry, I didn't mean to make you uncomfortable. I'm not really used to company. I understand if you don't want to work here, but I would appreciate it if you did." He looked anxious.

Suzy felt bewitched by his beauty. For a moment he looked young, vulnerable, hopeful of her answer.

The trance was broken as she said, "OK. And lunch would be nice."

She was aware of the tension leaving him and he smiled. "Come on over to the desk and I'll get you started." He directed her to the chair behind the desk and as he momentarily leaned over her, Suzy became aware of his fragrance. He powered up the laptop and loaded a document onto the screen. "You can work on this machine and take it home with you if you need to later; there's nothing else on it." His whole being seemed to have speeded up with excitement and yet he felt completely relaxed at the same time. It seemed the most natural thing in the world. She was seeing him again as he had been when he opened the door to her – and there was that smile.

"I'll let you get on. I'll be back in a couple of hours and then we can eat and get to know each other a bit more." He took this for granted, not waiting for any reply. "The bathroom is just next door, and you can help yourself to drinks and so on in the kitchen. Feel free to hunt around."

Suzy watched his back as he left the room and then stared at the computer screen. *What have I done?* she asked herself. She wasn't sure if it was better to be in this massive house with him or without him. But she was in her territory now, with a document to translate and a very impressive laptop to do it on. She sat back for a moment and considered recent events. His appearance at the bookshop, his email asking her to do work for him, how it had to be at his house, the offer of lunch and what looked like a brand new laptop at her disposal. Not to mention that she was alone in his house. She told herself to remain calm and not read too much into things. But still.

Lawrence got ready to go, grabbing his motorcycle helmet as he went out through the utility room, which opened onto the front driveway. Suzy caught a glimpse of him crossing the drive to the garage and heard the motorbike roar into life. She watched him, leather-clad, as he rode slowly towards the main road.

Lawrence activated his Bluetooth and waited for Lewis to pick up the phone as he cruised towards Manchester. "Have you got that date yet?"

"Hi, Lawrence. I've just emailed you. We think his release date is the twenty-third of January. Are you coming into town?"

"I'm on my way but can't stay too long. See you in twenty minutes." He ended the call and started to listen to Coldplay. He needed a bit of thinking time.

Chapter 4

Suzy needed the bathroom. She went into the hallway and tried the door next to the office. It was locked. There were seven doors leading off the hallway. Only the locked one looked remotely like a toilet.

She decided to try upstairs. As she got to the top of the stairs, she saw that the door on her right was slightly ajar. She pushed it open. It led into a huge bedroom with light pouring through double doors, which looked as though they opened out onto a balcony. Nervously, she stepped in and looked around her. The carpet was pale blue and springy to walk on. The ceiling was high and, together with the walls, was a stark white. There was a long side table against the wall, with a small candle, clearly frequently lit, a lamp and a book on it (she noticed it was the one he had purchased from the bookshop), and a soft grey leather recliner in front of the doors. She could just see out over the balcony, which had a view of the gardens and woods in the distance. It was beautiful. But there was something very odd about this room. There were no pictures or mirror and the only other furniture to be seen was a single bed. It looked totally out of place in these luxurious surroundings. The room cried out for a super-king-sized master bed. Could this be his room? Then she noticed a long thin mat running alongside the bed – perhaps for yoga? She opened a door, almost hidden in the wall, which led into a huge en-suite with exquisite white fittings, his and hers sinks, a sunken bath, separate large shower, toilet and bidet. And as she turned back into the bedroom she saw the dressing room, with rails of men's clothing hung meticulously in rows – all organised by type and colour. Suzy stared in awe and also fear. What sort of a guy was this?

She still needed to use the loo but felt too afraid to use this one. For goodness' sake, a house this size and she couldn't find a toilet! She went out onto the landing and along to the other end, trying a door that was set into a recess. Thank goodness;

it was just a bathroom, though there was nothing "just" about it. Again, it contained his and hers sinks, a large shower, a free-standing claw-footed bath, a bidet and, at last, a toilet she felt she could use. There was a large mirror above the sinks. She checked her appearance and went back down to the office to concentrate on her work.

As she went past the door to the downstairs toilet, she saw it was ajar. How could that be? She tried not to panic – was there someone else in the house? "Hello?" she called out. Surely he wouldn't have come back early and not told her he was back? Besides, she would have heard his motorbike. There was silence. She sat back down at the computer and tried to compose herself. She wondered about just leaving there and then. What would he think if he came back and found her gone? She knew she didn't want to leave; not yet, anyway. This was a new experience for her – she wanted to find out a bit more about this Lawrence Bane and, despite her trepidation, she actually wanted to see him again, smell him, have lunch and get to know him, as he put it. Focus on your work and see how it goes when he comes back, she told herself. She had never felt so excited before, and nothing had even happened!

Lawrence left the offices of Blue Securities, armed with information from Lewis. They had met about ten years ago, when Lawrence was "operating" in London. Lewis had been a cop then, a damn good one. He now owned his own security firm, with financial backing from Lawrence, and remained a very loyal friend to him. Lawrence Bane didn't have many of those. They had worked together to put Josh Black behind bars. Now it looked like he would soon be due for release on licence and no one doubted he would try to come after Lawrence. It would just be a question of how and when.

Lawrence's thoughts turned to Suzy Harper. He had some phone calls to make, but they could wait until later. He called in at a chemist and made two purchases. He tucked them inside his leather jacket and headed for his bike to go home.

Meanwhile, Suzy was progressing well with her translation and all thoughts of her "client" had been set aside for now. Suddenly she heard a door close; the sound seemed to come from the hallway. She was sure the motorbike had not returned. She went out of the room and called, "Is anybody there?"

A tall thin woman with short brown hair and a kind face appeared. Suzy guessed her to be in her mid-thirties.

"I'm sorry. I didn't mean to disturb you. Can I get you a drink or anything?"

"Er, no, I'm fine thanks. It's just ... I thought I was alone here." That explained the locked toilet door.

"Oh, I heard Lawrence go out earlier and thought I'd come over and do some ironing. I'm Christine. I suppose he didn't mention me. He's not much of a talker. Well, don't mind me, I'll just get on with it."

"Oh, OK." Suzy hurried back into the office and closed the door. She didn't know what to make of this woman – was she his girlfriend? Suzy had assumed he was single, and didn't he say he wanted to get to know her a bit more; and what was with the single bed? Alison was right – it was all a bit weird and she was beginning to think she had made a huge mistake replying to his email in the first place. *Just carry on with the translation and get the job finished.*

The sound of the motorbike broke her concentration and she looked out of the window. How mysterious he looked in the dark bike leathers. Mystery seemed to be his middle name.

She watched as he took his helmet off and glanced towards the window. He must have seen her watching. She fought her instinct to pull back from view and continued to observe him, as he seemed to hesitate for a second before turning towards the front door. She sat back down at the desk, too nervous now to actually work, but she went through the motions and tried to calm herself. He came straight into the room.

"Hi." He was still wearing his jacket and holding his bike helmet. He looked at her carefully and his eyes had such intensity, Suzy felt as if he was piercing through her mind to try to see what she was thinking. "I'm glad you're still here." There was no smile. In fact, Suzy perceived a look of relief flicker across his face.

"Yes. I've met Christine." Suzy had already decided she would confront him about Christine straight away; she had to know what their relationship was. From the moment she first saw him, the connection with the guy from her books, the mysteries that had then ensued, all these things had her yearning to know him better and to be with him. She needed to know if there was any chance, no matter how slight. This was such a new experience for her.

To her surprise he relaxed immediately. "Good. She's my housekeeper. I'm not much good at that side of things and it is quite a big place." Now he smiled like a teenager and gestured, looking around him. Suzy couldn't hold back a grin and hoped it didn't look too much like relief! "She can help us with lunch. Come on and let me introduce you properly." And he held out his hand for her to take.

Suzy looked down at it for a fraction of a second. It seemed the most natural thing in the world to wrap her fingers around his warm, firm hand and feel his grip tighten. She looked up at him and her insides tingled. Another new experience. This time he didn't look at her and she had no idea what was going through his head.

You are going to explode, Lawrence; take it easy, patience and gentleness. This feels so right; don't scare her off.

With feet as light as a feather, and despite having those cloppy court shoes on, she glided with him into the kitchen. She managed to compose herself sufficiently to prevent a gasp of awe at the huge state-of-the-art kitchen.

"Hey Christine, you've met Suzy Harper, I hear. She's doing some work for me, so will be around for a while." Suzy was wondering how she could stretch out the document to make it last "a while", but with the number of distractions she was getting it could easily be possible!

Christine had indeed been ironing, evidenced by the row of garments neatly folded on a worktop. She was now in the process of putting everything away. "Hi, Lawrence. I heard you go out so thought I'd get a head start on this. Hope you don't mind. I'll get off now." She glanced at Suzy. "Should I still come over as normal at five?"

"Yes, everything as normal. We're just going to have some lunch."

"There should be enough soup and bread for two. I hope you like carrot and coriander, Suzy. I'm sorry it's not something a bit more exciting." She continued gathering the clothes. Suzy remembered the neatly arranged rows in the dressing room – had that been Christine or Lawrence? "I'll no doubt see you again soon."

As Christine left the room Suzy couldn't help sensing how relaxed the relationship was between Lawrence and his housekeeper, almost like siblings; she couldn't have been much older than him, and it appeared she knew how he liked things.

Suzy looked at Lawrence and realised he was staring at her again. What was he thinking? They were alone now and she was beginning to feel a bit nervous.

"The document's coming along fine, although I haven't finished it yet. Would you like to go through it and see what I've done so far?"

"Let's wait until it's finished." He had his back to her as he rummaged through the fridge for their lunch. He put the soup on to heat and gathered the crockery and cutlery they would need. "We'll eat over here." He led her to a breakfast area off to one side of the kitchen. "It's a great view."

And it was. Suzy was looking out over the gardens she'd glimpsed from the bedroom, now seen from the other end of the house. He told her to take a seat and played at being waiter as he went to fetch the bread and soup.

"Christine is a good cook." He smiled as he sat next to her.

They spent the next hour chatting over lunch. Suzy was surprised how effortless it was to talk to him. He made her feel relaxed and confident. The conversation flowed, with no awkward silences, and any pauses were natural and easy. She had never shared a meal with a man on her own before, other than Dominic of course.

She wanted to pinch herself to make sure this wasn't just another dream with her Lawrence. No, this was real and she was enjoying being alive for the first time since her parents had died.

"So, Suzy, where do you come from? That's not an English or French accent."

Suzy smiled. "No, it's not. I grew up in Cameroon with my parents." Here she hesitated slightly and then continued, "I've only been in the UK for a year."

Lawrence listened, noticing how she sometimes dropped her "h"s, occasionally replaced "th" sounds with "d", and the soft lilt with which she almost sang some of the words. "I hope you don't lose it. Your accent," he added, as she looked a little puzzled.

Suzy blushed, wishing she didn't. "Well, I quite like living here, but I haven't decided what to do with my future yet."

"Would you go back to your parents?" His eyes never looked away from her.

"They're dead." Suzy couldn't believe she could talk like this to a stranger, to this man. "I miss them hugely, but life goes on. I need some new challenges in my life, and I'm hoping to make a success of the translation work."

"I'm sorry to hear about your mum and dad. We all need challenges, to keep us going. How many clients do you have?"

"Er, just you so far," she smiled, and took another piece of bread, concentrating on breaking it carefully, as if it were gold leaf and she didn't want to lose any crumbs.

He grinned a little smugly. "Good." He continued to watch her, amused by her concentration.

Put the damn bread down, you idiot! "What are your challenges, Mr Bane?" She was determined not to give him the upper hand.

"Oh, business, economics, boring stuff like that. Aside from that, I like to win races on my bike. In any case, all my challenges are better than the ones I used to have." Now he was shredding his bread, and it was her turn to watch.

"I take it you weren't born with a silver spoon in your mouth, then."

He laughed. "Nope – it's all bought and paid for by yours truly."

She thought, afterwards, he hadn't spoken very much about his personal life, and he never mentioned any family. She also realised what a treat it was to see Lawrence Bane smile. It was infrequent but genuine, and it served to intensify his beauty. She realised she was besotted with him. She found herself relaxing in his company and the mysteries surrounding him took on an intriguing quality, and no longer seemed threatening.

It was now 4 p.m. and Lawrence cleared everything away, having refused any help from Suzy. She followed him back into the kitchen.

"I think it best if I complete the work at home and bring it over in the morning." Of course, she could easily email it, but where would her excuse to come back be then? Besides, she was working on his laptop.

"Good." He had that intense look again. "You could stay here and have dinner?" This time it appeared to be a question.

"I think I should go now. I'll miss the traffic."

"Leave the work here. Then you'll have to come back. And wear something more comfortable tomorrow," he grinned like a schoolboy, looking down at her shoes. "Come in trainers and I'll show you something." And his eyes sparkled, as if he had some secret treat for her. She felt giddy. Was this what it felt like to have a teenage crush? Another new experience, and suddenly she couldn't wait until tomorrow.

Lawrence watched her leave and then went straight into the office and picked up the phone.

"Hi Miranda, it's Lawrence."

Chapter 5

As her car pulled up on his drive the next morning, he was already at the doorway as she stepped out. Today Suzy was wearing jeans and trainers, and she couldn't help smiling as she squeaked across his hallway. He was barefoot, in sweatpants and a T-shirt, and looked very sexy. He led her towards the study. She almost felt disappointed to be starting work straight away, but then he carried on past the office, to the door at the end of the hallway. It opened into a small lobby with two doors leading off it. He led the way through one of them and they entered a gymnasium, with several pieces of equipment around the outside of the room, a wall of floor-to-ceiling mirrors and doors leading off to what looked like his and her changing rooms.

"What do you think? Impressed?" The schoolboy grin had reappeared; he was obviously taking great delight in showing off. "It was one of the reasons I chose this house. And there's more." He led the way through the other door off the lobby into a beautiful room with a large swimming pool, hot tub and surrounding patio area. The water was shimmering off the walls and there was a fresh smell unlike that at any public swimming area. It looked warm and welcoming.

"Wow, this is amazing. You have all this to yourself? You could set up your own gym club here, it's fantastic!"

"I like my privacy, Suzy. And it makes me feel like a spoiled brat!" The grin was still there. "Next time, bring your kit and we can work out together." This was a statement, not a question. And Suzy didn't fail to register that there was going to be a next time.

"Right. Now I need to get on with my work." It was almost the last thing she wanted to do, but she needed to keep her feet on the ground and be focused in the safety of her own territory. His intense gaze was back and he seemed to be searching and trying to analyse every expression she made.

"You're right. Let me get you some coffee and I'll leave you alone for a couple of hours. Do you mind if I move you into the snug? I need to get some work done and you are proving to be quite a distraction."

He's calling me a distraction! What a nerve, but WOW! Suzy smiled and said sorry. Something told her this was going to be a good day.

Suzy read her translation through carefully and felt pleased with her work. She didn't pretend to appreciate some of the implications of the document, but was confident that her client would now have full knowledge of its contents. She was not surprised when, after exactly two hours had passed, he knocked on the door and walked in.

"Everything OK?" he asked, and Suzy perceived an anxiety in the question, and sensed something was distracting him.

"Yes, thanks. It's finished. Can I print it out and just do a quick check before I hand it over?"

"Sure, the machine should pick up the wireless printer – I'll go and get it." He observed her closely, unmoving. She lowered her eyes, a little embarrassed by the stillness hanging in the air.

He was about to say something but changed his mind and left the room, returning a few seconds later with the papers. He handed them to her and then went back out, saying, "Let me know when you're ready, I'll be in the office."

This had not gone the way Suzy had planned it. She hadn't expected him to leave the room, and he suddenly seemed aloof, after seeming so close earlier. She worried that he might not be pleased with the way she had worked today. She was beginning to feel uncomfortable in her jeans – they were hardly business-like. And what if he didn't like what she had done? She really wanted this to be right for him, then maybe there might be other documents to work on. Would he still want to see her again, as he had been implying? There was nothing for her to do except concentrate on scrolling through the transcript and presenting him with the completed document. She had calculated the cost last night, but had decided to leave the invoice until later. Was this really just going to be a work assignment?

"Come in," he called, as she stood at the open doorway of the office. He still appeared anxious and distracted as he looked up from his monitor. "You've finished, then."

"If now isn't a good time to go through it, I could just leave it with you and then you could let me know if you have any questions. I hope your purchase goes well." She didn't know what else to say as she placed the document on his desk, feeling awkward and as though she was intruding.

"No, no. I, er, I'm just a bit distracted. Let me get this email off and I'll be right with you."

She walked over to the window as she listened to the quiet clicking of a keyboard. Suddenly he was standing beside her. She could smell him and almost hear his breathing as he touched her arm. She turned to look at him. No smile.

"You are bewitching me, Suzy Harper. I can't get you out of my head. I think you know that and I think you have feelings for me too. Do you, Suzy?"

"I ... I like your company." She was shaking, and helpless to prevent him from knowing that.

"Will you stay and spend the night with me?"

Was that it? He just wanted to sleep with her? No romance, no friendship, no love? Why didn't he ask her out, ask her to be his girlfriend, take her on a few dates first? She suddenly felt naïve, stupid even, for thinking anything more could have happened. Who was she to him? She had been there to do some work, it was now finished, he wanted to take advantage of her and tomorrow she would be gone!

She felt his hand caress her arm, and he lowered his head towards her neck. She moved aside. "I don't think I can do that, not yet ... I've never ..."

"Never what?" His look was drilling into her mind and he held onto her arm.

She blushed, yearning to kiss his beautiful mouth, touch his beautiful face and feel his beautiful body. Her emotions were in turmoil, with her heart so desperately wanting to scream out yes, and to hell with the morning, but her pride telling her to leave with her dignity, and her virginity, intact. But what was she saving that for? Didn't she want excitement? Life wasn't going to get any more exhilarating than this.

"You're a virgin," he said softly and let go of her arm. He took her hands, lifting them to his lips, placing feathery kisses over her fingers and the back of her hands. He glanced up at her. "I didn't realise. How thoughtless of me. I think we need to talk. Can we do that?"

She nodded, fighting back the tears that had welled up in her eyes. His gentleness was so natural, a part of him, making her feel safe.

They sat on the sofa. "Do you want to be here, with me?"

His fragrance was intoxicating. Her mind swirled with memories of the bedroom, Christine, lunch, the gym and pool. Here was mystery, exhilaration, excitement. She was sitting next to one of the most handsome men she had ever seen and he had asked her to spend the night with him. She needed to know so much more about him. "Yes." The word boomed around the room. This was where she wanted to be right now. *Chill, Suzy, and go with the flow for once.*

"I have, let's say, an unusual history. I told you I like my privacy. There was a time I never had it – it wasn't allowed." He was looking intently at her face now, trying to read any reaction. "I have never pursued a woman – they have always come to me."

"I can believe that – you are so good-looking and I'm sure you know it. I think any girl would want to be with you." She smiled, but felt that this was not going to be a light conversation.

His expression was fixed and impassive.

"That wasn't quite what I meant. But never mind that for now. I started to take control of my own life when I was twenty-three, and made my first million when I was twenty-six. I'm thirty years old now and have been celibate for three years. You are the first woman I have wanted to take to bed in my entire life. I felt it the moment I saw you in the bookshop. And in a way that makes me a virgin – you could say this is my first time. Come with me." Still no smile. He let go of one of her hands and led her upstairs to the bedroom. "This is my bedroom and, other than Christine, you are the only woman who has seen it. Welcome to a part of my world."

Suzy's heart was suddenly pounding and she was desperately trying to fight a feeling of betrayal for having seen his room yesterday.

"I don't know what to say."

"Suzy, please. I'm not looking for a one-night stand – I want more than that. But right now, I don't know how much time I can give. I need to live in the now. Can you do that with me and trust me? You don't have to say anything, but …"

Amazed by her own confidence, she put her hand to his lips to silence him and nodded, hardly daring to make eye contact.

Her mind was spinning with his words – not a one-night stand, but unable to commit in the long term? What did it mean? Had she saved herself for this?

"Will you stay?" He was still looking at her. Suzy saw the anxious, pleading expression in his dark green eyes, and felt herself being drawn into him. He was holding one hand and she was willing him to pull her towards him and smother her with his lips and tongue. She had never felt her body yearn as it did right now and, if there was a risk this could all be over tomorrow, then so be it; she believed she could never feel this excited again and there was no way she was going to miss this chance.

"I want to," she whispered, and almost swooned as relief flashed across his face, his eyes shone and he smiled.

"I am going to take good care of you and we'll have the time of our lives." He raised her chin so she was looking straight at him, and leaned forward and lightly brushed his lips over hers. Slowly his tongue penetrated her mouth, just a little. She could feel it exploring lightly at first, and then getting more intense. She felt his body stiffen. Her eyes were closed and she could smell the woody, spicy fragrance that was him. *Oh my heart.*

He gasped and pulled back. "You taste wonderful." He lifted her up and carried her out of his room.

Chapter 6

Lawrence had decided he was going to ask Suzy to bed at some point, after they had had lunch together; he just didn't think he would do so this quickly. But as he lay in his bed after she had gone, he knew he wanted it more than anything else. He had left a dark life in London and immersed himself in work, gaining great self-control and respect from celibacy and meditation. But recent events had warned him that this life may not last much longer. He took stock of what he had, and this girl had made him feel he was missing a companion – a friend, a partner. He had never needed anyone before, but people hadn't let him be himself – he had even wondered who "himself" was. He remembered his sexual experiences. He had mastered the actual act of having sex, but he had never loved, nor been loved. He never believed he could love anyone, or that anyone could love him.

Meeting Suzy had awoken urges in him which he had suppressed for the last three years. Unable to sleep, he got up in the night and swam for a while, trying to interpret his thoughts and desires. Was he ready to make such a change? Was this the girl for him? He hardly knew her. Was it fair to her; how long could it last? He had woken at 6 a.m. and, as was customary, he meditated and cleared his mind. As he showered he made a decision. His fate would be in her hands, and if she said yes, then he was sure he would have a chance of some real happiness, for a short time at least. And he was confident he could make her happy – after all, he was trained to the highest level in giving women what they wanted, even though they may not have known that was what they wanted. And when his past caught up with him, and she would find out what a bad boy he really was, he'd be leaving the scene anyway and she wouldn't be hurt.

He thought he knew everything. He was wrong.

Chapter 7

Suzy couldn't believe she was doing this. This was what she had been saving herself for and she felt as if she would explode from excitement. They were in another bedroom now, and she caught a glimpse of the large bed enveloped by a dark blue duvet, as he gently set her down upon it.

"You are lovely, Suzy Harper. You know you are about to give your most precious thing to me." He spoke softly, confident now, and masterful. "Don't be afraid to tell me anything, even to stop, if you change your mind. I want to take you to your paradise, and I want to come with you." He looked at her intently.

"I want this," she replied. He moved onto the bed beside her and gently laid her down on her back. He put his arms either side of her and leaned in to kiss her, passionately, hard, tasting her mouth. She put her arms around his shoulders and arched her body up to him. They held this embrace, savouring each other, the heat of their bodies beginning to rise. He felt how lithe her body was; she really did work out. He pulled back and lay on his side looking at her and stroking her cheek.

"I'm going to undress us both now, slowly." He moved to the bottom of the bed and, holding one foot at a time, expertly undid the laces, removed her trainers and gently eased her feet out of her socks. He caressed each foot and planted feathery kisses over them. As Suzy raised her head and giggled, he smiled and said, "Ssshhh," He rested her feet back on the bed.

"Lie down," he said, and as she did so his hands moved to the top of her jeans and effortlessly unfastened them. She raised her bottom and he slid the jeans down over her legs, letting them drop to the floor. Nervous excitement was invading her body, creating a new arousal within her. She was succumbing to his seduction and wanted it with all her soul. He continued to shower her body with kisses as he moved smoothly along her shins, over her knees, caressing her thighs as he reached her knickers. Then he reached for her arms and pulled her gently up, lifting her sweater above her head. He ran his fingers along her arms and then over her shoulders. She was aware he was gazing all over her body, his eyes coming to rest on hers. She felt herself blush as she was sat on the bed in her bra and knickers.

"You're beautiful," he said, and he stood to remove his T-shirt and sweatpants, taking a small foil packet from the pocket and placing it on the duvet. Suzy feasted her eyes on his slim body, exhibiting toned muscles, with a shadow of dark hair showcasing defined ripples across his chest and trailing down into his trunks. He moved back onto the bed and lay beside her. She thought she was going to combust as he pulled her towards him and she felt the warmth of his skin against hers. He kissed her mouth, and Suzy felt his yearning and need, and surrendered to his demands, raising her hands to cup his face, to feel his soft cheeks. He closed his eyes as she gently traced her fingers over them. Then he took hold of her fingers and gently caressed their tips, as he gazed at her face.

"Do you like this?" His words broke her free from the trance he had put her in. She nodded, unable to speak. She was exquisitely nervous as he slid his hand inside the top of her bra, gently cupping one breast and then circling her nipple with his finger. He pushed the bra down, freeing her breasts. She responded by raising herself up slightly and releasing a barely audible gasp of pleasure. His hand moved around and expertly released the bra, casting it aside, and he lifted himself to straddle her body and lowered his mouth to kiss and suck on her nipples, pressing her into the bed.

"You taste exquisite and your body is telling me you are ready." He looked at her passionately, with an unspoken question in his expression, and her nervous smile confirmed he could make his move.

Slowly he eased her pants down and then brought himself up to kiss her lips again, as her naked body stretched before him. She felt vulnerable and excited, becoming aware that he was removing his own pants. She felt his naked body press against her own. She felt the hardness of his penis pushing against her thighs, but was so consumed by the passion of his kissing that her anxiety was replaced by intimate anticipation. Her body tingled from deep within her core and her arousal was almost exquisitely unbearable, telling her she wanted him. He hugged her close, pressing his body into hers, kissing her lips and exploring inside her mouth with his tongue, hard, demanding her to yield. His hands spread over her breasts and flowed over her body. Softly he moved his hand between her legs, stroking her inner thigh, slowly moving up to the opening into her body and then gently touching her clitoris. *Oh, my heart.* Steadily he stroked and circled, kissing her and taking her to the place of exquisite orgasmic sensation. Her body spasmed, and the rapture was beyond all her desires, rippling through her and leaving her feeling an all-consuming pleasure. So this was what it was all about – for her at least.

"Take it, Suzy," he was saying. "Enjoy the pleasure. Your body is beautiful, and so wet and ready and responsive." He had to concentrate hard to control his own urge to be inside her, to release himself from three years of total denial, to combine his desire with hers. *Patience, Los, this is her ecstasy. Gentle and easy does it. When the time is right...*

Then he rolled over, reaching for the foil packet, and unrolled the contents effortlessly over his penis. He felt himself relinquish his commitment to celibacy – now was the time, now was the moment. And he could wait no longer.

He gently held himself above her body. "I'm going to enter that part of your body I will cherish the most. I'll try to be gentle; it's been a long time for me." There was the smile to die for. *Oh my heart.* Suzy's heart was in her mouth and she tensed her body. "Relax, the first time will feel a little strange and may be uncomfortable, but let yourself go, give yourself to me and we will be in paradise." He gently eased his finger into her vagina and slowly circled around and around. He felt her body calm as she lost herself in this new pleasure. Hearing her faint gasps, he placed another finger inside and continued his movements to moisten her, to make her ready for him. "I want to taste you." He gently withdrew his fingers and put them to his lips, looking at her as he pleasured in her juice. "You are delicious." She felt herself blushing and tensing again. The apprehension was killing her, and she wanted him to be fully inside her, to feel what it was like. What was he waiting for?

"Easy, Suzy." Once more his hand went down between her thighs and this time his fingers gently opened her vulva and he slowly eased himself inside her. She could feel his penis begin to penetrate her, moving deeper and deeper. She started to feel full, tight; it was hurting. *Is this right?* He began to ease himself out, just to the edge of her, and then gently back inside. He was licking his fingers and rubbing them in her, lubricating her as he gently moved back inside. He showered her with feathery kisses and whispered murmurings of passion and need, and she felt herself relax, aware, as she did so, of the yielding of her body to his, the discomfort reducing. She was conscious of him speeding up, of an urgency growing inside him, getting closer and closer. Suddenly he gasped, softly, passionately, and his face was animated with pleasure. And they were one. Their eyes met and time stood still. He stayed inside her, revelling in his own sheer pleasure, for as long as he dared before he carefully withdrew from her, and cradled her next to him. They lay entwined for a few minutes before he stealthily removed the condom. "This is the messy bit." He raised an eyebrow and got off the bed to go to the bathroom.

Suzy lay back on the bed and stared at the ceiling. She wanted to cry – why? She was happier than she had ever been; she had felt his passion and yearning and it had been for her, she was sure of that. He had reached his joy inside her and she felt proud and as though she had some control over him; she was now a woman. So what was with the tears steadily creeping down her cheeks? He was by her side before she realised. He pulled her towards him and hugged her tightly, almost painfully. "Don't cry, you have just released my soul back to me and made me feel happier than I have ever felt." He spoke from his heart, vaguely aware of his head asking, *what the fuck have you done?*

He reached for a tissue from the bedside table and gently dabbed her eyes and cheeks. "Here, get under the duvet." They lay wrapped in each other, and Suzy felt wanted and cherished for that moment. "You will probably be a bit sore, but at least it will make you remember me. Sleep now." His face was concentrating on hers, as though trying to read her thoughts. Suzy was already feeling drowsy as she snuggled into him.

Lawrence carefully crept out of bed and slipped into his joggers and T-shirt. He went into his bedroom, lit the candle and got ready to meditate.

Chapter 8

An hour later, Suzy became aware of being naked under a thick duvet. It was still daytime. She turned to see that Lawrence was not beside her. She was filled with dread at the thought that maybe that was all there would be. He would see her only as a quick fuck. What had she done? What should she do now?

Well, she knew what she had been letting herself in for and had already resolved to live with any consequences. She had just hoped that it wouldn't have to be quite so soon! She was suddenly feeling invigorated and confident. Is this how women felt after sex? As she made to get out of bed she felt the soreness between her legs. Ooooooh – he had said she would remember him – too damn right. She needed to go to the bathroom. She looked around for her clothes – there was a soft white bathrobe laid over a chair, and that was all. She put it on. It smelled of fresh flowers. *Oh, this is lovely.*

She walked through the door off the bedroom into another luxurious en-suite. She tried to tidy her hair and gather herself together.

She went onto the landing and down the stairs into the hall. There was no sign of life – where was he? The office door was closed. She knocked, and as she entered he was by her side.

"Hi. Are you OK? You seemed sound asleep. I thought it would be at least another hour or so before you woke. Let's go and get a drink." He took her hand, and was about to lead her to the kitchen.

"Where are my clothes?" Her voice was quiet and impassive.

"I thought you would like the robe. Are you mad at me?"

She tried to stop her voice from trembling. "I don't know how I feel. I wake up in one of your beds, you're not there, I don't know what to think." She pulled her hand away from his and put both hands to her face. *I will not cry.* "Have you had what you wanted? Should I go now? I don't even know you." Her voice trembled, and she admitted defeat as she felt indignant tears start to roll down her cheeks.

Lawrence stepped back and gazed at her, caringly and confidently. "You sweet woman. I don't want you to go anywhere. I have put your clothes in my bedroom. I thought you were going to stay tonight. I have just had a wonderful experience with you, and I hoped it was the same for you – your body language certainly encouraged me to think that was the case. If I've got that wrong, Suzy, you must tell me."

Suzy looked at him almost imploringly. "It was wonderful for me; you made me feel amazing, and so alive. I am just afraid of what will happen next. This is all new for me."

"You are right. We need to get to know each other more. And I have already learned what a bright woman you are." He turned to the paperwork on his desk. "Your translation is excellent. And I'm looking forward to confronting my prospective partner with a couple of the clauses the bastard's trying to sneak in. It'll be a bit of fun for tomorrow. But right now I want to concentrate on you."

Suzy's mind was spinning. *He doesn't want me to leave, he's pleased with my work, and he's so forceful in business mode!*

He was looking optimistic and – oh – she thought, mischievous? His eyes twinkled, one eyebrow raised, but he didn't smile. He shifted his weight to rest on one leg. "You will stay." There was no inflection. It was not a question, it was a statement. She felt weirdly appreciative towards him for making the decision for her. She really didn't want to leave him.

"Ha," she said, a little too weakly. "You have me at a disadvantage. I am standing virtually naked in your house." And her eyes widened as he approached her and undid the belt of the robe.

"Just how I like it, except you're wearing one thing too many." He slipped his arms inside her robe and around her waist, lowering them to caress her behind, bringing his lips to hers as he did so. He was sensual and intense as his head lowered to her breasts and he circled her nipples with his tongue, all the while gently fondling her buttocks.

Oh my heart, I want him.

"Are you sore?"

"A little," she murmured. "I'm not used to this, but wouldn't mind some more, umm, practice?" She had thrown her head back and revelled in the intoxicating sensation of having this man touch her so intimately. His hands had moved round and were fondling her pubic hair, and she could feel the softness of his palm on her pubis. She moaned, unsure how much more she could take before she would scream out with carnal lust. She was tingling, her senses going off the Richter scale. *Goodbye, virgin!*

"You are so ready." He looked up at her. "But not yet. You have to wait." It was as though he were talking to an impatient child. "Now stop spoiling my plans. Come on." He took her hand and they went back up to the bedroom. "Take the robe off and just lie here and relax."

He started to light the candles that he had positioned around the room. The fragrance of lavender and vanilla filled the air. She felt very nervous and too self-conscious to even attempt to take the robe off. She stood motionless and her eyes followed Lawrence as he lit more candles. He then picked up a bottle from the dressing table and turned to face her. "Take the robe off." His voice was gentle but masterful, and he moved towards her. He was still wearing his joggers and T-shirt and shyness consumed her. She hugged the gown to herself.

"Suzy, I want you to feel comfortable with your body. It's beautiful and you obviously take good care of it. We will both get to know it. Please take the robe off and lie down. I want to give you a massage." His look was tranquil and serene and his eyes were on her constantly.

Oh my heart, can I do this? Where is he taking me? Suzy tried to take control of the situation, realising what a vulnerable position she was in. "I'm not sure I should stay – I haven't got any clean clothes or a toothbrush ... and I'm working tomorrow – I need to be at the bookshop before nine." Her gaze held his and she straightened her posture in a vain attempt to appear composed.

He smiled. "Much as I don't like your delaying tactics, or spoiling the fun for tomorrow, I will take you to get your things and make sure you get to work on time. You have my word."

He was deadly earnest. "But take the damn robe off and let me massage you, *now*."

"If this is your attempt at making me feel relaxed, you're not doing a very good job." Her voice had raised, and the audible tremble betrayed her nerves.

Before she knew it, he had taken hold of her and was kissing her, hugging her to him and she felt his protection, excitement surging through her body.

He felt her tense. This was not going to plan! He continued to kiss her while furtively sliding the robe from her shoulders.

Suzy felt her resistance desert her as the robe fell around her feet. He sighed with relief. Then he led her to the bed.

"Lie on your front. I promise you will enjoy this." He poured oil into his hands. She became aware of the aroma of lavender and vanilla again, coming from the oil this time, and then she felt his hands, warm, strong and large. He began to use soothing, tapping and kneading strokes over her upper body, relieving tension and invoking a hedonistic sensation. He moved downwards, stroking here, lightly pummelling, grabbing and lifting there, working with his thumbs and fingertips in deep circles, penetrating her muscles. It was exquisite and she lost herself in the indulgence, closing her eyes and drifting into semi-consciousness. He was forgiven and she desperately wanted to be with him.

Half an hour later he ceased and lay next to her on the bed. "Hey, sleepyhead, feeling more relaxed now?" He had placed a sheet over her and she turned onto her back and gazed at him, smiling.

"That was wonderful. You are a man of many talents, Lawrence Bane." Her eyes expressed her adoration for him.

"I like to think so. And I have had a lot of practice – I trust you like an experienced man." Again, he raised an eyebrow, this time with a grin. "I was beginning to think I was never going to get you back on the bed. Do you like to play hard to get?"

"I don't want to be easy," she teased. "And I haven't actually got any experience, but I am finding you hard to resist." *At some point you are going to have to analyse what he is doing to you.*

They lay quietly for a few minutes and then he got up. "I'll get you your clothes, and then we'll go to your place for your stuff, OK?"

"Yes." She waited a moment, aware of feeling peaceful and calm. No more negativity for today. *Enjoy.*

He held the door for her to climb into his Jaguar XKR-S. She felt confident she could get into it effortlessly, having had plenty of practice in her MX-5.

Chapter 9

At the cottage, she made him a cup of tea to drink while she got her things together. She included her swimsuit, as his pool had looked so inviting earlier.

"Nice place you've got here." He was standing by the fireplace, looking at some photos. "Are these your parents?"

"Yes," she said, still surprised that she could mention them in front of him. She was trying to think what other photos he may have seen. She hated dusting and tended to keep ornaments to a minimum, but there were about six frames at various intervals along the mantelpiece. "That photo was taken at Mount Cameroon. Shall we go now?" She had just remembered the photo of her and Dominic that Richard had taken when they'd gone bowling one night; she wasn't quite ready to give explanations just yet, not sure if it would spoil the mood.

Lawrence replaced the picture of her parents and smiled. "Sure. Come on."

Back at The Sway, he told her to put her things in the bedroom and to make herself feel at home. "Fancy a swim?" His eyes held hers, expectant and hopeful.

"That would be lovely." She followed him towards the pool area. "Oh, I need to fetch my costume. I took the liberty of bringing it." She grinned.

"No need. I swim naked – it's so much more liberating and invigorating." His face displayed his pleasure at shocking her.

"Oh." Was she ever going to keep her clothes on in this house?

He pulled his T-shirt over his head. She looked appreciatively at his firm chest. He unfastened his jeans and stepped out of them. He kept his eyes on her as he took his Armani trunks off and then he slowly walked over to a bench and placed the neatly folded clothes on it. She noticed a tattoo on his left shoulder. She had had sex with this man and yet she knew so little about him, and hadn't even really seen his body – at least, not totally naked as he was now. She felt very nervous as he turned and walked towards her, his eyes not leaving her face, and she not knowing where to look.

"Your turn, Suzy." And he went to the edge of the pool and dived in with such ease and perfection, gliding under the water and coming up for air halfway down the pool. He knew she was nervous, and he wanted to encourage her to be confident with her body, her sexuality, and with him. Then they could both have more fun. He continued swimming up and down the pool. Suzy walked over to the bench and gingerly took her clothes off, her back to the pool. She looked over her shoulder – Lawrence was still swimming. She quickly walked to the edge and slipped into the water. It was warm and she became conscious of the water lapping at her breasts and between her thighs. It was like being in the bath, but more intense, almost thrilling. He was right about swimming naked. She began to get into her stride, passing him as he came down one side and she swam up the other. As she came up for breath she kept glancing to see where he was. Still swimming. She wasn't nervous any more – this was wonderful. After a few lengths she started to tire, and, looking round, she saw him continuing to swim, apparently effortlessly. She floated on her back, feeling totally at ease sharing this intimate time with him, knowing he was so close and naked and yet not being able to fully see him. Suddenly she realised she did want to see him, completely naked, exposed, exhibiting himself for her, to admire his body, to search for the perfect and imperfect parts, to see his penis, the hair that crowned it. *Oh my heart, I want to touch him.*

And, floating in her reverie, she was suddenly aroused by a gentle stroke of her foot as she looked down at Lawrence and righted herself. He embraced her and kissed her, before he playfully lifted her high out of the water and threw her, splashing, back into the pool. She scooped a handful of water over him and they fooled around, both laughing, relaxed and very happy.

"Let's go and shower." Lawrence was at the poolside in a couple of smooth strokes and lifted himself out, then leaned down to help Suzy out. Getting out respectably in a swimming costume is tricky enough, but naked it was impossible, and Suzy tried to retain as much dignity as possible as she scrambled onto the side.

"His and hers showers?" She laughed and headed to the female changing room as fast as she dared on the tiles.

Lawrence caught hold of her arm and she turned to face him.

"No," he said. "I am going to wash you." He cupped her face and kissed her until she was breathless with desire.

Fully clothed now, minus footwear, Suzy followed Lawrence into the hall. Neither of them had eaten since breakfast and it was almost 6 p.m. They walked into the kitchen, where Lawrence opened another door, standing aside to let her go through first. She gasped with delight as she entered a softly lit dining room, with a huge table laid intimately for two. There was a candelabra with five burning candles, a large vase of beautiful rich brown roses and calla lilies, interspersed with green and vermilion foliage, a hostess trolley to one side and an ice bucket of champagne on a stand, the likes of which Suzy had only ever seen in a restaurant before. It looked divine, and she realised just how hungry she was.

She turned to Lawrence, and beamed like a child receiving a most coveted toy. "How did you do this? It's fabulous."

"We have Christine to thank." He walked over to an iPod docking station and the room was filled with soft, romantic music.

"You planned everything? This must have taken her ages. I must thank her. Is she still here?" Suzy looked back into the kitchen, suddenly realising she had not heard or seen anyone, and wondered if Christine came in at 5 p.m. every day.

"She's gone. We're alone. Take a seat, my lady." He was grinning as he held her chair out and shook out the napkin before placing it on her knee.

"I'm feeling very inappropriately dressed, Mr Bane."

"You and me both. And you are way overdressed for my liking!" Once again, the raised eyebrow and no smile. "But we'll leave that for now."

What? He looked at her face and burst out laughing. "Relax, Suzy, you'll get used to it." He popped the champagne cork and poured the sparkling fizz into two champagne flutes.

"Here's to us, Suzy. You can't imagine how happy I feel having you here." His face was earnest and incredibly seductive.

Oh my heart. They clinked their glasses and held each other's gaze as they sipped and savoured the sparkling liquid.

"I don't normally drink champagne; this is a real treat. I hope you're not trying to get me tipsy."

"As if I would dare. I've already had you try to walk out on me today. So I think we'd better fill you up with some food, too. Now let's see what we have for starter." He started to pour roast parsnip and spiced apple soup into bowls.

"This is delicious."

"Mmm. I don't have many guests at The Sway, so Christine doesn't often get the chance to show off her cooking skills, poor lass. So what do you like to drink?"

"Oh, bottled beer usually, and the occasional house wine if we push the boat out."

"Who's 'we'?" His soup suddenly seemed to require all his attention and he stared at it thoughtfully.

"Just a few friends, mainly Alison from the bookshop, and her boyfriend, and a few people I've got to know at the gym. I don't actually know that many people in the UK." *You should mention Dominic.*

"I guess it's not so easy when you haven't any school or college friends." He looked up and it was obvious something was bothering him. *How much are you going to tell her about your sordid acquaintances?* He pushed his chair away from the table.

Suzy became anxious that the atmosphere was beginning to change. They were having a lovely time, talking more than they had done the whole time they had been together. She felt sure they were growing closer to each other and believed he felt it too – it was in their body language. But now something had broken that. She was determined not to let anything spoil tonight. *Is he the jealous type?*

"They're just friends, Lawrence. I wouldn't be here if there was anyone else. Look what you have taken from me today." She looked down at the table and collected their empty bowls together. "And it was wonderful. It's all been so lovely. I don't want this day to end."

Lawrence looked at her. "I'm sorry. I just want to know as much about you as possible. I don't do 'one step at a time' stuff. Once I know what I want I will endeavour to get it the quickest and easiest way I can. I guess I feel more driven because I was never allowed to make my own choices when I was younger. Look, I don't want to get too heavy – we are having a good time, aren't we? Are you ready for the main course, and one more glass of champagne?"

"Yes, I can't believe how hungry I still am. Can I go and get some water to drink, too? I have got to drive to work tomorrow."

"You just sit down. I'll get it." He placed plates of roast chicken, dauphinoise potatoes, carrots and green beans on the table and went to fetch some water.

They continued chatting, and she revelled in watching him eat, hardly believing this was happening to her. He told her about his love of fast cars and motorbikes, chocolate and strawberries. She spoke about cycling around the Cheshire countryside, amazed that he didn't even own a bicycle.

"Maybe you could take me cycling one day." His gaze was intense, burning into her.

"I'm sure I could borrow a bike for you – if you could keep up with me," she challenged him.

"I'll take you up on that, Miss Harper, and I frequently cycle up mountainous courses in my gym." He looked smug, and suddenly very fit.

"So do I!" she retaliated, and he laughed, enjoying seeing her become more confident.

You have chosen the right one.

She discovered his favourite place was the zoo and his eyes shone as he spoke of liking the simple pleasures in life.

"There doesn't seem to be anything simple in owning a house with its own pool and gym," she protested.

"I was a kid with nothing, from nowhere, and spent most of my childhood in children's homes being a pain to everyone. My first trip to a zoo was Chester, after I had moved here, at the ripe old age of twenty-seven. I think I'm entitled to call that a simple pleasure."

Suzy looked at his face. He had a faraway look, as if remembering something he would rather forget. She wondered what memories he had and had a feeling she wasn't going to find out.

"Well, I was twenty-three before I bought my first pair of knickers from Marks and Spencers, so don't feel too sorry for yourself." The mellow tones of Michael Bublé singing "Hold On" flowed quietly from the iPod, and they were both relaxed again.

"Do you want dessert?" He spoke quietly, his eyes fixed on her, and she knew what he wanted her to say: time was pressing on and soon there wouldn't be much of the evening left.

"No, thanks, I'm done. Hope Christine hasn't done anything that won't keep." She got up from the table. "Let me clear the dishes." Without waiting for a response, she gathered the plates and carried them to the kitchen. Lawrence remained seated and watched her every move. She shimmied as she went, swaying to the music, and he could hear her humming as she left the room.

Suzy opened cupboard after cupboard and eventually located a dishwasher, and while bending to put the crockery in, she felt his arms around her waist, pulling her up and in to his body. Oh, his fragrance was wonderful, his hold so firm, and she was suddenly swooning as he kissed her longingly, so assured she would respond to him.

"Time's too precious – leave this. I want to take you to bed now."

She looked up into his eyes, feeding on his confidence, her own nerve holding strong, her desire becoming more intense. She touched his cheek with her palm and reached out to hold his hand. She couldn't bring her mouth to utter her thought: *Take me, please.* He gently kissed the hand holding his, and they walked up to the bedroom.

The lavender and vanilla aroma still lingered in the air, creating a sensual aura around them.

"How do you feel?" His voice was hushed and tender. He moved to sit on the end of the bed. Suzy remained standing near the doorway.

"Alright." Scared stiff was probably nearer the truth, but she so wanted to be here and she felt exhilarated knowing they would make love again.

"Let me look at you. You have a lovely figure, you know. Size eight, right?" She nodded. "And my favourite colour would really suit you." She looked at him quizzically. "Skin colour. I want to watch you take your clothes off." She had a feeling this wasn't open to debate. His face was expressionless, but his eyes were burning through her clothes and into her flesh. *Oh my heart.*

He started to smile at her nervousness. "Wasn't it Aretino who asked why should we not look upon that which pleases us most?"

Who the hell is Aretino? Her nervousness was evolving into tension so sexually bound, with such sensation between her legs, she thought she would have to visit the bathroom. Well, sod this, she wasn't some silly teenager, and now she wasn't a virgin. Stay strong – she would show him.

Trying not to tremble, she undid her jeans and quickly stepped out of them. She stood up straight, leaned her head back slightly and stared at him. His eyes had not moved from her, and he leaned forward, resting his elbows on his knees and interlocking his fingers, slowly circling his thumbs. He was looking very comfortable.

Her resolve to be strong was starting to desert her. She slowly lifted her sweater above her head and stood in her bra and knickers. He continued to watch and circle his thumbs. She had no idea what he was thinking. She reached around her back and released the fastening of her white bra. She looked down as she slipped her arms out of the straps and it fell to the floor. She then pushed her white knickers down to the floor and stepped to the side. She felt herself blush, but the arousal within her was creating a yearning that made her body ache with anticipation. With her head still lowered, she glanced towards him and their eyes locked on to one another. His mouth formed the faintest of smiles and, as he stood, she saw his chest expand as his lungs filled with air.

"You are beautiful. You should come with a health warning." His voice was quiet, smooth and sexy. She felt he wanted her as much as she wanted him. And this feeling gave her confidence in her body. He made her feel she could look graceful, feminine and attractive. He moved towards her and gently ran his hands down her arms and kissed her neck, and she could feel his T-shirt sweeping over her breasts. His head moved lower and his tongue began to circle her nipples, followed by sucking and nibbling. His hands moved around her and stroked her buttocks, and he bent his strong legs, until he was crouching before her, rubbing his nose in her pubic hair. *Oh my heart.* He placed his hand in between her legs and gently moved his fingers to reach that most intimate part. She wasn't sure she could stay standing any longer.

"Put your leg over my shoulder."

I beg your pardon! She slowly lifted a leg and reached for his body for support. And his face moved under her. She felt his tongue touch the top of her inner thigh, and move slowly into her, gently lapping at her clitoris. *Oh my heart.* She felt she could take no more and she murmured his name, pressing her hands onto his shoulders, her straight leg trembling.

"You taste divine." He moved aside, lowering her leg gently to the floor, and as he straightened he lifted her into his arms and placed her lovingly on the bed, moving her legs apart and continuing to lick and lap at her. Her hands clenched the duvet, her back arched and she steadily peaked at the top of an electrifying orgasm, screaming out with ecstasy and pushing him back as her body trembled on the edge again. He was then on top of her showering her lips with kiss after kiss, and then slowing to make them linger on her lips, her cheeks, her eyes. "I want you now." His masterful voice sent a thrill through her. "Watch me." And he moved off the side of the bed so she could see him as she curled up onto her side. He lifted the shirt over his head, slowly and deliberately. He untied his joggers and pulled them down to his feet before stepping aside. Then he lowered his trunks, bringing his knee up to finally kick them off, the whole time looking at Suzy. He stood naked before her, holding his hard, erect penis in his hand. "This is the best part of me. I've not really paid much attention to it for the last three years but you have aroused it, reigniting its fire. I am indebted to you for that, because I feel fucking brilliant." And he grinned, full of confidence and composure.

She smiled and leaned up on her elbow, clearly admiring the view. *Wow, you've done this, not any other woman!*

He turned around, exhibiting himself for her approval. "You see, Miss Harper, there is nothing to be shy about."

He reached into the drawer and pulled the condom on before getting back onto the bed. She could feel him enter her, moving slowly at first, and then more urgently, thrusting harder and deeper until he called out and she could feel him giving in to his climax. He kissed her, ran his fingers through her hair and hugged her to him. They lay like this for a few minutes, words unnecessary, each savouring this feeling of pride and contentment.

"You're one hell of a woman. Would you like a drink or anything?" He went to leave the bed.

Suzy shook her head and followed him into the en-suite. They faced the mirror, watching each other as they brushed their teeth. He watched her taking her make-up off and putting moisturiser on. She pulled her nightdress from her bag and held it up, looking into the mirror. Lawrence shook his head.

"I didn't think so," she replied to his reflection, and then watched as it moved closer to her and she felt his arms hug her. She continued to gaze at them through the mirror, his face nuzzling at her neck. Had she really only known him a couple of days? Wait until she told Alison, if she dared.

He led her back into the bedroom and pulled the duvet back. "Much as it pains me, I think we both need some sleep now. Do you want me to draw the curtains? I don't usually bother in the winter as it's still dark when I get up."

"Oh, I suppose you don't have to worry about nosey neighbours. And it's so dark and peaceful here. There isn't even any moonlight tonight. It's fine by me." They got into bed and curled into each other, with Suzy facing away from him. As he held her pressed to him, she could feel the hardness of his penis. *Will he come inside me again?* She felt a slight soreness, but it made her feel fulfilled and gratified to be able to pleasure him. It was the least she could do after the way he made her feel. Although she had no prior practical experience of sex, she knew that, in general, women found it harder to reach a climax than men, with some women never encountering the full sensation. She was certain it didn't get any better than the sensations her own body had felt today. She wondered how long her relationship with Lawrence could last. Could she even call it a relationship? She hoped with all her heart it wouldn't become a one-day thing. With these thoughts filtering through to the depths of her consciousness, she slowly drifted to sleep, vaguely aware that Lawrence, still curled around her, his body heat like an electric blanket, was already asleep.

Chapter 10

Lawrence woke at 6 a.m. and lightly touched the woman lying next to him, studying her face, her hair, one bare shoulder. She started to stir and opened her eyes. "Good morning, beautiful," he whispered.

She smiled. "Good morning. How lovely to wake up to such a view." She eyed him with a coy smile.

"For you and me both." He reached out to stroke her body. "Are you a bit sore?" He leaned up on his elbow.

"A little."

"Can I save you for tonight?"

Wow, what a question. "I go to the gym on a Friday after work."

Suddenly he was out of bed. "Work out here. Tell me what time you finish work and I'll pick you up. Come and shower with me now."

"But I have my class." She was talking to his back as he headed for the door to the landing. "I'd rather not miss it. I could come over on Saturday night, if you like." There was no response. She wasn't even sure if he had heard her. She went into the en-suite and started to brush her teeth. Then she saw him in the mirror.

"Come and shower in my room." For a moment, he almost looked embarrassed as he added, "When you're ready." Then he leaned against the wall, Mr Confident, and waited until she had finished.

Having completed her task, Suzy looked at the toilet and stared questioningly, directly at him. He held his hands up in mock surrender, smiled – *Oh my heart* – and went out of the room, closing the door behind him.

Was he mad at her? Did he want to see her on Saturday, or was it tonight or nothing? *You knew it could all be over by morning.* But for goodness sake, it wasn't even 6.30 yet!

Still naked, she walked into his bedroom. He was looking at his phone but put it down as soon as he saw her.

"Look, I wasn't expecting to not see you later. I'll take you to your class and then bring you back here. Have dinner with me and stay."

Was he trying to run her life all of a sudden? They really didn't know each other. Her gym class was her territory, a routine she had followed virtually since she moved into her cottage nine months ago. Shouldn't she try to retain some of her own life, even in the early stage of a relationship? She still wasn't even sure if this was a relationship. Was this a compromise she was willing to make?

"It seems a lot of trouble for you to go to."

"Suzy, I need to see you." He took her hand and led her into his shower.

She started to protest, but he pushed a button and water jets spurted around them, a soft rain poured down from above, coloured lights glowed and, with the flick of a switch, Nat King Cole started singing "What a wonderful world". Of course he would see her, and she felt his hands massaging heavenly-smelling soap all over her body. "I want to feel you on my skin, is that OK?"

She hesitated a second, unsure of his intention. Then she felt him, hard against her, and he pushed her, lifting her carefully against the shower wall – oh, unprotected, raw and pure.

"Yes," she panted.

"Relax, Suzy." He steadily eased himself into her, whispering soothingly as she drew back, feeling the initial sting as he penetrated her most intimate part. He moved himself slowly back and forth, his face contorted with exquisite pleasure, followed by fear – *Don't come inside her* – testing his own self-control. He looked fixedly at her closed eyes, seeing her pleasure mixed with slight pain, and pulled her towards him, on the verge of losing himself in her beauty and the ever increasing hold she had on him. *I want to keep you*. Then he withdrew, gasping, and released himself into the flowing water from the shower. He paused a moment, letting the hot clean water run over his penis, cleansing him, and he turned to look at her. She was watching him, not conveying disapproval, or offence, but innocent curiosity, and a simper, knowing she had done that to him. They looked at each other, their silence broken by the music and the streaming water, the jets continuing to shoot at them.

"You felt gorgeous," she whispered. He held her hands out in front of him and then took the soap and poured some into her palms.

"Feel me some more," he commanded, and she placed her hands on his chest, gently at first, gliding over it in small circular movements. Then she moved up to his shoulders, applying more pressure now. She turned him, so his back was facing her and steadily, with exaggerated sweeps of her arms, she covered his back with a trail of soap, over the small jaguar tattoo on his shoulder and then back down towards his buttocks, gently running her hands over them. He quickly turned to face her and placed her hand at the top of his groin. "Don't forget to clean here." Tasting the water, he kissed her longingly, moving his own hand down, in pursuit of her point of ecstasy. As if entranced by him, she widened her legs slightly and his finger entered her vagina, circling gently and then retreating to find the place where he knew he could make her scream, and rhythmically he touched her again and again, until she gave herself to him completely and cried out in pure pleasure.

"Good girl," he said. "You come so easily. Are you sure you want to go to work?" And there was that half smile, one raised eyebrow, and his arms enveloping her and hugging her to him.

"I have to. And if I stay in here much longer, I'll look like a shrivelled old shrew."

"I could tame you." He nibbled at her ear.

She looked up at him and her expression told him it was over, for now.

He stepped out and grabbed towels for them both. She started to dry herself.

"No," he said, and put his own towel around her. "That one is for me." She realised they were going to dry each other.

Back in the guest bedroom, she looked in the mirror. Damn, she had forgotten to wash her hair and it resembled a bird's nest. She frantically sprayed hair mousse and tried to comb it through, finally tying it in a ponytail in an attempt to look presentable enough to be seen in public.

She reflected on how erotically he had dried her. How did he manage to be such a sexpert? Was there a school one could go to? She had enjoyed herself so much she thought she would Google it later and find out!

She started to get dressed, wondering if Lawrence would make some comment about her putting clothes on. He made it obvious he preferred her naked. She had left him in his own room, completing his own morning routine, although she wasn't sure what that was. It was 8.15 and they still hadn't had breakfast. She was due in work by nine. Fully clothed, and laden with shoes and overnight bag, Suzy made her way downstairs.

She walked along the hallway past the dining room. She had a quick glance in – everything had been cleared away and it all looked tidy. *Christine?* She headed towards the kitchen. There was no sign of Lawrence. Christine was standing at one of the worktops, chopping vegetables. She turned around on hearing Suzy come in.

Suzy wasn't sure what Christine made of the fact that she had spent the night with Lawrence. She still wasn't sure what the relationship was between the two of them – simply owner and housekeeper? Suzy had been the one to bewitch him into forsaking his celibacy. How would Christine feel about someone who did that to her employer? Someone who would sleep with a guy without even being his girlfriend at all, let alone a long-term one? What must she think?

Suzy braced herself for a reproachful glare. But she was surprised.

"Good morning, Suzy. It's nice to see you." Her smile was genuine. "Lawrence asked me to tell you he's really sorry, but he had a phone call and has had to go into Manchester."

Suzy's face dropped and she felt a discomfort in the pit of her stomach. *So it really is a one-night stand, and he never really wanted to see me again. I never heard a phone ring or car leave. He could even still be in the house, for all I know – bloody stupid mansion!*

Christine could tell Suzy was uneasy. "Suzy, he couldn't avoid leaving, and it was important he left as quickly as possible. He said you would be leaving for work shortly, that I was to see what you would like for breakfast, remind you that he will take you to the gym, and tell you that it will be chicken casserole for dinner." She displayed such a genuine smile that Suzy couldn't help thinking she liked her. "So what can I get you? Would you like some cereal or toast? Or I could do some eggs?"

Suzy's emotions were in turmoil. She didn't know what to think.

"No, it's OK. I think I'd best be off." She felt herself reddening.

"Well, at least let me get you a drink – tea, coffee, juice? I was just making myself a cup of tea."

There was no sign of a cup out ready, and Suzy had the feeling Christine was trying to make her feel a bit more at ease.

"I'll have a cup of tea, then, thank you."

She watched as Christine moved around the kitchen and set the cups on the island. It was then she noticed the end of an ugly, deep scar protruding from her sleeve. It looked brutal. What had caused that? From its thickness, Suzy guessed it was quite long. Christine noticed Suzy's pained expression, and quickly pulled her sleeve down to cover the scar. She looked embarrassed, and Suzy suddenly felt an unexpected compassion for this woman.

After a moment Christine continued. "Lawrence takes a bit of getting used to. He likes to know what's going on and to be in control, in case you haven't already noticed. He doesn't like surprises."

Well, maybe Suzy could take advantage of the situation here and find a bit more out about the man she had just had sex with, several times. "How long have you known him?"

"We go back a long way." Christine suddenly became very focused on making the tea, avoiding eye contact with Suzy. "He brought me here to Cheshire and gave me this job. I would like to think I've turned out to be quite good at keeping house. We get on well together, having got to know each other's ways. Lawrence is very protective of his privacy, so I'm not in the house much when he is. I keep on top of the cleaning and laundry when he is out, if possible, and then just make sure he's got some food. It was a treat to cook for you both last night. I hope it was all OK."

"Oh, it was lovely. I'm sorry, I meant to say thank you for that." *Does she know we didn't eat pudding?* "You're a good cook."

"Actually, Lawrence and I learned together. When he decided to buy this place, he said he would need help keeping it, and I ... er—" She focused on her cup again. "I needed a job, so it worked out well. We went on a cookery course – can you believe him doing that?" She laughed and suddenly Suzy felt she may be much younger than she had first assumed. "He turned out to be really good. As he is at most things. I cook mainly when he has guests over, but that's not often." She looked over at where she had been chopping the vegetables. "In fact, I suspect he would have cooked for you tonight if he hadn't had to go out. But these things can't be helped." She pulled her stool away and made to return to her chopping.

"Well, thanks for the tea. I'd best be off now." Suzy put her cup in the dishwasher, pleased that she'd remembered where it was. "I'll let myself out," she added. "Maybe see you again. Bye."

"Oh, I'm sure you will."

Suzy wasn't so sure.

Chapter 11

Lawrence pulled into the car park of the Hilton Hotel at Manchester Airport. Miranda had said that she would be in about 9.30. Hopefully Lewis had booked them a room. He checked his phone. Room 311. He headed straight there. He was still annoyed at having to leave Suzy without warning. But at least this time he would be going back to see her later!

He entered the room, and was greeted by Lewis. "Coffee?"

Lawrence nodded.

"Miranda's going to be about ten minutes." Lewis poured fresh coffee and held out a platter of croissants, cheeses, cold meats and fruit.

Lawrence helped himself to some pieces of fresh fruit and sat on the end of the bed. "Has the release date been confirmed?"

"It's the twenty-third."

"Does she know?"

"Yes. She's nervous, Lawrence, and she's missed you."

"I'm not turning the clock back, Lew. I told her that on the phone the other day, but I'm not going to desert her either. Have the provisions we discussed been made?"

"Yes. Directions and keys are already in place in the secure storage area. Will you be ready?"

"Yes." *But a complication has come into my life. God help me.* "But I need a bit more time. Put everything back a week. I can't go back to London until then."

"That's cutting it fine, Lawrence. What's wrong?"

"You don't need to know. Just do it. I'll sort out the bank accounts."

"What about The Sway and Christine?"

"I'll arrange something with the house, but I want to keep it."

"You know that's not going to be easy. He may be able to trace ownership."

Lawrence stood up and started to pace round the room. He looked out of the window. "Then we'll have to make sure he can't. Christine stays with me. I don't want any chance of that bastard getting to her, not without me there! And I don't want Miranda to know anything about my life here. Let's stick to what we planned."

"I think she might find out you're back in London."

"Maybe. I'll cross that bridge if and when I come to it."

There was a knock at the door and, as Lawrence opened it, Miranda walked in. He took her coat and closed the door.

Chapter 12

Suzy flew into the bookshop dead on nine o'clock. Alison was about to put the 'open' sign up.

"Sorry I'm a bit late – traffic." She spoke hurriedly, trying to avoid eye contact with Alison until she had regained her composure. She had already decided in the car not to mention Lawrence yet. For a start, she wasn't sure what to say about him, except that he was pleased with her work, and oh, by the way, he took my virginity, I made him give up celibacy and it was all fucking brilliant – literally!

"Did you get cakes, Alison? I'm starving." Alison couldn't believe it was Suzy saying this and not Mike. The owner wasn't actually in yet, having phoned to warn Alison he would be late due to some problem with his bike – flat tyre, probably, she had thought.

"Are you telling me you didn't have breakfast – are you hung over?"

"No, just overslept this morning, that's all." Suzy grinned now, feeling a bit more relaxed and, having spied the bag of pastries, she helped herself to a jam doughnut and passed one to Alison. "I'll make some tea." And it was a good job she did, as a steady stream of customers came to the shop and neither of the girls had a chance to catch their breath until after lunch.

Later in the afternoon, Suzy's mobile rang. It was Dominic. "I'll just take this, if that's OK, Alison."

"Sure, no problem. If it's Dominic, say hi to him for me."

Suzy nodded, indicating it was him, and walked towards the back of the shop.

The doorbell sounded as another customer walked in.

"Hi, can I speak to Suzy?"

Alison recognised the weird stranger from the other day.

"Oh, I'm sorry, she's just on the phone to her boyfriend, Dominic. Can I give her a message?"

Lawrence's face remained emotionless, but he stared intently in the direction of Suzy's barely audible voice. He tried to focus on what she was saying, but he was unable to make out any part of the conversation.

"I'll wait." He walked directly to the sports section he had been in on his previous visit.

Well, thought Alison, he looks like he's here for more than a French translation! She looked out of the shop window and saw a sleek white sports car parked on the double yellow lines outside. Was that his? What a nerve, hope he gets a ticket. She was about to try to warn Suzy he was here, but it was too late.

Suzy had finished talking and headed back to the counter. Lawrence was there as she approached. Her face lit up, seeing him in a light grey suit, with a pink shirt and dark grey tie. Wow, he knew how to dress to thrill.

"Hello, Suzy. I need to talk to you."

She looked over at Alison, who was just serving a customer. "We're a bit busy. Why don't you have a browse and I'll come over when we're both free." His face was stern and she worried that something had happened in his meeting in Manchester.

He moved towards her, discreetly gripped her elbow and started to march her to the back of the shop. "She'll manage." His grip was tight and almost hurt. *What's his problem?*

He then pulled her round the bookshelves so they were out of sight.

"Lawrence, you're hurting me. What's wrong?"

"Who the fuck is your boyfriend, Dominic?" He spat the words out and they hit her like a tidal wave.

Suzy had not told Alison about Lawrence, and she knew exactly what her friend would have said to him.

"Well?" He let go of her and stepped back, his eyes never leaving her face.

"He is not my boyfriend, Lawrence. It's complicated." She was playing with her fingers, but her eyes held his. He was even more handsome when he was angry.

"Have you lied to me?"

"No. I have no partner, Dominic is my cousin."

"Then your friend has a serious issue with incestuous thoughts." He had visibly relaxed, and his eyes softened. With relief? Suzy wondered.

"Look, I can't talk right now." She peered round the bookcase to see what was happening in the shop. "Go and grab a coffee and a book upstairs. We'll be closing in half an hour and I'll come and get you."

He pulled her towards him and kissed her with a vigour that left her breathless. "Don't leave me, Suzy," he whispered. He turned and made his way to the staircase. She stood for a moment trying to regain her composure. She had to talk to Alison.

The two girls were attending to customers for all of the last half hour of the day. Alison was desperate to ask Suzy about the stranger; she could tell that her friend was flustered and uneasy. Was the guy harassing her? Mind you, he was incredibly good-looking; a girl might like to be harassed by him!

Finally the 'closed' sign went up, and Suzy locked the door. Alison had done a march around the shop checking for straying members of the public and had been surprised to find Lawrence reading *The Economist*. He didn't even bother to look up at her.

She went down to Suzy. "You do know he's still here?"

Suzy nodded. "I'm sort of seeing him." She grinned, and savoured the look of horror that shot across Alison's face.

"You're joking! What's been going on since Tuesday? I thought you looked different this morning. Hell, Suzy, you didn't come from his house, did you?"

Suzy started laughing. "I've a lot to tell you, but right now I need to go and see him. Can you spare me a minute?"

"Go on." Alison watched in disbelief as her friend ran up the stairs. She couldn't wait to hear about this.

"Hi." Suzy walked over to the sofa. Lawrence stood up, without smiling.

"Hi." There was a pause. "I really only called in to see what time you go to the gym. I wasn't expecting to hear about a boyfriend."

"Look, I said it's complicated." She was beginning to feel a bit sheepish about the whole Dominic thing. "He is not my boyfriend. I rather thought you might be?" This was a definite question and she studied his face for a reaction.

He smiled. "I guess so. I like the sound of that."

Oh my heart.

"Can we get out of here now? My car's on double yellows."

"You idiot – you're bound to have a ticket! Look, I need to help Alison finish up here, and my car is in the car park." She gazed at him. "Can you remember where my cottage is? Take my keys and let yourself in – make a drink or something, and I'll be with you as soon as I can."

"Yes, OK." He kissed her lightly on the cheek.

They walked down the stairs holding hands, and Suzy let him out through the front entrance, watching as he nonchalantly grabbed the parking ticket from his windscreen and got into his car. She felt weak at the knees as the car roared into life and zoomed down the street. She really was going to see more of him.

Back in the shop, she and Alison went through the closing routine before heading back to their cars, all the while Suzy was filling her friend in on the translation work, the lunch and the dinner, and – without going into any detail – the fact that they had slept together. Alison was gob-smacked.

"We need to go for a drink – I want to hear all about this. Can you make it tonight after the gym? I'll let Alex know I'll be late."

"I can't. Lawrence is picking me up straight from the gym. Let's do one night next week." By then, her romance could be over. She intended to make the most of it. After all, he had just asked her not to leave him.

Chapter 13

As Suzy pulled up outside her house she could see the lights on inside. No curtains were drawn. *He really doesn't know what it's like to have neighbours.* His car parked outside was enough to get their curtains twitching.

She walked in through the hall, and discovered him in the kitchen. He was sitting at the table with a cup of coffee and tapping on his phone, emailing no doubt, she thought.

"Hi." He stood up and walked over to her. He kissed her lightly, removing her coat, passing his lips over her neck towards her shoulders. "What time do you have to be at the gym?"

"I need to grab my things and go," she gasped. He smelled divine as he continued to try to remove her clothing, and she was beginning to succumb to his demands. But she had fought with him earlier to hold on to her right to go to the gym; she couldn't give in to him now. She ducked to slip away from him.

He sighed and reluctantly followed her upstairs. Suzy had gone into her bedroom to get her gym kit ready and some things for that night and tomorrow. Lawrence headed to the bathroom and glanced in. He spied the shower gel and shampoo for men; the toilet seat was up; there were two towels on the rail. Slowly he walked back into her bedroom and eyed the double bed.

Suzy turned to face him and saw him frown. *What's wrong now?* "I'm nearly done. Are you OK?"

"Does he live here?"

"No. But he does stay over." She was trying to think what he might have seen in the house. "When his boyfriend is away on business." She looked fixedly at him to gauge his reaction.

"He's gay?" A definite question, asked in disbelief.

"Yes," she smiled. "And he has been my guardian angel ever since I came to the UK. I never wanted men pestering me – I didn't think I was ready for a relationship. Dominic was my decoy. And I had a pact with Alison that any guys asking for me were told about my 'boyfriend' Dominic." She watched as a look of incredulity appeared across his face.

"Are you bullshitting me?"

"And why would I do that?" Her voice was getting louder. She had had enough of him not believing her, and she could feel her anger building up. He didn't trust her! "I am who I am, Lawrence, and if it wasn't for that, you wouldn't have got your virgin yesterday. Do you want to leave?"

He sat down on her bed.

"Only with you," he muttered, his confident and controlling manner momentarily deserting him.

Suzy sat beside him.

"I didn't think I wanted a relationship until I saw you in the bookshop on Tuesday." Was it really only four days ago? "You are beguiling me. I don't know what we have, or even if we have anything, but at the moment I think I want whatever you can give me. But if there is somebody else in your life, then I would rather know and leave you alone. I couldn't handle that and it definitely isn't what I want. But I can honestly tell you, there is no one else in mine."

"I have nobody else, Suzy. Trust me. Maybe we are two of a kind." And he thought how she had suffered the loss of her parents. He had never even known his.

"You must trust me, Lawrence. Isn't that important, if we are to have any kind of genuine connection?"

"Yes. I've just never been here before."

"Then maybe we are more alike than we thought. We will have a million and one questions for each other, and probably won't always like the answers. But I think we should always remember our friendship started yesterday – anything before then is history."

He took hold of her hand. "You wise old sage." He smiled, sadly, knowing his history was catching up with him, and beginning to feel much less certain that he could walk away from her when the time came.

Suzy's heart shuddered with anguish, as she perceived the sadness in his precious smile. Something was bothering him. She needed to lighten the mood. She wanted to see his eyes brighten, hear the masterful tone in his voice, have him be the Lawrence she was enjoying getting to know.

"Come on. Get me to the gym, pick me up at eight and take me to yours. I've got a surprise for you." And from the back of the wardrobe, she grabbed her long raincoat.

Chapter 14

Lawrence was leaning on his car, watching, as Suzy came out of the gym, laughing with a couple of friends. She said her goodbyes and waited a moment before walking over to him. He took her bag and put it in the boot as she went round to the passenger side and slid in.

She grinned at him as he got in beside her and glanced down at her black-stockinged legs peeping out from her long coat, her feet encased in kitten-heeled shoes.

He looked at her quizzically, with one raised eyebrow.

"Home," he said.

Oh my heart, that sounded nice.

The car purred out of the car park, followed by several admiring glances, and Duffy's melodious tones flowed out of the speakers.

"I'm sorry I spoke harshly earlier. It's not been such a good day so far. We'll have to do something to change that." He went to put his hand on her knee. She boldly put it back on the gear stick.

"Not yet," she murmured, steadily watching the buildings pass by as they headed to The Sway.

Standing in the hallway, she turned her back to him to allow him to take her coat. He gasped as he revealed her standing in stockings, basque and small black panties, and she secretly congratulated herself for keeping them after attending a *Rocky Horror Show* with Dominic and Richard some time ago, remembering that she never dared take her coat off that night!

"Well, you certainly know how to make the day get better!" He laughed, and stepped back, admiring the view. "Very nice."

She blushed, feeling inwardly smug, awarding herself eleven out of ten for having aimed to make him smile and actually getting him to laugh!

Oh, but she hadn't thought this through fully. As she looked at him his mouth widened with a superior grin and he held his hand up, circling it, silently instructing her to turn around. As she did a 360-degree turn and came to face him again, he shook his head and gestured for her to turn again. *He wants to see my behind.* Suddenly very conscious of the tiny thong she was wearing, she bravely turned her back on him. She heard him move, his arms touched her shoulders, and he kissed her lightly, gently stroking his tongue across the back of her neck. She moved her head, desperately wanting to kiss him, but he nudged her back to face away from him. She could hear him doing something with his clothes and she saw his grey jacket fall to the ground in front of her. Then she realised he had dropped to his knees and began to nibble at her bare buttocks. She flinched as she felt his teeth pull at her skin. "Ouch."

"Ssshhh," he growled and continued to bite and suck. "Touch your toes," he ordered.

Oh shit! Nervously, she leaned forward, and then risked crouching down.

"Straight legs ... and open," he added.

Anxiously, she raised herself up and moved her feet apart. She bent at the waist and held her ankles. Her behind was stinging slightly from the biting and she held her breath in fearful anticipation of what he was going to do next. Steadily, his hand moved the string of her thong to the side and she felt his tongue move from the top of her buttocks to the lower parts, circling around her anus. *Aahh, is it meant to feel this erotic?* He reached the tip of her vulva, then located her most sensitive part, and she moaned involuntarily as he aroused her so intensely, raising his hands to part her flesh. *Oh my heart.* She gripped her ankles as her orgasm raced to take her, so fast, her knees weakened as she was enveloped in that most desired sensation, and she screamed, casting aside all constraint. He lay on the floor and pulled her towards him. She could feel the coolness of the parquet flooring, and then she tasted herself as he kissed her. Oh, how she wanted him to do that, to feel his lips on hers, to feel his tongue inside her mouth, to breathe in his fragrance. As their bodies clung to each other, she could feel the hardness of his erection, and she rubbed her hand forcefully over his trousers, arousing him further. He took her hand and led her into the office, gently pushing her down onto the chair. He unzipped his trousers and, without taking them off, he let himself free.

"I really want you to do this, but you don't have to if you don't want to."

Oh, but she was desperate to. She took hold of him and gently rolled his skin back and forth. Her eyes were closed now and she couldn't see him watching her, admiring her, longing for her to take him. He didn't have to wait long. Hesitantly, she put the tip of his penis in her mouth. She moved her tongue over him and felt the very end, prodding it with her tongue. She heard his gasps and he exclaimed, "Oh, baby." Continuing to move him in and out of her mouth, rhythmically, persistently, she suddenly became aware of him thrusting himself to her rhythm, until he let out one heavy exhalation, and she felt his sperm rush into her mouth. She swallowed, curious at the salty taste.

Slowly, she let go of him, and as she wiped her mouth with the back of her hand, she raised her eyes to his face. His smile shone like a beacon and she met it with her own.

"That was wonderful. You have made my day." He lifted her to him and kissed her lips passionately and longingly. "What am I going to do with you, Suzy Harper?"

"Feed me with something a bit more filling." She smiled shyly at him. She hoped she had found something else she was good at.

"Come on." He led her into the dining room, where the casserole was keeping warm in the trolley.

"Shouldn't I get changed first?"

"No." He served dinner and poured the wine.

Suzy blushed slightly as she pictured the two of them eating chicken casserole, he in his pink shirt and grey tie and trousers, and she in her basque, tiny panties and stockings, and tried to think if she had seen anything similar in a movie. She didn't think so. She was also glad Christine didn't live in.

"I suppose this is a futile question, but do I have to take you to work tomorrow?"

"Yes, unless you want me to get a taxi." Suzy suddenly

thought of his early departure that morning – would he do the same tomorrow? "Maybe I should go back home tonight, I'm going to need to get my car anyway." She felt as though a bubble was bursting – and she was sticking the pin in it.

"Suzy, you're not going anywhere tonight." Lawrence was thinking ahead, way ahead. "I'll drop you at yours in the morning so you can get your car. I need to attend to some stuff tomorrow, as long as I get you to myself on Sunday. And I'll need you to do some more work for me on Monday."

Suzy was trying to digest this information. He didn't want to see her on Saturday night, so was it back to a translator/client relationship? She started to shuffle her food around her plate, and she felt his hand cover the top of hers.

"Are you OK, baby?"

"Sure. Good plan. You could come over to mine, and I'll cook dinner." She became reticent and drank some more wine.

Lawrence squeezed her hand. "Can I be smug and think you don't want to leave me?" His eyes twinkled and she felt a thrill run through her body. She shifted in her chair, a little embarrassed, and then she winced as she was reminded of the biting her behind had suffered.

"Ouch." She gave him an accusing look. There was his schoolboy grin.

"Let's finish here and I'll make you feel more comfortable." He got up from the table and, taking hold of her hand again, he led her along the hallway to the poolroom. "Let me make it up to you in the Jacuzzi."

"Well, that might do for starters." She smiled and he raised his eyebrow.

"That sounds like a challenge to me. Let's get you ready." He turned her to face away from him and started to undo the basque. "Who fastened this?"

Why is he so jealous and suspicious? "My dishy personal trainer, who'll do anything for a small fee!" She glared at him.

Then she felt his hands tighten on her shoulders, almost digging into her skin. She winced. "Damn it, Lawrence, that hurts. I fastened the damn thing myself from the front and twisted it round." *What is his problem?*

"I don't joke about paying for services rendered." His voice was impassive, and Suzy instinctively stepped away from him. He released his grip and met her gaze as she turned to face him.

"What are you trying to say – you use prostitutes?" Suzy suddenly started to shake and felt her legs weakening. Who was this man and what was she doing? She thought of the way he had got in touch with her, setting things up so that she had to come to the house; the sex which was so expertly done; he wanted her naked all the time; and look at what she was wearing! But she had wanted to meet him, she had wanted to have sex with him, and she had taken it upon herself to dress like this – to cheer him up! What a fool she was. She made her way to the side of the poolroom, sat down on the bench and held her head in her hands. Tears were forming – anger, humiliation or heartache that her dream of happiness was being shattered – she just didn't know.

He knelt in front of her. "It's not like that, Suzy. I have some issues in my past, God only knows, but I didn't mean it like that."

He yearned to reach out and touch her, comfort her and hold her close to him. The thought of her leaving him now consumed him like some incurable disease which was going to take his last breath, and he was staggered by the depth of his feeling and his fear of how she would judge him if (or when) she knew his secrets.

The seconds ticked away, and he was aware of her quiet sobs. She didn't look at him. She raised herself from the bench, feeling humiliated by her attire, and headed for the door. How could everything suddenly seem so wrong?

"I think it best if I leave. We don't know each other well enough for this. You ask me to trust you and believe you, but you don't seem able to do the same for me."

He stood between her and the door. "Suzy, please. I don't want you to go. I'm a stupid bastard at times and I have had very little experience of trusting people and not being let down by them. It seems I'm not very good at relationships, full stop." His eyes met hers, and there was the trace of a smile in his.

"Quite frankly, I'm not used to not being good at anything." A smile flashed across his face, briefly breaking his sombre look. "I think I need you in my life right now. I was afraid I might hurt you if anything happened – now I think I am afraid of being hurt by you."

Suzy looked at him. His hair was ruffled from running his hands through it; his eyes suddenly looked lost, and his usual strong, confident posture had become listless. He looked like a schoolboy, afraid of his first girlfriend breaking up with him.

"I never meant to hurt you in any way and you are right, I need to learn to trust: we need to get to know each other. We can't do that if you leave me. I really want to be with you, Suzy, and I hoped you wanted to be with me." He moved and grabbed a towel from the bench. Gently he put it around her shoulders. "I would like to touch you, just take your hand." He hesitated as his eyes held hers. "But I understand if you don't want me to." His voice was calm and quiet, and he straightened himself, almost like someone accused, awaiting a verdict, knowing that he could do no more to prove his innocence.

"Oh, Lawrence." She hugged the towel around her, recognising the clean smell which was becoming the trademark of this house. *How did Christine do that?* She reached for his hand. *Oh my heart.* "I don't want to be away from you, not right now. You enrapture me beyond anything I could have imagined, and I had agreed with myself to live for the now and enjoy it. Didn't I say anything before we met was history? Let's stop beating ourselves up with our suspicions and get back to enjoying each other and learning to trust."

Lawrence took hold of her hand and gently raised it to his lips. "Do you want to get in the Jacuzzi and I'll get some wine?" *Wow, a question!* "I could do with a drink, and I did say I would make it up to you." He looked nervous as he waited for her response.

"Yes, I would like that very much." She smiled, squeezing his hand before releasing it as she went to climb into the hot tub. Her bottom was still hurting from his bites, and as she finished undressing she tried to catch her reflection in the mirrored wall – about eight small marks. Love bites. She climbed into the tub and pressed the button. The water was warm and frothy and luxurious. Lawrence came over carrying two glasses of Chablis. He handed a glass to Suzy, then proceeded to take his clothes off, watching her all the while. He shrugged as he followed her gaze down to his erect penis.

"What can I say? It's the effect you have on me." Finally, there was the genuine smile to die for that endowed his face so enigmatically. He was forgiven. Again.

Taking hold of his wine, he climbed in beside the woman he couldn't keep his eyes off. "I don't want to make any more mistakes with you, baby. So tell me, what does Miss Suzy Harper like doing in her spare time?"

"Oh, I quite like doing some French translation, among other things, for this new client I have. In fact, he's my only client!" She smiled coyly.

"So I can demand your very best customer service treatment!" Now he had a real schoolboy grin. "I don't recall receiving your invoice yet!" He raised his eyebrows and lowered his chin as though he were reprimanding her.

"Don't think I have forgotten about it – you'll get one. And the way my behind feels, I'm inclined to charge my top rate!" She splashed some of the frothing water over his chest.

Lawrence laughed and pulled her towards him. Suzy was captivated by that laugh, their earlier antagonism forgotten. Her lips found his and she kissed him, long and passionately. He sat her on his knee and the water bubbled and lapped around them. Their arms were wrapped around each other and there was a calmness between them.

"Come on," he said, as they finished their wine, and he stepped from the Jacuzzi and held Suzy's hand, helping her out. They put bathrobes on. "Go on up to bed, I just need to get something." He headed towards the kitchen.

Suzy was drying herself when Lawrence came into the room and placed a glass of ice on the bedside table.

Asking her to lie on her front, he took an ice cube and lightly trailed it over her buttocks, precipitating shivers and tremors through her bottom, but it was weirdly soothing and a little tantalising. Then he tenderly dabbed her with the towel and softly massaged a little arnica onto her behind. "Does that feel better?"

"Mmmm."

He pulled back the duvet and they slipped in and lay together, the room bathed in moonlight, shining in a cloudless sky.

"Thank you for staying."

Chapter 15

Lawrence woke at 6 a.m. and breathed deeply as he took in the view of Suzy lying beside him. She had her back to him, and the duvet hugged her waist, leaving her upper body and shoulders exposed. Her top arm was resting near her head. He gently reached his arm out and over her back to lightly trace the soft dome of her breast, and as he moved closer and cupped it in his hand, Suzy shifted slightly, bringing her arm down to rest on her side. He quickly withdrew his hand, not intending to wake her just yet. He breathed in the smell of her hair and lay deep in thought. Today was the twenty-fourth of November. How much more could they have of each other? Was she happy to be with him on his terms? She seemed keen for him to stay at her house tonight. And could he do that, on her terms, for a whole evening? He hated to be away from The Sway. Would he really do that for her?

He quietly climbed out of bed and crept to his own room. He lit the candle and sat in the lotus position to meditate.

Feeling calm and sure, he climbed back into bed with Suzy and gently stroked her shoulders, her back, and moved round to her breasts as he straddled her body, placing soft kisses on her face, eyes and lips.

"Good morning, baby," he whispered.

She smiled, eyes still shut, and replied, "What a wonderful way to wake up."

Slowly she opened one eye and grinned like a small child being told she could have a chocolate. She put her arms around his neck, giving her lips to him as they shared a simple kiss. Then she felt his erection as he stretched himself out on top of her body, and she felt the tingling inside her, as the desire to feel him there became stronger and stronger. He moved his hand down her abdomen, tracing his finger through her pubic hair, travelling lower, slowly and deliberately placing it inside her.

"Does it hurt? Tell me to stop if you would rather." His eyes held hers and she felt herself succumb to his need, exhilarated by the promise of the pleasure her own body would receive. She said nothing but her response was clear. She wanted him.

"I'm going to come on your stomach, OK?" he whispered, and she was so caught up in her own sensations that she couldn't get the words out to question what he meant. Slowly he entered her, going deeper and deeper, until she could feel his fullness, delighting in the sensation as steadily his movement created a rhythm that excited them both. As she screamed out in climax, he quickly withdrew and his juice flowed onto her stomach. Gently and erotically he smeared it over her, making small circles with his hands, letting her skin absorb it like some organic moisturiser. Suzy lay back and relished in the lubricious act he was performing, feeling there was something naughty about it. Something kinky. *I like that.*

As he rested beside her she asked him why he had withdrawn at the moment of release.

"I didn't have a condom to hand. Did you mind?"

"I liked it." She smiled and put her hand on her stomach. He had caressed her so intimately, and knowing it was part of himself that was visible for once she felt excited by what he had done.

"I will remember that." There was that smile again. "But it's the hardest thing to withdraw at that moment, when really I just want to stay inside you."

Oh my heart. "It would probably have been OK, I think I'm due my period in the next couple of days."

"It wouldn't be fair of me to take that risk. I do respect you, you know." He ran his fingers through her hair and twirled the ends around. "And I love to be with you." He lay on his side, and propped his head on his elbow.

"Stay with me at mine tonight," Suzy suggested. "Let me cook you dinner. We still have so much to learn about each other."

"You don't want to know too much about me, Suzy. I don't want to lose you, you know."

Oh. What is he hiding, and is it so bad that I wouldn't want to be with him?

"I need to get ready for work." She felt nervous about where this conversation was going. Part of her was desperate to know more about him, but with his threats of it all being over between them if she did, she had no desire to let it end just yet.

"Let's shower." He kissed her passionately, before taking her hand and leading her to his bathroom.

He had finally agreed to come to hers tonight. Suzy tried to imagine why he had been so reluctant. She felt confident he wanted to be with her now. After all, they had been intimate with each other for the last three days, and he had given her no cause to think that he didn't want to see her any more; quite the contrary, in fact. Yet he seemed to think their time was limited. What did he think was going to happen? What did he know?

It was a typical Saturday in the bookshop. Suzy had little time to go through things in her head, but for her lunch break she took herself off to a nearby coffee shop and began to make some notes while enjoying some soup. She hadn't written for over a week now, which was unusual. Since she had been living in England she was always writing her stories or journal. But, somehow, she knew she would probably never write about her old Lawrence again. She had a new, real one to consume her thoughts – for the moment, at least. The thought of writing about Lawrence Bane in the past tense flashed through her mind. *Just be sanguine about it, girl.* She just needed to get a few things straight, and seeing things in black and white usually helped her to do that.

Sexpert but no girlfriend. "Women came to me." Oh dear God – did he use prostitutes? You have worked for him! You really must give him that invoice, and be careful how you describe your services!

Masseur – where did he learn that, and why?

Celibate – why did he become celibate after what seems to have been a very active sex life – and he must have taken that path at twenty-seven!

Smart - computers and money markets.
Christine - he gave her a job; there's some history between them.
Friends - has he got any?
Work associates - who?
Fast cars and bikes.
"Not much time"? Why did he say he didn't know how much time he could give?

The more she wrote down, the more puzzled she became. She didn't feel fearful, other than of not seeing him again, but she did want to understand what sort of man she was getting involved with and if there was any chance of a longer-term relationship – she already knew in her heart that was what she wanted.

Chapter 16

Suzy had no intention of spending too long in the kitchen tonight. She had bought some chicken, peppers and onions and was going to make fajitas, followed by strawberries and chocolate mousse she had bought, and serve with a nice bottle of Sancerre. She was acutely aware she knew very little about what he liked, but felt sure this was a safe bet, from her experiences with him so far. Shouldn't that be part of the fun of starting a relationship with someone, finding out some of their culinary likes and dislikes, in addition to the sexual ones? She blushed slightly, thinking how quickly their acquaintance had become so intimate, and she was glad he wasn't there to witness it. After all, she wasn't a teenager. At twenty-three, she felt she had some catching up to do, and she was sure as hell going to make the most of it!

She had changed her bed linen in anticipation of their night together. In her small dining room she lit candles. Looking at the table she had laid, she was quite pleased with the ambience she had created. She had a playlist of "easy listening" music, and she put her iPod on and started to prepare herself to see him. He said he would come at eight. Fifteen minutes to go. She poured herself a gin and tonic.

She heard his car prowl to a halt outside the cottage and could picture the neighbours' curtains twitching. They would know this was not Dominic! She didn't wait to hear him knock, but went and opened the door and watched him effortlessly extricate himself from the Jag. He was wearing his black leather jacket, a light grey crew-neck sweater, black denim jeans and grey leather chelsea boots. He looked stunning. *Oh my heart!* Suzy was beginning to wish she hadn't had the G&T. She wanted her wits about her tonight.

He approached her carrying a bunch of beautiful bright orange Asiatic lilies mingled with silver birch, and a small gift-wrapped box.

Suzy stepped aside to let him pass into the hall. He gave her an enigmatic smile and quietly said, "Hi, you look lovely," as his eyes soaked up the vision of her in a cream-coloured woollen jumper, black leggings and black ballet pumps. She wore a small gold chain and studs in her ears, and her hair was scrunched up in a bun with wispy tendrils escaping to fall around her face. She had light make-up on.

She closed the door and turned to face him. His face gave no insight as to his thoughts. Well, she wasn't going to let him intimidate her.

"Shall I take those? They're beautiful." She headed to the kitchen to get a vase. He followed her and took his jacket off, placing it on the back of a chair.

He said nothing, and did not take his eyes off her. He placed the gift box on the kitchen table.

"Are you ready to eat? It's all done. Go into the dining room and I'll bring it through. Pour the wine, if you don't mind." Suzy was desperately trying to keep an awkward silence at bay. Why was she feeling so uncomfortable? Surely they would relax over sharing the meal together. He hadn't moved.

"Have you had a busy day? It was hectic in the shop. I think it's great that people still want to buy paper books, and not just electronic media. Did you enjoy the one you purchased by Sir Steve Redgrave? Perhaps I could check out some others for you?" *Suzy, you're rabbiting on.*

The flowers made a gorgeous autumnal display, as she positioned them in the middle of the kitchen windowsill.

"I'll see them the most in here, I think." She turned to retrieve the chicken mixture from the oven.

As she was about to say that she hoped he liked fajitas, Lawrence reached his hand out to her, pulled her towards him and silenced her with an intense, passionate, lingering kiss. His tongue thrust deep into her mouth, a strong hand held the back of her neck, pressing her to him, and the other circled around her waist, lifting her effortlessly off the floor, before setting her back down, breaking the kiss and standing back to search her with his eyes.

"Do you know how long I have waited to do that to you?"

She shook her head, still reeling from the intense passion in the kiss. "Since I dropped you off here this morning. I'm not sure I can get through dinner." His gaze was so sincere Suzy knew he needed her as much as he wanted her. She felt inspired to adore him. She reached up and wrapped her arms around his neck.

"I'm so glad you're here. But let's eat first." She led him into the candlelit dining room with Andy Williams crooning "Can't Take my Eyes off You". Lawrence took her in his arms and started to gently sway with her to the music, singing the words softly in her ear. *Oh, what a wonderful voice! The boy can sing!*

Finally he said, "OK, let's eat. And thank you. I don't often have lovely women cook for me!"

Oh. Don't read too much into that.

The fun of making the fajitas together created the perfect atmosphere to let their conversation flow, allowing them to continue to get to know each other.

Chicken was his favourite meat, chocolate his favourite sweet, he didn't mind the odd glass of a good wine, but hated to drink to excess. He only drank the occasional beer or lager, though he did enjoy draught Guinness. His taste in music was eclectic, but probably his favourite band was Coldplay. He loved fast cars and bikes. He was particularly fond of his latest acquisition, a BMW S 1000 RR, which he was looking forward to taking on the race track at Oulton Park, to put the bike through its paces. She should come along and watch. He had a soft spot for jaguars, the four-legged kind, especially the black ones known as panthers.

"So that explains the tattoo," Suzy said.

"Yeah, I had it done about seven years ago, you could say to celebrate my freedom." His eyes studied her even more intensely than usual. "It reminds me of Bagheera, the black panther in *The Jungle Book*, and how he tried to get Mowgli to go and live with his own kind, the humans."

He was suddenly miles away from her, looking straight through her. It had been a long time since he had used the name Panther.

Suzy wanted to ask what he meant by celebrating his freedom, but she didn't want to interrupt what seemed to be a trip down memory lane for him. So far, he had not talked about any family or childhood memories, other than mentioning being in and out of children's homes.

"Did you like that story as a child?"

"Yes, I think I knew it word for word. So what about coming to the race track with me one day?" It was a quick change of direction but Suzy was glad; she just wanted to see him relaxed and, she hoped, happy.

"Sounds fun. I've never been to a race, and never really paid much attention to motorbikes."

"Would you like to find out a bit more about them? I had an idea for tomorrow, that's if you trust me and are up for a ride?"

She remembered he had said he wanted her to himself on Sunday. "OK – what exactly did you have in mind?"

"Now that would be telling." He hesitated before pouring another glass of wine. "Are you sure you want us to stay here tonight? I am still OK to drive us back to The Sway."

Suzy thought she detected a hopeful look, but, in deference to equality, shouldn't they spend a night at hers? "No, please let's stay here. I want you to feel at home here. You are relaxed, aren't you?"

"Surprisingly, more than I expected to be." There was a hint of a smile as he poured the wine. "You can be persuasive. So, do I get you for dessert?" His smile widened.

"Wouldn't you prefer strawberries and chocolate?"

"No."

"Well, I don't think we should waste another pudding."

"The last one didn't go to waste. Christine ate it with Dave."

"Who's Dave?"

"Oh, he's her partner, and he helps out with the maintenance and garden at The Sway. They make a good couple."

Suzy couldn't help thinking Lawrence had a real soft spot for Christine. She was pretty certain it was almost in a brotherly way, rather than anything more, though she was sure there was some history between them he wasn't prepared to discuss with her. Maybe she would learn a little more from Christine sometime.

"Please let me tempt you with the pudding. You said you love chocolate."

"Go on, then. Then I get to call the shots." He raised his eyebrows, looking at her salaciously.

What's he thinking of now?

As they cleared the dishes from the dining room, Lawrence followed Suzy into the kitchen. He picked up the box from the table. "I would like you to go upstairs and get changed. Just put this on, nothing else, and come back down to me. I'm sure it will suit you, but I need to know." His expression was blank, no smile, and no response from her was expected.

Full of his usual confidence, taking the statement she had made earlier about wanting him to feel at home very literally, he watched her. Suzy was beginning to feel that she was the guest! The box could only contain a scanty bra and pants at most.

"I'll wait for you in the lounge. I noticed you've drawn the curtains."

What?

Obediently, she went upstairs with the box. She sat on the edge of her bed as she unwrapped the paper and opened it, revealing a bottle of perfume, Vanitas by Versace. *Oh.* Still fully clothed, she sprayed some on her wrist and inhaled. It was divine! She had never known a perfume could smell so good on her skin, and she had tried many in various boutiques. How did he know this would be so lovely on her? He wanted her to wear just this! Had she the guts to walk naked down her own staircase and into her own lounge, to him? Would he be fully clothed?

She went into the bathroom and began to undress. She realised she wanted to please him. She would do anything he asked of her. She looked at her reflection. Her figure wasn't too bad, and she was thankful she went to the gym regularly. She removed her jewellery too and sprayed herself extravagantly: arms, wrists, neck, shoulders, abdomen, even her feet. She breathed in. Had she overdone it? Would she knock him out? What if it didn't suit her as much as she thought it did?

Feeling very self-conscious, she slowly walked down the stairs and stood at the doorway to the lounge, in full view, as she didn't want to appear to be hiding round the corner. Perhaps that first G&T had come in useful after all.

He was leaning back in the armchair directly facing the door, his legs crossed so one ankle was resting on his other knee, his arms forming a triangle on his stomach, with his fingertips touching at the apex and his chin resting on them, much as one might see a lawyer contemplating whether or not his client was telling him the truth. Oh boy, did he look at home now. His eyes penetrated her body, and already he could smell her, and the perfume. He was silently waiting to see what she did. When she did nothing, he broke the silence.

"Sit down Suzy, and relax."

Relax? How the hell did he think she could feel relaxed, being so vulnerable in front of him? He had the upper hand here!

She looked at him, exasperated. "I don't feel very relaxed, Lawrence." She glared, and tried not to raise her voice, which was quivering a little.

"You need to be comfortable with your beautiful body. Don't be shy, it isn't becoming." His voice seemed devoid of passion. How could he be so composed and in control? Was he not excited, seeing her like this? Was he playing some sort of game?

"I can see this is hard for you. I really want you to be totally relaxed and confident with your body. We can have much more fun that way." Now his eyes twinkled, as his own excitement began to build. He slowly stood up and strode the three paces it took to reach her. He took her hand firmly in his and brought her towards the sofa. "You can do this for me."

Suzy wasn't so sure. She lowered her head, and pulled back against his grasp. She could make her feet go no further.

"Close your eyes then, it will be easier."

She did as he instructed. He was still holding her outstretched hand and, as he pulled, she made her way to the sofa. Eyes still closed, she tentatively sat down. Well, he was right about one thing – it was easier. She could almost forget he was in the room with her. Until he spoke.

"Just sit back and relax, baby."

She opened her mouth, about to say she just couldn't do this, when she felt his hands on her face, his fingers very gently tracing lines along her cheekbones, down the slope of her nose, along the curve of her lips, brushing over her eyebrows and gently stroking her eyelids. He touched every part of her face with sensual indulgence. This was for his pleasure. She could smell him, that spicy wood fragrance that was his signature and, slightly in awe of him, she felt her whole body unwind, like a rope that had been twisted and then released as it hung in mid-air. She could luxuriate in simply sitting there, feeling his hands move down her neck, onto her shoulders, travelling in light whispery movements to her breasts. Here his fingers barely skimmed them, leaving her feeling the slightest of touches, and now she tensed with wanton anticipation. Then she felt the pressure from his hands enticing her to lie down. She kept her eyes closed. Now she could feel his hands move over her abdomen, and he was trailing his fingernails up and down, circling her belly button, tracing the edge of her waist. She felt his nails scratch a little harder, and let out a moan as the sensation teetered between pain and exquisite relief. He reached her pubic hair, his fingers pressing lightly on her soft mound. His hands moved lower, gently pushing her legs apart. *Oh my heart, I can't wait for you to touch me there.* She moaned softly and murmured his name. Suddenly she felt his tongue, lapping at her clitoris time after time, and she scaled her own parapet, climaxing with such intensity she was left breathless, in awe that her orgasm could reach such a height. She screamed and laughed and arched her naked body, and as he released her, she opened her eyes, urgently reaching for him and kissing him desperately, as though her next breath depended on him.

"My beautiful baby."

"Oh Lawrence, what are you doing to me?"

"Making you happy and making you mine. Can I take you to bed now?"

Wow, another question! "Yes."

This time he had a condom.

Chapter 17

"Come on sleepyhead, let's not waste the day."

Suzy blinked to adjust to the light he had turned on and saw that he was dressed and holding a tray with toast and orange juice on it.

"Don't expect this every time you let me seduce you, and I trust it is to your liking for breakfast. I couldn't see much else in your cupboards." He had a reprimanding expression on his face.

"No sir and yes sir," she conceded. "And thank you very much, sir! This is lovely."

"Well, let's hurry up and eat. We've got places to go and the weather is perfect."

"Where are you taking me?" She felt excited at the prospect of having a whole day with him, at being a couple on a date.

"I'm going to get you kitted out, and then we are going out for a play."

"And am I permitted to get dressed?"

He looked at her to judge her expression, and as she smiled he seemed to let out a sigh of relief, and he smiled back.

"Wear warm layers and keep it casual. Do you have any thermal underwear?"

"If I did, I wouldn't let you see me in it!" She feigned a look of flirtatious shock.

Settled in his car, with Coldplay drifting from the sound system, she realised they were travelling into Manchester. Lawrence left the car on double yellow lines and, wrapping his arm around Suzy, walked across King Street to Belstaff's.

"We are going to get you kitted out, baby, starting here."

Leaving with a gorgeous black leather motorcycle jacket and trousers, Suzy battled with mixed emotions; she was thrilled at the prospect of being on the back of a motorbike with Lawrence, but she had argued with him over his very expensive choice of clothing, there being no way she could have afforded the £1,500 he had just spent on her. For something she was anticipating she wouldn't be wearing more than a few times, she found this expense totally over the top.

"Just indulge me, Suzy, I want you to be safe and look good. I don't have that much to spend my money on, and I'll enjoy seeing you in these as well as getting you out of them." He flashed that schoolboy grin.

They set off to the motorcycle shop at Delamere and acquired an Arai helmet emblazoned with a Union Jack, together with gloves, boots, and thermals.

"Now, let's go home and have some fun!"

Suzy didn't think she had seen him looking so relaxed and happy before.

Feeling slightly overdressed by the sheer weight of what she was wearing, Suzy had to admit she did look good. So did he! Black leather definitely suited him, and he had a behind to die for. Lawrence had fitted an intercom into their helmets so they could communicate with each other, and he carefully helped her to put hers on, together with the gloves. She was well and truly padded up! She had already warned him not to get cross, as she explained she had previously only been on the back of a college friend's motorbike several times in Yaoundé. She climbed onto the pillion seat of one of his bikes, a Triumph Speedmaster.

"Good to go?"

"Yes."

"Remember, go with the bike, try not to over-lean. Just relax and enjoy, baby! Here we go!"

Effortlessly, Lawrence rode down his driveway and out onto the roads of Willowford. Suzy experienced a feeling of freedom. She could feel the air around her as they zipped along, yet she was warm in her clothing. She felt high up, able to see over fences and hedges. It was exhilarating. She watched as they passed beautiful gardens, busy farmers' fields, people queuing for a bus, all the time the bike just gliding along.

"Happy?" Lawrence asked over the intercom.

"Yes!" Suzy said exuberantly, and as they approached open countryside, Lawrence warned her to hold on. He twisted the throttle and let the bike soar along the highway, turning effortlessly. Suzy beamed with delight as they cruised around sweeping bends, roller-coastered along dips and rises in the roads, zigzagged through twists and turns, speeding past the beautiful Cheshire countryside. She revelled in the intimacy of being so close to him, totally in his care, and she trusted him implicitly.

"Don't you just love the sense of freedom you get from being on a bike?"

"It's fantastic! Lawrence, I'm having a really lovely time."

"Good. We'll head over to Bakewell and get something to eat. Hungry?"

"Yeah, sounds like a good plan! I've never been to Bakewell."

By 6 p.m., they were pulling up outside Suzy's house, after an exciting and very happy few hours. Conversation flowed easily and they enjoyed finding out more about each others' tastes in cars and bikes, food, music, clothing, films, all the things any new couple might start out discussing in a relationship. But Suzy was aware of a lack of history, gaps not being filled in, and still no mention of friends or family by Lawrence. She wasn't letting it spoil the feeling of joy she had for now, but she kept the thought at the back of her mind, to try to understand why, and analyse it in her own way.

They had arranged that Suzy would collect her car, dictionaries and so on, and then drive over to The Sway for the evening, with a view to looking at some more work for Lawrence the next day. Lawrence went straight off on the bike and Suzy went in to change.

She checked her answerphone and there was a message from Alison.

"Hi Suzy, it's Alison. A few of us are going out for a drink next Friday night. Can you and your guy" – her tone expressed impish curiosity – "join us? It'll be great fun! See you Tuesday."

Suzy wondered how Lawrence would react to such an invite. She liked the idea of introducing him to her friends, it seemed to add credence to the girlfriend/boyfriend relationship, which she was confident it had now become. Maybe she would check with Alison who else was going before she spoke to him.

She gathered a few overnight things, doused herself in his perfume and, with cheerful anticipation for the evening, set off in her car to The Sway.

Meanwhile, Lawrence had phoned Christine, via Bluetooth, on his way home.

"Has it been delivered and set up?"

"Yes, Lawrence, though how you persuaded them to do a Sunday delivery I don't know! I've made it up just as you asked, and dinner is in the fridge. Take care on that bike."

"Yes, don't worry. And thanks, Christine. Can you come over in the morning and sort breakfast, about 7.30?"

"Of course. I'll see you then."

Lawrence wondered if he had gone too far with his plan for a surprise, but he couldn't wait to get home and he was suddenly smiling from ear to ear.

He parked his bike in the garage and raced into the house and upstairs. Perfect. He changed into sweatpants and vest top and went down to the gym. He had let his usual workout routine slip a little since he had met Suzy Harper. He was still afraid to think too far ahead, but he was certain he wanted it to be a longer-term association with her, and not just on the work front. He longed to be with her all the time, and he was struggling to concentrate on his normal business and routines. Not to mention the preparations that had to be made after Christmas. He needed to buckle down and focus on what still remained to be done. He wasn't used to having such a distraction consume his thoughts in this way. His work, fitness and planning to get justice for Jimmy had been his sole objectives in life since he left Miranda. And he was accustomed to achieving those objectives. So how had he allowed this young woman to come into his life and take over? Did she have any idea what a hold she had on him? He knew the answer to that was no, in just the same way that neither of them could know what would happen in January.

He was now focused on his workout, punishing himself for skipping a couple of sessions. Inverted row, bench press, lat pull-downs, squats, underhand pull-ups, reverse crunches, leg press and fingertip push-ups. He showered as quickly as he could and, wearing just a pair of dark blue lounge pants, he went to sit at his computer in the study to listen for Suzy arriving.

There was an email from Lewis – this time encrypted via PGP Mobile. Lawrence read the decoded message and sat back in his chair as he thought through what still remained to be done. He sent an email to Richard Groves to arrange a meeting for Tuesday.

Chapter 18

Suzy's car pulled up at 7.30 and he met her at the door. Taking her bag, he put his arm around her and she pressed her cheek against his warm chest, breathing in the fragrance of his body, this time without his cologne. It was still heavenly.

"You're wearing the perfume. It's beautiful on you." Putting her bags on the floor he pulled her to him and kissed her lips with an urgency that exposed his fear of losing her. Suzy sensed this and wrapped her arms around him, binding him to her. *Would it ever feel normal just to walk up to him and say "hi" with a kiss?*

"I just need to get the motorcycle gear out of my car. I thought it best to keep it here, and then we'll be ready to go, assuming there will be a next time. I have had such a lovely day."

"Me too. I'll get the kit. Give me your car key and then go and get warm in the snug – I've lit a fire."

Suzy felt her heart leap at the prospect of a romantic evening by a real fire.

She crossed the hallway and opened the door. The flames flickered yellow and orange, creating dancing flashes around the unlit room, the smell of the burning wood enticing her to enter and embrace the warmth. The sofa had been moved a little closer to the centre of the room to tempt them to snuggle up together, sharing the heat from the fire and each other's bodies.

The next minute, he was by her side, hugging her to steal her warmth, his bare chest testament to the drop in temperature outside this evening.

Suzy looked up at him. He was excited about something, and she was intrigued.

"What are you planning?" she asked playfully. "Have you done a workout?"

"Yes!" he said. "And I have a surprise for you, but let's eat first. Christine has made some chilli. I'll just go and put some rice on, and then we'll sit in here and eat when it's ready." With a quick kiss on the top of her head he left the room, grinning. He returned after a few minutes with two glasses and a warmed bottle of Campo Viejo Rioja.

"Let me just get changed," Suzy said, and she turned to go and get her bag to take up to the bedroom.

"Do it here," he ordered, with a glint in his eyes. "Entertain me!"

Suzy thought for a moment. Her self-confidence was growing, and she was beginning to like his little games. Her insides started to tingle. She wasn't sure if she could wait until they had eaten! She brought the bag into the snug and fumbled for a moment to retrieve a pale blue silk wrap. She had intended to wear it as a dressing-gown in the morning, but the warmth of the room and the nervous excitement which was building up inside her compelled her to feel relaxed and seductive. She looked straight at him. He was sprawled on the sofa, one leg tucked up and the other extended leisurely before him, watching her with just the faintest trace of a smile on his lips.

Slowly she removed her cream sweater, revealing a pale yellow vest top, which she eased over her head, extending her arms up to the ceiling as she cast it aside to float down to the floor, revealing a cream bra with tiny red roses over the cups.

"Very nice," he said, his smile growing.

She turned her back on him and he watched her unclasp the bra and let it fall. Without turning around, she crouched down and removed her ankle boots and socks, and then she stood up and unzipped her blue denim jeans, swaying her hips slightly. She exaggerated a wriggle to extricate herself from them and glanced over her shoulder at Lawrence, her eyes bright with excitement. He held her gaze and slowly she turned to face him as she lowered her panties and stepped out of them, holding them up in her right hand. She then tossed them to him and quickly grabbed the wrap she had positioned at her side and covered herself in it. Lawrence was beaten to it, having delayed to hold the knickers to his face before he had the chance to reach her while she was still naked.

"You cheated!" They were both laughing as he strode over and held her in his arms.

To Suzy's surprise he did not attempt to undo the wrap.

"Now you know how to distract me, Suzy Harper. I'm not sure I like you having that power over me." He raised his eyebrow, his smile gone.

Oh my heart! Suzy was feeling anything but powerful, more like weak at the knees. How did he do this to her? She still couldn't get over how beautiful he was, his enticing features as his brows danced above his eyes, saying you know I am going to have sex with you ... and that was exactly what she wanted! But when?

He released her and poured the wine. Then he sat on the sofa and patted the seat beside him, silently asking her to join him. They snuggled into the corner, he put his arm around her, and they could almost taste the seductive anticipation between them. They sipped their wine and chatted about the bike ride.

After they had eaten the chilli and the dishes had been cleared away, he took her hand and led her upstairs. Suzy turned to go down the landing to the guest bedroom, but he stopped her and pulled her towards his bedroom door. "My surprise, remember. Now close your eyes."

Suzy tightened her grip on his hand and allowed herself to be led by him, as he gently guided her past the dressing room and manoeuvred her further into the bedroom. He then turned her around, and Suzy imagined she now had her back to the balcony, and he lowered her hand to her side. "OK, you can open them now." He stood at her side, carefully studying her reaction.

She was standing in front of an enormous wrought-iron bed. The elaborately woven iron top of the headboard just peeped up from behind the large square pillows carefully positioned on the mattress. There were graceful mixes of dark and pale grey Japanese birds soaring across wispy Japanese foliage in the silk of the duvet and the pillows. The effect was a stunning romantic scene set against the beautiful backdrop of the view out onto his balcony and beyond, to which the fortunate occupant of the bed would awaken. *Oh my heart.*

After a few moments of absorbing this exquisite vision, Suzy turned to face him. "Lawrence, it's beautiful. I'm stunned.

When did you arrange this?" She thought of the private man standing beside her and his single bed. Had he kept it, relocated it to another room?

"This is for us, Suzy. You have bowled me over and I want to be able to make love to you in the most beautiful setting I could imagine." He slowly eased her wrap from her shoulders, releasing the tie, letting it fall at her feet. He started to kiss her, gliding his hands over her shoulders and down her arms, smoothing them over her abdomen, cupping one breast in his hand and nuzzling at the other, softly nibbling and then biting a little harder, and yet harder, his hunger growing. Suzy yielded to his touch, electric shocks surging through her as she fed on his power, her head arching back, wanting to feel the pain of her nipples under his touch. He tugged his own jogging pants off and pressed his erection against her, moving his hand down between her thighs.

"I need you," he gasped.

He laid her on the bed and she shivered as she felt the coolness of the silk on her skin. He straddled her, his fingers moving urgently inside her, and she screamed at the intensity of her orgasm. She had come so quickly, the delicious sensations lingering as she continued to moan, and he kissed her fiercely, as though draining the air from her. Then he rolled to the side and reached for a foil packet. Suzy moved onto her side, watching him place the condom over his penis. She moved her hands to smooth it on and continued to rub him up and down. Now she was feeling her power! As he lay on his back, he lifted her onto him and she steadily raised and lowered herself, getting faster as she saw his excitement growing, until he cried out loudly, threw his head back and closed his eyes, arching himself further into her. *You are mine now, Suzy Harper. How can we ever release each other? I want to keep you.*

He grinned up at her. "That was all a bit too quick; now we'll have to go again." He pulled her towards him.

As Suzy lay back she couldn't believe she had orgasmed three wonderful times. She'd had the thrill of seeing him climax twice, too. Yes, that gave her a sense of power, power over him...

"It's been a wonderful day. I would love it to be my groundhog day, just like in the film." Suzy was looking up at the ceiling, as they lay under the soft duvet.

"I think you'll find the expression is to do with little groundhogs predicting when spring will start, but I know what you mean." He leaned over her and started to tickle her.

"OK, smart-arse," she retorted between giggles. She could never imagine getting enough of this man.

Chapter 19

"Come on, sleepyhead, let's swim." It was 6.30 a.m. and Lawrence had been up, brushed his teeth and meditated, and was now ready, with just a towel hung sexily around his neck.

How can I resist that? Suzy climbed out of bed and utilised the en-suite before following him down to the pool. She knew it was pointless to wear anything and, besides, swimming naked was liberating!

At breakfast, both fully clothed, Lawrence explained about the work he hoped she would do today.

"I want to give you the wording to go into that purchase document, and also a covering note. I want the guy to stop trying it on with me by using French. If it wasn't such a good project I'd tell him to go to hell."

"What exactly is it?" Suzy asked, genuinely interested to know what sort of businesses he wanted to be involved in.

"This guy has a small laboratory and has created a compound to increase the efficiency of fuel, make it go further. One of his main ingredients is urea, from none other than good old urine. I'm interested in getting the production and distribution into Third World countries, particularly in Africa. I have some other business interests there that could facilitate this. This guy is a good chemist, but has no idea how to progress the product and the business beyond his laboratory. He's trying to tie me into his own naïve business model, which won't work, and he thinks he can run rings round me using French. Well, baby, your skills are making sure that doesn't happen." He kissed her lovingly. "And he doesn't realise I have exclusivity – with my get-out clause. So he has nowhere else to go. But I need to seal this quickly now, and I'm running out of time. Luckily, he doesn't know that."

Suzy couldn't help noticing that he tried to fake a smile, and that was not like him; it wasn't his style. He was quiet for a few minutes and she wondered if he was thinking the same as she was – how long did they have together, and why did it seem it had to end? Something was bothering him and every now and then it reared its head between them. Would he tell her what it was? Could she help at all?

Lawrence set Suzy up to work in the snug. He didn't want any distractions in his office. Suzy wondered if he was just safeguarding his privacy, but that was understandable; after all, he wasn't used to having anyone around at all, other than Christine, and it seemed that she was in the house mostly when he wasn't. Suzy focused on translating the documents he had written into French. She didn't see him until he walked in with coffee about 11 a.m.

He had spent most of the morning at his computer, and having a teleconference with Lewis.

"Christine and I are ready to come down to London on the fifteenth. We'll take the train from Crewe and should be at Euston just after two o'clock. We'll go straight to the room and check the area out, then meet up with you."

"Good, we'll meet in the Black Dog. It's usually quiet and there's a room at the back we can use if it isn't. Don't go wearing any of your smart clothes, remember."

"Don't worry, Christine is going to vet everything I want to bring – she's already limited me to a holdall. Make sure the phones are sorted and the PGP loaded so we are ready to go with communications. And I want someone up here with Suzy, just to be on the safe side."

"Have you spoken to her at all?" Lewis sounded anxious.

"No. And I'm not going to. I don't want her involved. God, I don't even know if I will see her again." The conversation halted.

After a moment, Lewis responded. "It may not be that bad, Lawrence. I've heard Black has logged a call with Harry Rawlins, and as soon as it's made we'll know what he's planning."

Harry Rawlins was a sleazy private investigator, an ex-cop who had been kicked out of the police force. He was suspected of using and abusing young girls in a deal he had with Josh Black, but nothing could be proven and the girls were so afraid of Black that no witnesses would come forward. Now he would do any measly job for any dirty bastard who would pay him! It would appear that the dirty bastard was Black now.

"Thanks, Lewis, I know you've got everything covered. I'm meeting Richard tomorrow and, hopefully, I can start to tie things up at my end. I'll email the info through by the end of the week." He ended the call, then sat back, thinking of Jimmy.

Jimmy Havers had been his best friend at the children's home, and they had run away to London together. Homeless, penniless and desperate, the two fifteen-year-olds were prime pickings for the likes of Josh Black, who had offered to "look after" them. Lawrence was taken in by Miranda Cleveley. He knew he had been the lucky one. Jimmy, though, became devoured by a life of male prostitution, physical violence and drug abuse. Lawrence had first become suspicious that Jimmy was dead and that Black was involved, on the night the cruel pimp had attacked Christine. Lawrence had been warned that something was kicking off and he had shot straight over to Black's place in Whitechapel. He had managed to wrestle the pimp to the ground, but not before he heard him threaten, "You'll end up like Jimmy when I get my hands on you, Bane," and seen a menacing grin flash across the evil bastard's face. Lawrence was sure that Jimmy was dead and that Black had killed him. His purpose in life now was to prove it, and get him put behind bars as justice for his friend.

Lawrence needed a drink. He made some coffee and, leaving Suzy to continue her work, he went back into the office and started to scan through his financial files in preparation for the meeting with Richard Groves in the morning.

Lawrence had what was often referred to as a photographic memory. He was able to quickly absorb large quantities of data and recall even the smallest of details. He had also discovered his ability to apply the data he took on board. He hadn't really thought much about this gift until he had started to read almost whatever he could get his hands on during his time with Miranda. The real advantages came when he developed an interest in computer science, and began considering how data could be stored, transferred, coded and decoded. This ability culminated in him becoming financially secure and leaving his life in London. He realised his abilities and his own strength of character were going to be put to the test again. This time, lives could depend on it. He carried on reading.

Chapter 20

Dominic picked up his phone and scrolled through the text he had just received.

> Hi Dom. Have to cancel holiday tomorrow. Lawrence Bane coming into office and I must see him. Catch up with you at dinner tonight, but you may as well go into work tomorrow too and we'll rearrange. Rick

Dominic Cook and Richard Groves had been seeing each other for the last five years. They didn't date other people – with the exception of Dominic spending time with his cousin Suzy, helping her to create her own life in the UK, but that didn't count! Richard was head of his own wealth management company, which looked after rich individuals and their money. One of his richest clients was Lawrence Bane.

Dominic hadn't seen Suzy all week. He knew she was smitten with Lawrence Bane. The girl had waited for the right guy to come along, and he just happened to be one of the richest guys in the area! He wasn't particularly worried about her. They had texted each other and spoken on the phone and, truthfully, he was glad she had found someone she wanted to be with. It was all just a bit intense; he hadn't even been able to arrange to meet up with her since the beginning of last week, she just wasn't around. And now this guy urgently wanted to see his financial advisor. It was unethical of Dominic to expect Richard to discuss any of his clients, but he needed to know that this guy was trustworthy, and not going to let his cousin fall from a great romantic height into a pit of despair.

He tapped his phone.

> Hi Suzy, how is it going? Are you still seeing your client? What are you up to tomorrow night? I thought we could go for a drink

and I could stay over. Richard might come with me. Let me know; would be good to catch up. Dominic

He then let his office know that he would be in work tomorrow after all.

Suzy heard her phone beep and checked her messages. She suddenly felt a bit guilty about Dominic. To any onlooker, it seemed she had dropped him like a ton of bricks the minute Lawrence had come on the scene, but she knew her cousin was glad she was actually seeing someone at last, even though he would no doubt have been shocked to know what his cousin was getting up to so early in a relationship. She smiled at the thought.

She wasn't sure what Lawrence wanted to do for the rest of the week. There was certainly no pattern to their "dates", and she felt quite excited at the thought that he seemed to want to see her as often as he could. Then she remembered Saturday night, when Lawrence had been reluctant to stay at her house. But surely that was just because he was so used to being at The Sway? And what about his bed? That was a huge commitment – she was still bowled over by what he had done. She was having such a wonderful time with him, and was even enjoying doing this work for him. She was going to check if he had any plans before she got back to Dominic. Maybe the four of them could get together.

Lawrence entered the room. "Do you fancy a breath of fresh air in the garden?" He was holding a large grey cable-knit sweater and sporting a cream-coloured one around his shoulders – dashing!

"Sounds lovely. I've nearly finished this so we can go through it when you're ready. Have you had a productive morning?" She didn't expect him to discuss anything with her, but she checked for any giveaway look. There was none.

"Pretty good," he responded cheerfully. *Seeing how you are planning to leave her!* He pushed the thought instantly out of his head. "Here, let me see you in this." He held the sweater up to lift it over her head.

Oh, dear God, am I allowed to love him? Or not?

There were French doors from the snug into the garden, and it was a cold, bright, sunny day. They stepped out onto one end of a huge patio area that stretched along the back of the house. A manicured lawn gave way to an unkempt stretch of grass, interspersed with shrubs and flower beds, decorated pagodas and garden chairs and tables, arranged to catch the best aspects of the garden at different times of day throughout the seasons.

As a backdrop, there was mature woodland, with a variety of trees, the light glimmering off the reds, oranges and browns of the autumn leaves, interspersed with evergreens. Lawrence led her along a walkway and she could sense a feeling of uplifting calmness and optimism. Did he come out here to relax, or forget?

They passed through an open meadow and headed into the wood, smelling the foliage and hearing the crunch of the leaves, twigs and bracken at their feet. It became darker, with the stillness and watchfulness of deep woodland. Up ahead was a clearing and a bench in front of a pond. The pond was strewn with water hawthorn and a few fallen leaves. It was like a magical retreat. There was a large plastic drum on one side and Lawrence wandered over and removed the lid. He scattered food over the pond.

"For the sturgeon. They eat all year round, you know." He stared thoughtfully into the water.

Suzy kept silent, admiring the vision of him dressed in his dark brown walking boots, jeans and the thick cream cable-knit sweater, and taking in the beauty of his shining golden-brown hair flicked casually across his forehead, a shadow of stubble, and his dark green eyes looking intently into the water.

Oh my heart, I want to lie here with you.

She walked over to him and stood at his side. He didn't look at her, but reached out to take her hand, squeezing it hard.

"I'm glad you're here, Suzy." They walked around the pond, trying to spot any fish lurking beneath.

The mood was relaxed and romantic, just the two of them in this private space. He pulled her to him, and she felt his hardness against her abdomen. Slowly, she moved her hand to touch him, caress him there. He moved her towards the wide trunk of a mountain ash. She felt him tense, his breathing quickened, and she could smell his fragrance as he lowered his head to her and began to unfasten first her jeans and then his own. He eased hers down and slipped his hand inside her knickers, eagerly pushing his fingers up into her vagina, feeling her warm and moist. He brought his fingers to his lips and tasted her, looking at her. She slipped her hand inside his pants, released his penis and held it firmly, desperate to feel him, to taste him. She lowered her head to move her mouth down to him, but he stopped her.

"No. Put this on." He reached into his back pocket and took out a condom, taking it from its foil packet and handing it to her. She looked down and took it in her hand, feeling the soft, slippery rubber, with the harder outer ring. She had never held one before.

She looked up at him. "Er, I'm not sure which side."

He smiled, and tenderly showed her how to hold the end and ease it onto him, softly moaning as she did so. Then, her jeans and panties discarded, he lifted her up and pushed her back against the tree. She wrapped her legs around him as he pushed himself into her. She braced herself against the chill on her bare buttocks, and the discomfort of the tree, but felt the warmth of his breath, and she moved with him and against him. They became more desperate and it was feral and coarse, but she so wanted him, to feel the power of making him climax. As he cried out, spent, he lowered her and pulled her down onto the moss, kneeling over her. She felt prickles and bumps and undulations in the ground, and he leaned forward to cover her mouth with his, thrusting his tongue inside her, leaving her breathless and full. His hand moved to arouse her and she screamed in ecstasy as she climaxed with a new intensity.

Finally, they dressed, and lay side by side, gazing up at the canopy of branches.

"I wasn't intending to do that." He broke the silence, but continued to look up. She felt as though she were being kept in the dark, unable to see his expression. Was he glad it had happened? She sure was!

"I liked it."

"I wasn't sure if I would hurt you." He sounded anxious. "Remember, I never want to hurt you." He still didn't turn to face her.

Suzy shuddered as though someone had walked over her grave. He sounded so far away. He wasn't lying next to her. Was he thinking about the future? *Is he going to hurt me? Is he planning to end it?*

She turned on her side and propped herself up on her elbow. Struggling not to allow her voice to quiver, she demanded, "Why do you say that, Lawrence?"

He sat up and pulled one of his knees up, placing his arm around it, like a cowboy in an old Western as he surveys the cattle, with a strand of grass between his teeth.

"I'm sorry. I should have checked you were OK with it. It can be a bit rough that way." Then there was that schoolboy grin. He was not going to let her know what was on his mind. "But good, don't you think?"

He pulled her up and started to run back down the track.

"Last one back to the house makes coffee," and he sped off.

She had no chance of catching up with him, and she followed him into the kitchen, breathless and windswept, looking decidedly unkempt. She pulled bits of moss from her hair, glad Christine wasn't there.

"You can bring the drinks into the snug, and I'd quite like a biscuit with mine." His eyebrows moved cheekily, and he left her to fumble through the cupboards.

Oh my heart, this is so feeling like home!

Having managed to put everything together, she went into the snug and they checked through her work. She thought he was pleased and ready to proceed with the deal.

Later, as they ate the dinner Christine had prepared, she decided to ask him about meeting up with Dominic. She was going to be working the next couple of days, and again on Saturday. She thought about the night out with Alison, and friends from the gym. Alison had texted to let her know who was going, and Suzy thought it might be quite nice for Lawrence to meet a couple of her friends.

"Would you like to come over tomorrow night and meet Dominic? I haven't said very much about you but I think he would like to meet you."

"Check me out, you mean?"

Suzy couldn't be sure if he felt annoyed by this, or even threatened.

"I think he would just like to meet someone I am actually seeing! He's been looking after me and, yes, he probably does want to make sure you're not some sexed-up bastard who's just using me." *Oh, she hadn't meant it to sound like that.*

Lawrence stopped with his fork in mid-air. "Is that what you think?"

Suzy had stopped eating "How can you even ask that? Do you think I would still be here if that's what I thought? I thought we were getting to know each other." She looked down and added quietly, "And I, for one, am enjoying it."

She felt his hand on hers.

"Me too, baby, I'm sorry." He carried on eating. "Why not? I'll do you a deal. I'll come over and meet him. What do you normally do – go for a drink somewhere? Then you come home with me for the night." His face was determined. This was not a proposition up for discussion, it was a done deal! It would give him a chance to check this Dominic out, to help him decide how much protection he wanted Lewis to give Suzy.

"I have a meeting tomorrow, but I'll come over to yours for seven."

After they had finished their meal, for the first time since she had met him, they sat and watched TV together, *Top Gear*, his favourite programme. It gave her an idea, and she snuggled up to him contentedly.

Chapter 21

Suzy was really busy in the shop the next day, and she hadn't had the chance to let Dominic know Lawrence would be coming over. Dominic had texted to say Richard would be with him and they would both stay over, rather than travel back into Manchester. Well, that should be fine, they would have the house to themselves.

Lawrence parked his car in the underground car park of Groves Investors in Manchester. He was shown into the boardroom, which had panoramic views across the city, and coffee and biscuits at his disposal. He stared out towards the horizon as he sipped his hot drink. Richard didn't keep him waiting long.

"It's good to see you, Lawrence."

"Thanks for seeing me at such short notice. I just want to check that everything is in place, as discussed, and to keep you posted on the new deal. I'm hoping to sign by the end of the week. Otherwise, I am going to walk away from this one. I'll call to confirm everything anyway. I think the holding will just sit under Topco. It'll be sixty per cent and I'll let you and Frazer deal with it from there."

Frazer Meadow was Lawrence's solicitor.

Richard poured himself a coffee. "Do you want a top-up?"

"I'm fine, thanks."

"Well, everything is in order in Luxembourg. I presume you have the latest financials for the holdings there."

"Yes, I was checking everything out yesterday. I don't see anything slipping, but I need your guy out there to start implementing the arrangements we discussed."

"It's all ready. The structure's set up so your name will not be visible, and all records will be in French. Jacques has already been working on the programs you set up for him, and the network should be secure for the three of us. We can trust him. Are you sure you want to play it this way?"

"Look, I know you and I go back a long way now, but I don't want any cock-ups on this, Richard. I need to be able to rely on you. I'm not going to be in contact for a while, I can't say for how long, but I'll communicate via Lewis and he'll let you know how to get in touch with me, if needed. I don't want anyone to be able to trace my assets, or even the fact I'm living around here. I'll be around till mid-January anyway, so you can give me an update after Christmas. I've made a list of the payments I want maintaining." Lawrence took a paper from his briefcase and passed it over the table.

Richard was not surprised that the Julia Kershaw Children's Centre, Fairchance, was top of the list.

"How is Julia?"

"She's fine. I'm seeing her next week, as I want to make some arrangements for The Sway. It will be good to see the kids again." Lawrence sounded genuine and Richard wondered, as he always did, why a man such as Lawrence Bane would want such a close, and costly, connection with a group of drop-out kids. He knew they were regular guests at his home.

The rest of the list comprised the normal monthly outgoings, including Christine and Dave.

"I noticed the D fund had slipped into the fourth quartile. Who's managing it?"

"I know." Richard replied, as he checked through his papers. He had always been envious of Lawrence's ability to recall so much information from memory, and he had to admit to being wrong-footed by him on more than one occasion. But Richard knew his business and he knew how to identify the needs of his clients and find bespoke solutions. Over the years, he had come to realise Lawrence's needs were very bespoke, and Lawrence knew he could rely on Richard to provide solutions and assist in managing his affairs. He also knew he could trust him.

"The fund manager has changed. There's been a bit of a shake-up, and we're monitoring it. Will you leave it with me?"

Lawrence looked directly at Richard. "Let Lewis know if it's not back up by next quarter, and I'll get in touch to discuss what's going on."

Richard had no idea what Lawrence was planning or why, but he knew their conversations for the past few months had been leading up to Bane not being around. He made it clear that he didn't want anyone knowing anything about him. He seemed to be trying to disappear. He wasn't overly worried, and knew his client well enough to trust him and appreciate he must have a good reason for this strange behaviour. He was pretty certain there was nothing fraudulent going on. Lawrence wasn't like that. Was he?

"By the way, I'm organising a track day, for the bikes. Do you want to join us?"

"Sounds good – have you got a date?"

"It'll be early December. I'll send you the info as soon as I've finalised it. There'll be the usual suspects. Thanks Richard, and I'll be in touch."

* * *

Suzy was exhausted from her day in the bookshop, and she was glad she hadn't arranged to cook tonight. They would have a takeaway at her place and then walk down to the pub. She was excited at the prospect of Lawrence meeting Dominic and Richard, and was sure they would get along. She remembered Richard liked motorbikes, so they would have that in common, at least.

She got straight in the shower and lingered under the water, wondering what to wear. She walked downstairs in her denim jeggings and a dark grey polo-neck sweater. She would wear her knee-length black leather boots.

Lawrence arrived a little earlier than expected. "I wanted to have you to myself for a few minutes," he said as he walked in. "So, I'm going to meet the gay guys then?" He had a playful glint in his eyes, and Suzy knew he wasn't being malicious.

"Have you met many others?" she asked out of genuine curiosity.

His expression suddenly changed and she knew he wasn't with her for a moment. He walked into the lounge and slouched on the sofa.

"One or two," he said quietly. Then he stared up at her, looking adorable in his leather jacket over a pale green sweatshirt, perfectly setting off the colour of his eyes.

"Let me take your coat. Do you like Indian or Chinese?"

"Are we talking gay guys still?" he teased.

As Suzy leaned towards him to take his coat, he pulled her onto his lap and kissed her hungrily. "I'd rather be at home, with you naked." He grinned wickedly.

"You'll just have to wait." She pulled herself away and went to the door, hearing a car pull up outside.

Richard stopped dead in his tracks, recognising Lawrence's Jaguar outside Suzy's house. "Has she got company? I'm pretty certain that's Lawrence Bane's car."

"She didn't say, but I think she has been seeing him. Does it matter? If this is awkward for you, I'll make excuses."

"No. I, er, just wasn't expecting to see him here. I don't think he knows about us. In fact, I'm bloody sure he doesn't. But what the hell – it's none of his damn business. But I hope Suzy knows what she's doing. I didn't even know she had a boyfriend. When did she ditch you?" He punched his partner on the arm, trying to lighten the tension that was suddenly looming over the evening. He gritted his teeth as Suzy opened the door.

"Hi guys!" She pecked each of them on the cheek. "I'm sorry, Dominic, I didn't have a chance to let you know I invited Lawrence over tonight too." She took their coats, not sensing the atmosphere surrounding her cousin and his boyfriend.

Lawrence stood up as Dominic walked into the lounge, then went as white as a sheet as Richard walked in behind him. He immediately walked over, a little too quickly, and shook Dominic's hand. "Pleased to meet you," he said, trying to regain his composure and analyse the implications of his financial advisor knowing his girl.

Richard looked at him, as though searching for direction on how to handle the embarrassing situation. He didn't know whether to be more concerned about the fact Lawrence would now know he was gay, or that he now knew Lawrence was dating his partner's cousin, and obviously their relationship would not continue smoothly, at least not based on the conversations they had had and the plans that were being put into place. Hell, this was awkward.

Suzy noticed something wasn't right. There was a silence hanging in the air. Why hadn't Lawrence said hello to Richard?

Dominic broke the tension. "Hi Lawrence. Not sure if you have met my partner, Richard Groves." *I may as well come right out with it – we are not used to living in the closet, though work and relatives don't usually clash for us*! Richard, for his part, was glad Dominic had rescued him, as it put the ball in Lawrence's court whether to admit that they knew each other or not. Either way, though, he knew he had some explaining to do to his client.

"Hi Richard, it's good to see you again," Lawrence said, and the ice was broken.

"You two know each other?" Suzy was flabbergasted, and relieved. "Well, that's great. Let's order some food, I'm starving." She felt delighted that it seemed they would all get on fine.

Dominic glanced at Richard, who glanced at Lawrence, who raised his eyebrows and said, "Good. And I need a drink." He made his way into the kitchen to find the fridge. He wished he were at home, where it would have been a longer walk to the kitchen, as he would have been grateful for some more time to think. He knew he had some explaining to do to his advisor!

Not knowing what everyone drank, he took four bottles of Budweiser out of the fridge and opened one for himself. He took a few swigs, contemplating what other surprises could come out of this evening, and then made his way back to the lounge.

"Not sure if this is what everyone wants." He placed the bottles on the coffee table.

"It's good." Dominic took the bottle opener and handed the drinks round.

"What do you fancy?" Suzy passed Lawrence the menu.

Taking you home and having you to myself for the evening. "I'll go for sweet and sour chicken, and whatever rice is going."

The conversation flowed remarkably easily for the next hour, moving from motorbikes, to food, to the state of the UK economy. At this point, Suzy suggested the men walk to the pub, while she dealt with the dishes and followed them down.

Lawrence immediately said he would wait with her, not wanting her to be walking in the dark on her own, though he was assured the pub was only a short distance away. Dominic then suggested Lawrence and Richard go on ahead, sensing the two of them needed to talk, and he would follow with Suzy.

It was cold and wet as they walked to the Red Fox.

Lawrence got straight to the point. "I presume you are wondering what the hell I'm doing dating your boyfriend's cousin?"

Richard noticed he sounded more bitter then angry. "Look, I didn't know until tonight – I was as surprised to see you here as, no doubt, you were to see me! But I do want to know what you're playing at – she's obviously besotted with you. Does she know you're not intending to hang around?"

"No!" Lawrence was glad of the dark – he wasn't sure if he was controlling his expression sufficiently to prevent Richard Groves knowing how much pain this was causing him. "It's complicated." *And I don't want her to get hurt.*

"Well, I don't know what you're up to, Lawrence, but maybe you should do the honourable thing and break up with her now. Give her the chance to hate you for a while." His bitterness hung in the air.

They reached the pub and Lawrence followed Richard to a table in a quiet corner. He sat on the bench and leaned back, not removing his coat just yet. He stared after his advisor, as Richard went to get the drinks. *How could you possibly leave her now? God knows how you're going to leave in January. Maybe by then she might hate you anyway. Would Richard tell her anything?* Lawrence played with a beer mat, absorbed in his thoughts.

Richard placed four pints of lager on the table. Lawrence wondered if now was a good time to mention he was going to drive Suzy back to his house for the night!

"I know I owe you an explanation. Something from my past has caught up with me and I need some time in London to sort it out. I don't want Suzy involved: I care too much for her. And I can't leave her now – that's not an option." *I want to keep her.*

Richard knew his client too well to try to change his mind. He didn't interrupt him.

"I will see that she is well looked after. I have already asked you to look at the implications of changing my trusts, in case anything happens to me, and – well, part of that is for her. At least I will have peace of mind that she will be financially secure."

Richard was stupefied. Lawrence couldn't have known Suzy for more than a couple of weeks! Surely the two of them hardly knew each other?

He was about to say something when Lawrence continued.

"I would appreciate it if you didn't mention anything to her. Let me handle it my way. I assure you, I will keep you informed of my intentions, as far as she is concerned."

"I won't let you hurt her, Lawrence. And money doesn't compensate for everything, you know."

Just then Dominic and Suzy appeared. "I think we need to talk more about your arrangements." Richard was conscious he could be seriously pissing off one of his best clients, but Suzy and Dominic were more important.

"We'll speak tomorrow." Lawrence looked anxious as he stood up for Suzy, and leaned over to kiss her gently on the cheek. She blushed slightly, and squeezed along the bench to sit next to him. Richard noticed she looked happier than he had ever seen her.

Dominic and Suzy continued their conversation about Suzy's translation work. Lawrence glanced at Richard, and then said he had a contact in a company based in Nantwich with French subsidiaries, and had informed them of Suzy's work. He was arranging for Suzy to go and see them, with a view to some regular work translating inter-company correspondence. He apologised to Suzy that he hadn't had a chance to tell her about it.

Suzy was obviously excited at the prospect of more work, but also made every effort to hide her concern that he was going to put an end to her working for him, and that he might put an end to their relationship, too. Richard studied her expressions intently. Clearly she felt very deeply for Lawrence Bane, but there was something worrying her, too.

Lawrence put down his half-empty pint. "I'm sorry guys, but I'm driving." He looked at Suzy.

"We're going back to Lawrence's place tonight, so you guys get the cottage to yourselves."

Dominic laughed. "I think my cousin has grown up all of a sudden. You'd better take good care of her, Bane."

Lawrence glanced at Richard as he said quietly and resolutely, "I will." He picked up his coat and, taking Suzy's hand, they said their goodbyes.

"I'll call you tomorrow about that outstanding information," Lawrence told Richard. He breathed a sigh of relief when the two of them were alone outside.

Suzy had noticed some tension between him and Richard. "Are you OK?"

"Sure," he replied. "I can see they are very protective of you, and also very discreet for a gay couple." He forced a grin, desperate to lighten the conversation. He did not want the evening ruined.

She punched his arm and chastised him, "What did you expect? That they'd be all over each other? We weren't, so why should they? And don't forget, people around here think Dominic and I are a couple and Richard is just a friend! They could even think you and he were the gay guys!"

"Hey!" He put his arm around her shoulders and pulled her to him. "I was only joking." *I know they will take good care of you, my darling.* He kissed her hair, breathing in her fragrance. He was desperate to get her home.

As they walked into the hall he took their coats, then got some ice and water from the kitchen before leading her upstairs.

"You're not too tired are you?" He started to remove his sweatshirt, looking at her constantly.

Suzy caught her breath, a feeling of tingling excitement forming between her legs.

"Not at all." Her eyes met his. She removed her sweater, revealing a plain black bra against her ivory skin.

He moved over to her. "Let me undress you." With a flick of his wrist her bra fell to the floor. He grabbed at her breasts, desperate to feel them, pulling at her nipples and twirling them between his forefinger and thumb, until it hurt and Suzy gasped at the delectable pain.

"OK?" he whispered, and she moaned, "Don't stop, please don't stop."

He moved his mouth down and pulled at her nipples with his teeth, then sucked her breasts, hungrily taking in as much of her fullness as he could. "I need you, Suzy."

He removed his T-shirt and she felt the warmth of his torso and its subtle ripples. She smelled his body and tasted his hair as she kissed his bent head. He moved his hands to her jeggings and knelt to roll them down her legs, running his tongue down the front of her right leg and lifting her foot, then lifting her left one to free her from the trousers and socks, his tongue gliding over her feet. She ran her fingers through his hair, pulling as his touch sent quivers through her feet, enthralled by the exquisite delight he seemed to be taking in tasting her, inch by inch. As he knelt before her he reached up, slowly easing her black panties down, and as she stepped out of them he held them to his face, smelling her scent and revelling in it. She sensed the thrill he was getting, and time seemed to stand still as he was consumed by her sex. He gently tugged her down to him and they knelt facing each other. He moved his hands along her arms and nuzzled at her breasts again. She moved her hand down and felt his penis, erect and hard through his jeans. She undid his zip and pushed her hand inside, desperate to feel him. He gasped at her touch, delighted in her initiative and her own need. He helped her to push his jeans down and quickly raised himself to remove them, together with his trunks.

"Wait a moment, baby." She watched as he walked over to the bedside table and removed a piece of cloth. He then crawled back to her.

"Can I put this over your eyes? I want you to use your other senses to feel and enjoy." It wasn't really a question. He began to cover her eyes, until all light was gone and she couldn't see anything. She was still kneeling upright, and suddenly felt slightly unbalanced.

"Don't move," he commanded, and he calmed her with his hands on her shoulders. Then he left her. A moment later he was in front of her again. Suddenly she gasped as he slid some ice over her left nipple and then began to lick at the droplets of water. He rolled the ice around her breast and she shivered and pulled back from its coldness and paradoxical burning.

"Ahh, Lawrence!"

"Sshhh, Suzy," he continued, bringing her towards him with his arm at her back, moving the ice to her right breast. It was burning and freezing and driving her crazy. Then he took it away. Suddenly she was aware of the ice on her forehead and again he lapped up the water droplets. Then nothing. Then she felt it on her stomach, followed by his mouth. Gradually, in a random pattern that left her guessing where she was going to feel it next, he iced and lapped her cheeks, her neck, the centre of her chest, the line down to her pubis. Then he spread her knees apart and she felt the ice along her inner thighs, followed by his tongue.

"Now lie down."

She obeyed, feeling him position himself between her legs, pushing her knees apart. She lay back, trying not to feel embarrassed at how they must look, which she was unable to see. Then she cried out as she felt the now watery ice cube being pushed gently inside her body, stimulated by the cold and wet of the ice and warmth of his fingers. As he withdrew it he rubbed it against her clitoris and she arched her back, raising herself up to him, oscillating between bearable and unbearable, desire and fear. The sensation was mind-blowing and he moved his head down to add the feel of his warm tongue to the melange. Then he coaxed and teased her, bringing her to the edge of climax, then pausing, letting her ebb and then flow again, as he restarted his actions, forcing her to beg, "Please … don't stop."

"What do you want to do, Suzy? Tell me what you want."

"To come, I want to come."

He moved up a gear, roughly spreading her legs, lying before her on the carpet, and flicking her clitoris with his tongue, over and over. Her sensations were going into overdrive, and she quivered with the intensity of it, trying to pull back and escape that feeling of extreme, unbearable sensitivity.

"Lawrence," she whispered, "it's too much!" She leaned up to push at his head for relief, but he kept hold. Then he slowed and ceased, placing his body over her, quickly rolling the waiting condom over his penis, and entering her. She was so ready for him. He pinned her arms above her head and in the darkness she felt him thrusting in and out and then throbbing inside her as they came together, crying out loudly.

He gasped "Fuck, that was incredible. Suzy, you make me come so easily and intensely; it's like I have never come like this, ever. What are you doing to me?" He removed the blindfold gently as she lay beneath him.

"I love you," she said, and ran her hands up and down his spine, reaching his coccyx, caressing it and then leaving a white line with her nails as she scratched her way back up – agony and ecstasy, and he arched his back upwards to feel her nails travelling along him, his eyes closed and his furrowed brow revealing his intense pleasure.

After a short while, she watched his graceful, defined body go into the bathroom, returning condom-less, and he lay by her side.

"I've been to the doctor, and I should be able to start taking the pill in the next few days." She had turned on her side and was playing with the hairs on his chest as he lay on his back.

His expression became impassive, all signs of the joy and pleasure of a moment ago gone. He took her hand and moved it away, before getting off the bed. Richard's words came back to him. *Maybe you should do the honourable thing and break up with her while you're still around, give her a chance to hate you for a while.*

Suzy stared up at him. "What's wrong?"

"Nothing. It's OK, baby, try and sleep. I just need to do a bit of work before I come back and join you." He leaned over, kissing her cheek to reassure her everything was OK, before grabbing his jogging bottoms and leaving the room.

He sat in the dark at his desk. The TV screens were all blank and there was an eerie glow from the moonlight shining through the window. With his elbows on the desk, he clasped his hands as if to pray – for help, divine inspiration, forgiveness? He thought about his expectations for the future: was he being too defeatist? Did he believe he had no right to happiness, so could not expect to keep it once he found it? Why shouldn't things work out? He should trust Lewis and his team to do their work, trust himself to see everything through to the end – the just and honourable end. He realised he had more to fight for – his own future and his choice to keep what was his. He would not desert her; he would come back, no matter how long it took, and maybe she would still have him. He would try to regain her love.

He flicked on the desk light and powered up his computer. He checked his email and entered the PGP code to open one from Lewis.

> Lawrence, Harry Rawlins snooping around and fishing for info. Seen meeting a Charles Rigsby – does this name ring any bells with you?

Lawrence leaned back in his chair and ran his hand through his hair. Fuck! He remembered Veronica Rigsby. This could be confession time, and he needed to see Lewis. He sent an encrypted email to say he would be over in the morning.

He wasn't sure he could sleep now. He was sinking into despair and his head was beginning to throb. He walked into the kitchen and poured a glass of ice-cold water. *Come on, get a grip.* He drank some of it and splashed the remainder over his face, then went back to the bedroom.

Suzy was fast asleep, and he realised how relaxed and comfortable she now was with him. He had to keep her out of his mess, protect her from his past. But he also wanted to try to hold on to her. *Were these two objectives mutually exclusive? How could he be honest with her?* He slid into the bed next to her and curled himself around her. She shifted slightly at the contact with his skin, but remained asleep.

Chapter 22

Suzy was surprised to wake up and find Lawrence still asleep beside her. She gazed at his face, so calm and peaceful, and watched the duvet rise slightly in rhythm with his breathing. She leaned in to smell him. This man was beautiful, exciting to be with, successful at what he did, and she felt safe with him. She should be very happy, but there was a gloominess lurking within her. She couldn't really comprehend this feeling; it wasn't despair or desolation, just a shade of sadness dampening her joy.

She slid from the duvet and took her phone from her bag. She angled for the best shot of his face and clicked. He turned over but remained asleep. She set the photo as her screensaver and smiled. *Don't let anything spoil what you have now. Enjoy it while you can. Didn't he ask you to live for now?*

She went into the bathroom and closed the door, hoping not to disturb him, but as she turned the shower on he was beside her.

"Got time to come back to bed for a quick play?"

Oh, he was definitely awake now!

She eyed him mischievously. "We could play in the shower. I'm not at the bookshop today."

"Damn!" he exclaimed, grinning. "What a waste! I have a meeting in town. Still, let's not waste the time we've got now." He carried her, naked, back to the bed. "Let's do it in comfort."

They made love at a leisurely pace, taking time to feel each other's bodies, taste each other, and pleasure each other. Suzy's gloomy feeling slipped into the recesses of her mind for the time being.

* * *

They were later than usual going down to breakfast and Christine was in the kitchen. She looked at Lawrence as she asked, "What can I get you for breakfast?"

Suzy sensed she was a little uneasy. Maybe it was because it was still so unusual for someone to be with him.

"Eggs and bacon would be nice." He glanced at Suzy, who was surprised at how relaxed he seemed. He was expecting concurrence from her, and as she smiled he added, "Then I'll take you home, if you like. Or you could stay here till I get back." He seemed to be trying to decide which option he preferred.

Is he regretting giving me the choice?

"I'll go home. I would like to hear more about the possible work with the company in Nantwich that you mentioned last night, though." *Gotcha, Lawrence Bane – you can't have everything your own way!* Suzy looked smug.

His lips tightened slightly as he knew exactly what she had done. "Mmm. OK. Let's take a walk for a few minutes. Give us fifteen, Christine." And he led the way through the breakfast area into the garden. It was another sunny autumn day and the air was still. They crossed the dewy grass and headed to the left, following a rough path leading through a shrubbery. Suzy caught sight of someone pruning a cherry laurel hedge.

"Is that Dave?"

"Yes." Lawrence's monosyllabic answer was followed by silence.

What's wrong with him now?

Suzy walked with him in silence for a few minutes before asking, "What are you thinking about, Lawrence?"

They had reached one of the many benches positioned around the grounds. He took a seat and beckoned her to sit on his knee. "I'm thinking about how I can get to see you as much as possible. It seems you are keen to get away from me today. I don't know when I will get you back – and I need to know."

"It's lovely to be wanted," she whispered, as she nibbled his ear. He turned and kissed her.

"Are you happy?" He looked expectant, nervously awaiting her response.

"Can't you tell? Of course I am!" *Don't tell him about the gloomy feeling.*

"We need to arrange when we'll next meet – a diary, showing where we'll each be and when we will be together. I'll put something together and let you know when I'm happy with it." He was deadly serious and his expression was one of determination.

"Oh, will you? And what if I don't like it?"

He gently eased her off his lap and took her hand as he started to walk back towards the house, rubbing his damp jeans. "Don't worry, you will." He wasn't smiling, and Suzy knew he was deep in thought. Something was bothering him and it was as if he needed to have some sort of peace of mind with regard to her place in his life, so he could deal with something else. She had a feeling it would be pointless to ask him about it now. But she would. Later.

When he dropped Suzy off at her house, she sat in her kitchen with a cup of coffee and started to make some notes.

> *What is he so secretive about today?*
> *What is his meeting about?*
> *Why does he want an arrangement with me? - Is he checking up on me?*
> *Does Christine know anything? - Arrange to have tea with her again.*
> *He is still not talking about family or friends.*

She had probably missed a trick by leaving the house with him this morning when she could have had a chance to have a chat alone with Christine. Well, never mind.

Lawrence had given her a phone number and contact name to see about working with the Nantwich company, so she shifted her focus by giving them a call.

Chapter 23

Lawrence drove straight to the Blue Securities offices.

"Good morning, Mr Bane. Mr Deane is expecting you. You can go straight through to his office. Can I get you some coffee?"

"Thank you, Angela, that would be nice." Lawrence was wearing a black wool trench coat over jeans, with a checked shirt in shades of blue and white, and black leather boots. Angela swooned as she went to make their favourite customer, and effective company owner, his coffee just the way he liked it.

"Hi, Lewis, don't get up." The men shook hands as Lawrence sat opposite his friend at the desk. He leaned back in his chair and rested one ankle on his other knee. "I presume you know by now why I have come over."

Lewis leaned forward and pushed a vanilla-coloured file over the desk to Lawrence. He took a sip of his coffee and waited while his client scanned through the contents.

Angela brought Lawrence's coffee in, checked whether the two men needed anything further and then left the room, closing the door behind her.

Lawrence ran his hand through his hair. He spaced out three photographs of two men meeting in a bar. He recognised one of them as Harry Rawlins. He didn't have to guess that the other was Charles Rigsby, even though he had never met the man. There was the transcript of a conversation between the two men. Lawrence skimmed through it, picking out details referring to Charles accessing his wife's bank account, the need to speak to Josh Black, and a discussion about the police.

"Care to elaborate?" Lewis looked attentive but calm, sipping his coffee and wrapping his hands round the cup to keep them warm. It was cold in his office today. He always claimed he could think straighter if he was cold. The heating was only ever up if he didn't have any pressing business to attend to. Lewis obviously felt this was serious!

Lawrence stood up and walked to the window, which overlooked the next office block. The Blue Securities office windows were all reflective glass, so an occupant could see out, but no one could see in.

"I need to find Veronica Rigsby. She was one of my – I mean, Miranda's" – he shot an apologetic look at Lewis – "clients. I took some money from her. It was all repaid, together with a fair share of the profit I made on it. I just need to talk to her. I'm sure she…"

"Did she know you were going to take the money?"

Lawrence shook his head. "I was stupid, I know. I thought, provided she got it all back, it would be OK. She never spoke to me about it, and she will have known exactly what I did, and why!" His voice was raised, but more out of desperation, from a feeling of needing to justify what he had done, rather than anger. "She hated her husband. She would have left him if it hadn't been for the kids. She kept coming back to me. It was good between us. I'm sure she would talk to me."

"She's dead, Lawrence."

Lawrence staggered back over to his chair and fell into it. Lewis went round the table and sat on the end in front of him. Experience had taught him to give Lawrence a few moments to take in what was happening. It seemed to enable his friend to see the bigger picture, and invariably he would know what he was going to do about a situation.

This time, as Lewis looked down at him, he couldn't see the life that usually beamed out of his eyes, indicating what he had decided, declaring, *Fuck it then, we'll do this or that or the other*.

This time, all he could read in Bane's eyes was *I'm fucked*.

Lewis picked up the papers and photographs and put them back in the envelope. "I've got copies for you to take. We're tracking Rawlins and we've got his phone tapped. And we'll get help from the guys if we need it. He's got no friends left in the police. We'll get to know any contact he has with Black. Don't worry, Lawrence, we'll get this sorted." He put his hand on his friend's shoulder.

"Thanks mate. I'll let you know if I can come up with anything."

Lewis thought he had never seen him look so despondent. "Did Miranda know about the money?"

Lawrence looked up, clearly not comfortable with this conversation at all. "I don't think so. I don't see how she could have. It was such a shock for her when I left, and I made sure she knew nothing of the money I had made. Unless…" He was thoughtful, with a more determined look, which gave Lewis hope that there was spirit left in the boy to fight. *Did she have any contact with Veronica after I left? I need to speak to her.* "How did Veronica die?"

"Natural causes. I've checked it out and spoken with the pathologist myself. We are just waiting to find out what her relationship with her husband was like at the time she died. We suspect they were estranged and he has taken advantage of her death to dig stuff up that she kept secret from him when she was alive. If he knows about you and her and he's talking to Black, then they may well think they have a mutual target. It's just an added complication, but nothing we can't handle. But we can be more effective down there. Are you sure about that extra week's delay to go?"

"Yes. But I need to speak to Miranda before then."

That's more like it, thought Lewis, and he saw the more familiar glow in Lawrence's eyes now.

As Lawrence drove home, he had a sick feeling in his gut. He had always considered the money he took from Veronica to be a loan – £100,000 just sitting in her bank account. She wasn't even getting a decent rate of return on it. He took it, invested on the stock market, and got out just before the big dotcom bubble burst, having made £500,000. He returned £200,000 to her. During his subsequent "appointments" with Mrs Rigsby, she never mentioned anything, but he did remember noticing she wanted to increase the number of meetings, and there had been a tenderness between them; on both sides, he admitted. She had been old enough to be his mother, but the sex had been good, and she never played dirty.

Speaking to Lewis, and surmising what Mr Rigsby would deduce from the bank statements, he felt like a common criminal. Did Suzy really want to get to know him better?

He thought of what Richard had said about ending it, about Lewis not wanting to delay things by a week. But this was his life, and at the moment he was still in control. He knew what was best for both him and Suzy.

He dialled Miranda Cleveley's number.

"Miranda, it's Lawrence."

"Well, hello, darling. You know, you leave me for eight years and I hear nothing! Then suddenly I meet you, and you start ringing me. My my, you are a busy man, Lawrence."

The sarcasm and mocking tone permeated his ears, but he knew how to handle this woman now. Number one rule – make her think she was in control.

"Hey," he replied, feigning laughter, "You know how it is, Miranda. Just like the buses. Look, you know I'm going to be coming down to London soon. I'd like to see you." He hesitated for a nano-second. "Do I need an appointment?"

"For you, darling, I would drop everything." She laughed salaciously.

His face twisted in disgust, but his voice continued to sound interested. "Great, glad to know I haven't lost my charm. I'll look forward to it. I'll give you a date as soon as I can confirm it. By the way, can you get in touch with Veronica Rigsby? You know, for old times' sake." Lawrence was turning on the charm and sex in his voice.

"Well, you are full of surprises! I haven't kept in touch with so many of them, you know, but I know a man who can help if I can't locate her. Don't forget your promise to come and see me. I'll have the apartment dusted, darling! Ciao." And she hung up on him.

Miranda tapped her long red nails on the telephone table in the hallway and smiled. She thought back for a moment to her relationship with Lawrence. He had been by far her best prostitute, male or female, and had earned her the most money. More than that, he had enjoyed it. That was what made him so good at it, and why all the ladies wanted Lawrence, and why they kept coming back for more. He made it easy for her. Not only that, but he let her play with him, allowing her to do what she wanted, taking it, enjoying it, even – well, most of the time at least. Even her current partner couldn't match him for that!

Last week she had been thrilled to see Lawrence Bane at the airport, but had left Manchester feeling short-changed. He was on a mission with Lewis to ensure Josh Black would finally be convicted for the murder of Jimmy Havers. She herself could be vulnerable to Black once he was out of jail, and Lawrence clearly wanted to make sure she was protected, but secretly Miranda had hoped for more than that. She had allowed herself to believe that he might still want to play a little, for old times' sake, as he had put it. She had not expected it to be with Veronica Rigsby! She had always thought there was something special between the two of them, something more than a rich, sad housewife with her high-class gigolo, but Miranda had never been able to find out what the connection was. Now she knew something must be going on. She already had her bait lined up for Lawrence. It looked like she was going to be able to increase the enticement and, in so doing, snare a bigger reward from him. She unlocked the drawer and drew out her black book.

Rigsby, V. : Tel. 0207 434585.

It took her an hour to find out that Veronica had died, and another ten minutes to talk to Paul Irvine, Veronica's solicitor. Irvine told Miranda that Veronica had left a letter for Lawrence. Now she couldn't wait to see Lawrence again!

Chapter 24

Lawrence sat in his office, studying the timetable he had just created. He had included some key events he was planning: the bike track day; a dinner with his pharmaceutical company – *Are you sure you want to include this, Los?* – going to the farmhouse in the Peak District for Christmas. He decided not to let it extend into the new year. After all, he may no longer be a part of her life by then.

Today was Wednesday, the twenty-eighth of November. His intention was for Suzy to stay at The Sway every night when she wasn't working at the bookshop the next day, and they would try to be together as often as possible around that. He would take her to the farmhouse for Christmas. He realised there would also be times when he would have to stay at her house.

He picked up the phone to make one of his rare calls to Suzy. He had seen so much of her since they met, he had little need to telephone her. Besides, he much preferred to see her in the flesh. This was the first time he didn't really know when he would next see her. He had been so wound up this morning about meeting Lewis that nothing had been arranged when he dropped her off at home. It was now five o'clock and he hadn't heard from her.

"Hi, baby. How's your day going?" His confident tone did not give away his anxiety that she didn't want to see him as much as he wanted to see her.

"Lawrence, I've been waiting to hear from you. I didn't want to disturb your meeting, you seemed so preoccupied with it this morning. Did it go OK?" There was genuine relief in her voice.

"It was good, everything is OK," he lied. "I want to see you. Actually, I want to make love to you. What are you doing now?" His voice had lowered, and he sounded enticing.

"Oh," said Suzy, slightly taken aback by his directness, although she shouldn't have expected anything else from him.

"I'm working on my website and updating my CV. I've got a meeting with that company in Nantwich on Friday. And I'm going to the gym at seven. My routine has slipped a little; I can't think why!"

He knew she would have a big grin on her face. He was more concerned with the big member beginning to throb between his legs.

"You're not making it easy for me, Suzy," he scolded. "When can I have you?"

"I'll be home by half eight."

"I'll be there." He hung up.

For the second time Suzy was taken aback by his directness, and his assumption that this would be OK with her. Well, actually she couldn't wait to see him, but now she wondered what mood he would be in. Had the meeting really been good, as he said? Startled by the phone ringing again, Suzy thought he might be calling back to explain his abruptness.

"Hi Suzy, it's Dominic. I've just seen your email about your website. Did you need me to help with something?"

"Oh, hi, Dominic, yeah. Thanks for ringing." At least this would take her mind off her boyfriend! *Boyfriend! Oh, that sounds nice!*

Lawrence came to the end of his one-mile swim and stood under the shower, letting the water ease his muscles and soothe his head. He had gone over the issues of the day as he pounded through the water. He still hadn't rung Richard Groves. It was none of his damn business what he did with Suzy! He respected the concern the guy had for her, but he had convinced himself he wasn't going to hurt her. It would be a temporary parting, and he would do his damn best to get back to her. However, that was before he had heard about Veronica Rigsby.

"Richard, it's Lawrence. I said I'd call you. I can only say I've got the best of intentions for Suzy. I am going to try to get back here … to her, as soon as I possibly can, and I'll make sure she is safe while I'm gone. I won't stop her from meeting anyone else – but if that happens, I'll do everything I fucking can to get her back."

"You can't—"

"I can and I will, but she mustn't know that anything is going on – it's just better that way." *Safer for her, you mean!* "I have client confidentiality, so I'll sue your arse off if you tell her anything."

"Damn it, Lawrence. Sounds like you're being a selfish bastard."

"I'm not, because I know I am good for her – I can look after her and make her happy, and just knowing that she's there means I'll get my job done quicker."

There was a loud sigh on the other end of the phone. "Listen." Lawrence's tone eased. "You and I go back a long way, and it would be crazy to let our feelings for someone we both care deeply about make us do something we might regret. I trust your integrity and judgement, Richard. I need you to trust me on this. If I make a complete mess of things, you can ruin me, and there would be plenty of ways to choose from, believe me, but quite frankly, I don't know what I would do without her. I'm just asking you to cut me a bit of slack here."

Richard had been ready to tell Bane to go and fuck himself with his client confidentiality if he hurt Suzy, but now he was put off balance by the emotion and candour with which his client spoke.

"Look, we need to be sensible about this. I haven't a clue what you've done or are going to do, but I need a link to you – I need some way to be able to get in touch, and not just about Suzy. Your estate is too big for you to just walk away from, no matter how long you're planning to be gone. Let me have a contact number, Lawrence."

"As I said, Richard, do it through Lewis. I'll tell him to tell you what you need to know if the situation arises." He paused, not wanting to commit to anything he couldn't deliver. "I'll contact you myself if I think the worst will happen." He thought of Black. He remembered his cruel treatment of Christine, and he was convinced he had murdered Jimmy. And then there was the threat of prison now hanging over his own head. He wasn't ready to give in yet, though. Suzy was his inner strength; he wanted to live, for her. He hung up.

Chapter 25

Lawrence's car pulled up at 8.30. Suzy was wearing just a dressing-gown and perfume when she opened the door to him. He had brought her a small pot of winter daffodils.

"I thought you would like these on your windowsill." He kissed her gently on the lips. "You smell divine. I've missed you today. It's funny how quickly I have got used to having you near me." He looked intently into her eyes. "Is that a problem for you?"

Suzy was again concerned by the anxiety in his tone, and now she could see his face, she felt he seemed uneasy. Something was troubling him, and she was sure there was more to it than just not seeing her all day. What had his meeting been about?

She remained silent but shook her head – *Of course it's not a problem* – not wanting to blacken his mood by asking too many questions right now.

He responded to her quietness, placing the flowers on the side, removing his coat and driving gloves and placing his cool hands on her warm skin through the opening of the gown. She shivered slightly at the coldness of his touch and brought his fingers to her lips, kissing them, and telling him, "These need warming up."

He picked her up and carried her upstairs. "This will do it for me, baby."

They fell onto the bed and kissed passionately and longingly, Suzy scrambling to get his clothes off, to feel his skin and his hardness, anticipating him being inside her any second. He relished her desperation for him. They were soon both naked, and he straddled her body, kissing her more forcefully, tasting inside her mouth with a brutal hunger, not holding back as he moved to nibble at her shoulders and chest, at the same time tweaking her nipples between his fingers until she moaned, hovering between excitement and pain. As he held her harder, she dug her nails into his back and he groaned with pleasure and excitement. They both needed this, and he wanted it hard and rough. *Will she play?*

He grabbed her arms and pinned them above her head, positioning his legs in between hers, using their strength to part her knees, pushing them vigorously down on to the bed.

"Do you like this?" he asked hungrily, and she could sense a danger and urgency in him, his desperation to have her, and his growing forcefulness. *Oh, this is a bit different!* She was apprehensive, and a little fearful, but she didn't want him to stop. He read her face, her responses, tuning in to her expressions and her movements, watching to see if she cowered, attacked, tried to push him away, or if she was as hungry for it as he was. He entered her then, forcefully and roughly for the first time, and she tried to pull back, squirming beneath him, attempting to alleviate the discomfort she felt from his size, as she wasn't quite wet enough for him. But he kept her pinned down, her legs apart and her hands restrained above her head. "I will stop if you want me to, Suzy." His eyes searched her face. "But you are so good for me. I need you. Do you need me? Do you?"

"Yes." Her response confirmed her own need of this, right now.

Quickly and fluidly, he turned them both over so she was on top of him, with his penis still inside her. He scraped his fingers down her back and watched as she held her head back, eyes closed, biting and licking her lips and arching her back up to his hand. He loved that she wanted him to do it again. He pulled her down onto him, roughly. He wanted her to slam herself onto him, and she lifted and pushed herself up and down, lustfully wanting to feel him and to see the pleasure in his face. Her hands pulled at his chest as she pinched his nipples, and he whispered, "That's good, baby, I need this. Fuck me."

She continued to bang down on him. Then he flicked her back over and thrust himself deeper inside her, hard and unceasing, and she held his shoulders, pulling him, raising her hips to take more of him.

"I want you, Lawrence, stay inside me," she gasped, almost breathless.

He moved a hand to her clitoris and she came, long and loud. He quickly withdrew and spurted his semen onto her stomach and proceeded to massage the thick white liquid into her. She curved herself sensually up to him, her muscles pushing up as his hands pushed down.

They lay, spent, on the duvet.

"I love you, Lawrence Bane."

He looked into her eyes. "I love you, Suzy Harper." They kissed and hugged and dozed, stirring just before midnight to go to the bathroom and brush their teeth, before returning to bed, contentment hanging in the air around them as they drifted into a deep sleep.

At 6.30 a.m. Lawrence woke Suzy with breakfast in bed. He was naked, and she watched him, admiring the view, as he walked into the room and placed the tray on the bed in front of her.

"I am not making a habit of this," he reproved mildly. "Move over, 'cos it's flipping cold!" He climbed into the bed, put his arm around her waist and fed her a buttered muffin.

"I could get used to this." She smiled, and fed him his muffin.

"I want to wake up to you as often as I can." He placed a grape in her mouth, then trailed a piece of pineapple over her breast, up the centre of her neck, and slipped it into her mouth to follow the grape.

"Where did all this fruit come from?" she asked, gazing at the grapes, pineapple, strawberries and kiwi fruit in the bowl on the tray.

"I brought them with me. They were in my car. I thought I should come prepared, remembering what little you had last time for breakfast." He raised an eyebrow, but there was a hint of a smile on his lips.

"Did you just get them from your car, naked?" Suzy was shocked, immediately wondering if anyone had seen him. "I do have neighbours here, you know!"

"Not many are up at 6 a.m.!" he laughed. "And it was dark … and freezing, so there wasn't much to see anyway!"

He popped a grape into his own mouth.

"You brazen idiot!" she admonished playfully, and was then

silenced as he leaned over to kiss her, sliding the grape into her mouth.

She stirred and kept her mouth over his until he said, "Careful, or you'll have a wet bed."

He moved the tray with the breakfast things onto the floor. Then he took some kiwi and trailed it over her abdomen, before putting it into his own mouth. She replicated his movements, and together they trailed the fruit pieces over each other, eating some and feeding each other with some, until he began to caress her thighs, moving his hands over the tops and trailing his fingers along the insides. She lay back as he moved closer to her vulva, patiently waiting to feel the coolness and wetness of his fingers inside her. He could feel that she was already wet and waiting for him, and he moved over her and gently pushed himself into her. As he withdrew his fingers, he saw some redness and looked at her.

"I think your period has started," he whispered in her ear.

"Oh." She looked embarrassed. "Can I carry on?"

Her concerned, blushing expression told him she wasn't sure about this, and he moved to the edge of the bed. With her legs wrapped around him, he remained inside her, carrying her carefully into the bathroom and stepping into the shower cubicle. "Turn the water on," he commanded, and they embraced as the initial cold water drenched them, before becoming warmer. He pushed her gently up against the tiles, shushing her as she whimpered at the coldness on her skin. His face creased with his ecstasy as he came inside her, unprotected, skin on skin, and he held her tightly as the ecstasy lasted for as long as he could possibly make it. He gently withdrew from her and massaged himself under the water, cleaning himself. She moved her hands onto him and bent to kiss his penis.

"Do you want to get a tampon?"

Suzy loved him for his directness. He didn't get embarrassed, but spoke and acted with frankness and a lack of unnecessary restraint. She quickly located the packet in the bathroom cabinet and went over to the toilet. Lawrence thoughtfully turned away and started to wash his hair.

"Come back in here when you are ready," he instructed.

As she stepped in, he embraced her body and began to share the lather from his body with hers, washing her provocatively. She moved her hands over his chest and shoulders and across his back as he knelt to wash her feet and legs, adding soap and massaging the creamy lather as he continued with his task. She gloated at the pure pleasure of watching him and feeling him; at her sensation of such intimacy with this man she was now head over heels in love with.

Finally they dried each other and started to get dressed. She noticed he had brought an overnight bag out of the car too, and watched as he placed a toothbrush and a silver shaving set on the ledge in her bathroom.

He saw her face in the mirror. "It's OK for me to leave these here. Looks like I may be using them quite frequently." He was confident, no question, just took it for granted that he would stay here sometimes.

Is this part of the arrangement he wants between us? "I'm glad you're able to feel at home here." She gazed at him, feeling he belonged in her life now.

"The Sway is home for us for now, Suzy." No smile, and no room for discussion. "But I realise I will have to be here sometimes if I want to see you as much as possible." He took half a dozen clean pairs of underpants and socks from his bag. He held them up and looked at her questioningly.

Suzy was deciding whether to retaliate about his assumption that The Sway was now her home: it was still only just over a week since they had met, and once again he referred to something that could separate them. *Home for us for now.* More than that, though, he was actually telling her what to do! She wasn't used to this and she wasn't sure she wanted to be! But she knew it made good sense, really. She loved The Sway and no doubt they would end up spending more time there than here. Deep down, she knew she felt the same as he did. She wanted to be with him as much as she could. She remembered something he had said when she first met him – he didn't do one step at a time stuff.

She quickly looked at him, waiting patiently, and emptied

the contents from one of the bedside cabinets, from the side which he appeared to have now claimed as his own.

"You know, I've never done this before. I think it's called commitment." He placed his things in the drawer and closed it slowly. Then he turned to face her, and she saw a look that she wasn't expecting – pride. He seemed to be proud to be doing this, as though she were bestowing some sort of honour on him in allowing him to be part of her life. *I don't recall having much say in the matter, actually!* She smiled to herself, before beaming at him, seeing his face light up in a smile that exuded relief and happiness. They were committed to each other!

"Let me cook dinner tonight and perhaps we can discuss our arrangement. I need to know your timetable at the bookshop and any other commitments." He looked at her, hesitating for a second, trying to read her expression for any signs that she might have any tasks he may not know about. "What time is your interview with Winstons tomorrow?"

"Oh, for the translation work? Two o'clock." Suzy pondered over the reference to their "arrangement", not sure if this would further cement their "commitment" or if he was treating it like some business deal. *You really don't know this guy you've fallen in love with.* She needed some space to think, and analyse what she did know.

"I need to be heading to work now, and dinner sounds lovely. You have to let me help, though. I'm not too bad at cooking, you know." She glanced at her watch. It was coming up to 8.30. "Alison has asked us if we want to go for a few drinks tomorrow night, about six people, plus us. It should be nice." She hesitated slightly. "If you would like to?"

"Why not? I guess I'll get to use my toothbrush here, then." He was genuinely relaxed.

"Great, I'll let Alison know." Suzy was relieved he'd said yes so easily. She knew everyone would be curious about Lawrence, but she wasn't too sure what they would make of him. "What are you doing today?"

"I'm hoping to complete on the deal you've been helping with, and I have a board meeting this afternoon, one of my non-exec director roles. They're trying to convince me about a new MD."

"Sounds important. Tell me about it tonight."

"If you like, though I don't want to bore you. Don't want you feeling sleepy on me." He gave her a knowing look. "That reminds me; don't forget to take your pill. If you're sure you want to, that is."

Suzy's heart fluttered at the concern for her in his voice. "Of course I do! I've already taken it."

Chapter 26

Suzy's interview with Winstons went really well. The engine lubricants company had a subsidiary in La Défense in Paris, and the UK owners wanted to improve the *'entente cordiale'*, as it were, between the companies by having more communications in French. There was no one in the UK company sufficiently competent in the language, and Lawrence Bane, who happened to be a non-executive director for this company too, had suggested getting a freelance translator in to do ad hoc correspondence, emails, group newsletters, and so on, and to help with any commercial document translations as necessary. The managing director confirmed that the arrangement could work well and advised Suzy that he would draft a service agreement for her to consider at the beginning of next week. Most of the work would be done remotely by Suzy, and her main contact would be the UK sales director, but it was envisaged it would be useful for her to meet the French team within the next month or so, to put names to faces and to demonstrate the UK's commitment to improved relations with their French colleagues. The MD informed her it was never clever to let the French think the English were taking over anything, otherwise any translation would be a waste of time because they wouldn't read it anyway! He was certain Suzy's friendly manner and professional ability would be appreciated by all concerned, and he was hopeful that she would contribute to the success of this initiative. It sounded ideal for Suzy, and she was buzzing about it as she chatted later with Lawrence while they got ready to go out with her friends.

Lawrence was also pleased with the deal, as it would give Suzy additional work while maintaining her flexibility, as she would be able to work from home. Being apart from her while she was at the bookshop was bad enough for him. However, he wasn't sure about a trip to Paris to meet the French team, and if the trip took place early in the new year, where would he be? Unable to go with her?

Chapter 27

The pub was buzzing on Friday night, with young and old alike battling at the bar for drinks, voices raised to be heard, and all swaying to the music that was blasting into every crevice of the building. It didn't lend itself to intimate chat, but conversations were just about manageable and the banter was friendly and humorous.

Lawrence was engrossed in discussing various fitness regimes and martial arts disciplines with Alison's boyfriend, Alex, and another friend, John. Suzy was happy to see him looking so relaxed and comfortable with people he didn't know. She found herself telling Alison and their gym buddies, Jane and Lizzie, about being with Lawrence, about The Sway and the pool and gym, and how he was helping her to get more translation work with Winstons in Nantwich. There were various inferences to sex, but Suzy wouldn't be led into giving anything away, other than a beaming smile across her face!

Then the karaoke started, with a Rhianna not-sound-alike blasting through the air. Suzy shot Lawrence a glance, expecting him to be signalling that it was time to leave, but he suddenly got up from the table and, after giving her a quick kiss on the cheek, and with a knowing wink, he headed over to the DJ.

What's he up to?

He returned with a round of drinks for everyone and she thought no more of it. She noted Lawrence was drinking his fourth pint of Guinness. Was he a bit tipsy?

After a few minutes he got up again and Suzy looked stunned as she watched him walk over to the microphone. Duffy's "Breaking My Own Heart" started to play and, with his eyes firmly fixed on her, he started to sing.

Suzy stared at him, frozen, and feeling totally alone in the crowded pub. The words swam around in her head, his beautiful, mellow voice resounding through her body. The room had gone quiet as the audience acknowledged this guy could sing, and Alison reached for her friend's hand as she realised there was some sort of bond between the two lovers, perfectly aware that Lawrence had not taken his eyes off Suzy.

The spell was broken, there were claps and cheers and Lawrence played to the audience with a mock bow and a huge smile before making his way back to the table. Amid the friends' remarks of "Great voice ... where d'ya learn to sing like that? *X Factor*, here you come...", Lawrence downed the remaining third of his pint and looked over to where Suzy had been sitting, seeing only her vacant chair.

He glanced at Alison. Clearly, the two of them were never going to be bosom pals. Alison viewed him as rude and arrogant, but she could now see his concern for Suzy, and was well aware that Suzy was besotted with him, even in love with him (if that were possible after such a short time), and she leaned in towards him.

"She's just gone to the ladies. She'll be back in a minute."

After a minute Alison got up to go and check on her friend. Suzy was standing in front of the mirror, trying to remove black smudges from under her eyes.

"Suzy, are you OK?" She put her arm around her, and tears started to run down Suzy's cheeks again.

"I'm fine, really. I'm just being silly, you know, period and all that..." She dabbed at her eyes again. "I look a right mess!" She laughed, a quivering, tearful laugh.

"Come on, Suzy, it's alright. He's worried about you, you know." She hugged her friend for a minute. "You look fine, and it's dark in there. Everyone thinks you just came for a pee. Why don't you go back now and I'll follow in a mo? No one will think anything of it."

"Thanks, Alison. I feel better now."

Lawrence stood up as soon as he saw her walking back into the room. He looked at her anxiously, and as she smiled at him he visibly relaxed and returned her smile with a subtle yet loving one of his own.

She took her coat from the back of her chair and picked up her bag, mouthing to him, "Take me home, please!" He didn't hesitate, collecting his own coat and handing Alex a twenty-pound note, telling him to get another round in, and saying that it had been good to meet Suzy's friends.

The cold fresh air hit him as they stepped outside and he wobbled slightly as he wrapped his arm around Suzy, clutching her to him tightly, as they walked in silence to the cottage.

"I'll make some coffee," he said as Suzy took his coat. "I need some." He looked at her, with a sad expression creeping across his handsome features.

Oh my heart, how I love this man. The words of his song kept echoing in Suzy's head.

She followed him into the kitchen. "Why did you sing that song?"

He had his back to her as he filled the kettle and began to look through the cupboards for cups, then for coffee. "It sums me up, don't you think?" His voice was unemotional.

She was on autopilot. She passed him a spoon from the drawer and watched as he filled the cups and stirred and stirred and stirred. He couldn't face her.

"I think it's done," she whispered.

She wanted to touch him, to kiss him, to feel his hands on her, but she felt as though she didn't know him. The atmosphere was tense, and neither of them seemed to know how to break this feeling of sadness. She sat down at the kitchen table. He finally turned around and brought the coffee over, sitting next to her. He stared into his cup.

"I think I've had a bit too much to drink." His voice was apologetic and he kept his head down.

With her voice a little too shaky for her own comfort, Suzy said, "I don't understand why you chose a song about breaking your own heart and feeling ashamed." She quietly added, "Is it me, Lawrence?"

He looked up to see her gazing at him. He shook his head and sighed. "No, baby, it's not you. It's me. I'm not good enough for you."

Oh, dear God, he's going to break up with me; please, no. Suzy put her elbows on the table and sipped her coffee, focusing on swallowing and trying to repel the feeling of sickness welling up inside her.

Lawrence ran his fingers through his hair and cursed himself for feeling a little woozy from the alcohol. This was why he never drank much!

He breathed in deeply, then took the coffee cup out of her hands and held them between his, caressing the backs of her hands with his thumbs. She succumbed to the comfort she felt from this loving gesture. "I've done things I am ashamed of in my past, and I don't want you to know about them…"

"But I don't know what to think, Lawrence. I can't shut it out of my mind, it's eating at me and I'm going to end up thinking the worst. Surely it would be better to tell me and not have secrets between us." She looked at him imploringly.

"You can't imagine anything worse than it actually was, Suzy. Please, don't make me tell you."

He looked dejected and she realised he was begging her.

What have you done, my boy?

"I can't stop my imagination running away with thoughts. I—"

He interrupted her. "Have you ever meditated?"

She looked puzzled. He suddenly sat up straight, and appeared brighter, optimistic even. His mind drifted back for a moment, to when he first moved into The Sway. At the time he felt undeserving of such a beautiful home. He rarely went out and only had contact with Christine when she came over to carry out chores around the house, and with business acquaintances when he had to. Then he met Steve Jameson when he was out on his motorbike; a fellow biker who just happened to be the local vicar. A friendship developed, and Steve introduced Lawrence to meditation, to help him tackle the issues he had with his previous lifestyle and encouraging him to focus on who he was, what aspirations he may have, and to look inwardly at why he felt self-loathing, and what he could do to turn that around. Lawrence Bane had never looked back. Until now.

"I meditate every day. Well, almost every day since you came into my life." He raised his eyebrow, with a slightly scolding look.

Am I supposed to know I'm preventing him from performing a daily ritual?

He continued, "It really helps me to focus on the positive things in life, and experience genuine feelings." He looked at her intently. "Including love, compassion, and forgiveness." He raised her hands to his lips, gently sweeping them along her fingers. "I can teach you some exercises, Suzy." He was pleading with her to accept his help to cope with him. "I can teach you to love and accept me." He studied her expression.

"Lawrence, I already do," she exclaimed, perplexed at his lack of self-worth. Why did he think so little of himself? "You've already taught me to live for the now. I confess to finding it a bit difficult at times. But history is just that and yet I get the feeling something is going to come between us, and it scares me."

"Don't worry. We will be together." He emphasised the word *will*, sounding more like his assertive self. Suzy wasn't quite so confident.

They finished their coffee and he got up. "Let me take you to bed now. We both need to sleep. Things will look brighter in the morning, I promise." *You hope!*

In the morning they found themselves back at the table in the kitchen, eating breakfast. Neither of them had slept very well. They had showered together and the intimacy was tender and reassuring for both of them. The fear from last night was gone. They both now had their own challenge of how to make their relationship last. Suzy needed to focus on trying to give him what he wanted and what she felt capable of giving, Lawrence needed to figure out how he could make her wait for him and be confident he would return to her.

"How was your board meeting?" Suzy wanted to focus on something that would help her to learn more about him – his present life at least, leaving him with the secrets of his past, even though they were tormenting her mind.

"Well, it's clear the other directors want me to accept the proposed candidate. On paper, he seems the man for the job, but I'm just not sure. The company is working with a pharmaceutical giant with a view to subcontracting for them. I'm concerned this guy isn't that well known in this particular field. His background is oncology, and this new contract is working with coagulants. But I'm no expert, and—" he smiled smugly, "being the youngest member of the board, they tend to listen to my money, not me. And, sure, I need them on top form to make more money … it's just how it is! Anyway, I'll probably go with it, but they're arranging a dinner so I can meet him in a relaxed setting, would you believe."

"Wow, what it's like to be important!"

He grinned and they both began to finally relax and feel at ease with each other.

"That reminds me, we need to discuss our arrangement."

Suzy looked at him as she started to clear the dishes away. "What exactly does that mean?"

"I just need to know when I will be with you, where we will be sleeping, what we will both be doing – you know."

"Sounds a bit formal. Isn't part of the fun the spontaneity of our relationship?"

"Well, yes, but we need some routine."

Suzy glanced at him, looking down her nose as if to say "speak for yourself".

"OK, *I* need a routine. I need to know where you are."

"Why?"

"Because I can't stop thinking about you, worrying about you, if I don't."

"Why on earth should you worry about me?"

He was beginning to get annoyed with her lack of cooperation. "Damn it, Suzy, it's how I feel." *I need to know I can protect you and that you will be here when I get back.*

She ignored his tone and carried on tidying the kitchen. "It sounds a bit Big Brother-ish, Lawrence." She tried to keep the disquiet from her voice, not wanting to jeopardise the fragile calm that was now between them, and not really sure why she was beginning to feel uneasy. Their relationship was still so young, but she knew they were both in deep. Should she be annoyed that he seemed to want to protect her?

Lawrence was also aware of the delicacy of the atmosphere between them. He did not want to part with ill-feeling between them, and he now felt he had to see her tonight and try to reassure her of his commitment to her. He was taken aback as she continued, as though she had read his mind. "Look, we are already committed to each other, aren't we? We're not going to stop seeing each other or suddenly start seeing anyone else." She stopped wiping the table and looked across at him. "But don't stifle what we have with rules and timetables, hey?"

"You think I'm stifling you?" He stood up and began to pace around the room. "Because I want to be with you as much as I can, it makes you feel stifled?" He didn't take his eyes off her, nor did he try to hide the concern in his voice.

"No, no, I didn't mean it like that. I want to be with you, I love being with you. You make me feel alive and beautiful." She was blushing and speaking hurriedly, urgently. "But I have lived on my own for the last six years, not answering to anyone, and now you want to know what I am doing, where I am, when I'll be back. I just don't think we need to change anything at the moment." She looked around her, waving her arm. "Look, I haven't properly cleaned around here for two weeks!" She looked at him and started to laugh. "I can't believe I just said that. It sounds like I'd rather be cleaning than be with you!" She went up to him and put her hands on his chest, playing with the zip of his sweatshirt, and whispered, "Of course I wouldn't."

He kissed the top of her head. "What are we playing at, Suzy? I think we both want the same thing, really, but maybe I'm just rushing forward too soon. I'll try to be patient. But, remember, I don't do one step at a time." He put his arms around her. "Just promise me you'll stay with me as often as you can, especially when you're not in the bookshop the next day." This wasn't a question.

"I will. I'll buy a new toothbrush today and bring it over tonight?" There was a slight pause. "Oh, and I'm not in the bookshop on Monday or Tuesday." She beamed.

Chapter 28

Lawrence drove home fast, with Amy Winehouse drawling from his iPod. He skipped the track "You Know I'm No Good"!

He stripped off when he reached The Sway and dived into the cool water of the pool, pulling himself punishingly through the water, adding another ten laps to his usual routine. Then he sank into the Jacuzzi and closed his eyes, letting the bubbles pummel his flesh and the fresh, clean smell cleanse his thoughts. He struggled to clear his mind, re-energising himself to concentrate on what he needed to do over the next few weeks. He dressed, drafting his action plan in his mind, then went into the study and sat down at his laptop.

The couple spent the next three days in each other's company at The Sway. They only dressed to go out walking in the grounds or to take a ride on the motorbike in the mild December sunshine, Suzy relishing the intimacy of being so close, her body moving in sync with him and his bike. Mostly they lazed around in bathrobes, reading, watching a bit of TV, swimming and then relaxing in the Jacuzzi. Lawrence massaged her, and she was left feeling serene and content. She learned from him, improving her own technique, massaging his body and bestowing on him something close to the pleasure he gave her. He taught her the basics of meditation: how to clear her mind, achieve deep relaxation, focus clearly, accept life, and accept him.

Her confidence in herself and their relationship grew as she found herself able to wield her power over him, as she aroused him with her hands, her lips, her tongue and her vagina. He made it so easy for her, as he was always ready and waiting, but never persistent or needy. It was just how he was. He, in turn, aroused and excited her with his penis, his fingers, even his toes, never wanting her to miss out on that fulfilling sensation of climaxing, yet ensuring she was at ease, with her body, with him and with their being together.

Before they knew it, it was Wednesday morning, and Suzy would be going to work shortly.

"Leave me your house keys, will you, and I'll meet you there tonight." Lawrence was tapping away at his phone over breakfast. Suzy presumed he was checking his emails; he tended to do this every few hours, rather than flicking through them every minute of the day. She wondered if he was expecting something in particular, but he had seemed so relaxed these past couple of days that she wasn't really worried about it. He seemed more willing to stay over at her house, too.

They had agreed that their "arrangement" would consist of planning for the week ahead, to check when they would see each other and where they would sleep, both agreeing that they would be sharing a bed every night. Lawrence viewed this as a compromise he was willing to make for the next couple of weeks. Then he hoped he would get more information about her routine and whereabouts, with or without her knowledge.

In the meantime, he had a surprise for her when she returned to her cottage that night. He had arranged for cleaners to come in and do a full clean on her house. He wasn't prepared to risk such mundane chores preventing her from seeing him!

Chapter 29

Suzy drove to The Sway after work on Thursday, as arranged. She had the agreement for Winstons and was going to review it, ready to sign and return. The work would start at the beginning of January, and she was excited at the prospect of her new venture, not least because she would have the opportunity to go to Paris for a couple of days. *Maybe Lawrence will come and meet me, and we could stay for the weekend?*

Lawrence opened the door and took her coat and bags from the car. "Good day, baby?"

Suzy followed him into the hallway, sensing an air of excitement about him.

"I'll be back in a minute!" He ran upstairs with her things, returning straight away. He was barefoot, and dressed casually in jogging bottoms and a T-shirt. "I thought we could eat in an hour or so. Do you fancy a workout in the gym?" He was charming her into saying yes, with a smile to die for.

"You seem very excited." Suzy removed her shoes and looked up at him. "I haven't brought my kit."

"That's OK." He beamed, and she knew he was up to something.

She hadn't been in the gym since he had first shown it to her. It was bigger than she had remembered, and her reflection gazed back at her from the floor-to-ceiling mirrors. *I look tired after work. I hope he's not expecting me to do a full circuit routine!* Then she folded her arms as she watched him undress. "You must be joking!" she exclaimed, grinning appreciatively at his muscular body. *Can I ever stop admiring him?*

"It's perfectly natural to exercise naked." He grinned back. "*Gymnasium* comes from the Greek word *gumnos*, meaning naked, you know."

"You don't say. And just what do you expect me to do? I did my workout last night, in appropriate attire, in a registered place of exercise, I'll have you know." She was trying to ignore the fact that he was lifting her sweater over her head, and in one swift move her bra was on the floor.

"Don't try to get round me!" she laughed, as he started to nibble her breasts while unfastening her jeans and pushing them down, along with her pants. *Oh my heart.*

She wasn't sure about feeling this erotic in a gym, but she did know she wanted him to kiss her, to be in her, as she felt the titillating tingling well up inside, and the wetness between her thighs.

"Why don't we go upstairs?"

"This will be fun, trust me!" They stood naked in the middle of the room. He held her shoulders and positioned her so they were both looking straight ahead into the mirrors. "Look how beautiful you are," he commanded, and his lips caressed her shoulders and his hands ran down her arms. "Let me take you to some new heights." His hands moved down the sides of her waist, creeping towards her pubic hair, slowly moving between her legs.

"Lawrence!" she gasped, almost drowning in the sensual tide that was washing over her. She turned to face him and held on to his upper arms, feeling his firm biceps, as she slowly moved her legs apart to give him access. His lips found hers, his tongue gently exploring her mouth, and he gently inserted a finger into her vagina, exploring around the sides and then deeper within. She moaned, ready to climax at the slightest touch.

"You've finished your period," he stated, and she could only manage to murmur "yes" as her whole being succumbed to the exquisite delight of his touch.

"Not yet, baby," he whispered, and withdrew his finger, licking it and watching her expression. He then placed his finger in her mouth and she sucked on it provocatively.

"Come on." His voice was low and seductive. "You have to earn this." He led her over to a bench.

She watched as he lay back on the seat and started to lift the steel bar holding forty kilos of weight. His breathing was controlled and it appeared effortless to him. He did ten lifts and she remained still and silent, admiring his flexing muscles, the veins standing out on his arms and chest, the silence broken only by his steady breathing. She was in a trance, until he stood up. *What is he going to do now?*

"Your turn." He removed the weights from the bar. "Let's keep it light, baby." He gestured for her to lie back on the bench and, as she did so, hesitantly, he handed her the bar. She looked at him, questioningly.

"Lift it," he quietly ordered.

As she raised it above her head, watching him, he knelt beside her and traced his finger from the base of her neck, down between her breasts and over her abdomen, very lightly, leaving a tickly trail of senses down her body. Then, as she lifted the bar up, he leaned in and began to suck at her breasts.

"You're ... er ... distracting me." She tried to focus on raising and lowering the bar, and counting to ten. Although the bar was relatively light, her arms were shaking and her body tingled expectantly. Then he stood up, and she was very aware of his erect penis as he stood over her.

"That's the idea. I want you to enjoy this. Come on." He raised her up from the bench and walked over to a piece of equipment with a seat in front of a bar, and a pad on which to rest your arms. The aim was to curl your arms up, to exercise your biceps and triceps. Suzy guessed the bar had fifty kilos on it. Lawrence sat down, grasped the handles and started to curl the bar up. She moved to caress his shoulders but he looked directly at her, his face impassive.

"No," he said, in a low, even tone. "I want to pleasure you in here. It can be my turn later." His lips momentarily formed a smile, before straightening in a concentrated effort once more. When he had completed ten lifts he got up from the machine and looked at Suzy.

She tentatively sat down and watched as he removed the weights, leaving fifteen kilos on the bar. She wasn't surprised that he had guessed the weight she normally used. His ability to be right about so much associated with her was just one of the many things she admired about this man.

As she began her ten curl-ups, he slowly traced her spine with his finger, with feathery movements at first, up and down, then she could feel his nail scratching, lightly at first, then getting more and more intense as it all but tore into her flesh. It was exquisite. She couldn't concentrate on her counting and she didn't want him to stop.

"That's your ten," he said. "No cheating!" He grinned as he led her to the next piece of equipment.

This time he waited as Suzy studied the adductor before her. It consisted of a seat in front of two pads, with the mechanics connected to weights. The pads formed a support to hold each leg, with the aim of squeezing the thighs inwards. They were positioned approximately seventy centimetres apart, ready to be squeezed together to tone the inner thigh. Suzy reddened as she realised what position he was now expecting her to sit in.

He waited a moment. "Sit down, Suzy."

Slowly, she sat down, and placed each leg in the supporting pads. She felt vulnerable and uneasy in this exposed position, wondering what he had in mind. She was about to say something when he knelt before her, and the feel of his lips on hers kept her silent.

He spoke in a calm, matter-of-fact manner. He was so confident that she would do as he asked, and enjoy the experience, that it put her at ease.

"I'm going to lower the back and restrain your arms, if that's OK. I want you to have a mind-blowing experience, which should be intense and stimulating. Then we can make love."

Oh my heart. She turned her head and watched him, holding herself up as he lowered the back of the seat. He instructed her to lie back, and she made contact with the cool leather, surprised to find herself at a very comfortable angle. Her senses were heightening, and she closed her eyes, giving into the sexual arousal rising within her, the tingling around her vagina and the quivering through her lower abdomen. She felt she would scream out at the mere anticipation of what he was about to do. She couldn't see him now, and wondered if he had left the room. A moment later he was standing beside her with some soft rope in his hand. His eyes held hers momentarily and he smiled, with desire in his eyes. To have her? Or to make her happy? She wasn't sure which. He knelt again and took hold of her arms. Suzy watched him painstakingly bind them together, using an intricate pattern of knots and layers of rope. The rope felt soft and comfortable, and reminded her of the handles on gift bags. The rope formed a type of gauntlet around her wrists, and they were now firmly, but not too tightly, bound together and she was completely immobile, with her legs resting apart in the pads of the adductor.

"Try to keep your eyes open, and place your hands above your head." Suzy elongated herself along the back of the seat as she lifted her arms up and back, resting them on the cool leather. She felt libidinous and horny, desperately wanting him to touch her, devoid of all self-consciousness.

"Good girl." His voice was low and sexy, and he smiled appreciatively, loving her confidence and her need for him. He slowly knelt in front of her and gently began to feel around the tops of her inner thighs. She felt his fingers lightly brushing over her skin and she tingled, desperately wanting to feel him inside her, and at her clitoris. As if at her bidding, his fingers separated her lips, his head lowered and his tongue began to stroke her, slowly, intimately and unceasing, moving over her clitoris in a steady motion so that there was not too much intensity, just an unfaltering, growing feeling of pleasure and ecstasy. She shut her eyes tightly for a second before opening them to observe him pleasuring her tirelessly and energetically. She was completely at his mercy, unable to touch him. *Wow, this is some workout.* Her orgasm got closer and closer, and he was making the build-up last longer and longer. It was mind-blowing, and she finally screamed out, long and totally gratified. He quickly untied her hands and smoothed his hands over her arms, pre-empting any cramping or itching from the rope, and gently lifted her legs from the pads. She murmured softly and leaned into him. He cradled her, kissing her hair, her cheeks and her lips. She could taste herself on him, and she thought she would melt under the heat of his breath and his hold on her.

"That was wonderful." She smiled, and his face beamed with pleasure for her.

"We aim to please." He took her hand and slowly led her up to the bedroom. Candles were burning and their fragrance was intoxicating. Suzy fell onto the bed and grinned up at him as he started to laugh. "Well, you really did like that. You're grinning like a Cheshire cat."

"I can't help it!" With a wicked grin, she added, "I need to repay you now. Come and lie down." Then, more quietly, "Where is the rope?"

He looked directly at her as she lay on the bed "Oh!" His expression was one of salacious expectation! He went into the dressing room and returned carrying a shoebox. He looked at her with one eyebrow raised.

"I rather hope you don't know what you're doing." He handed her the box, folding his arms and looking mildly amused.

Suzy looked inside and was taken aback at the quantity of rope, several pairs of handcuffs and various eye masks. She glanced up at him questioningly.

"I used to like it." The amused look was now replaced with hesitancy and apprehension. "I'll put it away if you prefer." He sat down on the bed and leaned forward with his elbows on his knees. His eyes hovered between Suzy and the carpet. *Why the hell did you get that out?*

Suzy held up a pair of black leather handcuffs. The leather was soft, and there were brass studs around the cuffs, with a gold chain linking them. There was a key in one of the locks. The gold looked real, and the cuffs looked brand new.

"Is this your history?" Her voice was quiet, calm and clinical. While Lawrence looked at her and admired her self-control, he was also fearful of how she was analysing this situation.

"Yes." He stood up and walked towards the balcony, gazing out onto his woodland, and with his back to her he added, "Actually, no, not entirely. I bought those things when I arrived here. I thought I would want to use them. And I did at first – want to, that is." He paused. "But it just never happened. And then I met Steve, from St Lukes, and he taught me how to accept who I was and not just torture myself with the lifestyle fate had dictated for me. He helped me find a way to repay the debt I felt I owed, and be thankful for the comfort I could now afford to live in." He turned to face her. She remained sitting on the bed, the handcuffs in her hand, her eyes on Lawrence. She had so many questions for him, but did not want to interrupt, for fear that he would close up on her again.

"That's when I chose to be celibate." He looked at her, pleading for acceptance.

She needed to know more.

"Did you handcuff the women you slept with?" Her clinical tone was still there, and her eyes searched his face for a reaction. She did not doubt he would be honest with her.

"I don't want to talk about it." He stared at her, a defiant look in his eyes. *I don't want to lose you.*

"I need to know, Lawrence. What did you do to them?" It was her turn to stand up.

His voice rose as he felt anger building up inside – was it with himself for getting the damned box out, or her questioning a past he so wanted to leave behind, but which was beginning to penetrate his present, with a power capable of destroying all he now had, including her love for him?

"If you are asking if I hurt anyone, then the answer is no, I did not fucking hurt a woman!" *Unless they wanted it. Does that count?* He was standing beside her, towering over her.

Suzy felt indignant at his anger. "Don't get angry with me, Lawrence. You have just given me a box of ropes, handcuffs and blindfolds. What the hell am I supposed to think? You have too many secrets! Why?"

"I liked it! I liked to be cuffed and hurt!" His stance was solid and his face looked icy-cold.

Oh, you are beautiful when you are angry! Suzy felt glued to the spot, unable to move or speak. Lawrence moved his arms out to touch her, then stopped and walked into the en-suite. Suzy heard running water as he splashed some over his face. Then she watched as, wearing a bathrobe, he left the bedroom. She heard him go downstairs.

What has happened? We were having such a wonderful time. He had just made her feel like the most important thing in the world to him, in his gym, and he was the most important thing in her world. She didn't want to even begin to think of being without him. He liked to be hurt … he liked to be hurt … Why had he chosen her? What could she do for him?

She grabbed a robe and made her way downstairs, feeling gloomy and fearful. The door to the snug was ajar. She hesitated at the entrance as she saw him standing in front of the fireplace, a whisky tumbler in his hand. He turned to face her but didn't approach her.

"OK. I've fucked up now, haven't I? I presume you're going to leave me." He spoke quietly and took a sip of his whisky.

"I wasn't thinking of going anywhere. I thought we had an arrangement." She leaned against the door jamb, feeling strangely confident, and continued, her voice steady, "I said I was committed to you, didn't I?"

He took another gulp and placed the glass on the mantelpiece. Then he brushed his hand over his mouth, pensive, anxious and regretful. "I'm sorry." He walked towards her and she looked up and gently kissed his lips. He closed his eyes, breathing deeply, and slowly put his arms around her, pulling her to him.

"When you asked for the rope, I..." He hesitated and hugged her tighter, preventing her from looking at him as he spoke. "I thought you might want to play. I don't know why I remembered the box. I'd forgotten I'd even kept it." He waited a moment. "Say something, Suzy, please."

She pulled away from him and gazed at him with an intensity that made him feel vulnerable and not in control.

"I wanted to please you, Lawrence. I wanted you to have a mind-blowing experience, just like you gave me in the gym." She blushed slightly as she continued. "I've been in awe of your sexual expertise." She smiled coyly, her confidence increasing. "I've been doing my own research." Now she boldly took his hand and led him to the sofa to sit down. She sat on the floor at his feet and smoothed her hand over his knee. "That's why I asked for the rope. I asked for the rope, Lawrence, remember." And she smiled to herself as she parted his robe and kissed his knees, remembering the copy of *The Joy of Sex* she had secretly purchased from the bookshop. She had studied the chapter on "Slow masturbation for him", and after his display with the rope she felt determined to give it a go tonight. She knew several knots from her sailing trips in Cameroon. She looked up at his face as she untied his belt and exposed him, lowering the robe from his shoulders.

"We could carry on where we left off." Her eyes were hopeful and expectant.

Lawrence felt a surge of relief, respect and love for her sweep over him. *I knew you were the right one for me, Suzy Harper. I can't let you go. I have to keep you.* His eyes glistened like emeralds, and his face softened, the glow of the fire reflecting off his golden-brown hair, and Suzy felt his love.

"Make love to me." His command was quiet, mellow and softly spoken. He raised her up from the floor and removed her robe. He lay back on the sofa and pulled her onto him. "This is what I need right now." It was slow and passionate, hushed and pleasurable, and their relationship moved on to new heights.

Chapter 30

As they discussed their "arrangement" for the following week, Lawrence asked her to join him for the dinner to meet the prospective new managing director.

"It's on Saturday. Dave will drive. We'll pick you up at seven. It will be formal, and there'll be about twenty people, mainly the senior management and their partners. We'll stay in town that night; I've booked the Hilton on Deansgate."

Suzy was used to his unilateral decision-making, rarely needing to protest as his judgement was, annoyingly, nearly always right, and she wasn't one for being petulant and bloody-minded.

She began to think about what she was going to wear, mentally going through her wardrobe. She had the obligatory LBD, which she loved. Lawrence hadn't seen her in it yet. With her black kitten-heel shoes and her golden shawl she was confident she would look good enough to face his colleagues. She was looking forward to seeing Lawrence in business mode, not to mention attire. There was something about him in a dark suit!

It had been a long day in the bookshop, and she put the kettle on to make some tea before going upstairs to shower and dress. It would be a bit of a rush to be ready for seven, but there were no distractions and she had got everything ready on her bed earlier.

Feeling happy with her appearance, she grabbed her clutch bag and went downstairs, with ten minutes to spare for that cup of tea. As she turned to take her drink to the table, the sleeve of her dress caught on a cupboard handle and she heard, with horror, the fabric tear. *For fuck's sake!*

She lifted her arm up and could see her pale skin showing through the plainly visible hole. What the hell was she going to wear now? The doorbell rang. Upset and annoyed with herself, she opened the door, immediately displaying the damaged goods to Lawrence as he walked in.

She felt slightly annoyed as he smiled at her predicament.

"I don't know what there is to smile about. I haven't got anything else I can wear." Her annoyance was just enough to stop her swooning at the vision of Lawrence Bane in a dinner jacket, dress shirt and bow tie. *Daniel Craig, eat your heart out!*

He raised his finger to her lips to quieten her and disappeared back out to the waiting car, returning after a moment carrying a large white box, and a very broad smile.

"I hoped something like this would happen. Miss Harper, please do me the pleasure of wearing this." He feigned a very dignified and gentlemanly bow.

How could she resist? She was relieved that this box had to contain more than just a bottle of perfume!

She looked at him quizzically and he removed the lid, pulling golden tissue paper aside. Her mouth dropped as she saw the deep red velvet fabric and, smiling from ear to ear, she followed him upstairs.

In her bedroom, Lawrence leaned against the wall, standing on one foot, with his ankles crossed, looking very much at ease, pleased with himself and faintly amused.

Suzy lifted the fabric from the paper and her smile grew wider as she gazed adoringly at the Christmas-red velvet dress in front of her. It was knee-length, with only one sleeve, and decorated with beautiful diamante studs depicting holly leaves above the left breast. She glanced in the box and saw a long red velvet glove for the right hand and arm. They looked and felt exquisite. Hurriedly, she pulled off her damaged black dress and stood in her bra, knickers and hold-up stockings. Lawrence came forward and deftly removed her bra, cupping each breast from behind. He leaned into her ear and whispered, "Take the pants off too." She glanced over her shoulder and saw him lick his lips provocatively. Without hesitation she did as he bid, and then pulled the red dress over her head. He helped her to put her left arm in, and tenderly pulled up the side zip, smoothing the dress down over her breasts, her waist and her hips. The fit was perfect, as she knew it would be. He nuzzled at her bare right shoulder momentarily, and she melted at his touch. Then he took the glove and expertly pulled the fabric up her arm to complete the picture of his beautiful girl in this ravishing outfit. He stepped back, holding her outstretched hand tightly. She knew he was excited, but she was desperate to see herself in the mirror, and she moved to pull away to go to the bathroom.

"Not yet." He looked around and spied her open make-up bag on the dressing table. "Sit down."

As she sat on the end of the bed, wondering what he was going to do, the dress rose up her thighs. I must remember to keep my legs together!

She watched Lawrence remove his jacket and study the contents of her make-up bag, and she sat in awe of the many talents of her guy, as he expertly touched up her lightly applied make-up, emphasising her cheekbones with blusher, defining her eyes with liner and a touch more mascara, and transforming her rose-pink lips into a deep red, accentuating them to complement her dress. Where had he learned to do this?

Then he led her to the bathroom and stood behind her, watching her expression as she studied herself in the mirror. The total effect was stunning, and they both knew it.

"I can't wait to get you out of this, you know," he whispered, and she moaned softly as he peppered her bare shoulder with soft kisses. "Now let's go. Dave is waiting."

As they got into the back of a sleek black Mercedes, Lawrence introduced Suzy to Dave, as they had only seen each other from a distance in the garden before. Suzy imagined him to be a very private man, as he smiled and said "Hi" in a kindly voice.

Sitting as close to Lawrence as a seatbelt would allow, she turned to face him, her mouth almost aching from smiling so much.

"The dress is beautiful, perfect – thank you. How come you bought it and never said anything?"

He smiled mischievously. "I didn't dare presume that you would wear what I told you to. I know I can be a little controlling at times…"

"A little?" she interrupted, laughing.

He raised one eyebrow in the special way that she had come to love. "I just hoped the situation would arise and you would want to wear it. And before you say it," he continued, grinning,

"I did not tear the sleeve of my voodoo doll. Even my considerable talents don't stretch that far." He pulled his arm back as she playfully punched him.

"Dave, put the radio on. I'm just going to put the panel up, as I need to talk to Suzy." Suzy looked at him, puzzled. Why the privacy?

Lawrence then pushed a button and a privacy panel rose between them and the driver. He removed his seatbelt.

"What the hell are you doing?" she exclaimed.

"Open your legs." He was smiling, but spoke with a firmness that compelled her to do as he said.

Then he moved right up to her and placed his hand up into the dress, between her legs.

Suzy looked anxiously towards Dave.

"He can't see or hear anything. Just enjoy, baby." There was no kiss, he just watched her intently as his fingers continued to move up and then she felt them enter her vagina. *Oh my heart!* She leaned back, closing her eyes as she felt his touch, his fingers wet from her juices, gently caressing her clitoris. Could she come, here in the car, with the traffic going by?

"You can come for me. Take it." It didn't take long for her to find herself on the precipice, and as she reached her orgasm, he placed his hand over her mouth and muffled her moans. She licked his palm, relishing its taste and revelling in the moment. Then he removed his fingers and brought them up to her mouth.

"Now open your mouth and lick them clean. Taste how good you are."

And she did. *You naughty girl!*

The company had hired a private room above an Italian restaurant in Piccadilly. They were the last to arrive, and Suzy felt confident and very happy as, with his arm firmly around her waist, claiming her as his own, Lawrence led her through the mingling crowd to the bar. Conversation momentarily stopped flowing as the inquisitive audience admired the stunning woman physically bound to Lawrence Bane.

The chairman broke the silence. "Lawrence, good to see you." His eyes immediately shot to Suzy, waiting for an introduction.

"Tony, this is my girlfriend, Suzy Jones. Suzy, Tony Cross, our chairman." He winked at Suzy, as though this was the most natural introduction to make, and he pulled her close and whispered, "Go with me on this", while looking at Tony and smiling.

Tony shook Suzy's hand. "Delighted to meet you, Miss Jones, and I hope you don't mind me saying, you look beautiful." He thought about introducing her to some of the other staff, but looked at the firm expression on Bane's face and thought better of it.

"The bar's paid for. Let's get you both a drink, and then let me introduce you to Kevin Underwood."

Suzy felt Lawrence's grip tighten around her waist and instantly knew his mood had changed – was it the mention of this guy's name? She assumed it was the soon-to-be-appointed managing director, the reason for the dinner.

Lawrence interrupted her thoughts. "What would you like to drink, darling?"

Oh, he hasn't called me that before. She felt disappointed that her relaxed, friendly Lawrence was gone for now, replaced by the formal businessman, and she perceived an added guardedness that she knew accompanied him withholding something from her.

"Er, gin and tonic, please. No ice."

"And I'll have a martini," he informed Tony, clearly expecting him to get the drinks. Tony didn't bat an eyelid, so it was presumably business as usual.

Armed with their drinks, with Lawrence's arm firmly tucked into Suzy's gloved elbow, they followed Tony through the gathering, towards a tall, grey-haired man, whom Suzy imagined to be in his late fifties. He was talking animatedly with a man she later found out was the production director.

Tony interrupted them and made the introductions. Suzy still didn't know whether to be cross or concerned at the sudden use of "Jones" as her surname. He could at least have chosen something more original!

Again, Lawrence's grip on her elbow tightened, and she almost winced. He momentarily released her to give Kevin Underwood a very firm handshake.

"I'm pleased to see you again, Mr Bane. Many thanks for holding this dinner, and for giving me the opportunity to show you my potential to successfully work with your management team and take the company forward. I'm sure I can allay any concerns you may have."

He paused, and Suzy thought he seemed a genuine guy, ready to prove his worth. She expected him to continue, but almost cringed for him as Lawrence interrupted very curtly. "Call me Lawrence, and I'm sure we'll have lots to discuss over dinner." With that, he grabbed Suzy's elbow and led her over to a very tall, thin, blonde-haired woman, whom he introduced as "Linda, the finance director, and her husband Simon." Both immediately complimented Suzy on her beautiful outfit, but her mind was spinning at the way this evening was going. She felt it wasn't going to be a pleasant one, as Lawrence was clearly pissed off about something. Was it just Mr Underwood?

Lawrence started to talk to Simon about his new car. "Linda tells me you've just purchased a new Audi A6 – how do you like it?" Suzy hoped he would relax a little, talking about one of his favourite subjects. He was holding her hand and his grip was firm and reassuring. She squeezed his fingers, interlocked with hers, to let him know she was there for him.

Suddenly Lawrence felt a light tap on his shoulder and he and Suzy turned to face a woman in her early fifties, with short brown hair, wearing a cocktail dress of silk ochre. Suzy thought she looked sophisticated and wealthy.

"Well, Lawrence, what a surprise! I didn't realise the Lawrence Bane Kevin was introducing me to tonight was you!" Suzy stared at her, a chill running through her at the drawl of this woman's voice, the mocking tone, and the almost derogatory way she said "Kevin". Was this Mrs Underwood, and how did she know Lawrence?

Lawrence's face became veiled in a hard, impassive expression. He immediately let go of Suzy's hand, but made no attempt to shake the woman's. He was silent.

The woman then blatantly looked Suzy up and down, and in a sickly voice, heavy with sarcasm, she turned to Lawrence and whispered. Suzy only just managed to make out the words. "Oh dear, can she afford you, darling? What are your rates these days?" A disingenuous smile crept across her face, and she looked again at Suzy.

Lawrence's expression was like thunder, and he remained silent and immobile. Suzy quickly glanced at Linda and Simon, and then around at the other guests. No one seemed to notice the friction between these two. Suzy looked at Lawrence, hoping he would just take her arm and lead her away from this woman, but he appeared to be frozen to the spot.

A second later, he made to turn away and suddenly his martini spilled over the ochre dress. Suzy stared in horror as the woman glared at Lawrence, looked down at her dress and marched away, in the direction of the ladies.

"Mingle with the others," Lawrence instructed Suzy, as he regained his composure and left her standing alone. She stared after him, knowing he was following the woman. *Can she afford you ... what are your rates now?* Her head started to swim. She realised Tony had come up to her and was asking if she would like to come and sit at the table, as they were getting ready to serve dinner.

Concentrate. Concentrate. She sat down, finding herself sitting next to the production director and an empty chair, which she prayed would soon be filled by Lawrence.

Elizabeth Underwood had gone into the ladies' toilets. Lawrence walked straight in after her, closed the door and stood leaning against it.

"What the hell do you think you are doing?" His voice was filled with anger, hate and contempt.

"I ... I was just joking. Hell, look at the state of my dress!" The drawl and sarcasm in her voice were gone now and, looking at Lawrence in the mirror, she was hesitant, unsure of what to say and fearful of his anger.

"Running out of pocket money, are you? He needs another job to accommodate your lifestyle, doesn't he?" Lawrence spat the words at this woman in front of him.

He suddenly moved forward, as someone was trying to come in to use the facilities.

"Male cleaning in progress. Find an alternative." He did not take his eyes off Mrs Underwood.

"You keep your fucking mouth shut and your husband can keep paying your bills, and remain in the dark about your hobbies." He walked out and closed the door quietly behind him.

He sat down between Suzy and Kevin Underwood, apologising for the delay. He placed his hand on her knee and left it there for a moment, as he started a conversation with Kevin about the prospective new business the company was embarking on, accurately reciting the target sales, profit margins, licensing issues and distribution challenges. Half an hour ago, Suzy would have listened with pride and respect as Lawrence talked confidently, animatedly and with passion about this business. But, whereas he appeared to be able to carry on as usual, she could not. She played with her starter of mozzarella, buffalo tomato and avocado, and was grateful for the constant chat from the production director seated at her other side. She only had to say the occasional "yes" or "no" and smile automatically.

Afford you? Your rates? Really, she just wanted to throw up.

Lawrence had finished his starter. He excused himself from the table for a moment and asked Tony to have a word with him at the bar.

"I know enough, Tony, and he's got my vote. Did you bring the offer and draft contract with you?"

"Yes, Linda's got everything." He looked puzzled, but not really surprised at Lawrence Bane's unorthodox way of appointing the new managing director.

"Good. I'm sorry, but Miss Jones and I need to leave now. Arrange a board meeting for the first week of January, I'll want to go through things with Linda a couple of days before it. Have a good Christmas, Tony, and give my regards to your family. Thanks for all you're doing for the company. You've got a good team, and I'm sure Kevin is going to strengthen it."

"OK, we're leaving," he said quietly to Suzy, placing his hands on her shoulders. She turned and looked up at him questioningly, glancing along the table at Mr and Mrs Underwood.

"We are leaving now," he said firmly and, taking hold of her hand, he looked around the table. "I'm sorry, folks, we have to leave. Welcome to the team, Kevin. Have a good Christmas, everyone, and thanks for all you've done. It's been a good year. I'll see you in January. Enjoy the rest of the meal." With that, he led Suzy out of the restaurant.

"You…" She was shaking, and pulling her hand from his grasp. He was not letting go. "You owe me an explanation."

Lawrence raised his other hand to hail a taxi, and then ran it through his hair. She now recognised this as a sign that he was troubled and closing up on her. But she had no intention of letting him get away with this. *Miss Jones … afford you … your rates.*

"Lawrence, talk to me." She climbed into the taxi and he followed her.

He pulled her towards him. "I will, just give me a little time. Let's get to the hotel," he whispered and she breathed in his smell.

"We've got a reservation. Mr and Mrs Jones."

Suzy stared at him as he took the keys from the desk clerk. *Can there be any more surprises tonight?*

In the room, their overnight bags had been placed on the luggage rack, thanks to Dave, who had brought them round to the hotel.

Lawrence went straight to the mini bar and studied the miniature whiskies.

"Do you want a drink?" he asked quietly.

"No thanks." She sat on the bed, watching him empty the contents of one of the bottles into a glass before taking a long, slow sip of the golden liquid, savouring the taste and, no doubt, preparing himself for the unavoidable speech he knew he was going to have to make.

"Who was she, Lawrence?"

He recognised the clinical tone she had used before. He knew she wouldn't let him stall her now, not this time. He also appreciated that she deserved to know. She had the right to make her own judgement of him. He would be on trial.

"Her name is Elizabeth Underwood." He thought for a

moment about his reluctance to appoint, or even meet, Kevin Underwood. He had asked Lewis to confirm it was the same person: the cuckolded husband of one of his former clients. He knew the risks involved in taking Suzy to the dinner tonight, but what the heck, his demons were starting to flood out of his closet and he needed to face the truth – with her.

He sat on the bed next to her, and took another couple of sips of whisky, studying the glass thoughtfully, watching the remaining liquid swirl around inside.

"What did she mean when she asked if I could afford you and what were your rates now?" Suzy's voice was devoid of emotion and, as he looked at her, he wondered if she had already prepared herself for his answer.

"Just promise me you will remember our deal about the past being history." His voice was hushed, and as his eyes softened she could sense the pain he was feeling; guilt and regret enveloping him. He put the glass down.

"She was a client." He paused, staring at her intensely, trying to read her thoughts and waiting for her reaction.

"Go on, Lawrence. I need to know what you mean." She took hold of his hand, squeezing it as if to reassure him she knew how hard this was and that she wanted to help him.

"She paid to have sex with me. It was my job." His voice hardened, as though he was trying to remove himself from this confession, unwilling to be a participant. He let go of Suzy's hand, feeling that he didn't deserve to hold her. "My only excuse is that from the age of fifteen I had no choice. A madam took me in and she became my employer. She taught me to please women, and punished me if I stepped out of line."

Suzy sat still and silent, as her worst fear was confirmed. He used to be a male prostitute.

"You knew she would be there tonight. Why did you bring me along?" Suzy was stupefied.

"I want you to be part of my life, Suzy, and I know you feel you need to understand where I'm from as well as where I am now. I couldn't be afraid of meeting Elizabeth, or let that stop me from involving you in my life. I realised that when I gave you the box from my dressing room." He smiled at her, ever so faintly. "Of course, I expected her to be more discreet and dignified. But I guess some people never change."

He stood up and walked over to his overnight bag. He went through its contents and, with his back to her, he continued, "I never really wanted you to find out about my past, but I realised I couldn't live with you honestly and openly if I continued to try to hide it all from you." He turned and faced her. "This is really hard for me, Suzy, but I need you to understand how I feel. I can't live with you and fear you finding out and hating me. But I also need you to accept what I did, what it has made me, and what I need now."

Suzy sat motionless on the bed, watching him and wondering what on earth he was going to do. He had already said more than she had expected. She felt numb inside. Nothing could shock her now, or so she thought. Then she saw him take something from his bag and an expression of shock and fear froze on her face.

He had pulled out a brown leather flogger. He studied the handle and fondled the strands with his fingers. His breathing was calm, and he was totally in control. His voice was firm and she became anxious as he approached her.

"I need you to do this, Suzy." His eyes were determined and he stared at her face, perceiving her fear and dread. "I need to be punished and I want you to do it, baby. You can, and your forgiveness can let me move on…"

She interrupted him, her voice trembling, and looked down at her shaking hands, unable to meet his stare. His words "I liked to be hurt" were swirling round her head. "No, Lawrence, I can't hurt you, I can't do it."

"Don't cry, Suzy. You must do it." His voice was instructional, devoid of emotion. "I've hurt you and my guilt would only become greater, as my past is catching up with me. I can't live in fear of some other woman coming and tapping me on my shoulder. I realise I was a fool to think I could live in a cocoon with you and that no one would ever find us. I can cope better knowing you have punished me and that I am forgiven…"

Again she cut in. "I don't need to forgive you, Lawrence; it's history, remember. And you said yourself, you had no choice. I love you and I want to be with you, no matter what happened in your past. I do want to share the truth with you. We shouldn't have secrets from each other, and I really appreciate your honesty. Don't be afraid to talk to me, tell me anything. But I don't need to punish you, Lawrence."

"Suzy, I need you to punish me." He looked desolate as he slowly started to unfasten his bow tie. He placed it carefully on the bed. "This is who I am."

She watched him unfasten his dress shirt, take it off and place it on the back of a chair. "I will never demand too much from you, baby, but I have to have this, and I am begging you to do it." His look was solemn, dark and intense. She was in this weird paradoxical world, feeling afraid of him, yet safe in his presence.

"Will you, please?"

She lowered her head, unable to look at him, and nodded, with a barely audible whisper. "Yes."

It was enough.

He took her hand and removed her glove. Then he placed the flogger in it and picked up his bow tie.

"Come," he ordered and, holding her other hand, he led her into the bathroom.

As she followed him, she observed his upper body; his powerful shoulders; his sleek, smooth back; his soft, unblemished skin. It was a stunning, heavenly vision, completed by his black trousers and bare feet. Could she go through with this? She understood that if she couldn't do this for him, she would never be enough for him. It would be a chasm between them, something they could never bridge. She felt it wasn't primarily a sexual thing, though inevitably there was something carnal about the whole situation. No, it was his own perception of what he believed he had to put himself through in order to be cleansed, accepted and forgiven. What did he say? *She taught me ... and disciplined me if I stepped out of line?* Who was she? What did she do to him?

He watched her as she looked at the flogger in her hands. She twirled the handle and stroked her hand with the long tails. They felt soft and innocuous. She fought back tears as she realised what she was going to do and gazed up to see him looking at her imploringly. *What do I do?*

He read her mind. "I promise it will be OK, Suzy. Don't be afraid of it, and don't be gentle. I want you to strike me fifteen times: lash out and use your energy." A brief smile crossed his lips and his eyes glistened with compassion: he was conscious of the enormity of the task he was asking her to perform, and how alien this was to her. "Try to think of how much I annoy you sometimes. You say I never trust you enough."

Oh my darling, you are trusting me now, to do this to you!

Her lips moved as she tried to say something, but he placed his finger on them, compelling her to remain silent, alone with her thoughts.

"I will hold on to the rail and I will count. If it's not hard enough, Suzy, I will let you keep going. Please, don't hold back on me. It will be over when I let go of the rail. Do not stop until then." His voice was controlled and authoritative and Suzy couldn't begin to imagine how he was feeling or what was going through his mind. Was his meditation helping with any of this?

Then she gasped, as he gagged himself with the bow tie, pulling it tight at the back of his head. He never turned to face her, but leaned forward, positioning his right foot slightly in front of his left, and she saw his muscles flex as he gripped the sides of the rail in front of him.

Suzy was motionless for a moment. Then, trying to think of nothing but a countdown from fifteen, she raised her arm and lashed out at him.

She whipped and flogged and lashed and thrashed her beautiful, masochistic man with as much strength as she could muster. The tails of the flogger wrapped around his waist and over his shoulders, increasing the pain he experienced. She saw his body tense, his veins stand out, his legs reposition themselves to maintain his balance, and his head reel back and then lower forward, as he braced himself for the next lash. She saw faint red lines appearing on his graceful back, and she put her hand over her mouth, determined not to sob. *Focus on the task. You are doing this for him.*

Fifteen.

He let go of the rail, his whole body heaving in a massive sigh. He removed the gag and crouched down on the floor.

Suzy saw the redness of the marks across his back deepen, and it was over. She could take no more.

She was exhausted, drained of energy and emotion.

Quietly, she moved to place the flogger on the washbasin and went, alone, into the bedroom.

Lawrence stayed motionless for a few moments and then he stood under the shower, letting ice-cold water fall down his back, alleviating the swelling. After the initial shock of the coldness on his burning skin, his breathing slowed and he began to feel calm.

Naked, he walked into the bedroom and found Suzy curled up on the bed, still wearing her beautiful dress, facing away from him. He moved around the bed, knelt on the floor beside her and took her hand in his, caressing it gently.

"Thank you," he whispered with warmth and passion, and slowly he climbed onto the bed and lay facing her, continuing to caress her hand while the minutes slowly passed.

Eventually, Suzy opened her eyes and surveyed her man. He was staring at her intently, his hand stroking her hair and her bare shoulder. He smiled at her hesitantly.

"Are we good?" His voice was hushed and anxious, his eyes pleading.

Suzy gave the faintest of nods, and whispered, her voice quivering as tears fell onto her cheeks, "I'm so sorry, Lawrence. Please hold me."

He stretched his arm out and wrapped it around her, hugging her to him. She placed her hands on his chest and suddenly winced, as she opened her fingers in his dark, wispy hair. He studied her palm, seeing the swollen redness from her tight grip on the leather flogger. He lowered his head, placing his lips over her palm, covering the swelling in soft, moist kisses. Then he moved off the bed and fetched a small tube of ibuprofen gel from his bag.

"I'm not sorry for this, baby," he said as he massaged the cream into her palm. "It shows that you love me, Suzy." He walked back over to the bag and took out a small gift-wrapped box. She looked at him questioningly. "An early Christmas present," he explained.

"Wait." He gently took her hands, beckoning her off the bed. He brushed away the tears from her cheeks before lifting the dress over her head and rolling the hold-ups down and over her toes, leaving her standing naked before him. He then handed her the gift. "Suzy Harper, I give you my heart." He watched fervently as she opened the box and gazed admiringly at a beautiful platinum heart-shaped locket on a chain of platinum rope. It felt heavy as she removed it from the wrapping, examining it appreciatively. Hesitantly, she opened it, expecting to see a photograph but unable to recollect when they had had one taken together. It was empty, and she looked up at him.

"Wait a moment." He went into the bathroom. Suzy's smile faded as he returned with the flogger in his hand. *Oh, what is he going to do now?* She watched with curiosity as he took a penknife from his toilet bag, carefully cut a tiny piece of leather from one of the strands, and placed it inside the locket.

"I..." He hesitated and began to fasten the chain around her neck. "I know how hard this was for you and, no matter what happens in the future, I will never forget it or stop loving you for it. I'm yours for as long as you want me, Suzy. You look beautiful." He stepped back to admire his naked girl wearing his gift, and then came forward to wipe away the tears that had started to fall again.

She whispered through her sobs, "You planned all this, didn't you? You booked the hotel so I couldn't escape to another bedroom or get in my car, you brought the flogger, and this gift..." Her voice was trembling and she gave way to her emotions. He sat down on the bed and cradled her on his lap, gently stroking her hair, and she could hear his steady heartbeat.

"It wasn't planned, Suzy. I just came prepared. I didn't know how Elizabeth would react. I haven't seen her for over eight years. But I knew what I would have to do if my past profession came out, so I was prepared. You're right about the hotel. You don't need to associate The Sway with any of this. That's the place only we truly know, where we can be together and shut out the world for a while if we want to. It's my sanctuary, Suzy, and I hope it can be yours."

She had stopped crying now, but stayed on his lap, breathing in his smell and feeling his warmth. He was still the same man she loved, and she suddenly realised that now she knew him more, she loved him more. Her fingers clasped the platinum heart.

"It's beautiful," she said. "Why did you introduce me as Miss Jones, and use Mr and Mrs Jones here?" The calmness in Suzy's voice was enough to dissipate his fears of her rejection.

"There are certain circles where I think it best that Suzy Harper isn't seen to be connected with the big bad Lawrence Bane." There was the trace of a smile on his kissable lips. "At least not just yet," he added, as if to quell any feeling that they couldn't have a future together.

Her crying over, Suzy felt a bit stronger. "You're too mysterious for your own good. Maybe now you don't need to be so cagey. I think I've earned that." She looked composed and in control, knowing she had the upper hand.

"Mmm." He raised one eyebrow, secretly in awe of her handling of the situation, and energised with determination to see him through the next few weeks and ensure he comes back for her.

She studied her palm, touching the small blisters that had formed.

"Stand up," she said quietly but firmly. He got up from the bed and stood in front of her. "Turn around," she added, gloating at his puzzled expression. She took the ibuprofen gel and started to gently rub it over his back, lightly tracing the red lines with her fingers. "Lawrence Bane." She was beginning to enjoy this feeling of new-found power, as her fingers continued to massage the cream into his damaged skin, seeing him flinch at her touch. "I am sorry for this. I will never want to hurt you." He sensed her smile fading as she finished her task.

I think you might. He experienced a paradoxical sensation of the pleasure she could give him, and the pain she could inflict if she were to abandon him.

It had been a long evening and, having decided they were not in the mood to eat, they had a glass of wine each from the minibar before crawling under the duvet, Lawrence carefully lying on his stomach, still smarting from his flogging. Suzy drifted uneasily into sleep and for the first time since Lawrence had known her, he was awakened by her sobs. The alarm clock read 4 a.m. She was not fully conscious and he gingerly raised himself up and tried to hug her to him. Still not properly awake, her crying subsided and he could make out her words, "I can't do it." He hugged her more tightly, his thoughts filled with guilt. He took comfort from the fact she was grasping the heart pendant around her neck, but he did not sleep any more that night.

As she stirred, a couple of hours later, she reached out and stroked his face.

"You're awake," she smiled warmly, and he eased himself onto his side to face her.

"Yes, baby, and I'm sorry, I don't think you slept too well." He was anxious, and she knew he was feeling guilty and nervous.

She wanted to reassure him of her acceptance of who he was and what he had been. She wanted to reconnect with him in the way that she knew would convince him that she still loved him. She wanted him to be inside her, to feel him, and for them both to feel pleasure and feel that everything would be alright between them. She reached her hand towards his penis and began to gently stroke it, waiting for it to harden. His eyes drilled into hers intently, and then he closed them as his arousal started to consume him. "I don't think I deserve this." He smiled weakly.

"You don't," she agreed quietly. "But we both need this now, and I think you owe me." She smiled coyly, determined to move on from last night. *Or else why did I do it?*

He straddled her and leaned forward to kiss her lips, taste her mouth, his tongue hungry and demanding. He cradled her face in his hands, and his hold was firm. She knew he was desperate for her, and eager to please her. She wallowed in the pleasure of his tongue invading her mouth, curling around and touching her own tongue. As they released each other for air, he eased himself into her, gently at first and then harder and more forcefully. She lay back, surrendering to him, her body moving in rhythm with his. She reached up to pull him further into her, but as her hands made contact with his back, he cried out in pain. "Aarghh! Easy, baby." His contorted expression betrayed the discomfort he felt.

"Will you trust me?" He was breathless with anticipation, continuing to move in her. "Say you will trust me," he ordered, and she whimpered, "Yes."

"I'm going to turn you over and come from behind, Suzy. Let me know your pleasure, tell me." As he spoke, he turned her onto her stomach, while staying inside her and continuing to thrust backward and forward. His hands moved down to her hips and he firmly raised her onto all fours.

"Do you like this, Suzy?" She could feel more of him now, as she arched her back, pushing herself onto him, feeling his testicles making contact with her opening.

"Oh yes, yes." She was relishing this sensation and losing herself in the wild lust it aroused in her. She wanted to feel him touch her clitoris; she so wanted to come.

"What do you want, Suzy? Tell me!"

"I want to come," she moaned, trying to turn her head to see him, and he leaned forward to kiss her.

Then she felt his hand touch her, right where she wanted him to, right where he knew she would reach her climax in seconds. He teased her, getting close, then pulling away and leaving her crying out, "Don't stop!"

"You want me to do this?" His fingers began again, bang on target.

"Yes, please." She pushed back onto him as he thrust into her, still stroking her clitoris. They came together, intensely, and as his climax subsided, he worked to ensure hers lasted, never wanting her ecstasy to end, and only ceasing as she shuddered and the sensations became too much for her.

Lawrence eased himself onto his side, not quite comfortable enough yet to lie on his back, and gently circled her nipples with his fingers, playfully making figures of eight, and Suzy sighed with the pleasure of the morning so far.

"Should we think about getting up and leaving?"

He continued making patterns on her body. "Not just yet. We have time for a shower and breakfast." He reached for the phone and ordered light continental breakfasts to be sent to the room in forty-five minutes. "Come into the bathroom." He slid off the bed with the grace of a dancer and Suzy's heart leaped as she watched him walking away from her, the red marks on his back somewhat diminished, but adding a darkness to his character which was somehow unthreatening. She still had many questions, but she was trying to subdue them, not wanting to spoil the lovely start to the day.

As she approached him in the bathroom, she saw the enticing glint in his eyes. *What are you up to?* His hands were behind his back, and his lips formed a lascivious smile.

"Put your arms out and stand with your feet apart. I owe you a treat." She peered at him anxiously, and did as instructed. He pulled a small brush from behind his back, and slowly and meticulously began to tenderly, but firmly, brush every inch of her body, the strokes always going towards her heart.

"This should energise, detoxify and radiate your skin. How does it feel?"

"Wonderful," she exclaimed as she stood watching him kneel before her, brushing her feet, moving up her legs, enjoying the sensations he was creating as he reached her upper thighs and buttocks. Skin brushing was not something she had experienced before. In fact, she had never even been for a spa treatment, and had only been massaged by Lawrence. What sort of male prostitute learned how to do this?

As he brushed her arms, he kissed her lightly, revelling in delighting her. She was stimulated with pleasure at the invigorating, tingling feeling all over her skin. Once the skin brushing was complete, he led her into the shower, and under the hot steamy water, he proceeded to cover her body with foaming lather from the bottle of Chanel shower gel he had bought for her. The sensation was luxuriously hedonistic, and she loved him a little bit more! As he continued, she reached for his Chanel body wash and roamed his body with her hands, delicately polishing his back, and slowly cleaning his penis and balls. He stopped for a moment, allowing himself to be pleasured, then took her hands. "Enough, I think. Let's get ready for breakfast. We've got a lot to do today."

"Oh? Are you going to tell me what can be so important to entice us out of here?" Her curiosity was barely enough to break her away from the shower.

As they dried each other, and she carefully rubbed some more of the ibuprofen gel onto his back, she couldn't help asking, "Lawrence, did Elizabeth flog you?"

He froze. She couldn't see his face. *Why did I ask that now? I could have waited!*

"No." His monosyllabic answer betrayed the fact that he was deep in thought. He wasn't telling her everything.

The playful, sensual atmosphere of the brushing and showering was gone.

The innocence of his relationship with her was gone.

Soon I could lose you. He observed her in the mirror.

"I won't talk about it now, Suzy. Please don't let it spoil this time we have."

He walked out of the bathroom and slowly began to get dressed. She reached for her own clothes, a little surprised he didn't want them to stay naked for breakfast. After all, wasn't that why he had ordered room service?

She opened the door as a knock told them the waiter had arrived. As she picked at a croissant, she asked, "So what are the plans for today?" in a desperate attempt to break the cold atmosphere with which her earlier question had engulfed them.

He answered curtly, "Dave should be here at nine, and we're going to buy a Christmas tree!"

"Oh, that sounds lovely. Are we going to decorate it? I could do with one for the cottage too."

"We need to discuss our arrangement and plans for the holidays, synchronise our diaries up to the new year." His tone was cold and controlling, and he ignored her comment about a tree for her cottage. He started to eat some of the fresh fruit and pastries, and poured them both some coffee.

What's happening? What's wrong with him?

He continued to eat and drink. Suzy watched him, her mind trying to decipher the reason for his mood change. She picked at some of the food to distract her from her own thoughts – her question about Elizabeth.

He continued in the same controlling manner. "I rent a farmhouse for Christmas and the new year, in the Peak District. I want you to come with me."

Suzy finished her coffee and was about to suggest that, if they spent Christmas at his holiday farmhouse, they could have New Year with Dominic and Richard; maybe a party at The Sway?

Then she realised he did not expect a counter-proposal, or a protest.

He started to pack both their overnight bags. He put his jacket on, carefully. Then he stood and faced her. She had remained seated at the table, watching him. He looked gorgeous in black jeans, a pale coffee-coloured crew-neck sweater and a luxuriously soft brown leather jacket. He picked up her coat, holding it open, waiting to help her put it on. "Come on, let's get out of here."

He was authoritative, unilateral in his decision-making, and he did not wait for any response from her. Suzy was baffled by this sudden change in him. She felt at a loss to understand why he was suddenly dictating to her, her opinion not considered, not even expected.

Mindlessly, she followed him out of the room. She hadn't even checked to see if he had packed everything, but somehow she knew he would have done. Before she realised it, he had checked out and they were sitting in the foyer waiting for Dave. She had still not spoken to Lawrence.

In the parking zone was an old red pickup truck. There was no driver in sight, but the engine was still running.

Dave suddenly appeared from round the corner. "I was just checking if I needed a ticket to park the truck."

"I'll drive," said Lawrence, and he turned to Suzy and kissed her cheek.

He climbed into the driver's seat, as Dave held the passenger door for Suzy, then got in to sit beside her. So they really were going to get a Christmas tree!

Suzy was still feeling annoyed at the way Lawrence had dictated to her, but she knew now was not the time to make an issue of it. She needed to think about what had been said and how he had said it. She would pick her moment. In the meantime she started to consider her options for Christmas. Other than gate-crashing at her cousin's, again, she didn't actually have any. A farmhouse in the Peak District did sound lovely. Somehow, the thought of the two of them being alone for a whole week was very appealing. *But what if he's going to be in this sort of mood? We could go in separate cars, so I could leave at any time if I wanted to.*

"Thanks for coming to get us, Dave." She decided to try to make the journey a bit more pleasant, hoping he did not pick up on the atmosphere between her and Lawrence, who had turned the radio on and was driving in silence, while Slade's "Merry Christmas Everybody" blared out over the engine noise.

Dave glanced at Lawrence, who appeared to be concentrating on the road. Dave had never seen him so unimpassioned. Lawrence loved driving, and this old ex-racing pickup truck was a favourite of his. Usually he never stopped going on about the hum of the engine, the torque, the suspension.

"You're welcome. It was no trouble." This was the most Suzy had ever heard him say in one go.

"So what are you and Christine doing for Christmas this year?" she continued, determined to keep some sort of conversation going.

Another glance at Lawrence, almost as if he were asking permission to reply. Lawrence glanced back, raising one eyebrow. His eyes avoided Suzy.

"We're going away."

"Oh, that sounds good. Where to?" *The Peak District?*

"St Lucia, for some sun."

"That sounds fabulous!" She appeared excited. Lawrence looked at her and she tried to gauge his assessment of her response. *Does he think I would rather be in St Lucia than the Peak District? Well, let him!* "I had a lot of Christmases in thirty-degree heat when I lived in Cameroon. Do you normally go somewhere hot for the holidays?"

"Yes, it's a Christmas present from Lawrence." At this he turned to his employer. "Cheers for that."

The driver kept looking straight ahead. "You're welcome."

The truck turned into a garden nursery, the driveway lined with Christmas trees.

As Lawrence got out of the car and went round to the passenger side, Dave had beaten him to assisting Suzy down from the high step to the cabin. Lawrence was stony-faced as she walked past, following Dave inside to the sales counter.

Well, you've pissed her off now, you controlling bastard! He marched after them.

"Hi Mr Bane, we've got the tree you ordered all ready for you over here. The large one has been delivered and should be being erected now. Will you come in for a drink and a mince pie?"

Suzy stared at the tree that was ready for them, and found it hard to imagine a bigger one. Just how high were the ceilings at The Sway?

"That would be nice, thank you, John. And do you have a smaller tree for my girlfriend's cottage?"

Is he trying to make up for his behaviour? Or is this his way of telling me I may as well stay at home alone? Do I care?

"Sure, something like this, perhaps?" and John went over to a four-foot Nordman Fir. "This won't drop its needles too easily and is our most popular tree this year."

"It looks lovely. How much is it?" Suzy asked.

"Just put it on the bill, John, thanks." Lawrence was not in the mood for discussion and Suzy didn't want to make a scene, but why the hell was he being so rude?

She thanked John and then felt Lawrence take her hand as John led them to a counter laden with mince pies and an urn of warm mulled wine. She pulled away from him as she accepted some wine and a pie. His eyes stayed on her, drilling into her, and she wondered if this was still over the Elizabeth question. Perhaps she should ask to be taken home with the little tree, but this would break their arrangement to spend the nights together. Maybe it would be better, but she felt a chill run through her at the thought of not being with him. She was vaguely aware of him asking John if business was good, discussing a chainsaw Dave was after, and then some reference to pond plants. She remembered their walk and passion at the pond. How she wished they were there now, alone, happy and carefree. It had been her first time putting a condom on him. Mmmm…

"Suzy, time to go." His words broke her dream, and she felt his fingers tighten around her hand, warm and firm. *Oh my heart, where are we going with this? Love or destruction?*

The truck was loaded with the two trees, and they took their seats again, Suzy watching the traffic around them as Lawrence and Dave discussed the grounds at The Sway and what needed to be done over the winter. She admired Lawrence for his knowledge of trees and shrubs, and the passion with which he spoke about his land. Was he like that with all his possessions? Was that how he saw her? She thought about his protection of The Sway, the flogging at the hotel, not at his home. Would she feel better when she got there?

Then she realised he had pulled up outside her cottage. *Oh. He's going to leave me here, with my tree.*

"Take the truck home, Dave, and we'll follow in Suzy's car. Just give me a hand with the trees." They got out of the truck, Dave moving the larger tree to enable Lawrence to take the smaller one into Suzy's cottage, and she followed with the bucket he had added to the purchase. How did he always think of everything?

As the truck disappeared, she closed the door and went into the lounge, where Lawrence was securing the tree upright in the bucket. Then he went and fetched a jug of water from the kitchen. He worked in silence.

Suzy felt exhausted after all the events of last night, her disturbed sleep, and now, trying to determine his mood and where today was going. She stayed in the kitchen. Looking around, she remembered that her whole house had been cleaned by the Merry Maids cleaning company, thanks to Lawrence. That was the sort of control she didn't mind! She went into the lounge.

"I didn't thank you for the cleaning the other day." She spoke quietly, trying to quash a nervousness within her.

He looked up, his face masking any thoughts or feelings. There was a brief silence, then his mask fell away, revealing sad eyes and a tiredness.

"Would you rather go to St Lucia than the Peak District?"

So, has this been bothering him too? He thinks I don't want to be with him!

"No, I wouldn't." She spoke in a hushed tone, her own emotional exhaustion beginning to consume her. She sat on the sofa. "I would love to come to your cottage, and I hope it snows." She smiled nervously. The air between them needed to be cleared, the atmosphere refreshed, and that "something" which existed between them restored. He must talk to her now.

"Why did you talk to me like that, at the hotel? You were laying down rules, with no intention of asking what I wanted to do for Christmas. You practically frog-marched me out of the hotel. It was like you were trying to show me who was master. I know you were cross when I asked about Elizabeth, and I'm sorry. But after last night..." Her glance pleaded with him to respond to her, to explain, make excuses, whatever, just to say something to put things right between them. "It wasn't easy for me, you know." She glanced down at her hand, feeling the small blisters on her palm, and fighting back tears.

He came to sit beside her, and took her hand, making gentle, featherlike circling motions with his fingers.

"I wanted to make you angry with me because of who I am now, not because of what I was. Now, I like to be in control and I like people to do what I tell them. I needed to be in control of you earlier, Suzy, I know it was stupid. But you couldn't stop thinking about Elizabeth, about the old me, could you? Suzy, you said the past was history. Why are you asking me to bring it into our present?"

"I'm sorry. I'm trying not to think too much. But my thoughts are driving me crazy – am I like one of your clients, or one of your possessions? I can't help it."

"Suzy, you are my girlfriend. I want to share my life with you, not to own you. I know I was inconsiderate today, and I'm sorry. But that was my way of coping, and trying to regain control. I gave up my celibacy for you, Suzy. I love you and I have never loved anyone before. Can't that be enough?"

She lifted her face to him, displaying her desire and need for him.

"Yes, it can, Lawrence. I love you." *Please kiss me.*

He reached his arms around her, hugging her tight to him, kissing her lips, draining her breath for his own survival.

"You need to get us home."

She looked at him questioningly.

"You're driving, remember. Much though it pains me to give you the controls." There was that smile again. "Your tree will be fine for a few days. We'll decorate it later. Come on."

Peace had been restored between them and they found themselves singing along to all the old Christmas favourites on the radio. As Suzy drove up towards The Sway she gasped with delight and wonder at the huge Christmas tree erected in the middle of the drive outside the front of the house, multi-coloured lights sparkling and a huge silver star glowing on the top. It was beautiful. So this was the large one! In addition, there were glowing reindeers and a sleigh, a shiny white snowman and icicles hanging from the eaves over the front door. The scene was magical.

She got out of the car and walked around the statues and the tree, smiling from ear to ear and exclaiming how lovely everything was, like a child in a sweet shop.

"A bit over the top, I know!" laughed Lawrence, delighting in her excitement. "It's for the kids." He looked at her as she stopped in her tracks.

"Kids? You have children and you didn't tell me?" Her expression was one of incredulation and needy curiosity, not fear or accusation.

She would accept the fact I had children! "They're not mine." He laughed. "It's a group of youngsters from a children's centre called Fairchance. I try to support them, and they come and take over The Sway each Christmas, and during the summer too. The centre's run by a woman called Julia Kershaw; a good friend of mine. I'd like you to meet everyone when they come." He gave her a questioning look – did she want to?

"I'd love to, Lawrence. Tell me more about it." They entered The Sway together, the unity between them restored, flogging and ex-clients put to rest for now.

They spent that evening cuddling naked, wrapped in blankets, on the sofa in front of the glowing fire in the snug.

"Before you ask," he whispered, "I never did this with Elizabeth, or anyone else!"

Chapter 31

Sunday morning found Lawrence doing his 6 a.m. meditation and Suzy grabbing a little extra sleep before joining him in the pool. Today was track day for Lawrence and his biker buddies, and he was brimming with excitement. He had spent most of Saturday polishing and tweaking and doing whatever motorbike enthusiasts do in preparation for a big event. His BMW S 1000 RR was the very latest in racing power, with its aluminium bridge, radial brakes and super sporty tail-up nose-down design. He couldn't wait to get on the track with it.

Suzy drove to the racecourse in her Mazda, following Lawrence on his bike. With his helmet under his arm, he caught up with her at the meeting point, beaming as he introduced her to some of the fellow racers for the day: Lewis Deane of Blue Securities; Frazer Meadow of FM Lawyers; Steve Jameson, local vicar; and, of course, Richard Groves of Groves Investors. There were ten riders in total and the air was buzzing with roaring engines and enthusiasts' chat.

Suzy wished Lawrence luck and then went to find Christine, who was ensuring there was an abundance of coffee and bacon butties.

"Does he do this often?" she asked when the racing had begun, and they had a couple of hours or so before they would be surrounded by hungry men.

"It's been a biannual event since he came to live up here, during the summer and just before Christmas, weather permitting, of course. He'll be full of it when he comes in."

"Does he usually win?" Suzy was determined to find out as much as possible from Christine: having an opportunity to spend time with her alone didn't present itself very often.

"I think he'll have a tough time beating Steven, even with his new toy!" Christine smiled fondly, backing up Suzy's belief that she genuinely cared for Lawrence, almost like a sibling.

"How did you meet him?" She wasn't going to hold back on her questions this time.

Christine hesitated a moment, turning to face Suzy.

Suzy had the feeling she knew that she was on a fact-finding mission. She wondered how much information Christine was prepared to share with her. Had she earned some of her trust yet?

"You love him, don't you?"

Of course, Christine knew she was practically living at The Sway nowadays, and she had heard Lawrence discussing arrangements for their Christmas in the Peak District with her, so she would know they were going to be spending it together.

"Yes."

"We were both dealt a rough hand when we were young. Sometimes you have to do what you can to survive. It's not something we would have chosen." Christine could have been a million miles away, talking to herself, as she sipped her tea, but she was an astute woman, and greatly protective of her saviour, his privacy, and the respect he had earned for himself here in Cheshire. Neither of them wanted to return to London, but she knew it was coming, and she had her own world to safeguard; her life with Dave. Could she say anything to Suzy that she wouldn't want to say to her lover? "Experience has taught us to live for now, and not to dwell on the past, if to do so would be futile. But sometimes, when things need to be done and wrongs need to be righted, if we have the ability to do that, then God would want us to try, don't you think?" She seemed to come out of her reverie as she stared at Suzy.

Is she talking about her and Lawrence, asking for my agreement, warning me they both have to do something? Suzy felt chilled by her words.

"I guess so." She was nervous of Christine ending the conversation when she wanted to know so much more. Keep her talking. "Do you like living here?"

"Yes, very much. The gatehouse at The Sway is perfect for me and Dave, and I love going into Nantwich."

"Are you ready for your holiday in St Lucia? How long are you going for?"

"We come back on the fifth of January, and I was pretty much packed weeks ago. After all, we're only taking summer clothes, and it's not really the weather for them here at the moment." Her eyes sparkled with excitement at the thought of the holiday, and she seemed much more relaxed. Had she lowered her guard slightly?

"I was wondering about asking Lawrence to go to Paris at the end of January. Do you think he would be up for that?" *Will he (you?) still be here then?*

Christine's face dropped as if she'd just been given some tragic news! "I don't think that would be a good idea." She busied herself unnecessarily clearing the two cups away. "You must speak to him before you book anything." With that, she hurried away to await the return of the racers.

Suzy followed and said, as calmly as possible, "Sure, thanks, I will. I'm not bothered either way. Like you, I like to live for now and am really looking forward to Christmas. Here, let me help you with those bread rolls." She started to assist Christine before there could be any protests, and she made sure their conversation was light-hearted and cheery.

The tell-tale absence of motorbike revs indicated the men were on their way for lunch, and Lawrence came over to Suzy, kissing her and handing her his helmet as he helped himself to some food.

"That was brilliant! The bike did me proud and rode like a dream." He was beaming, his eyes bright, and his hair deliciously messed up. He winked at Christine. "I beat him at last!" He patted Steve on the back, as he appeared at his side.

"Come on, I was beaten by the bike rather than the rider, I think!" The two men teased each other and, as the others joined them, they became a group of animated experts discussing every bend and dip of the course, the use of revs, brakes and knee sliding – kids in their element! Very hungry ones, at that. Suzy helped Christine to make sure there were plenty of bacon butties and chips, and a few pieces of fruit thrown in.

As eating overtook talking, things quietened down for a while, and Suzy went over to Richard for a chat.

"Looks like you all enjoyed yourselves."

"Bane knows how to host a good race day," he complimented her boyfriend. Suzy couldn't help feeling she was being scrutinised by her cousin's partner. She remembered the evening the four of them had spent at the pub and wondered what Richard and Lawrence's relationship was really like. Richard smiled, to put her at ease, as he sensed her concern. "How are you two getting on? Dom seems to think it's serious." Well, Richard's expression certainly was.

"Yeah, I guess it is."

She saw him shake his head slightly in disappointment. *What's that about? Can't you be happy for me?*

"Richard." She raised her voice slightly. "I'm really happy, happier than I've ever been, since I came back to England. I thought you might be pleased."

Richard looked around, not wanting to be overheard by anyone. "Suzy, you've only known him a few weeks. He's not exactly your Mr Average! I just don't want you to be hurt." There was a real unease in his eyes.

"For goodness' sake, why should I be hurt? We're having a great time." She laughed, hiding her own concerns about what the future held for the couple, Christine's words and reactions clear in her mind.

"Are you coming to stay with us for Christmas? My brother and his wife are joining us."

Suzy remembered Richard's brother, Tom, and his wife, Angela. They were great company and last year the five of them had had a fab time.

"Lawrence has invited me to the Peak District with him." She frowned as she recalled the way he had practically ordered her to go with him. She certainly wasn't going to tell Richard that. *Change the subject.* "What's Dominic up to today?"

"He's meeting us at Bane's place later. He's been catching up on some work this morning."

"Do you know if he managed to get the *Top Gear* tickets for me from his contact at the studio? I'm hoping to take Lawrence, for his Christmas present."

"Yeah, he's got them – a great gift for someone like Lawrence. I bet you'll have a fab time."

There was a sudden guffaw and Suzy turned to see what was going on, when Richard grabbed her hand. "Suzy, be careful. We don't want to see you get hurt. You know Dom and I are here for you, any time."

She was startled at the sincerity of his words. He was pretty much family, being practically married to her cousin, and she didn't have any other close relations.

"I know. Please don't worry, it's fine." Then she saw Richard's expression change and felt Lawrence's hand on her shoulder.

"Hi baby." He leaned in and kissed her cheek lightly. "Richard." He gave a slight nod. "You were good on the track. How are you finding the Ducati?"

"Hey, I'll leave you two to talk bikes." She touched Lawrence's arm, feeling the hardness of his muscles through the softness of his leather suit. *I can't wait to get you home, and ruffle your hair up some more!* Hips swaying, she made her way over to some of the others.

"I'm looking after her, you know."

"That's the trouble." Richard's eyes followed the girl he regarded as his own cousin. "I wish you weren't." He hesitated. "Look, I know you've got to get through some stuff. Maybe you trust her enough to keep her informed, take her with you, I don't know, but don't hurt her, Lawrence, please."

She's not the one I can't trust. "I'm making sure she will be safe until I get back. Come on, let's join the others and start getting back to the house. Is Dominic coming?" Lawrence laid his hand across his advisor's back as they strode over the tarmac, determined not to let this affect their professional relationship. Richard Groves was highly regarded in the investment world, and Lawrence had been impressed with the management of his portfolios and the advice he had been given for his "temporary" absence. Not to mention his hopes for a closer relationship with Suzy's family in the future.

* * *

The men and their partners, now dressed for dinner, were assembled in the dining room at The Sway. Christine, with the help of outside caterers, had prepared a four-course meal. Lawrence had arranged for transport home for all the guests, and the champagne, wine and whisky flowed. There were large floral displays, with poinsettias, red roses, thistles, fir cones and different shades of green foliage displayed elegantly around the room, and a Christmas tree decorated with garlands of berries and fairy lights in the corner. The table places were set in black and white and there was a table gift at each setting. It looked beautiful and the atmosphere was brimming with anticipation for a lovely reception.

Introductions were made all round, and Suzy felt very happy, confident in her red velvet dress, with her platinum heart adding the finishing touch, and revelling in the stunning beauty of her man, who was dressed in a black Hugo Boss dinner suit, with white shirt and a dark grey floral tie with dashes of red. Mmmmm.

Suzy was seated next to Lawrence, with Steve and then Jane on her other side. Opposite were Richard and Dominic, while Lewis's wife, Sally, was seated on the other side of Lawrence. Suzy got the feeling the two of them didn't really know each other that well, and she wondered how he knew Lewis from the security company. Another non-exec director role? This group were seated in the middle, and the other guests occupied the remainder of the two sides of the long rectangular dining table.

The vicar proved to be very communicative. She guessed he was about forty-five. He had curly blond hair and a very friendly smiley face, the sort you could tell all your worldly secrets and fears to, confident that he would listen, and give advice only if you wanted it. The best sort of vicar.

"It's a pleasure to meet you, Suzy, I've heard a lot about you. I must say, you look fabulous. How's the translation work going?"

"Oh, Lawrence is still my only client, actually, but I do have a new contract starting in January, although that's through Lawrence, too." *Controlling?*

"He's a good bloke to know," Steve cut in before she could get too uptight about her thoughts. "But then I guess you already know that."

Suzy was surprised at his confidence and support of his friend, and she took an instant liking to this man of the cloth. "How long have you known him?"

"Oh, we go back a few years."

At this point Lawrence leaned in to join their conversation. "I trust you're not going to tell her about all the embarrassing moments we've shared." He laughed, raising an eyebrow, far too relaxed to be afraid of any secrets Steve may give away. There was obviously a great trust and comfort between these two men.

"Don't worry, Bane, your secrets are safe with me, for now! But I might change my mind if you keep beating me and ruining my track record. So, Suzy, just how do you put up with him?"

"Oh, that's easy." She gave Lawrence a sly look as she reached into her clutch bag. "When he starts giving his orders, I just put these in." She placed two earplugs, commonly used by bikers, on the table.

Steve laughed. "She's got you weighed up, mate!"

Eyebrow raised, Lawrence raised his glass. "Cheers for that, baby!"

"Don't worry, I think she used to do that to me too." Dominic joined in the banter and everyone appeared relaxed, with conversation flowing as strangers got to know each other and old acquaintances caught up on recent events. Inevitably, the main chat among the men was about the racing. Suzy loved to see Lawrence so relaxed and happy.

As coffee was served, the gifts were opened. The ladies all received Crème de la Mer hand cream, and the gentlemen were given Waterman black rollerball pens. Thanks were said all round, but Lawrence interrupted the chorus of appreciation as he stood up and thanked everyone for coming, both to the dinner and the races. He had an air of authority, which Suzy was now getting used to, and admired in him. It made her feel safe, although sometimes it infuriated the hell out of her. In her mind she tried to reconcile this with the image of him leaning against the rails in the hotel bathroom, his back covered in red marks, but this wasn't the place for analyses. She realised he was still talking – he was saying how happy he was to have met Suzy, and that they were looking forward to sharing Christmas together. He ended by wishing everyone a very pleasant Christmas and a happy and prosperous new year.

Slowly, coats were collected, taxis arrived and the friends got ready to leave. Steve's wife said she hoped Suzy and Lawrence would join them for lunch or dinner one day soon. Suzy thought that would be lovely and promised to arrange something with Lawrence. There was something intimate about getting to know his friends. Steve pulled her to one side at the doorway.

"He's a good man, Suzy, and I know he gives himself a hard time about his past. It may be difficult for you sometimes, too. Please don't hesitate to come and talk to me, Suzy. Any time. About anything. With him or alone. You're obviously good for him. I've never seen him so happy!"

Suzy smiled, wondering if he actually knew all of his past and his sexual tastes. Possibly the former, but she very much doubted the latter! However, she did know she liked this vicar, and his wife seemed really nice and friendly, from the little she had spoken to her. She hoped she would see them again.

"It would be good to see you in church – I hope it's not just you that's been keeping him away recently," he shouted, still smiling, as they climbed into the taxi.

As they left, she looked around for Lawrence. He was just leaving the office with Lewis Deane. She wondered why they had been in there. What could be so important that it would prevent Lawrence from saying goodbye to his guests?

In fact, Lawrence had been instructing Lewis to place one of his security firm's best men to follow Suzy. He wanted him to start learning her routines, to identify any areas of risk or vulnerability, and, in particular, what precautions might need to be taken should someone make a connection between her and Lawrence Bane. Lawrence was determined to ensure Josh Black would not get to Suzy, especially as he would not be there to protect her.

Suzy watched as the two men shook hands. She had not really had any opportunity to speak to Lewis, and she couldn't help but notice he made no attempt to speak to her alone. Having said that, she perceived that he preferred to observe everyone rather than be engaged in conversation. She wasn't sure why, but she felt that he was acting more like someone observing the guests, rather than being a member of the party. Maybe security people just never stopped working.

Chapter 32

"It's been a lovely day." Suzy was taking her make-up off in the en-suite. She studied Lawrence as he stood naked, brushing his teeth. Her eyes scanned the muscular ripples of his slender abdomen; the firm biceps, buttocks and thighs; even his feet were beautiful. *You were so created in my dreams, and now I am here with you...*

He smiled at her through the foam.

She was desperate to please him. "Are you tired?" she asked seductively.

"Never too tired, baby." He wiped his mouth and replaced the brush. A wicked gleam was in his eyes. "What did you have in mind?" *You've done enough controlling lately. Let her have a go!*

She walked into the dressing room and opened the box. It was the first time either of them had referred to it since its first appearance. He leaned against the door jamb to the bedroom, his ankles crossed and arms folded, watching her as she took two lengths of rope, running them through her fingers as she walked over to the bed. She looked over to him, serious, determined and beautiful.

"I have some unfinished business with you."

"Oh?" He walked over to the bed. "Tell me, have you got your ear plugs in?" His eyebrow was raised and he licked his lips.

Oh my heart. Concentrate, girl!

"Now let me think, who's giving the orders here? Oh yes, it's me. So, no. No earplugs. Now lie back."

He stood, looking slightly amused.

"Please!" She started to giggle.

He lay on the bed on his side, and observed her mentally measuring the lengths of the two pieces of rope. His amusement was increasing. "Can I help at all?"

"No, no," she said, trying not to laugh or appear confused. "Now, you have to remember I've never actually done this before, but I have been studying it."

He had a huge grin on his face. "A theory lesson, I hope, and not a practical! How do you want me?"

She couldn't stop giggling as she saw the look of cheerful expectation on his face. "Just lie on your front a moment. And stop distracting me. I am trying to get you all aroused and feeling sexy, and you're making me laugh!"

"Come and give me a kiss first," he commanded.

"Ear plugs!" she whispered. "Now turn over and clasp your hands together at your back, please."

"Legs together or spread?" he asked, trying not to laugh.

"It doesn't matter for a moment." He remained quiet as she straddled his back, and bound his hands together with one piece of rope. He felt the tightness of it and the rubbing as he pulled at it gently. His hands were held fast.

His voice was now deep, husky and inviting. "You know how to tie a knot." He arched his back, feeling her vulva on him. He tried to move his hands up to feel her, but she slipped off.

Then her cheek was at his and she whispered in her sexiest voice, "I sailed a bit with my parents, and I found tying knots very easy."

He turned his head back to bite at her neck. "I'll take that as a warning then."

There was no laughter or giggling now, just erotic expectation for both of them.

"Turn over and cross your ankles," she commanded.

He rolled onto his back and saw her eyes stray to his penis. He was struggling not to get too hard just yet. *Let her do it.* He tried to concentrate as she bound his ankles together, watching her naked back and buttocks as she faced away from him. His senses were heightening.

"Now open your knees." He did as she instructed.

Then his eyes followed her as she went over to her bedside drawer and pulled out a red lacey thong. She stepped into it and returned to the bed. Their eyes made contact and she felt an urge to kiss him. But not yet.

She mounted his body, facing him this time, and slowly, holding his hair in her hand, she rubbed her breasts firmly over his mouth, letting him lick at her and taste her body. Then she shimmied forward, with her legs pushing lightly against his neck, and pressed her thong-covered pussy onto his mouth. He pulled at the soft cotton with his teeth, trying to get his tongue around the material to taste her. He had never been teased in this way before, and he was in ecstasy. He pulled at the rope around his wrists, and felt a burning sensation, slight enough to be highly stimulating. She lifted herself off him, with a smile that betrayed her desire to have him. *Patience. It's going so well.*

She stood on the bed looking down at him as she lowered the thong and stepped out of it, and he watched with a lustful hunger as she placed a finger in her vagina and then licked it, their eyes not breaking contact. Then she lowered herself onto him again, this time facing away from him, and he could feel her lips brush over the tip of his penis, and then her mouth taking in more of him. His foreskin was pulled back, and she was doing her job brilliantly so far. He was aroused beyond belief and desperate to come. She stopped and sat up on him.

"Baby, I need…" He began to move his knees together.

"Apart," she commanded, and he did as he was bidden. She turned slightly, placing one palm over his mouth, while working his penis with her other hand. She worked him slowly, insistently, using her hand, then her mouth, cupping his balls, stroking his perineum, that most sensitive part between his testicles and anus. Then she lifted her head. "Now, let me taste you." His semen shot into her mouth, his eyes shut tight, his cry expressing the rapture of his orgasm. Quickly and efficiently she untied him, and as she began to rub his ankles he grabbed her, squeezed her to him and kissed her passionately. Within minutes, his fingers ensured she was coming in her own orgasmic joy. Neither wanted the night to end, but they were both soon consumed by a peaceful, deep sleep.

Chapter 33

"Hi Suzy, it's Dominic. You OK?"

"Yeah, good. You? I'm sorry we didn't get the chance to speak much at dinner the other night, but it looked as though you were having a good time." Suzy was trying to keep the guilt out of her voice.

"It was a good do, and you looked beautiful. Nice pendant. Guess I don't need to ask who got you that!" He waited a moment to see if there was a response, but Suzy just blushed on the other end of the phone, remembering what she had to do for the gift.

She tried not to think about it too much. Things had been going really well between her and Lawrence.

"Richard told you I got you those tickets for the *Top Gear* show. They're for January the fifth. We were hoping we could take you to dinner, for a Christmas treat, and I can give them to you then. Are you doing anything on Thursday?"

He sounded a little nervous, and Suzy wondered if it was because it seemed he had deliberately not included Lawrence in the invite or because he thought she wouldn't come without him.

"Yeah, I think that should be fine. I will just need to check with Lawrence."

There was a pause at the other end of the conversation. Then came a reluctant and unenthusiastic invite for the "boyfriend".

"Dominic, we're not joined at the hip." Suzy tried to sound genuine and shocked. "I just meant to check he hasn't arranged anything." She quickly tried to recollect anything in their arrangement. "I'm sure it will be fine, and it will be lovely to catch up with you guys."

"Great. I'll come and pick you up from yours at about six on Thursday evening. Stay over, then we can all have a drink. Maybe you could have a look around the Manchester Christmas markets, and I'll take you home after work on Friday – I'll finish early."

"Sounds great. I'll look forward to it. See you on Thursday."

Suzy put her mobile back in her bag behind the counter.

"Sounds like you've been offered a night out." Alison was just closing up the till, and the girls were getting ready to go to the gym.

"Yeah, I just need to let Lawrence know."

"Glad to hear you say that and not that you 'need to ask him'. He is a bit controlling. But that's rich men for you." Alison tried to keep the sarcasm out of her voice, but she was concerned at how much independence Suzy had given up for the man she had only known a few weeks. Still, at least she was still going to the gym.

Suzy was heading home from the gym, still trying to decide how to tell Lawrence about Thursday night. *Just come straight out with it. You don't need his permission!*

Things had been really good between them, with his recent insecurities and tensions laid to rest, for now, at least. He had seemed more relaxed, as though something had fallen into place and he didn't need to worry any more. They had even been to a carol service at St Lukes and gone back to Steve and Jane's for a drink. She was beginning to feel they were a normal couple at last.

His car was outside her house, and he had actually drawn the curtains. She wondered if he was already naked.

As she walked in she was welcomed by delicious smells drifting from the kitchen, and a huge smile and kiss from the chef.

"Go and put your things away. It's nearly ready."

She came down to see the dining table laid for two, candles burning, a red poinsettia in the middle of the table, and artistically presented plates of salmon fillet with pea and lettuce fricassee and baby roasted potatoes. Lawrence was pouring two glasses of red Merlot, while wearing superhero lounge pants, with a white T-shirt and bare feet. *Mmm, how gorgeous.*

"Wow, this looks lovely. You've been busy. Good day?" They sat down and started to eat and drink.

"Not too bad, and how about you?" His mind drifted a moment, as he thought about his discussions with Lewis and Dan, the ex-detective security guy who was going to start shadowing Suzy tomorrow. He would be checking up on her whereabouts, who she came into contact with, and anyone who may be paying particular attention to her, all of which he would then report to both Lawrence and Lewis. *It's for her own protection, and my piece of mind.* He tried to convince himself of this, and to deny himself the pleasurable feeling of control this was giving him.

He watched her as she ate. She was a little quieter than usual and he wondered what was bothering her.

"Good session at the gym?" he asked. "I would love to give you another workout at The Sway. Shall we try to fit something in before Christmas?" His eyes read her reaction, as she smiled and blew him a kiss over the table.

Then she became serious, and he detected a nervousness in her voice. "I'm going to go over to Dominic's on Thursday night. He and Richard want to take me to dinner." It was her turn to study his face for a reaction. His mask went up. Was he angry or anxious? Why couldn't she read him as well he seemed to read her?

He remained silent, and sipped some wine. She continued. In for a penny... "Dominic will pick me up, and I'll stay over. We're going to go round the Christmas market on Friday. He said he'll bring me home, probably in the afternoon." She tried to carry on eating, but the suspense of waiting to hear him say something was making it difficult for her to chew. Her turn to sip the wine now.

He resumed eating and said calmly, "I'll take you. I can bring you home too, on the Thursday night." He suddenly thought about earplugs and added, "If you like."

"No, it's OK. You don't need to go to that trouble. I'll be fine, and it will be nice to have a look round Manchester on Friday. A chance for me to do some Christmas shopping." She looked at him and smiled. "You don't mind, do you?"

"No. It's fine. I guess you've seen a lot less of your cousin since I came along."

Wow, he's taken this well. All through her gym session she had been preparing for a battle, armed with a right to her independence and her need to see her own family and friends, playing out the imaginary conversation in her head.

"He did say you could join us if you wanted." Her voice gave away her own lack of enthusiasm for this. She was looking forward to having some fun with the guys, and things always seemed a little strained between Lawrence and Richard. She still had no idea why.

"I bet he did!" He sounded a little bitter, realising the tension between him and Richard in such a personal setting would probably spoil it for all of them. "But I will take you there. And keep your mobile with you." That was an order!

Suzy let it go, relieved it had been a relatively painless discussion. She wanted to check the evening wasn't going to be spoiled now, and was determined to keep the conversation light.

"No problem. It'll save Dominic a trip out, anyway." She gave him a seductive glance and started to rub her foot along his thigh. "What shall we do later?"

He smiled and grabbed her foot, gently stroking the instep, and then moving it to feel the hardness of his penis. "I'm sure we'll think of something." He was relaxed in the knowledge that, with Dan in place, he would know exactly where she was and what she was doing.

Chapter 34

Lawrence pulled up outside the boys' apartment in Manchester, and savoured Suzy's kiss, before getting her bag from the boot and walking her to the lift.

"I've put a gift in your bag. Please don't open it until I tell you. I'll call you later. Have a good time."

He watched as the doors closed. He wanted to say *don't go*, and he suddenly felt lonely. How had this girl got so deep under his skin, become so much a part of him, part of a family he had never had?

He got back in his car, glancing round for any sign of Dan, not sure whether to be impressed with the guy's undercover work because he couldn't see him, or to wonder where the hell he was. He drove across town to meet Lewis in a bar for a quick drink before heading home.

His phone alerted him to a text message, as he sat in bed reading.

Good night. I miss you x

He replied:

Miss you too, baby. x

It was 1 a.m. and he didn't know if he could sleep. This was the first time they had not shared a bed since their first night together back in November. He was about to get up and go for a swim, but he'd had a couple of whiskies when he got home and thought better of it.

He put his book down and flicked the lamp off. He was suddenly aware of the vast size of his bed and he thought momentarily of his single bed. He turned over, and the next thing he knew it was morning. He reached across the bed, expecting to feel Suzy next to him. Then he remembered. He reached for his phone and texted.

Good morning, baby. Are you alone?

She replied:

What do you think? I hope you're smiling. And missing me?

He pressed Call.
"Hi."
"Good morning. Are you OK?"
"Fab. Did you have a nice time?"
"It was great. We went to a lovely restaurant. It was really good to have a bit of time with them. Thanks for understanding." *You do understand, don't you?*
"Have you got the gift box I gave you?"
"Yes. It's on the bedside table." Her curiosity was becoming unbearable. "Can I open it?"
It went very quiet on the other end of the phone.
Then she heard his voice again. "When I tell you. What are you wearing?"
Oh, he suddenly sounds provocative.
"Pyjamas, not that you've ever seen any of mine!" She couldn't help wondering where this conversation was going, and what was with the mysterious gift.
"Take the bottoms off. Slowly," he commanded, his voice low and sexy.
Now it was Suzy's turn to be silent.
"Talk to me while you are doing it. Describe what you're doing."
"I think I've got a look of shock on my face!" She gave a small laugh.
"Excite me, Suzy. Tell me what you are doing and I'll tell you what I'm doing." He was serious and passionate.
"You first," she whispered, not sure what game he was playing, and glancing over at the bedroom door to check she had closed it properly, glad that the guys' room was down the hall

on the other side of the apartment. It was a very large apartment, thank goodness.

"I am lying naked in our bed, under the duvet, leaning up on my elbow looking out over the balcony."

"I am kneeling on this BIG bed." She emphasised the word *big*. "OK, I am pulling my pyjama bottoms down to my knees…" *I can do this.*

He interrupted. "Stop there. Cup your pubis in your palm. Tell me how you feel."

"It's … it's a bit silly. It's not the same on my own, Lawrence."

"Keep going, baby, I'm picturing you. Pretend I am with you. You sound lovely, soft and hot. Are you still kneeling and holding yourself?"

"Yes."

"Now take your hand away and slide it up inside your top and pinch your nipple. Tell me you're doing it."

"I'm putting my right hand inside. My skin feels warm, Lawrence. I can feel my nipple; it's getting longer and harder." Her voice was hushed, and he knew she was relaxing, ready to be pleasured.

"That's good, baby. Now cup your breast and feel its volume, its silkiness." There was a moment's pause and she was holding her breast, fondling it gently, curious at the pleasure she was feeling.

"Now take your hand away, and put your middle finger inside yourself. I want to hear how it feels."

She did as he asked. "I'm wet, Lawrence, it feels moist and tingly."

"I'm on top of the duvet now, Suzy, and I'm holding my favourite body part. It's long and hard. I'm pulling my skin back and I wish I was inside you. What do you want to do?"

All the while, his tone was full of passion; sexual, erotic and slightly forbidding. She pictured his eyes drilling into her.

"I want you here with me. I want you inside me." Her voice was trembling, aroused and fearful of her own sensuality, her own act of masturbating.

"It's OK, baby, it's good. I'm rubbing myself and picturing your beautiful face. Take your finger out and let me hear you lick it clean."

Slowly she withdrew her finger and tentatively put it towards her lips. She was still apprehensive of tasting her own juices, but there was something really erotic about the way he was talking to her, and she felt her inhibitions begin to fall away. She smacked her lips together and then, as she placed her finger in her mouth, she sucked with exaggeration, her eyes closed, and it was as if he were in the room watching her.

"That's my girl. Tell me how it tastes."

"It's sweet, not as salty as you."

"You taste much better than me, baby. Now I want you to put your phone on speaker. OK?"

"Yes."

"Good. Take off your pyjamas, slowly." He paused. "Keep talking to me, I want to hear your voice."

"I ... I'm pulling my bottoms off and folding them. I'm just putting them on the floor ... now I'm lifting my top over my head and looking down at my breasts." She was beginning to enjoy this game. "I'm going to hold them in my hands."

"No! Wait until I tell you what to do." This was his game!

"Spoilsport." She was in too good a mood now to think about annoying him. "I am naked with the phone in my left hand."

"Take the gift box and then kneel on the bed. Tell me when you are ready."

"OK. I have it in my hand. Can I open it?"

"Yes."

Suzy pulled on the bow of black ribbon wrapped around the rectangular box, which was encased in gold paper. She tore the paper away to reveal a matt black box with the words "*Je Voudrais Jouer*" in gold lettering on the top. Her heart began to race.

"Have you opened the box yet?"

"I'm just doing it." Her voice was a whisper.

She lifted the lid. Nestled among folds of black velvet was a black and gold vibrator. Above it, tucked into the folds, was a black card with "*Love Lawrence, x*" scrawled in gold lettering.

"Take it out of the box, Suzy." He waited a moment. "Take it out of the box."

Suzy could hear the smile in his voice. Was this for her pleasure or his? Or both? She had never thought of using one of these. *But why not? Is this his way of trying to make sure I don't need another man?*

"I'm holding it in my hands, cupping it in my palms and running it along my fingers. It feels smooth and hard. It reminds me of you."

"OK, baby. Take the lubricant and put some on yourself – tell me how you are doing it."

Suzy took the small bottle and glanced at the label – with ginseng and aloe vera, and added slipperiness to enhance your intimate play!

She whispered, "I am squeezing some on my right hand and rubbing it with my fingers. I'm putting my fingers inside myself. It feels cool and slippery!"

"Good girl. Now put some on your toy."

She did as instructed.

"Open your legs, baby. Place it inside you. Feel it, where I should be. Keep talking to me. You are making me feel so fucking horny, I can't hold back much longer."

"I am just putting it to the tip of my vagina, Lawrence." His name was as a breath of sensual exquisiteness on her lips, and he knew she was getting breathless. "Oh wow, it's inside me."

"Turn it on."

She had already located the on switch, and he heard the faint whirring sound down the phone. He could hear her sighing and moaning.

"Now lie back, baby, feel my fingers caressing you. I am feeling your hands on me, pulling me back and forth. Let's share each other's pleasure. Let me hear you."

"I … I can't talk … I want to come." She was lying back, the movement of the vibrator inside building her excitement to a pinnacle she couldn't wait to go over, and she placed her finger on her clitoris, replicating the rolling and gentle pushing motions he performed so brilliantly on her. "I want you, Lawrence, and I want to come."

"Come now, baby, climax and let me hear you."

Suzy screamed and he cried out as they came together, his release complete and hers lingering, her cries eventually subsiding, becoming soft laughter, and her confidence soaring as she pictured him smiling, contented, and loving her.

"How did you know that was going to be so wonderful?"

"I didn't. I just hoped you missed me enough to want to play. I miss you like fuck, Suzy, and I hated sleeping alone last night. You are under my skin, and I need you."

Oh my heart! There was a knock at her door. "Oh shit, someone's at the door! I need to go. I'll ring you later, honey." *Oh, I haven't called you that before!* "Just a minute!" she shouted, as she heard Dominic asking if she was OK!

Chapter 35

Lawrence got into the shower. It was the last Friday before Christmas, and he was going to check out his investment portfolios before getting things ready for the children's arrival at The Sway, and his week in the Peak District with Suzy. He was relieved she had taken his gift the way he had hoped she would, and that she enjoyed it. She was so the right girl for him. He reminisced about their first meeting and those first couple of days at The Sway. He contemplated how much a part of his life she had become, and wondered how much he meant to her. It hurt him to realise that his parting would hurt her, and it scared the hell out of him to face the fact she might not wait for him to come back. If he had any chance of getting Black back behind bars, and securing his own freedom from prison, he needed someone's help.

His thoughts turned to Miranda, and he recalled their last words in London.

"Lawrence, you can't leave. You need me."

"No, Miranda, I don't. It's time for me to move on. It's over."

Now he did need her, but he would never need that way of life again.

Reluctantly, he picked up the phone.

"Hi, Miranda."

"Ah, Lawrence, I've been waiting for you to call. I've been a busy girl."

"Did you speak to Veronica?" *Why do you think she doesn't know?*

"She's dead, Lawrence, but I think you already knew that. Don't play games with me. I'm not stupid, remember."

"OK. Look, I need your help."

"That's better. Good. Quid pro quo, Lawrence. You know me."

"What were you thinking?" He had no intention of committing to something he couldn't give. He would not return to her lifestyle.

"Just say yes, Lawrence."

"I'm coming to London in three weeks. I'll come and see you."

"That will do. I'll be ready for you, Lawrence. I won't let you down. Ciao."

She hung up.

Could she really help him? Did she know Charles Rigsby? What did she have on Black? Did she really have some evidence? And what price would he have to pay?

He was sitting at his computer when the phone rang. He hoped it would be Suzy, calling to brighten his day, but the display read "Lewis".

"Lawrence, I just got a call from the station. Charles Rigsby has accused you of stealing a hundred grand from his wife's bank account."

There was a moment's silence on the other end. Then Lawrence leaned forward onto his elbow.

"OK. Tell me how long I've got."

"I've asked Jack to 'misplace' the complaint for a while. He's given us until the end of January. Then they will have to ask you for an interview."

"Right. Thanks, Lewis. I'm glad you have your contacts. And thank Dan for his report last night. It means a lot to me."

"I know. Stay focused though, mate. Speak to you later."

"Yeah, see ya."

He pulled up his timetable on the computer.

Thursday the thirty-first of January – police will seek to interview him.

That gave him a couple of weeks in London to get information.

"Breaking My Own Heart" started ringing out from his mobile.

"Hi, baby."

"Lawrence, hi. You OK?"

"Great." He checked his watch. It was 11.30 a.m. "How's the shopping going?"

"Good. I've got gifts for the guys, and for Alison." She paused. "And a few other bits. I was wondering about getting some Christmassy knick-knacks for the Peak District. Then I thought it might be nice to get them together. What do you think? Are you busy?"

"I'll meet you in an hour. Where will you be?"

She was relieved he still sounded like he was in a good mood, after their lovely morning phone call.

"I'll meet you in Waterstones on Deansgate."

"See you there." He was glad to have something to cheer his day up.

* * *

Christine had made a fish pie, and they were enjoying its warm nourishment after their cold afternoon in the city.

"I'm glad you liked your gift." He watched her eat, studying her face as she blushed slightly.

"I wasn't expecting that!" She looked directly at him, determined not to feel too embarrassed. "I never realised I was that kind of woman!"

"And just what is 'that kind of woman', may I ask?" There was humour in his voice and eyes, and he continued eating.

"Oh, you know, sex-starved!" She laughed. "Although I hardly think that applies to me any more!"

"You can't beat a bit of phone sex, and I wanted you to get the most out of it, make sure you don't need to start looking around if I can't always be with you."

She stared at him. *Why can't you always be with me?* But he still had that humorous glint in his eyes, and she didn't want to voice her concerns right now. He was relaxed, and she didn't want him closing up on her. Maybe she might get more information out of him in this mood?

"And just how many times have you had telephone sex?" Trying to keep the mood light, she did not sound in the least accusatory, adding playfully, "I didn't even know it could be so much fun. Almost worth going away for."

"Never mind how many times – it's not relevant now." His eyebrow was raised, and his tone was slightly scolding, but his eyes still shone. "I won't appreciate you making the habit of going away. Give me your foot, and I'll remind you of the real thing you've been missing."

She lifted her foot to his lap, and he pushed it down onto his rock-hard penis.

She gulped some wine, her eyes keeping contact with his, her desire for him rising. "No pudding for me just now." She got up from the table, took his hand and, leaving the plates and the leftover food until morning, she led him upstairs. Whatever he was doing to her, her confidence was growing and growing.

As they lay in bed later, he asked how her evening had gone, not quite ready to drift off to sleep.

"It was fun. We met up with some friends in the Red House Bar and had a couple of drinks. It was good to catch up with everyone as I haven't seen them for ages. Then the three of us went to eat at the Yang Sing."

"Yeah, I know."

Suzy leaned up on her elbow and stared at him. "What do you mean, you know?"

The image of Dan's report shot into his head. Shit.

"I mean, I know it, I know the restaurant in Chinatown." *Back-pedal, Los!*

He can't have known where we were. Can he?

"Lawrence, just what did you do when you dropped me off?"

"I met Lewis for a quick drink, and then came home." *It feels weird being on the back foot with her. Stay calm.* "I was on the other side of Manchester, up by the MEN. What, do you think I was spying on you?" He laughed, a little more brightly than he intended.

"I bloody hope not, you idiot. You knew who I was with."

He leaned over and pulled her on top of him. "Of course I did. Now, are you ready to go to sleep yet or not?"

"Yes! I've got work tomorrow."

Chapter 36

It was Saturday evening, and they were wrapping presents in the snug.

After Lawrence had joined her in Manchester, Suzy had persuaded him to buy small gifts for Steve and Jane, and some pretty Christmas garlands and table decorations for the Peak District. He had already stated they would transport the tree from her cottage to the holiday let, though she had no idea how they were actually going to do that – there was hardly room for a packet of biscuits in his Jag, let alone a tree, and somehow she couldn't imagine he would allow a roof rack on top of his car!

He had then led the way in choosing gifts for twelve children between the ages of eight and sixteen, and he briefly described each child who would be coming from the Fairchance centre. There would be four girls and eight boys. Lawrence knew nearly all of them from previous holidays at The Sway and his own visits to Fairchance. There was an eight-year-old boy who was a newcomer for Julia. Apparently he had been abandoned by an aunt who had labelled him "unmanageable". Suzy couldn't help but notice the anger in Lawrence's voice that someone could do such a thing. There was a fifteen-year-old girl who self-harmed, and had been passed around various foster homes, hospitals and psychiatric units before being placed in Julia's care. Lawrence believed there had been some improvement in her life, and had recently seen her smile on the odd occasion, but she was a sad young thing and would need a lot more help with her self-esteem before she could really move on. This was one of Mike's strengths, and Julia was proud to have him on her team. He would be arriving with the others.

Within a short while a selection of computer games, DVDs, Lego, jigsaws and books had been purchased. Lawrence obviously knew most of the children quite well, and Suzy could only admire the care he took over what to buy, and the love he seemed to have for these kids. It was as though he could relate to them, and their problems, from his own youthful experiences. He also spoke very highly of Julia Kershaw and her staff. They were all due to arrive at The Sway tomorrow afternoon, and Suzy was looking forward to meeting everyone. The plan (or arrangement, as he kept referring to it) was they would all have tea together, and then Suzy and Lawrence would head off to the Peak District.

First, though, there was the soup kitchen.

Lawrence had mentioned that, every so often, time permitting, he volunteered at a drop-in centre in Manchester. He had talked about its aims: to give people dignity, self-belief and value. He was particularly keen on the ethos of trying to help people to move on, rather than just leaving them to live on the streets. Suzy wondered what exactly he had been through as a teenager and young adult, and was beginning to realise just how much he felt he wanted and needed to give back to society. She admired the fact he didn't seem bitter about why society had allowed him to end up as a male prostitute in the first place.

The plan was to be in Manchester for 7 a.m., and to start helping prepare food for whoever needed it. So they went to bed early on Saturday night, and at exactly 5.45 a.m. he gently, and then not so gently, tried to coax his girl out of bed. The highlight was a quick shower together, where Lawrence awakened parts of her that soap alone couldn't reach! Then she was stepping back and admiring "dressed down" Lawrence. He wore faded skinny jeans, a Jack Daniels T-shirt, a black hoody and grey trainers. His hair wouldn't quite lie down, and she wondered what he usually put on it. But somehow he still managed to look gorgeous.

"Come on, let's get going. We'll take the bike." However, closer inspection of the blackness outside revealed a light dusting of snow carpeting the grounds of The Sway. "OK, scrap that idea. We'll have to take the car." Suzy felt a sparkle of excitement at the thought of her first white Christmas.

With aching feet, and hands that screamed out they had just peeled half a ton of potatoes and scrubbed more carrots than she cared to remember, by midday Suzy was lying on the sofa in the snug, feeling on top of the world. The morning had been a wonderful philanthropic experience of meeting people who had nothing, and in some cases wanted nothing, but who were grateful, pleasant, polite and still, in most cases, glad to be alive, with some hope for the future – it was this latter point that impressed Lawrence.

It had been clear that spirits were high at the centre, as it was nearly Christmas. When they had arrived at 7 a.m., a young man had been sitting on the steps at the entrance, and food hadn't been due to be served until 9 a.m. Suzy had guessed he was about twenty-five years old, with long matted hair protruding from an old woollen hat. His clothes had been dirty and wet from the sleet. He had been clinging onto a small bag – she hadn't been able to make out its contents – and he had looked hungry and miserable. One of the other volunteers had talked to him, had explained it was too early to let him in, but it had been clear he was going to just sit there in the sleet and wait. After all, where else would he go?

Lawrence had gone over to him and the volunteer. "I'm sure we can find you somewhere inside to sit, and no doubt the showers do work before 9 a.m. Come on, mate, let's get you a cup of tea." Suzy had watched as Lawrence helped the young man to his feet and led him into the centre. She hadn't seen him then for about ten minutes, and she had realised he had taken the guy to the shower area, provided him with a towel and some toiletries, so he could bathe under hot clean water. Nick, as they discovered he was called, had joined them, and gratefully drank his tea while the volunteers had started preparing for the day.

On their way home in the car she had told Lawrence she would like to learn more about the centre in the new year, and become involved in the various projects going on in the area to help people who had been dealt a rough hand in life.

It made her reflect upon the death of her parents when she was just seventeen. Her school had been helpful, and the community in her village was a real source of unity and support in those early days. Of course, she had a small core of real friends and their families who had got her through the bad times. There had been times when she hated the world, the unfairness of her loss, and she had stopped going to church. But as time went on, and she was able to laugh and smile at things, she began to find her own way of coping and getting by, without being scornful and bitter about other people's happiness and luck. She discovered it felt better to share their happiness. So she could really appreciate the work of the people helping out at the drop-in centre, and more importantly for her at the moment, she was learning more about her guy, about how he saw the world – or at least this small part of it. It gave her hope for the future that she could get involved, with him, in something that was close to his heart.

In this contemplative mood, she was suddenly aware that she needed to drag herself off the sofa, as a minibus pulled up on the drive. The children!

"They're here!" Lawrence shouted from the hallway, already on his way to open the door.

Earlier, Dave and Christine had transformed the bedrooms with bunk beds and camp beds, to accommodate adequate separation of the sexes and allow enough space for the adults to have some peace and quiet. Lawrence's bedroom would be locked, as it always was when the children came to stay.

From one of the garages, pool equipment had been brought in, including floats and inflatables, together with table tennis and snooker tables. A swing and climbing frame had been erected in the grounds, although these were currently under the light covering of snow that had fallen in the night. There was also a selection of bicycles and go-karts in the garage.

Lawrence went outside to help get the gear from the bus, and greeted Julia with a big hug. "It's great to see everyone. Come on, let's get this stuff inside." He organised everyone in a human crocodile of baggage handlers to get everything into The Sway. The younger ones loved it and, as she peered out of the doorway, Suzy saw happy smiling faces and heard lots of giggles. Christine was then at her side, and the two of them set the bags in the hallway, ready to be dispersed into the correct locations for the next few days. She felt as if she was on *The Sound of Music* set!

Lawrence introduced Suzy to Julia, Mike and Carolyn, and of course to the children. It would have been handy for them all to wear name badges! Christine went to organise hot chocolate for everyone, and there was chaos as the children ran around investigating where they were going to sleep and what they were going to do next. The older ones tried not to appear too excited, but the strain of following the little ones at a more dignified pace was evident, as they, too, were eager to check everything out. Most had already been to The Sway before. Some of them lived permanently with Julia and her crew, and others came from elsewhere, with the excursion providing a break for their carers.

Lawrence had followed the kids upstairs, and Suzy could feel his excitement, as he cast a huge grin in her direction. It was clear Julia had issued strict instructions on acceptable behaviour, and the jovial chaos did not turn into accidental, or any other type of, destruction.

The remaining adults went into the kitchen to join Christine.

"It's lovely to meet you. Lawrence has told me you're from Cameroon." Julia had a warm voice, with a quality that made everyone feel at ease. It was immediately clear, however, that she had the requisite air of authority to run the children's home.

"Yes." Suzy had taken to this woman and her assistants straight away. "I've been here in the UK just over a year now. I have to say I am really hoping for my first white Christmas."

Julia then started chatting to Christine, and it was clear the two women knew each other well and got along easily. Mike and Carolyn both said hello, and how much they always enjoyed their stays at Lawrence's home, not least because of the pool. Mike made a point of stating that all the kids could swim. The atmosphere at The Sway was of one big – very big – happy family!

Lawrence came into the kitchen, followed by Daniel, a sixteen-year-old boy. The former appeared a bit stern, and Suzy sensed some discussion had taken place between them. In fact, Lawrence had just learned from Julia that Daniel had got a fifteen-year-old girl pregnant, and Lawrence was advising him that they needed to have a chat. Daniel was looking rather sheepish, though evidently trying to act naturally in front of everyone. He was a tall, slim, dark-haired boy, who had lived through more than he should have done in his sixteen years.

"We're going to eat first, and then make sure everyone is settled, before Suzy and I head off and leave you to enjoy your holiday," Lawrence announced chirpily to the crowd gathered in the kitchen, and he led everyone into the dining room.

The table had been laid out as though for a party, with Christmas crackers and party poppers, and the kids gasped with delight.

The older diners were seated at one end of the table, with Suzy next to Daniel on one side and Pippa, the eldest girl, on the other. Lawrence was on Daniel's other side and Suzy hoped Lawrence wasn't going to give the teenager too much of a hard time. Julia sat opposite Lawrence, next to Mike and Carolyn. The youngsters were happy to have their own company at the other end of the table, and Suzy couldn't help noticing the only sullen-looking face, which belonged to a fifteen-year-old girl, Melanie. She kept rubbing her hand along her sleeve as though something was itching, and Suzy remembered that this was the young girl who harmed herself. She tried to smile brightly when Melanie glanced her way, but the youngster merely gave her a scornful look and lowered her head.

However, Suzy did notice before too long that Melanie could hardly stop herself from looking at Lawrence almost the whole time, only taking her eyes off him if he looked in her direction. *Oh, you have a crush on my guy! Well, I can't blame you!* Suzy began to hope that a bond (possibly unwanted on the young girl's side) could be formed between herself and Melanie, and she made a mental note to talk to Lawrence about the sad soul.

Christine had prepared lasagne with baked potatoes and vegetables. Julia announced to all the children that the greens were to be eaten along with everything else. Other than a slight grumbling from the youngest end of the table, everyone happily tucked in and enjoyed the food and the setting. Crackers had already been pulled, poppers popped and tiny streams of paper were being picked out of food and drinks. It was great fun. Suzy whispered to Lawrence to pull Melanie's cracker with her, and he was rewarded with a beaming smile, revealing some of her hidden beauty, and her eyes shone for a moment as they made contact with his.

"I think she has a crush on you."

"I'm old enough to be her dad! Anyway, don't all teenage girls have crushes on handsome guys?" Lawrence flashed a seductive glance at Suzy, which was gone in an instant.

"Don't flirt with me in front of her or she'll hate me forever!"

After a pudding of chocolate cheesecake and strawberries, the gathering moved out of the dining room, and Lawrence led the way down the hall and opened the door opposite his office. Suzy realised she had never been in here before, and as she followed the troops inside she saw that it was a cinema room, with a huge horseshoe-shaped sofa surrounding a large screen suspended from the ceiling. There was what looked like a drinks cabinet on one side of the room, which she assumed was locked, and shelves covered with DVDs.

"What can we watch? What can we watch?" was all that could be heard, until Julia spoke, and everyone was quiet. Apparently, the younger ones would get to choose and the older ones would be having a late night and could make their choice later. Everyone seemed happy with this, and nearly everyone wanted to stay and watch the *Arthur Christmas* movie, with only Daniel, Melanie, Julia, Lawrence and Suzy leaving the room. This group made their way to the snug.

As the girls settled on the sofa, Lawrence tapped Daniel on the shoulder. "Come on mate, we need to talk."

Daniel's look betrayed his preference to stay with the girls or even go and join the youngsters rather than listen to Lawrence Bane, but he knew he didn't really have a choice. Lawrence led him into the office and closed the door. His computers had all been placed in his bedroom, out of the way, but Carolyn had set up some laptops for the kids to use. She was the IT geek of the group, as well as being a qualified child psychologist, and a great admirer of the way Julia ran Fairchance.

The two of them sat on the sofa. "Look, I'm not going to lecture you on what you have already done. I'm sure you've heard more than enough. But I need to say two things. One is: listen to Julia, Mike and Carolyn – these guys are on your side and will always be there for you. You need to take their advice and try to do what they say."

"I know, but I don't love the girl. It was a stupid one-night fling, and she was asking for it."

Lawrence stood up and started to pace the room. "Don't say that, Daniel, and don't try to pass the blame on to her."

"But you don't know what she's like." Daniel had stood up too now, and Lawrence knew this was not a kid standing in front of him any more. He had grown up, with a vengeance.

"Don't interrupt me, Daniel, and sit back down."

Lawrence's stern voice cautioned Daniel to do as he was told, and he sat at a desk, rebelling in his own way by not returning to the sofa.

"It takes two, Daniel, and you're old enough to know the possible consequences of careless actions. If you have to go giving it to someone who is 'asking for it', as you put it," Lawrence's frown and penetrating glare at Daniel were enough to have him holding his head in his hands, "you know what precautions you should have taken. Don't bloody forget them in future, if you can't keep it in your damn trousers."

Daniel looked embarrassed.

"So, the second thing I'm going to say is this. You need to face up to your responsibilities and pay towards the care of the baby." Lawrence paused, and Daniel immediately looked up at him, panicking, anxious and frightened.

"Who the fuck's going to give me a job? I haven't got any bloody money."

Lawrence looked at him, and felt huge pity for him. He almost wanted to go over and hug him, certain that Daniel would have had very few hugs, and unwillingly feeling conscious of being very like him when he was younger. *You were just lucky you never got any of them pregnant, you prick, and who are you to lecture him?* He knew he needed to be firm and try to encourage this young man to do the right thing.

He was also aware that Daniel had had problems with arson and the police in the past. He had been accused of burning down a disused garage. The story was that he believed it to have been owned by his father, who had murdered his mother. In fact, the garage owner was not his father, and had died intestate. The building had been left to become derelict and dangerous. These factors had helped ensure that Daniel stayed out of jail and was allowed to remain at Fairchance, but he had served his time with a curfew and community service. Working with Carolyn and Mike helped to steer him away from further arson attacks.

"I will give you a job, mate." Lawrence walked over and sat on the edge of the desk. "We need quite a bit of help around here, and the job will be waiting for you when you have finished your exams."

Daniel looked at him questioningly.

"When is the baby due?"

"June."

"Right. Just in time for you to get some qualifications under your belt. Then you can start earning some money here, doing the place up. You can start with the outbuildings, and let's see how good a handyman you are."

"How am I going to get here from Macclesfield?" Daniel sounded dejected and sceptical.

"We'll get you some bike lessons, and they'll be my treat. But if you fail all your exams, then you'll have to pay me back!"

Daniel sat up straight, as Lawrence's offer started to sink in, and he could begin to see some purpose coming into his life, and a sense of something to work for. He wasn't thinking just about a baby. He had seen Lawrence's bikes, and been on the back of a few of them over the three years he had known Mr Bane. He had even been allowed to help clean them. The thought of having the opportunity to pass his test and possibly own one was worth the effort he would have to put in to pass at least some of his exams.

"Look." Lawrence could see he had got through to him now. "Concentrate on schoolwork, and at least try to do what you are told at home, and we'll talk about this in detail when…" Lawrence hesitated. *Exactly when are you going to do that? You need to concentrate on getting out of your own shit!* "… when it gets nearer to June." Lawrence made a mental note to speak to

Richard Groves and Lewis. His to-do list for January was growing, and time was running out. "Come on. Let's go and join the others and enjoy our Christmas." Now he put his arm around Daniel, and the two walked back to the snug like old mates.

Suzy was painting Melanie's nails when the men entered the room, and Julia and Pippa, the sixteen-year-old girl who had just joined them in the room, were planning some activities for their break.

"Very nice." Lawrence smiled at Melanie, taking Suzy's cue from earlier at the dining table, and he sat down next to her.

"It's a lovely colour, isn't it?" Suzy sounded really cheerful, and Lawrence wondered whether he should have planned for them to leave in the morning. But he had never been in the habit of staying at The Sway when Julia and the children came. He felt it would be intimidating for the children, not to mention he was so used to living on his own that he would struggle with the noise and constant activities. But that might change now that Suzy could be a part of it with him. *No, let's stick to the plan.*

He nodded to Suzy's question, and turned to Melanie. "You've got lovely fingers and nails, Melanie. Are you looking forward to Christmas?"

Melanie blushed and looked down, whispering, "Yes, Mr Bane."

"Well, I hope you have a lovely time. No doubt you'll beat everyone at table tennis again, I hear you're quite a player!" He remembered Julia filling him in on the summer holiday's activities.

This time the young girl looked up, a little more confident now. "I hope so."

As the nail painting was completed, Lawrence stood up and looked at Suzy, saying, "I think we'd best be getting ready to go now. Make sure you don't smudge those nails, Melanie – it'll get you out of any chores for a while." He shot a playful, furtive glance over at Julia.

"Lawrence, don't say that or they'll all want their nails painting!" laughed Julia, looking at Daniel, who shook his head, smiling.

"I'd rather clean one of your motorbikes." He grinned at Lawrence, who felt the kid was going to be alright and would cope with fatherhood one way or another.

Lawrence couldn't help feeling pained that Daniel's stupidity could lead to another unwanted baby being born into the world, and he momentarily wondered how he himself had come into it. As he had grown up he had tried not to care. If his biological parents hadn't wanted him, then they were nothing to him. He was living in the now, and that meant with Suzy, at least for a bit longer yet.

He held his hand out to her, and she followed him into the hallway. Everyone assembled in the hall to say Merry Christmas and to see the couple off. Christmas presents had already been placed around the tree, and the children were under strict instructions not to tamper with anything, but to wait until Christmas morning.

Lawrence had arranged for Dave to load the pickup truck with their luggage and, as he saw the look of surprise on Suzy's face at not going in the Jag, he enlightened her.

"Well, it looks like it's going to continue snowing, and much as I'd love to be marooned with you, I don't think it will be very convenient if we get stuck for too long in the Peak District. I've heard being trapped in the wild can bring out the worst in you!" He leaned in and nipped at her neck playfully. "Besides, we've got a Christmas tree to collect!" He helped her into the cab then climbed in on the driver's side and they pulled away, amid cheers, waving and whistling.

Chapter 37

"At last, I've got you to myself!" He put his hand on Suzy's knee. She smiled and sat back in her seat, looking over at him.

"They're a great bunch, Lawrence. You care a lot about them all, don't you?"

"Yeah. I've known most of them for three years now, and watched them grow up and develop into good young people. They still need a lot of care, even the older ones. In fact, they sometimes need it the most. I really respect what Julia and her team do for them. Steve and Jane will be having Christmas lunch with them, and hopefully they'll have a fab time. It helps to give them some happy memories." He watched the road ahead, and Suzy wondered if he was thinking about his own childhood.

"Do you mind me asking … you don't have to say anything…"

He glanced at her, and she was sure he had guessed what she was going to ask.

"Do you have any happy memories, Lawrence, from your childhood?"

"Not really." His tone was very matter-of-fact, and then he had a mischievous grin. "Shagging a few girls, I suppose, and being sensible enough…" he hesitated and became a little more serious "… or lucky enough, I guess, not to get any of them pregnant. We'll need to watch out for Daniel."

Suzy loved the use of the term "we".

"I've offered him a job, once he finishes his exams. There's plenty of maintenance around the house that needs doing, and Dave could do with some help. I'm hoping if it goes well I may be able to get him working at Winstons or somewhere. The lad deserves a break, and I would rather it be a legitimate one, not like mine." He suddenly glanced at her again, apprehensively, as he thought about the money he'd taken to get his big break.

"Look out, Lawrence!" Suzy shouted, as the truck had started to drift into the middle of the road.

He pulled the wheel round and focused on his driving.

"Sorry. She sounds great, doesn't she?"

He gave a faint smile, but Suzy perceived he was remembering something, and by what he said, it wasn't something he would want to discuss.

They had collected the tree and secured it in the back of the pickup, complete with all its decorations, in the hope they could reinstate it once they got to the holiday home.

"What's the place like?"

"You'll love it. It's an old farmhouse, set in about ten acres." He was really relaxed now, enjoying the driving and relishing the thought of their week alone. Suzy had felt uncomfortable about asking Alison for all the time off between Christmas and the New Year, but she had said they would manage. They were only going to open for a couple of days anyway, as they were not expecting to be very busy, especially with the snow.

"It's in Hayfield. There are some lovely walks around there. Christine has sorted a supermarket delivery for tomorrow morning, so we won't need to go out at all if we don't want to. And no one can disturb us." He eyed her sexily. Then his look became serious and his voice hushed. "I have hardly had you to myself at all today."

Suzy waited to hear what he was going to say next, aware of the subtle change in his tone.

"It will take us about an hour to get to the house. It seems a shame to waste an opportunity." He gave her a direct, seductive look.

Oh my heart, you know I'll do anything for you when you look at me like that!

"What did you have in mind?" She felt a tingling between her thighs, and remembered their journey to the eventful dinner in Manchester, when he had been in such a lovely mood. He hadn't been driving then.

"Pleasure yourself for me, Suzy. Turn me on." It was an instruction.

Suzy stayed motionless, staring at the blackness out of the window, only broken by the odd house light where curtains hadn't been drawn.

His eyes were moving between the road ahead and the girl sitting next to him. He reached out and took her hand, placing it over his penis. She felt the hardness of his erection.

"I would rather pleasure you," she whispered, rubbing him slowly up and down over his jeans. He smiled. "Thanks for the offer, and don't worry – I'll take you up on it as soon as we get there. But you need your seatbelt on. Besides, I want to hear you having a good time. Undo your jeans, baby."

Her libido was rising, and she didn't want to fight it. It was warm in the truck, and she was aware of his fragrance. The spicy, woody smell that was so him. He had his iPod on, and Perry Como was singing "And I Love You So".

Slowly she eased her bottom forward on the seat and leaned back, slowly dragging her zip down. She looked over at him and met his gaze momentarily, before his eyes returned to the road.

"That's good, baby." His voice was so sexy she wanted to reach out and pull him on top of her. Instead, she moved her hand inside and closed her eyes. She gently touched herself, feeling inside her vagina. She was moist, and, inhibitions flung aside, she withdrew and put her finger to his lips. He licked it provocatively.

"You are so horny. Do you know how much this is turning me on?" He focused back on the road.

Suzy was caressing her clitoris, moving her finger over it faster, more intently. Her eyes were closed and she was ready to come. Soft moans escaped her lips, and she arched her back, sliding further forward, her body pulling at the seatbelt.

"Come now, baby, put me out of my agony. I want you to come."

She murmured as her orgasm took her to exquisite pleasure, and slowly, as she descended from its height, she looked over at him, her eyes half closed, peering at him from beneath her lashes, and pushed back up into the seat and fastened her jeans.

"What are you doing to me?" she whispered, huskily.

"Keeping you," he said. He was staring straight ahead and his voice was firm but quiet.

"Keeping me? What's that supposed to mean?"

Still staring at the road ahead, he explained, "I have you all to myself for a whole week, twenty-four/seven. You're mine."

"You're a control freak, Lawrence Bane." She could see his lips forming a faint smile, and knew he was enjoying intimidating her a little. As she was feeling so good, she was actually happy to play his game, and her mind was running wild thinking about what they might get up to over the next few days.

"I forgot to ask you something before we left The Sway, what with all the kids around." He glanced over at her. She looked contented, a girlish anticipation emanating from her face, her posture relaxed, and her smell heavy in the air.

"I've brought the box. I was going to ask if you wanted me to or not." He hesitated for a second. "We don't have to open it, if you don't want to." He could have sworn he saw her eyes twinkle, and she smiled, watching the road ahead and avoiding eye contact. He put his hand on her lap, and she put hers on top of his.

"I would have said yes." She carried on looking straight ahead.

Chapter 38

The farmhouse was situated down a long track. The flakes were falling thick and fast, and Suzy was hopeful of her white Christmas. Lawrence was glad they had come in the truck.

They finally pulled up in front of a stone building. Through a small leaded window, a pale light shone out. Someone had prepared for their arrival.

"They forgot to put the bloody outside light on," Lawrence grumbled, as he grabbed a torch from the glove box of the truck and started searching a post on the edge of the driveway, which held the secure key-box. It was now snowing quite heavily, and Suzy heard the scrunching of the snow underfoot as she scrambled out and started to grab some bags from the back.

Lawrence took them from her and placed them under the porch as he put the key in the lock. He then opened the heavy door.

"Welcome, Miss Harper, to our Christmas retreat." He scooped her up and carried her, giggling, over the threshold and into a small, dimly lit hallway. He set her down and brushed his lips over hers, and she closed her eyes and breathed in his scent.

"Let me get the bags in. Wait here." He hurried over to the vehicle and brought the remaining bags . "Sorry, but I'm gonna need your help with the tree!" He grinned as he took her hand, and they both plunged back into the snow, struggling to get the tree through the farmhouse doorway.

Leaving everything in the now crowded hallway, he took her hand again. "Come on, let me show you around."

There was a huge sitting room to the right. Thick, shabby red velvet curtains had been drawn, and there was a roaring fire casting a glow over the furniture. The fabric had seen better days, but the room was cosy and clean, with the smell of burning wood making for a pleasant ambience.

The kitchen cupboards were pine, and Lawrence flicked a switch, lighting up bright spotlights, giving a contemporary feel to the well-appointed room, which included a pine dining table, big enough for six. The appliances were modern, and there was an attractive white Belfast sink set in a light-coloured worktop. There was a box containing some breakfast things, a bottle of Shiraz and a box of chocolates on the worktop. Other provisions for the evening and for breakfast had been placed in the fridge.

He's thought of everything, as usual.

Off the hall, there was a small cloakroom with a loo, and a narrow, winding staircase leading upstairs.

She followed him, feeling her excitement grow, as she took in the intimacy of this place, secure in its isolation.

Upstairs, he walked past the first door and opened the door to the bedroom at the end of the landing. It was a large room with twin beds and a set of bunk beds against a wall. It was decorated in pale blues and yellows and looked like a children's room. He smiled at her as she looked at him in surprise.

"For kids." He shut the door.

He then led her to the end of the landing and started to climb a cast-iron spiral staircase. She followed him round and round. He had to duck through the doorway. He turned the light on. It shone dimly over a huge room that ran across the width of the house. There were two round windows at each gable end and a large picture window across the front of the house, each window letting in an eerie glow from the snowy sky outside. There were cupboards, boxes, an armchair, a rocking chair, a four-seater sofa and a huge TV, all randomly placed around the room. Suzy felt that all that was missing was cobwebs. This room, like the rest of the house, was very clean.

Lawrence switched the light off and walked over to the large window, beckoning her to join him, before staring out across the countryside. The glow of light from the evening sky was enough to cast shadows around the room, and Suzy made her way around the obstacles of furniture to stand next to him.

She smiled, captivated by the idyllic beauty of the fields with their white blankets, and the trees with their garlands of snowflakes, painting a picture postcard scene of romantic bliss. She felt his hand in hers.

"Lawrence, this is beautiful."

He pulled her towards him and kissed her, his passion growing, and she could feel his hardness as he pushed himself into her.

"Come on. I need you now."

They returned to the first door at the top of the main staircase. He opened it and then stepped aside for her to enter first.

The room was dominated by a large four-poster bed. It was curtained with rich Toile de Jouy, in hues of russet, brown and gold, showing ladies and gentlemen from seventeenth-century England, among trees and shrubs. There were a gentleman's and a lady's mahogany wardrobes, a dressing table and tallboy, and a door leading off into the bathroom.

With a huge grin on her face, Suzy flung herself back onto the bed and laughed. Then he was on top of her, laughing and kissing and rolling over. He started to pull at her clothes, and she tugged at his shirt and jeans.

"I saved the best until last," he whispered, erotically licking her earlobes, nibbling and tugging.

Now they were both naked, and he knelt up on the bed, pulling her up to him. She rubbed her breasts against his chest, and he closed his eyes and breathed in her air, his hands pulling at her hair. He looked at her intently, pulling her hair into a ponytail and tugging her head back, raising himself up as he did so.

"I'm keeping you." His voice was low and menacing, and her body quivered with anticipation. She knew she would do anything.

He sucked at her neck, giving her a necklace of his marks, slowly and thoroughly moving from one side round to the other. Then he traced his tongue down to her breasts, nibbling and sucking each one. She couldn't see his face as he moved lower, licking a trail over her abdomen. Soft moans escaped from her lips and she felt moisture between her legs.

Then he let go of her hair.

"Lie down," he ordered. He straddled her body, rubbing himself on her, his eyes drilling into hers. He moved forward and she saw his penis, long and hard. He stroked it, before pushing it into her mouth. She gagged, as she was pinned down on her back. He lifted himself up and down on her, his eyes still on hers. Then he moved her onto her side and she used her tongue, lips and throat to bring his semen gushing into her mouth. He gasped in pleasure, still thrusting. He withdrew, and slid down to meet her lips with his own, his tongue craving her, his arms pushing on her shoulders. She felt his hand take hers and move it down to the private entrance to her body, and he rested his head on his elbow and watched.

"I want to see you this time."

She looked at him, knowing he was now in control of her and she would obey him, as she began to feel herself, closing her eyes and working to make her orgasm surge through her. As he watched her excitement grow and get close to peaking, he took her arm away.

"No!" she whispered, exasperated and desperate. "Don't make me stop, please!"

"Ssshh, baby." His hands parted her legs and his head moved down, his tongue working its magic, bringing her close, then leaving her teetering on the edge, before taking her over it, as she cried out and pulled at him, before pushing him away with her legs, as she had gone beyond what was bearable.

They lay back, side by side, and laughed softly. He turned to face her. "Happy?"

Oh, a question! "Very!" She snuggled into him, the warmth of his body intoxicating her, letting him keep her. For now.

After a deep sleep, and feeling on top of the world, Suzy reached across the bed to find him gone. It was 8 a.m. and she wondered if he had been up since six. She looked around the room for her clothes. There was nothing, no bags, and her clothes from last night were nowhere to be seen. She checked the drawers and wardrobes. Empty.

She went into the bathroom, took a warmed towel from the heated rail, wrapped it around herself and went down to the kitchen. It was empty, but there was a note on the worktop.

Hi, sleepyhead. Will be back before nine. Make some coffee.
Love, Lawrence x

Suzy felt a little disappointed that he hadn't waited for her, or even woken her; she would have loved to have gone walking with him. Was he in a mood? The note was pleasant enough. She looked around and walked into the hallway and lounge – there were no clothes to be seen. She started to feel cross. What the hell was he playing at?

She went up to the bathroom. There were her favourite toiletries, her Chanel Coco Mademoiselle and Versace Vanitas perfume, together with their toothbrushes and all her make-up. Had he just left what he thought she needed?

She decided to have a bath, to pass some time, as she was apparently unable to go wandering outside. She looked up into the mirror.

"For fuck's sake!" she exclaimed as she saw her necklace of love bites, extending down over her breasts and abdomen. She remembered his words – *I want to keep you. Oh Lawrence, what the hell are you doing?*

She lay back in the foaming water and felt relaxed, inhaling the beautiful fragrance. There was no need to rush – and he could make his own bloody coffee.

He stood at the bathroom door. He was wearing his superhero lounge pants. His chest and feet were bare. She hadn't heard him come in, as she lay back with her eyes closed and head submerged in the warmth, only aware of the sounds from the water. She looked serene and pretty.

She sat up and started to wash her hair. He watched.

All done, she stood up and reached for the towel. He moved over and handed it to her.

"Oh! How long have you been there?" Her anger was already fading, from the pleasure of the bath, and the handsome vision now standing in front of her.

"Long enough." He smiled faintly, seductive and mysterious.

She stepped out of the bath and took the towel he held out for her.

"I see you have lounge pants on." She looked down at them.

"I was thinking not for long."

She looked up at his smouldering eyes. He was leaning against the door jamb again.

Suzy wrapped the towel around her body and walked past him. He pulled it from her and she stopped as it dropped to the floor.

She gestured towards her neck and breasts.

"Happy with your handiwork?" Her tone was sheepish, hesitant, wondering what he was intending to do, and she couldn't help feeling excitement run through her as she saw him take his trousers off.

He strode over to her confidently, masterfully taking her in his strong arms and kissing over all the marks. "Yes." His voice scorched her. "Very artistic, though I say so myself."

As he felt her arms rise to protest, he pinned them to her side. "They'll be gone by the time anyone else sees you." His voice smouldered away at her soul, diminishing her resolve to regain control.

Suddenly there was a knock at the door. He put a finger to her lips, then grabbed the towel, wrapping it round his waist as he ran downstairs to receive the supermarket delivery.

As she heard the van drive away, she went to the kitchen. He was sorting out what needed to go in the fridge and freezer. The rest of the purchases were left in the bags.

"Where are my clothes?"

"You don't need them."

"Lawrence!" She felt exasperated. "You can't expect me to be naked all week."

"Why not?" His voice was devoid of emotion; there was just firmness.

"Do I get to say what I want?" She was beginning to feel fearful of his intentions, and her voice betrayed her feeling of weakness.

He was feeding on it.

"I know what you want." He suddenly smiled, dangerously. "And you may need your earplugs, because I am going to control you here." He dropped the towel from his waist and took hold of her, pulling her to him.

Suzy was about to voice her protestations, her mind swinging between anger at his nerve, and the desire to see, feel and hear what he was going to do next. Did she want to be led? *Yes, I think so!* She felt him lift her and he arched his back, lifting one of her legs around his hips, and she raised the other to wrap around him as his penis entered her. Then he pressed her against the wall, the cool paper sending tingles down her back. As he thrust himself in and out their pleasure rose simultaneously, as they cherished each other's climax. They were hot and sweaty, their perspiration mingling as they kissed and stroked each other, their hold becoming firmer, each more urgent for the feel of the other's body.

After a few moments, they released each other and he stepped back.

"I want to show you something." Suzy followed him to the stable door.

He stepped outside, confident in his nakedness, and grabbed her hand, pulling her after him.

"Lawrence, it's freezing, and what if someone comes!" she shrieked as she ran, trapped by his grip, her feet burning with the coldness. "Are you mad?"

As they rounded the corner of the house, she saw steam rising just in front of them. They were on a paved patio area, and to one side was a bubbling, steaming hot tub.

"Jump in!" He practically pushed her towards it, as she was momentarily glued to the spot.

Her body prickled, in a provocative way, as the bubbles lapped over and into her, the clean smell of the chemicals clearing her head. She looked around and realised the snow had been cleared to make a pathway to the tub.

"I had to make sure it was all working properly this morning. I couldn't wait to get you in here, but we had important business to do first." He was being playful, and looked like a proud schoolboy who'd earned a house point for a good deed. He climbed in beside her.

"Why didn't you tell me?"

"I like seeing your face when I surprise you. You are even more beautiful when you smile spontaneously." He turned and looked out over the open fields, and she followed his gaze.

"It is beautiful here. Is this where you always come?"

"I came across this place last year when Julia and I were looking for another possible retreat for the kids. We decided the accommodation didn't really work, but I loved the solitude of the place and stayed here last Christmas."

Suzy thought how much he would love this isolated place, but she couldn't picture him sleeping alone in that four-poster bed.

"Were you all alone here?"

"Yeah. I drove over to The Sway to share Christmas lunch with everyone, but I spent most of the week here. I've never slept in the four-poster bed before, though. Remember, I was celibate then, and I was more comfortable in one of the single beds. Double beds used to bring back unwanted memories." He had raised an eyebrow, as if to say "what did you expect?" But then his expression changed, as he knew she was aware of what he was referring to. Some of his secrets were being laid to rest.

"Didn't you miss a profession like that?" Her tone made him think she found it hard to believe he could have left it all behind.

"I wasn't in control of what I did then, Suzy. I pretty much had to do what I was told, when I was told." Suddenly she knew he was far away with his memories.

He remembered Paul.

"Do you want to go exploring a bit?"

"Not dressed like this!" she retorted, mockingly.

"I will concede to ... let's call them tools for the job." He climbed out of the tub. "Wait here and keep warm."

A couple of minutes later he returned, dressed in chocolate-brown walking trousers, boots, a cream polo-neck sweater, a checked scarf and his leather Belstaff jacket, carrying a towel and clothing for his girl.

He helped her to quickly dry and dress on the patio, and she felt the warmth from her sweater and jeans as she hugged herself while he put her boots on her feet, toasty from the warm walking socks. *He's put everything in a drying room!*

They arrived back at the farmhouse about three hours later, after a good hike around Hayfield and out towards New Mills, exploring some of the Sett Valley trail. They were flushed and hungry, raiding the fridge and cupboards to prepare a quick, warm and filling meal.

Lawrence lit the fire in the sitting room, and he suggested they put bathrobes on and sit in front of the fire to drink some of the fine Chateau Petit Bocq, which was described as "sexy, fat and luscious" on the label, one of six bottles of red he had brought along.

They lounged on the sofa and watched an old Morecombe and Wise Christmas special on the TV. It was Christmas Eve.

Their enjoyment of the evening continued as he went into the kitchen and returned with a large box filled with an assortment of Godiva chocolates.

"Are you trying to fatten me up?" Suzy joked.

"It's nearly Christmas!" He opened another bottle of the red and they watched TV until nearly midnight.

They had both had quite enough to drink, and as they slipped into bed he put his arms around her. "You're the best thing that has ever happened to me, Suzy. There are times when I think I could die here with you and my life would have been worth it."

She felt frightened by the intensity of his words. "Well, you're my best thing too, but I'm not ready to die yet, Lawrence. I want to live my life with you, share your joys and try to take away your pains, whatever they may be. We're young and have our whole lives ahead of us. I feel like mine has just begun again. With you." She smiled, trying to lighten the mood. She touched his face and as he closed his eyes she yearned to know his thoughts.

I will leave you in three weeks and you will probably hate me. And if I don't come back you will never know how much I love you. This is the price I must pay. I'm going to make sure this week with you will be worth it!

Chapter 39

It was Christmas morning.

"Merry Christmas," he whispered, as he pulled her hair back from her face and gently brushed his lips over hers.

"Merry Christmas." She smiled at him, rolling onto her side and running her hands over his chest.

"Can I have you today, as a Christmas present?" He stared at her face, his own giving nothing away.

"You've always got me, Lawrence." She was trying to fight back the return of the fear she had felt last night. "I have a gift for you. Shall we get up now?" Her gaze held his.

He moved on top of her. "I want you as my gift." He took her hands and held them over her head. "Trust me," he said and he kissed her, holding the embrace for a few moments, before whispering in his sexy voice that melted her resistance, "Wait here."

He moved off the bed and opened the gentleman's wardrobe. The box was in the bottom of it. He placed it on the bed.

Suzy leaned up on her elbows. She was trying to decide if the excitement welling up inside her was through lustful anticipation of what would happen between them or feral fear, both of what he would do and of her weakness to resist. Her eyes were wide open and she watched as he opened the box and took out several lengths of rope. Then he picked up the black leather handcuffs with the gold chain.

"Let's play, baby," he said softly. "Let me play with you." It was not a question.

Suzy remained silent as he took her wrists and placed them in the handcuffs. He then looped a long piece of rope over the top wooden rail on one side of the bed, and secured it. He took the loose end of the rope and threaded it through the loop of chain of the handcuffs, before proceeding to wrap the rope around the rail on the opposite side of the bed, lifting Suzy up onto her knees, her arms being pulled above her head as he secured the rope. She was now captive, hanging naked from the rope, kneeling upright and facing the wall at the head of the bed, her arms stretched above her head.

"What are you doing?" she whispered, her voice dry and shaky.

"Trust me. If you want me to stop say 'red', OK?"

Since the night Lawrence had shown her the box, Suzy had read about games and safe words, the world of BDSM, and she had known deep down that this could come into their relationship, particularly after the night in the hotel. She had tried to determine in her own mind how she would feel. Could she accept it? Did she want that to be part of her relationship with him? She knew as he had fastened the platinum heart around her neck that night that the answer was yes. He had said he never hurt women. He liked to be hurt.

She stayed motionless. She didn't try to turn her head to see him, but kept her focus on the wall ahead, waiting and listening.

She felt his hands brush over her shoulders. She straightened herself up and he ran his fingernails down her back. She rolled her head back in rapture at the sensation it gave her, and moaned softly. Then she felt his hard penis rub against her buttocks, and his hands caressed the tops of her arms. He did not kiss her.

"I'm keeping you, Suzy," he breathed on her shoulder, and she could feel his want.

He raised her up onto her feet and pulled her bottom back, pressing it to his groin as she leaned forward, hanging in the cuffs on the rope. His hands roamed over her behind, moving round, his palm cupping her pubic bone. His fingers caressed her inner thighs, before trailing into her vagina, feeling her soft dampness, and stroking her clitoris.

Her moaning became more intense and she groaned in erotic pleasure as his penis lunged into her and he held her waist and pulled her onto him, his movements steady, the feel of his balls against her skin making her want him even more.

"You want this. You need this, baby." Still he didn't kiss her.

"Yes," she gasped. "I want you, please…" His fingers moved back to her favourite place. "Make me come," she gasped, and she knew she was so close. As he released himself into her she orgasmed exquisitely, savouring the exhilarating sensation. He pulled away, and she couldn't feel him any more.

She hung forward, feeling the strain on her arms.

"Lawrence, my arms ... they're hurting a little." She tried to turn around to look at him, but she was alone in the room. She called out his name. *Don't cry, don't cry!*

She knelt down, her arms beginning to ache. Then he was at the side of the bed. He adjusted the rope, so she could lower her hands onto the bed, but she was still captive.

"Can you let me go now?"

"No. Not yet." His voice was low. "We haven't finished. Lie down," he ordered.

"I don't think I can take any more."

"Oh, I think you can, Suzy. Remember, the word is 'red'. Now lie down." He looked at her darkly.

She wondered about yelling out "red". But she was curious, and now that the rope was lowered she was more comfortable. She eased herself onto her back and placed her cuffed hands on her chest, with her head at the top of the bed.

Lawrence then went to the bottom of the bed and moved her legs apart. He took two pieces of the rope and fastened each leg to a corner post of the bed, so his girl was spread out before him. Suzy felt vulnerable, the rope biting at her skin if she pulled against it too hard, but she was excited, completely under his control, and the sensations running through her body were driving her crazy. He positioned himself on top of her, head to toe, and as he gave her his penis to take in her mouth, he began to enjoy tasting her juices. The power and mastery of both acts were his.

After they were both pleasured he lay next to her, stroking her immobilised body, softly singing the words of Paul Weller's song, "You Do Something To Me".

Suzy closed her eyes and breathed deeply.

She felt him release her feet, tenderly rubbing her ankles and massaging her calves. He unlocked the handcuffs and peppered kisses over her reddened wrists, then kissed her passionately, hugging her to him.

"You've moved me to new heights, do you know that?" He continued to kiss her hands. "I will never have enough of you."

Suzy looked at him, loving his handsome face, melodious voice, mysterious character and inescapable magnetism.

"I never want to lose you." She sighed and started to sit up.

He looked away so she didn't see a darkness creep over his face. *What the fuck are you going to do now?*

"Why don't you run a bath and I'll go and light a fire." He went over to the wardrobe and handed her a red silk wrap he had secretly hung there. He put on his superhero lounge pants and a white T-shirt.

"Oh, you're going to let me wear some clothes today, are you?" she enquired, holding the wrap up, challenging him to say no.

"Don't be cross with me," he smirked. "We're having fun, aren't we?" He sought her assurance as he made his way onto the landing.

Her smile was enough for him, and he ran downstairs.

By the time Suzy came downstairs, Lawrence had made scrambled eggs, served with smoked salmon and bucks fizz.

"Lovely!" Suzy exclaimed as she sat at the table. She looked out of the window. "Look at all that snow! Let's build a snowman later – I've never done that!"

"Well, Miss Harper, there's a first time for everything!" He cast her a knowing look as she thought back to the beginning of their Christmas morning and blushed.

She was holding an envelope bound with a red ribbon. "Merry Christmas," she said, passing it to him.

"You were enough." He smiled, smoothing his fingers over her writing. He seemed relaxed and happy.

Oh my heart.

His face lit up as he saw two tickets to the filming of the *Top Gear* show. "Wow!" He exclaimed. "How did you manage to get these? That'll be great."

"Dominic got them for us. I hope the date's good for you."

He checked the tickets – the fifth of January. "Should be OK. I'll make sure it is, anyway."

As Suzy started to clear away the breakfast things, he went

into the sitting room. She joined him a few moments later, and found him leaning against the mantelpiece, staring at the flames.

"What are you thinking?" she asked.

"Oh, nothing. Just that I'm glad you came here with me. Here." He held a small golden gift box out to her. "Let's sit down." He placed his arm around her as she opened the box.

"Lawrence." She spoke softly as her eyes took in the ring seated in the velvet cushion. It was an elongated panther, its outstretched paws round to the tip of its tail forming the circle of the ring, fashioned in white gold with tiny emerald eyes. "It's beautiful."

He took it out of the box and placed it on the ring finger of her right hand.

"It's a bit big." He sounded disappointed, running his thumb over it on her hand.

"I'm sure we can get it adjusted. Let's try this." Suzy moved it onto her middle finger. It fitted perfectly. "There. It looks lovely."

"I just wanted you to have something to make you think of me."

She put her hand to her platinum heart pendant, which she rarely took off. "I already have." She smiled, and knew he still felt a little guilty about the restless night she had endured following his punishment in the hotel.

"I cherish this, you know. It's OK, Lawrence." She held his hand.

"I know I come with a lot of baggage. But you can handle me, can't you, Suzy?"

A rare question, and she sensed he needed reassurance. "Of course I can. I love you as you are, Lawrence: fun, sexy, even dark and mysterious at times; I never know what you are going to do next. I also know you are kind, thoughtful, compassionate, philanthropic. Your past, no matter how bad it was, has helped to shape who you are today, and I love every bit of you." However, she had no intention of letting anything dampen the happy mood of this special day. And she added, laughing, "After all, how bad can it get?"

Suzy had also bought him a copy of Rudyard Kipling's *The Jungle Book*, and *Seeing Red*, the photographic review book of the British Superbike Championship.

Lawrence opened *The Jungle Book*. "I haven't seen this for a few years." He flicked through the pages, admiring the pictures and, Suzy thought, remembering his own childhood memories.

"Let me read some to you."

He looked at her for a moment, and the image of a foster mother, one of many, flashed through his mind, as he lay in bed while she read to him. Nothing good ever seemed to last long in his life then. Was this girl going to change that?

"Why not?" He smiled. Suzy looked pleased as she took the book and sat at his feet. She began to read. He put his arm over her shoulder and peered at the pictures as she read. *Is this how family life should feel?*

Later, after they had worked together to prepare their Christmas lunch, they wrapped up and went outside to build a snowman and have the compulsory snowball fight. After he had rolled her round in the snow a few times, Suzy was glad to get back inside by the fire.

As they lay in bed that evening, having made love in a more traditional manner, they were each content with the joy of the day, each other's company, and both wondered what the future would hold for them.

Chapter 40

They were due to go back to the real world tomorrow, having spent their time making love, playing games and walking around the beautiful countryside of the Peak District.

It was a bright sunny New Year's Day, and most of the snow from the beginning of the week had melted away. Suzy had made them breakfast in bed and Lawrence was browsing through his new superbikes book. She couldn't believe how easy it had been to spend the whole week alone with him. It had been idyllic, and she was regretful in a way that they were returning to their two homes, wondering if they would be having the same battles over who had control of her life. She hadn't minded that so much here. In fact, it had added to the mystery and fun of being with him twenty-four/seven, but she knew it wouldn't be the same when things returned to normal. She smiled when she thought of the earplugs.

Then she became thoughtful, as she planned her last gift to him before they went home.

He was engrossed in his book and, for once, not paying too much attention to her.

She went down the landing into the bathroom. She had noticed a couple of days ago that he had put the box in the cupboard under the sink. She took it out and started to go through its contents.

There it was. The soft brown leather flogger. She put it back in the box. Then quietly she climbed the spiral staircase up to the attic room and looked around. There was a wooden beam spanning the ceiling. Perfect.

She went back down to the bedroom. Lawrence was still reading. He looked up at her.

"I'm just going to run a bath. I'll give you a shout when it's ready. Carry on reading – I'm glad you like it."

"I love all your gifts, Suzy, especially the first one – although I remember choosing that one myself." Now he had that schoolboy grin. "Let's play some more before that bath."

Oh no, you're not stealing my thunder now! "Oh, we've got all day for that." She tried not to sound as if she were putting him off – that would have been too much of a challenge for him to resist. He had already put his book down. She hurried on. "I want to feel nice and clean for it." She licked her lips, provoking a smile from him.

"OK, but don't keep me waiting too long," he shouted after her.

The bathroom had two doors, one from their bedroom and one onto the landing. She left the taps running slowly over the bath and went out through the other door, back up to the attic. Carefully, and as quietly as possible, she started to move the furniture out to the sides of the room. Then she took the longest piece of rope from the box and, climbing on to one of the chairs, managed to loop it over the beam. She manoeuvred the rope to the centre of the room and fastened the two ends together, pulling the knot as high as she could reach so that the loop of rope now hung above her head. She smiled, wondering if her parents would approve of the use to which she had put the skill for rope work they had taught her during their sailing trips. *If you knew how much I love him and how much I would do for him, then you might approve, Mum.* She couldn't be so sure about her dad, though!

She went down to the bathroom and turned the taps off. Then she ran down to the kitchen and took a white cloth from one of the drawers.

She went into the bedroom.

"Come to me in five minutes, OK?" She tried to sound seductive and tempting. "Don't forget me, or no playing later!" She beamed at him and lowered the shoulder of her silk wrap.

"I'll set my alarm." His voice was filled with desire as he put the book down and sat back in the bed with his arms behind his head.

She went up into the attic room and removed her wrap. Then she placed the white cloth on the floor in the middle of the room. She took the flogger from the box and displayed it artistically on the cloth. Then she took the leather handcuffs and looped them over the dangling rope. She placed the gold key on the cloth next to the flogger. Next she raised her hands up and carefully placed her wrists in the cuffs and fastened them shut. She was now imprisoned with her hands secured in the handcuffs, totally naked.

Oh, please let him come, and let him like it!

Her heart was pounding and she was fighting back the thought that he wouldn't like it. She was certain he would. She stood still and listened.

She heard him open the bathroom door.

"Suzy?"

She remained silent. There weren't that many rooms in the farmhouse to search.

Lawrence was puzzled for a second, then he looked up to the top of the spiral staircase. He smiled and slowly started to ascend the steps.

She was facing the doorway. She heard him gasp, and immediately saw his penis erect and waiting. He was naked, and his eyes darkened as he stared at her. His look moved to the cloth, and the flogger.

"Oh, baby," he said under his breath

"I want to play," she whispered, looking directly into his gleaming eyes.

He walked over and lightly touched her shoulders. "I should be standing there," he said quietly, and he looked up into her eyes.

"Your turn next." She let her head drop, the excitement and fear becoming too much. She glanced up at the cuffs and then looked at him. He was still standing in front of her.

Then she watched him as he bent down and picked up the flogger. He played with the strands and his fingers lingered on the one he had cut. He walked round behind her and unfastened the heart pendant. He placed it on the cloth.

"Are you sure you want this, Suzy? I don't need you to do this. You know that, don't you?"

"I want to know what it's like, Lawrence. I want it this time." She had turned her head to see him.

He looked thoughtful, almost hesitant. She knew he had made his decision.

"I won't hurt you, baby, and remember the safe word is 'red'."

She nodded and stood upright, the chain from the cuffs resting on the loop of the rope.

He moved to face her. He raised the flogger in his right hand and slowly trailed it over her shoulder, bringing the tails down to gently tickle her breasts. As the soft leather fell away he cupped one breast at a time with his left hand, and then lowered his head to suck on her nipples.

She murmured his name.

He held her gaze as he lowered the flogger and brought its tails up each of her legs, brushing them against her inner thighs, flicking them gently across from left to right.

The touch was light and feathery, and Suzy could feel herself getting excited and nervous.

He held the flogger upright now and lowered himself to his knees as he placed the grip up towards her vagina, the strands hanging limply down. Suzy felt the coolness of the leather, the hardness of the handle, and moved her legs apart ever so slightly, as if inviting him to push it in.

"Not this, baby," he whispered as he looked up at her.

He stood up and kissed her harshly, leaving Suzy taken aback by his force, conscious of his lust, sensing a feeling of anger. Suddenly she wanted to put her arms around him, and she pulled against the rope, leaning into his kiss, her own desperation palpable on his lips.

It was as if she had broken his trance and he was suddenly back with her, his desire replacing the anger which had threatened to envelop him.

You're doing this for her, for her pleasure.

He let the kiss trail off, luring her to beg for more. "Be patient," he ordered.

He moved round to her back, seeing her tense in anticipation of his next move. He would not keep her waiting.

Suzy felt the leather land on the right side of her back. Lawrence took care to avoid letting the tails wrap around her body, so she wouldn't feel any stinging. The thud had made her lurch forward, to instinctively try to get out of the way, but of course she couldn't.

Lawrence watched, excited by her reaction, and fearful of hurting her. "Enough?" he asked gently.

"No." She straightened, determined to continue the experience. "I'm OK." She waited.

The tails hit her next on the other side, a little harder, and she could feel pain on her back, but it was arousing her, she was tingling inside and she held her breath, desirous of more.

He now brought the flogger across her bottom, and she moved forward on to her tiptoes. He made one more move across from the other side, careful not to cover the area he had already struck.

"I think that's enough now, darling." He put his hands around her waist, kissing the back of her neck as she leaned into him. Then he slid himself inside her, and with rhythmical motions and stroking movements, they both reached their orgasm.

He took the key and unfastened the cuffs. Then he led her to the sofa.

"Wait here a moment." He went down the staircase and returned with some ibuprofen gel. She felt the coolness of it on her back and bottom, and she lay on her front while he gently rubbed a little onto her soft skin. There were no marks, and he was relieved.

"Why did you do this?" His whole expression was asking the question, and she still wasn't sure whether he enjoyed it or not.

"I was curious. I feel good, Lawrence. I feel exhilarated. I wanted this to be your last gift, before we go home tomorrow."

He sat down and pulled her onto his lap. "Would you do anything for me?" His eyes were sincere, and he rubbed his fingers over the panther ring.

"Yes." She touched his face. "Well, within reason!" She laughed a little. "I feel braver now, and you're training me well."

He looked over at her handiwork with the rope. "Do you think we really are two of a kind? You give me great sex, and you seem to know what I like."

She had never thought of it like that. Was she like him? Kinky? She didn't imagine for one minute that their games were the norm for the average couple, but who was she to know? After all, she hadn't actually slept with anyone else. She smiled as she wondered what games Richard and Dominic might get up to! Her bravado kicked in.

"Can I play with you now?"

"Oh. Is it my turn? I wondered if you were going to ask." He had a full-blown smile across his face and he pushed up slightly, so she felt his hard penis beneath her. "I'm not sure about the cuffs," he added. "I won't be able to let go."

"Trust me," she taunted him, echoing his own words. "You'll like it."

She was beginning to shock herself with her confidence, but what the hell – she was a quick learner and the setting was so much better here than it had been at the hotel. "This is for pleasure, not punishment, Lawrence." She boldly took hold of his hand and got off his lap to lead him over to the handcuffs.

If only you knew, baby!

He watched her face as she secured each hand in the cuffs.

"Now I'm yours," he said, his eyes twinkling with anticipation. "You may want to secure the rope higher."

"Are you challenging me, Mr Bane?" Now she had a schoolgirl grin.

She brought a chair over to stand on and skilfully she added another knot in the rope, shortening the loop hanging from the beam, and raising his arms higher above his head. She moved behind him and he struggled to turn to see her. He faced forward again.

"You're a good teacher," she whispered in his ear, and he turned to bite at her, growling softly, but she moved back. "Aha, not yet, sir."

"Oh, I like that title," he laughed.

She struck him hard across his right shoulder. "And does sir like that?" Her voice was sexy and confident.

"Oh, yes, more please, ma'am." He lurched back, straining on the rope, trying to turn, to reach her. He relished the pain as she struck him again with just the right amount of force. "I am so going to need to fuck you after this."

"I can't wait." She lashed out again and again and again.

Then he heard a thud on the carpet as she threw the flogger down, and she knelt in front of him and began to suck at his penis, desperate to possess him, to feel and taste him.

"Are you forgetting something?" he grinned, trying not to lose himself in the carnal desire she was inflicting on him, and he nodded up to the captivating cuffs.

"Sorry." She smirked, and stood on the chair to reach up with the key and release him.

He scooped her masterfully into his arms and made to go down the spiral staircase.

"Fuck," he muttered, as he realised there was no way he was going to be able to carry her safely down there. He took her back into the room and laid her down on the floor. Then he was on top of her, inside her, thrusting hard. She could only surrender her body to him, enraptured by the knowledge she had driven him to this need; this need of her. As he cried out, she came herself, with mind-blowing intensity.

Chapter 41

The truck pulled up at The Sway. Suzy gazed through the window. The house looked empty and lonely. The children were gone, and Christine and Dave would be enjoying the remainder of their holiday in St Lucia. The Christmas decorations had all been taken away and things were back to normal. She couldn't help feeling a tinge of sadness.

Still, it was a new year. She had Lawrence in her life and more work starting with Winstons. She was feeling good.

As they walked into the hall, Suzy hesitated a moment. His arrangement schedule had only gone as far as today. She was working tomorrow, and wondered if maybe it would be best if they had a bit of space to catch up on things. She knew he had a meeting to go to with Tony Cross and Kevin Underwood on Friday, and he was seeing Linda, the finance director, tomorrow. Maybe she should go home.

Lawrence was putting the luggage away and broke into her thoughts, suggesting she made some coffee while he checked his emails and post.

She made the drinks and joined him in his office.

"Have you got a lot to do?" She moved over to his desk, glancing at the TV screens he had turned on, providing updates on news and financial performances around the world. How on earth did he keep track of everything?

"I'm afraid so. Holiday period is over, baby." He reached out to take hold of her hand. "You made it my best Christmas ever, and we've still got Saturday to look forward to." He smiled.

He started to open his post. His face lit up even more.

"Look at this!" He handed her a homemade card, filled with sketches ranging from a mass of red and blue claiming to be Spiderman, to quite a good pencil sketch of a man standing next to a motorbike, and coloured flowers around what looked like a drawing of Lawrence's pond. "The kids have done this, and your name's on the card too. It looks like you made an impression on Melanie."

Suzy admired the thank-you card. The children had each done a drawing and written thank you for their gifts and for being able to stay at The Sway. It was lovely.

"I would like to be involved with them too, if I can. At least, with plans for when they're here." She hesitated a moment, wondering if she would be around long enough to get to know them better, and her face must have reflected her concern.

"Yeah, fingers crossed there will be lots of opportunities. Maybe we'll try and pop over to the centre on the bike sometime. I want to see how Daniel is, anyway."

She wasn't sure why he had mentioned going on the bike, but he had carried on opening his post and it looked as though he needed to concentrate.

"I think it might be better if I get out of your way for a bit now and let you get on with everything. I can go home and start to get things straight. I'm at the bookshop tomorrow and going to Winstons' offices on Friday, to put a schedule of work together. I think they want me to go to Paris at the end of January, to meet the French team." She remembered Christine's words from the race day. "I could arrange to stay for the weekend, and you could come over and meet me. What do you think?"

His expression hardened. He picked up his coffee cup and studied its contents.

"I don't think I'll be able to make it." *I'll be in London, in hell.* Then he thought of Dan and made a mental note to make sure he followed her out there, for her own safety, with the added bonus of checking she didn't meet anyone else. This did little to compensate for the fact he really did not want her going anywhere, let alone Paris, without him!

Now she knew something was wrong. He was expecting something to happen, and she suddenly felt a chill at all his talk about limited time and not always being around.

He saw a panic begin to rise in her. Should he start now to make her hate him? Could he leave her knowing she would move on from him? No. He wasn't that strong.

He pushed his chair away from the desk. "Look, don't go just yet. Let's at least eat together. It's been a lovely holiday. It's a shame work stuff is going to start getting in the way." He tried to make light of his inability to commit to her for the foreseeable future. He knew he had to start to let go.

Later that afternoon, Suzy brushed aside his attempts to get her to stay the night, and tried to appear cheerful as she waved and drove off in her Mazda. Maybe she was overreacting and he was just going to be too busy with work to go to Paris. He would be there for her when she got back. It need only be a day trip, anyway. But she was feeling far from at ease as she started to unpack her things back at her cottage.

She checked her emails, and saw one from Peter Dane, the sales director at Winstons. He was looking forward to seeing her on Thursday, and he attached a code for the car park, which was very thoughtful.

There was one from Dominic and Richard, thanking her for their gifts and hoping she'd had a good Christmas and new year. Dominic asked her to call him when she got back.

She suddenly felt the need to talk to her cousin. Would he even stay over, like the good old days? *Oh, how much life has changed – it hasn't all been for nothing, has it?* The thought of life without Lawrence made her want to cry.

She made a cup of tea and called Dominic.

"Hey, Suzy! Happy New Year! You had a good time?" Dominic sounded really cheery.

"It was great, thanks, and thanks for the woolly scarf and gloves, they're lovely. Did you guys have a good time?"

"Yes, and it was all over far too quickly. But things have to get back to normal, and it will stop me from eating too much."

Suzy laughed, finding it hard to imagine Dominic ever eating too much.

"Richard said why don't you come over soon, seeing as we didn't see you at all over Christmas. You can bring Lawrence. I was thinking of the week after your *Top Gear* show – the twelfth."

"Yeah, maybe. I'll need to check with him. I think he's got a lot of work to do at the moment."

"Are you not with him now?"

"No. I'm at home. I'm working at the bookshop tomorrow, and Lawrence has got a couple of meetings to prepare for, so I've left him in peace." She hoped her voice didn't betray her disappointment at being home alone.

"I guess he's a really busy guy. I could come over later if you like, and come into work from yours in the morning. Rick won't mind."

She really wanted to say yes, that would be great, but she had a feeling she might need to get used to being on her own, and she didn't want to fall back into the habit of having her cousin around to be her guardian angel. She had grown up quite a bit in the last few weeks, and it wasn't fair on him.

"It's OK, I need to get straight here." She looked around her kitchen and noticed it had been cleaned again. "And I start the contract with Winstons on Friday. I'm meeting their sales director to start going over a schedule of work. I think I'm going to be quite busy myself, and hopefully it will be fun."

"Sounds good. Well, let us know about the twelfth. Take care, Suzy."

"You too. Speak soon, and say hi to Richard."

She sat down, and noticed a business card from Merry Maids cleaning company on the table. *Have they been again? How did they get in, and how much did it cost?*

She thought of asking Lawrence but wasn't quite sure she could talk to him at the moment, not without sounding upset.

She rang the cleaning company.

"Yes, Miss Harper, that's right. Two of our girls are scheduled to do a fortnightly clean, one and half hours, giving you the equivalent of three hours. I've been meaning to speak to you to go through your requirements. Mr Bane said you would be away until January."

"Has he spoken to you?"

"Yes, Miss Harper. He has given us a set of keys, and the invoices are all for his account. I presumed he had spoken to you about it. The girls will come every other Thursday morning. When would be convenient for me to come and do a proper inspection and go through your requirements with you?

We tend to find that men are not as particular about standards as ladies."

Suzy was silent on the other end of the phone, taking in the fact he was still trying to control her life – her work assignments, her own house. She struggled to match this side of him with the side that seemed ready to leave her. His mysteries were far from being solved.

"Is everything OK, Miss Harper?"

"I'm sorry, yes. The house looks lovely." She couldn't deny it was a real treat to have her cleaning done for her! "I could meet you here on Monday afternoon."

"I look forward to seeing you then. My name is Marion O'Toole, by the way. Shall we say three o'clock?"

"That's fine. See you then."

She looked at the card, with Marion's name listed as proprietor. How much was this costing? She did need to speak to Lawrence about it. She drank her tea and then dialled his number.

"Hi. How's it going?" She tried to make sure she didn't appear too eager to talk to him. Her heart was pounding.

"Well, I'm getting back up to speed with things. I'm seeing Linda at three o'clock tomorrow afternoon. Can I meet you in Nantwich for lunch?"

"I'll probably be busy with book deliveries, so I might not be able to get away."

There was silence for a moment.

"Suzy, is everything alright?"

"Sure. I just don't think I can commit to lunch."

"I could meet you after work."

"Well, I'm going to the gym, and then having a drink with Alison. I probably won't be back until late." She had made no such arrangement with Alison, but suddenly felt the need to talk to someone other than Lawrence. She was feeling too confused.

"You didn't say you were seeing Alison." He sounded accusatory, even angry.

Why the hell should I? You don't control me!

"Well, I'm saying now, Lawrence. Don't start the controlling thing with me. And what's with the cleaning company?" She paused a moment, her own anger mounting out of sheer frustration with the hotchpotch of emotions she was feeling.

"I thought you'd be glad, seeing as you're going to have extra work now." He sounded exasperated, and Suzy thought this conversation was probably not what he needed right now.

"Look, I am glad. Thanks. You must let me pay you back, though, maybe out of my first cheque from Winstons."

"Don't worry about that." His voice was quiet now, pensive. "When can I see you?"

Oh my heart. She weakened her resolve to get to the weekend without him.

"Why not stay here Friday night?" *Is he going to argue about it?*

"OK. I'll drop you at the bookshop on Saturday and pick you up to go to the *Top Gear* show. Will you use your gift tonight?"

"What?"

"Just tell me if you do. I will want to hear all about it. See you Friday, baby," he said huskily and ended the call.

Suzy stared at her phone. The vibrator. What was she now – a sex addict? He thinks I can't go a couple of nights without sex? She'd used it before for him. Did she now want to use it for herself?

She rang Alison, hoping to have a heart-to-heart chat with her as well as getting rid of some of her frustration at the gym. Who knows if she would be in the mood to use her gift after that?

Chapter 42

Lawrence's mobile rang. He contemplated not answering it. It was an unrecognised number and he was in no mood to talk to anyone at the moment. He had just asked Lewis to instruct Dan to get back to his surveillance of Suzy. He was trying to come to terms with how he would manage when he was in London, never knowing what she was doing until he could read about it in a report!

Damn it! "Hello. Bane speaking."

"Lawrence, it's Elizabeth. Please don't hang up on me."

His brow furrowed. What the hell did she want?

"Why are you ringing me?"

"I'm in a bit of trouble, and I didn't know what else to do."

There was silence at the other end.

She continued, "I'm being blackmailed." She paused. "I don't want Kevin to find out. Please, Lawrence, can I come and talk to you?"

"Not here. I'll meet you tomorrow night. Do you know the Hanging Dog?"

"Yes, I think so."

"Half past eight in the bar." He put the phone down. He wasn't sure why he should contemplate trying to help her, or even if he could help her. Goodness knows what she was involved in, but he felt it could only increase his leverage over her, and, indirectly, over her husband. Besides, it might be good to hear of someone else's shit, to take his mind off his own.

* * *

He stripped and plunged into the pool. He pounded up and down, trying to induce a tiredness which would make him sleep. Then he resorted to whisky. A little too much. He met Linda in the morning with his head feeling a bit thicker than he had intended, but pleased with the finance figures ready for the board meeting tomorrow.

Now what on earth could Elizabeth Underwood need to see him about?

* * *

Suzy and Alison finished their aerobics class and decided to order some food in the pub, as Suzy started to tell her friend about how lovely everything had been over Christmas, but that something hadn't felt right since they had got back. There was nothing specific, and Suzy felt a bit silly telling Alison, but her friend was understanding, almost protective of her. After all, she had witnessed the innocent young woman from Cameroon suddenly becoming totally consumed by some egotistical rich bastard. She was fearful of her dropping from a great height of happiness, and would make sure she was there to catch her if necessary.

Suzy was at the bar getting menus when she heard Lawrence's voice. She turned and saw Elizabeth Underwood gazing into his eyes. He was raising a pint of Guinness to his lips when he froze.

Their eyes connected and he stood. Elizabeth turned to face Suzy and smiled, spite written across her face.

Suzy turned away and breathed deeply. Then she put the menu back on the bar, turned and walked over to Lawrence.

"Suzy, I…"

She lifted his pint and poured the contents down his checked shirt, then strode over to find Alison.

"Let's leave," she exclaimed, loudly enough for all those who were staring at her to hear.

"Lawrence, I'm so sorry!" Elizabeth's voice made him feel sick. "Let me get you a cloth."

"Don't bother." He rubbed his hands down his shirt and wiped them over the backside of his jeans. "We're done. I'll get someone on to it and they'll be in touch. Don't call me again." He turned to the group of spectators gathered to see if there was going to be any more action. "Show's over, folks!" With a face like thunder he walked into the street.

"Where is she?" he yelled down his mobile to Dan.

"They've gone into the Red Lion."
"What size shirt do you wear?"
"What?"
"Do me a favour and swap."

By now Lawrence had caught up with Dan and put his phone away. "Just help me out here." In the middle of the street the two men swapped shirts, Dan feeling slightly done by the deal, not to mention wet!

Alison saw him come in and she put her hand over the table to warn Suzy. Suzy's eyes were swollen and she had gulped down a large glass of Pinot Grigio.

He stood next to her and she looked away. "It's not what you think, Suzy."

"I don't want to know." Her voice was tearful and her eyes glistened.

Alison looked up at him. "I think you'd better go."

"I'm not going anywhere until you listen to me." He was looking directly at Suzy.

"Oh, and what were you going to tell me, Lawrence? You couldn't wait to go back to her, is that it? Is that why you keep implying you're not going to be around? Are you going to fuck off with her?" Suzy's voice was low but vehement.

"This isn't the place, Suzy." He glanced at Alison, who looked stunned. "Let me take you home. We need to talk."

"I'm having another drink!" She got up and headed to the bar.

Lawrence glanced over at Dan, who was standing at the side of the bar sipping a diet Coke, his jacket fastened over Lawrence's very damp shirt. Then he turned to Alison.

"She's got it all wrong. I just need to explain to her. Please, can I take you both home, and then perhaps she will listen to me." He looked anxious and tired, and Alison felt pity for him, sensing in him a genuine feeling of being wrongly accused.

"What were you doing with that woman?"

He was about to tell her to mind her own business, but thought better of it. He appreciated it didn't look good for him.

"I used to know her, way back. Now she's in trouble and she

was asking me to help her." His eyes pleaded for some understanding.

"Let me check with Suzy if she wants to go with you. I'm in my car, so I can just go home. But I'm not doing anything she isn't comfortable with. I think she's a bit drunk. I've never seen her like this before." She went over to her friend, who was gulping down another glass of wine.

Lawrence stayed back while the two girls talked for what seemed like an age. Then he saw Alison look over towards him, before she hugged Suzy.

"Call me if you need me, Suzy, promise? And it doesn't matter what time, OK?"

"I promise. Thanks Alison."

"I'll see you on Saturday. Take care, hon."

Alison walked back over to Lawrence.

"You'd better not hurt her any more than you already have, and don't let her down. She's too good for you, you know."

"I know. Thanks, Alison."

She watched as he walked slowly over to the bar, and then she left.

"Please come and get in the car." He reached out to take Suzy's hand.

"Don't touch me."

He was stunned by the bitterness in her voice. He put his hand down and stood patiently by her side as she gulped down the remainder of her drink.

She walked unsteadily into the street and looked around for his car. He caught her elbow and steered her to the right. She immediately shrugged him off and he let go, walking a step behind her. As she tottered in front of him, he signalled to Dan to go home. He wouldn't be leaving her tonight.

When they reached his car, he opened the passenger door. She started to slide onto the pavement, but he held her up and gently eased her into the seat, hoping she wouldn't throw up in his Jag.

"Drink the coffee, baby."

Suzy was slumped in the chair at the kitchen table. He wondered if there was any point in trying to explain to her in this state, but he was fearful of her reaction if he tried to take her to bed.

However, the decision was made for him as he realised she was asleep and wouldn't be drinking or listening, or consciously doing anything until the morning.

He undressed her and placed her under the duvet. *What the hell, I've got nothing to lose!* He climbed in beside her, gently stroking her hair.

He woke at six and watched the rise and fall of her breathing for a moment. Then he got up and went to shower. Once he was dressed, still in Dan's shirt but at least with his own clean underwear, he ran a hot bath and went back into the bedroom to wake her.

"Bugger, I feel crap," she whispered to herself, and as the memories of last night came back to her, she glanced over to where he was leaning in the doorway.

"I've run you a bath."

"Hadn't you better go running back to *her*?" The bitterness was gone from her voice now, just a sadness that wrenched at his heart.

"She is nothing to me, Suzy. She never was. She was someone I just fucked for money. Last night she needed my help and I said I would see what I could do. I have committed enough crimes, Suzy. For God's sake, please don't punish me for one I haven't committed. I don't want or need anyone else, just you. Please, go and have your bath." He turned and walked downstairs.

She heard him go into the kitchen. Then her phone pinged. It was a text from Alison, asking if she was OK.

She didn't feel OK. Was he being honest with her? He looked dejected, and she wondered if he might be telling the truth.

She climbed into the bath, and as she lay back, trying to numb the pain in her head, she tried to remember how he had seemed when she had seen him with Elizabeth. He was just drinking. He had been sitting opposite her. He wasn't touching her, at least not above the table. Then she remembered how capable he was with that toe of his, or taking her foot to push onto him! Would he lie to her?

She started to wonder if he had really only been trying to help Elizabeth. But help her with what?

His mysteries were becoming too much for her. She needed some fresh air and, since they had come back from the Peak District, she didn't feel she could breathe freely. It was as if she was suffocating.

Lawrence was sitting in the kitchen, flicking through the pages of one of her old magazines. She knew he wasn't even really looking at it.

He stood up. "Can I make some coffee?" He looked rough, with stubble and wearing yesterday's clothes. Was that the shirt I poured his beer over? Oh no, did I really do that?

"Please." She responded quietly and without emotion. "Do you want anything to eat?"

"No thanks."

She went over to the cupboard and took out some paracetamol and poured herself a glass of water. She sat quietly while he made the drinks in silence. He put the mugs on the table and sat opposite her.

"I don't quite know what has happened between us, Suzy." He looked at her intently now. "Can we start over?"

She looked straight at him and asked the question that had been slowly eating away at her since she met him.

"Are you going to leave me, Lawrence?" She had to get her fear on the table. She couldn't let it go on slowly devouring her, ruining everything.

He recognised the clinical tone she used when she tried to detach herself from a situation, as she had when he had first shown her the box, and she had tried to guess what he used to do with women.

"I don't want to, Suzy, believe me." How much dare he tell her? He looked into his coffee cup, then his eyes drilled into hers. "If I did need to go somewhere, I would try to come back to you. As soon as I could."

"When?" Her voice was raised a little, but her tone remained clinical, analytical, like a doctor asking when the test results would be back, while for the patient it was an emotional nightmare, a matter of life and death. "When are you going?"

He stood up and took their mugs over to the sink. He looked out at the small back garden, although it was still dark.

"In about a week." He kept his back to her, too afraid for her to see how hard this was for him. He wasn't prepared for this conversation.

"Where are you going? When will you be back?"

He took a deep breath and then turned to face her. He was closing up on her and she knew it.

"Enough. What time are you due at Winstons?"

She switched to autopilot, hardly aware what she was saying. "Ten o'clock. I'm going to the bathroom." He heard her run upstairs. The door banged shut. After ten minutes he called upstairs.

"Come and get your coat. I think we both need some fresh air; we're going for a walk."

How does he know that I'm suffocating? Is he?

She went to open the bathroom door and hesitated a moment. He was in control mode now, and she wasn't really in the mood for that. However, she thought it would be useless to argue with him, unless she wanted him to leave, and she didn't want that. Not ever.

They walked around the lanes for half an hour, the cold wind blowing away some fears, the memory of his words bringing new ones. *That's why he won't come to Paris. And Christine knows about it. Will she tell me more?*

Suzy suddenly felt eager to see Christine. They would be back tomorrow. Well, she wasn't just going to lie down and let her dreams disappear.

As she drove off to Winstons she looked in her rear view mirror and saw him getting into his Jag. She tried to be optimistic. He said he would get back as soon as he could. She could always phone and email him, maybe even Skype! Maybe there would be more telephone sex, and she'd have her new work to keep her busy while he was away.

But something was nagging away at her, a sense of foreboding that it wasn't that straightforward. Why wouldn't he tell her anything? Christine knew something, and Suzy had to find out what.

She turned into the car park at Winstons and entered the code Peter Dane had given her, shifting her focus to the meeting and wishing she hadn't gulped down all that wine last night.

She was shown into his office, and couldn't help being pleasantly surprised as she saw a handsome dark-haired man sitting behind his desk. He came over to her and shook her hand. He wore a navy pinstriped suit, white shirt and silver-grey tie, with highly polished black shoes. She guessed he was a bit older than Lawrence, and about the same height. It was clear Peter Dane knew he was a good-looking guy, and as he stared at Suzy she felt a little uneasy.

"Take a seat, Suzy. You don't mind me calling you Suzy?"

"No, it's fine." Suzy sat down, already hoping for the meeting to be over quickly.

* * *

Lawrence rang Lewis and passed on the information Elizabeth had given him last night. What a pain that bitch was. He explained that someone was threatening to tell her husband about some of her more kinky sexual habits. Lawrence was sure Lewis could come up with something on this guy that she could go back to him with, and that would be the end of the matter. No, he didn't want Lewis to keep him in the loop. He didn't want to know any more about it, and Lewis was to make sure he sent his bill direct to Mrs Underwood. He was damned if he was going to pay for any of it!

He then went to his board meeting with Mr Underwood.

Chapter 43

Lawrence waited in his car outside Suzy's house that night, nervous of how she would be feeling after their earlier conversation. He had already said too much and knew he needed to strike a balance. It was important that he didn't discuss things any further with her, but he didn't want to piss her off or frighten her. How to handle a woman? There could never be a book thick enough!

She parked her Mazda and walked over to him as he got out of his Jag.

"Fresh start." She smiled warmly. It was the best she had felt since they got back from the Peak District. After her meeting with Peter Dane, she couldn't wait to get back to Lawrence and try to put things right between them. *While you still can!*

"I'll go with that." He leaned down and kissed her.

As they walked into the house, he asked how her meeting with Winstons had gone.

"I met Peter Dane." She looked at him, waiting to see a reaction.

"Yes, I thought you might! So, do I have competition?" He raised an eyebrow, managing to mask the jealousy which was beginning to seep into him more and more as the fifteenth of January loomed nearer.

Suzy grinned. "He's a good-looking bloke." She thought about spinning it out so that Lawrence may think twice about leaving her, but she decided not to. Her vibes told her it was no joking matter, and she didn't want to risk causing any more friction between them. Instead, she stuck to the facts.

"It was a good meeting. I have copies of various templates for memos and newsletters, and a couple of examples to work on this week. He's also said he wants me to get started on translating the UK company's HR policies and procedures. I think they will need to consider French law and practices, but I'll discuss that more with Peter once I've started that project."

"So is he going to be your boss?" His playful look from earlier was now gone. There was only so much Lawrence could take.

"He's apparently my main contact, but I'm not an employee, remember? You're not jealous, are you?" She flashed him a flirtatious smile

"I'm very protective of what's mine, you know. And you are my most treasured possession!" He wasn't smiling.

She decided not to challenge him about his use of the word "possession" but, remembering the way Peter had looked at her, combined with her own feelings about Lawrence, she couldn't help feeling flattered at the forcefulness of his words.

After dinner, and having watched a bit of TV, Lawrence put his arm around her.

"I want to take you to bed now. I feel we've got some making up to do." He looked sincere and determined. "Come on." He led her upstairs.

He turned her docking station on and put his iPhone in it. Snow Patrol started playing "Chasing Cars".

He began to undress her, and she gave herself to him until she was naked. Then she slowly and deliberately undressed him, kissing his body as she did so.

They lay on the duvet, touching and stroking each other, kissing like lovers, building up to a union of passion and pleasure. It was gentle and basic, but they both reached orgasms that confirmed the love and power they had over each other. Suzy was aware of a new tenderness in him, and she fought back the thought that it could soon be over.

Chapter 44

Lawrence dropped Suzy off at the bookshop the next morning. She had taken clothes to change into for tonight. He was going to collect her from the shop, and they would go straight on to the *Top Gear* show.

In the meantime, he needed to complete some of the actions on his "to do" list.

He went into the office and began his encrypted message.

Hey, Dogtooth.
It's been a long time! I need a favour.
Panther

He pressed Send, then called Lewis.
"You want my bike, mate?"
"Are you kidding me? Wondered when you were gonna ask! But what's your price?"
"Treat it as a loan. I hope to be back for it before too long."
"I know. I'll take good care of it – just don't restrict my mileage allowance too much."
"Do NOT prang her!" This was a very clear order from Lawrence Bane, as his BMW S 1000 RR was his third-favourite possession, right behind Suzy and The Sway. "I'll sort out the paperwork to sign it over. Don't disappear on me when I want her back! And I need a buyer for the Triumph. Any of your guys?"
"I'll check for you, and see how much they're going for. What are you doing about The Sway?"
"I told you, I'm not getting rid of that. I'm going to shut it down. Will you come over and go through any security changes you want putting in place? Better leave the gatehouse so that Dave can carry on living there. Christine and I agreed that would be best."
"What exactly has she told him?"

"That we have to go away for a while. He knows a little bit about her past. You can imagine her scar took a bit of explaining."

"Yeah, I bet." Lewis remembered that fateful night in London when Lawrence had attempted to kill Josh Black after the bastard had cut Christine.

"Dave's a good guy. He keeps himself to himself. I think he'll be OK there, and he'll keep an eye on the place. You'll just need to monitor if Black or Rawlins get too close, and make a decision about it then. Just make sure I'm kept informed, and that means about everything, Lewis. Don't hold back on me."

"I won't, Lawrence. So when do I get the bike?"

Lawrence knew his friend was trying to lighten the conversation. "Don't worry, you won't have to wait till I'm cold in my grave. At least I fucking hope not." Neither man laughed at this weak attempt at a joke. "I'll let you know." He paused a minute and then remembered Daniel. "Oh, by the way, I'm on the lookout for a 50cc moped. I want to get a young lad started on his bike test before the summer. Let me know if you come across anything."

There was a short silence and Lewis wondered what Bane was thinking about, but he had a good guess.

"I'll need you to see this project through, Lewis, if anything happens to me."

"Better make sure it doesn't then, 'cos me and young kids on mopeds don't mix very well." He had seen enough traffic accidents during his time in uniform.

"I know, I know, but this kid was born to ride a bike – he's been out with me a few times and he's smitten. Just look out for a moped, OK?"

"Of course. Oh, I hear Dan's got a new designer shirt – a bit damp, by all accounts."

Lawrence could hear Lewis laughing on the other end of the phone.

"Hey, tell him if there's any reference to that incident in any of his reports, he's sacked!" At least some things could still make him smile.

Then Lawrence read the decrypted message.

Subject: Long Time
Good to hear from you, buddy. My records show you have a few favours to call in. What's happening?
Dogtooth

Subject: Re: Long Time
I need to disappear for a while. Need property recording under my other name.
Address 27 15 12 26 30 8 32 30 16 19 19 22 30 13 22 25 11 9 9 4 4 32 32.
Panther

Subject: Re: Long Time
No prob. Keep you posted. Take care buddy.
Dogtooth

Subject: Re: Long Time
Cheers mate. Will wire funds – treat yourself to a new toy.
Panther

Subject: Re: Long Time
You don't have to – but I can always find something new to play with. Stay safe.
Dogtooth

With a heavy heart, he went on to contact the Jaguar garage and arranged for them to take his car on Tuesday the fifteenth of January, the sale proceeds to be split between Fairchance and the drop-in centre in Manchester as anonymous donations. He wondered what Julia would make of that, and the fact that she wouldn't be hearing from him, for a while at least.

The pickup truck he was going to transfer to Dave for safe-keeping. He had already sold the Mercedes.

The Sway was the last thing he needed to secure. Christine had already arranged for the name on the utility bills to be changed. He had resurrected his fake passport and ID, and only Christine and Lewis (and its provider, Dogtooth) knew of its existence. His non-executive directorships were all in the name of his Luxembourg company, and it was unlikely anyone could trace that back to him, at least not without some legal contacts out there. He was confident that was beyond both Black and Rawlins. As far as they knew, Lawrence Bane was some has-been gigolo, with little to his name, who squandered other people's money – as they thought he'd done with Veronica Rigsby's. They would be more concerned about his hell-bent mission to prove Josh Black guilty of the murder of Jimmy Havers.

The next thing on his list was to access his bank account. He could see that the funds he'd arranged to be transferred had cleared. He instructed his bank to make a payment of £100,000. Payee: Miss Suzannah Harper.

He then emailed Richard Groves to contact him on Monday. He needed to make sure that Suzy knew what to do with the money, assuming she wouldn't go straight out and spend it all!

Later, he stood under his shower, letting hot water gush over his body, and thought about the night ahead, at the *Top Gear* show. It was probably just what he needed to take his mind off this ritual of erasing his existence. He didn't want to contemplate that it may not be temporary. Not tonight.

He deliberated more than usual over what to wear, finally deciding on his black Armani jeans, Chelsea boots and green Ralph Lauren sweatshirt. He knew he was going to miss his designer clothes, and he cast a derogatory glance at the Top Shop bag at the back of his dressing room, containing the cheap jeans and tops Christine had bought him ready for their trip. Well, sod it. He was still going to take his Emporio Armani underpants!

He went downstairs and grabbed his Belstaff leather jacket and went into the kitchen. Christine and Dave would be back tomorrow and he admitted to himself he was looking forward to seeing her. He hoped she had had a really good holiday. He knew this was going to be as hard for her as it was for him. They had each talked through the plans being put into place. Christine was frightened at the thought of Black being released, the painful memories of the night he had attacked her haunting her dreams more frequently as the twenty-third of January approached. Christine made it clear she was determined to go to London to try to help in any way she could. She needed to be with the man who had saved her, at the very least to take care of him. Lawrence was equally determined to take care of her.

He pulled up at the bookshop, leaving his car on double yellows, and went in. He hadn't seen Alison since the Guinness incident. Although he didn't really care what she thought of him, he didn't want her – or anybody else – thinking he would cheat on Suzy.

"She's just getting ready," Alison said, as she looked up to see him walking over to the counter.

"Thanks for letting her go a bit early." He spoke quietly.

Alison could feel his eyes penetrating her, and she took in his stunning looks, strong, lean physique and oh so expensive clothes. She couldn't help admitting Suzy had landed herself a good catch. She guessed he wanted to say something, as ordinarily by now he would have gone off to look at books.

She put her pen down and looked up at him again.

"Can I help you, Lawrence?" She didn't even attempt to hide the sarcasm in her voice, and he knew she was thinking about Elizabeth.

"I just wanted to thank you for enabling me to sort things out with Suzy the other night." His face was without expression and he spoke calmly and dispassionately. It was a very formal thank-you.

Alison softened. "She said it had been a misunderstanding on her part and she was good with it. It seems she trusts you." Her look was challenging.

"Most people do."

She was slightly taken aback by his confident reply, and then thankful to be rescued from him by Suzy.

"Lawrence, wow, you look fabulous!" She rushed towards him in a short black woollen skirt, with thick black tights and knee-length black leather boots. She wore a cable-knit mustard-coloured sweater under her biker jacket.

"Ditto, baby," he said in his sexy voice, and lowered his head, planting his lips on hers for a long-awaited kiss. "Are you ready to go?"

Suzy looked at Alison. "OK?" she asked.

"Sure. Have a good time. You both look great." She couldn't help smiling as she saw the young lovers leave the shop, and felt a little envious of the excitement emanating from them both. *Mmm, I must see about doing something different with Alex.* She felt herself flush at the thought.

"They make a good couple," Mike announced as he came up from the back of the shop. "Do you think it will last?"

"They're definitely serious, but who knows?"

Chapter 45

Lawrence held the door of the Jag for Suzy, and as he climbed in on the driver's side he was still smiling after the fabulous evening they'd had. The infamous trio were on top form, the Stig had made an appearance, and they had seen a couple of the fastest cars in the world. Lawrence had been in his element.

He held her hand most of the way back to The Sway, and Suzy was asleep by the time he pulled up on the driveway. He felt a little disappointed she was so tired, as he was wide awake and definitely not set on going straight to sleep. He wondered what his chances were…

She leaned against him as he led her into the house.

"Hey, sleepyhead. Do you fancy a drink?"

She eyed him cautiously in her languorous state. "I feel shattered. What did you have in mind?"

He walked her into the snug and she sat on the sofa. The room felt cold with no fire burning. He hoped the coolness would wake her a little. He took her coat.

"I'll go and make some espresso." He headed for the door and turned, saying seductively, "Don't go to sleep on me, baby. You know I won't be able to leave you alone tonight."

Oohh, I've been on my feet all day, I'm not sure I can stay awake.

He returned with two double espressos. Suzy was curled up on the sofa.

He placed the coffee on the table and knelt beside her.

He slowly started to undress her, lifting her arm and extending the sleeve of her sweater to free it, tracing his fingers along her bare flesh as he did so. Then he pulled her forward, removing the other arm and lifting the sweater over her head. She smiled faintly at him, lacking the energy to protest. He kissed her shoulders and his fingers lingered at the top of the cups of her bra. He ran his hand round her back and unclasped it, casting it aside with the sweater.

"Stand up," he ordered quietly, and he held on to her hands as she complied, seeking his support. He knew she'd had nothing to drink and she was just tired, but he was determined not to let it consume her just yet.

He slid her skirt, tights and pants down together, realising she may not be standing long enough for him to do it in stages. He then allowed her the comfort of lying on the carpet, naked now, only just awake, and feeling a little cold.

He straddled her and gently kissed her lips, eyes, ears and neck. Slowly he eased himself down her body and began to move his tongue steadily and sensually over her breasts and along her abdomen, moving down to the soles of her feet, nibbling her toes, returning to lick her shins and thighs. He needed her taste in his mouth. He wanted to savour her, and then release himself in her. She was rising to his bait, warming to his touch, allowing herself to be aroused by the eroticism of his attentive actions. As he reached her labia she unconsciously widened the gap he had made between her legs, inviting him in. He parted her erogenous lips and tasted her wetness, revelling in her need to come, and, as he felt her hands in his hair, he diligently brought her to her climax, before desperately unfastening his trousers and entering her now eager body to take his pleasure. His gentleness had gone, but she was alert and craving him as he pushed into her, rapidly and hungrily, until he quickly released his semen inside her. He withdrew and lay on his back laughing, as he put his arm around her and pulled her towards him, kissing her with a deep, long-lasting kiss.

When he finally released her, she lay back. "I think you just seduced me, Mr Bane."

"I think the lady did not protest."

"This lady would like some more." She rolled onto him. "We need to get rid of these." She slid his jeans and pants down, then removed his sweater, exposing his own nakedness. He held his breath as she slowly stroked his firm abdomen with her vulva, before sitting on his penis to take him again. He did not disappoint. Now he was totally exhausted and spent.

"Take me to bed, my insatiable darling, you have truly knackered me."

Chapter 46

It was ten o'clock on Sunday morning, and they were seated at the back of the church. From the welcomes he got, Suzy realised Lawrence was a regular attendee, and this was where he usually sat. No wonder Steve had suspected her of keeping him away.

She had been surprised when Lawrence had suggested they go to church, and wondered about her own relationship with God since her parents had been killed. She had acquiesced, and as she sat in the pew, watching Lawrence praying privately before the service, she gave up her own prayer of thanks, for the fate that meant she had been in the bookshop the day he walked in, and that they had got to know and love each other in this short time. She asked for him to be kept safe. Maybe her own faith would be restored.

At the end of the service, Lawrence lingered in the church until most of the congregation had left, then sauntered over to Steve.

"It's good to see you both," the vicar greeted them, kissing Suzy on the cheek. "Coming back to the vicarage for a drink?"

"No thanks, Steve, we're gonna try and get out on the bike while the weather's not too bad. But do you and Jane fancy coming over to The Sway for a drink and bite to eat on Wednesday?" He looked at Suzy, and to her surprise, he asked, "Is that OK with you?"

"Sure." She wondered what had brought on this need for her approval; she was so used to him making most of the arrangements unilaterally.

"That should be fine. I'll check with Jane, and look forward to seeing you both then."

Lawrence had not told Steve of his impending disappearance. There were some parts of his past that he only shared with God, and not the middleman, as it were, and he didn't want his friend worrying about him or, worse, offering to help. But he did want Suzy to get to know Steve and Jane better, knowing they would be here to support her if the need arose.

When they got back from their bike ride, Christine met them in the kitchen. Without any fuss or exaggeration, she spoke about what a lovely holiday they'd had, and hoped poached salmon with peas and bacon was OK for dinner that night, as it was quick and easy to prepare. Lawrence had intended that she should have the night off, but she insisted that she wanted to get back into routine. Only he fully appreciated the irony of this, as they would only be here a few more days.

"The cleaning company are coming to see me tomorrow," Suzy announced as they were eating.

"You're not seriously cross with me for arranging for them to come to you, are you?" His expression told her he wouldn't believe her even if she said yes on principle.

"No. But you should have told me, discussed it with me. I only work part-time – I should really be able to keep my own house clean! If I got to spend more time there, that is."

He looked down, pretending to rearrange his napkin on his lap, so she didn't see the frown on his face. *Soon you'll be spending all your time there.*

"Well, you've got more work now with Winstons, and have you had any more responses to your advert or website?" He was suddenly conscious he had forgotten about her efforts to get more work. Did he need to speak to Lewis and Dan about that?

"I haven't gone live with my website yet. I thought I would leave it until after Christmas, and also see how it goes with Winstons. I think I'd like to get into a routine with that and then see what I can do freelance, as it were. Do you think I'm doing the right thing?"

"I'd like you right here with me, naked and ready all the time!" He raised an eyebrow, but there was no smile.

"You'll be lucky."

"That's what I was hoping!"

"We'd drive each other mad. I need to make you wait, at least some of the time." She had a go at trying to raise her own eyebrow.

He laughed. "What will you do about the bookshop if your translating work takes off? I'm sure it will. You portray an intelligent understanding of what you translate. I was really impressed with the work you did for me. You'll be an asset to any organisation."

Suzy was genuinely flattered. "Do you really think so?"

"You've already picked up on the fact Winstons need to consider French law and customs, rather than simply dictate to their French colleagues. You might find your remit getting bigger than just straight translation."

"Mmm, maybe. I'm hoping it's going to be a good opportunity for me, and I have you to thank for the contact."

"I know you can do it."

She was pleased with his confidence in her abilities, and she wanted to show him it was well placed.

"Well, it all kicks off tomorrow. I'll be working on my first assignment for them."

"Do you want me to take you home in the morning?" *Start to let her go...*

"Yeah, I think so." She suddenly realised she was missing his "arrangement". *When will I see you again?* "Has Steve confirmed about Wednesday?"

"He texted me to say yes. They're coming over at seven. When are you going to come back?" He looked at her now, and she felt he wanted to say something more, but he remained silent.

"I could come over on Wednesday afternoon, if you like?" She wondered why he wasn't dictating when she should be back or protesting that she would be away for two nights.

"Do that, and we'll cook together. OK?"

"Sure." She needed to analyse what was being said here and, more importantly, what *wasn't* being said. Something didn't feel right, but she couldn't quite put her finger on it. *Two nights without him!*

Two nights without her! How many more will I have to endure?

They lay awake until the small hours of the morning, neither daring to turn to the other, each seeking their own solace, with their own thoughts.

Chapter 47

He hadn't phoned. There had been no telephone sex. He hadn't emailed or texted her. He didn't call in at the bookshop on Tuesday.

It was Wednesday lunchtime, and Suzy felt apprehensive about going to him that afternoon.

She had made some more notes:

> *He's let two nights go by without contacting me.*
> *He hasn't dictated what we do.*
> *Two nights without contacting me.*
> *He hasn't updated the arrangement.*
> *Two nights without him.*
> *He isn't coming to pick me up.*
> *Two nights!!*
> *He's stopped controlling me.*
> *Two nights!!!*
> *Something was wrong.*

Lawrence read Dan's report of her movements.

Monday
9.30 a.m.: telephone call with Peter Dane of Winstons
3 p.m.: woman from Merry Maids cleaning company arrived
3.30 p.m.: woman from Merry Maids cleaning company left
7 p.m.: went to the gym
8.15 p.m.: left the gym, alone, and went straight home
Tuesday
8.40 a.m.: drove to the bookshop
11.45 a.m.: went to the deli for sandwiches, which she took back to the shop
5.45 p.m.: left the premises, alone, and drove straight home.

Lawrence read the email that had just landed, from Dogtooth:

Subject: Long Time
Sorted.

Lawrence transferred £1,000 to Dogtooth's account.

He stopped himself from racing to the door to meet Suzy as he heard her car pull up on the drive. He had spent the last two nights in his old single bed, which was now in the attic room, trying unsuccessfully to get a good night's sleep.

He stared out of the window and watched her get out of her Mazda with the grace he had come to love. He was regretting having this last week with her, thinking it would have been better to have just gone to London on Monday. Now he had to put himself, and her, through the next six days.

"Hi baby." He leaned in to kiss her tenderly on the lips, breathing in her smell. She was wearing his perfume. How long ago that evening at her cottage seemed.

"I … I've missed you." She spoke quietly and moved away from him, taking her coat and shoes off.

He watched her for a moment.

"I know," he said at last. *Do something, for fuck's sake!*

"Come on, we've got chicken fajitas and chocolate mousse to prepare." He grabbed her hand and led her into the kitchen. Suzy was relieved it was nothing too taxing. She was finding it very hard to concentrate.

"I've given Christine the day off." *Letting her have more time with Dave, before she has to leave him.*

"So what are we waiting for?" He held up "his and hers" chef's aprons. Suzy reached her hand out to take her apron. He shook his head and managed to display his schoolboy grin. "Not yet. You're overdressed." He raised his eyebrow.

Oh my heart! She beamed at him.

"We're going to cook naked?"

"Yep. First time for everything." For her, that is. He frowned slightly, trying to evade the memories.

They stood a few feet apart and watched each other as, hastily at first, they removed their outer clothing, and then worked in unison, each slowly revealing their bare torsos, and then finally facing each other naked. He stepped towards her and gently rubbed her body with his own, and they kissed each other appreciatively.

He fought back the urge to take her to bed.

He took hold of the apron and slid it over her head, tying it behind her back. She turned and stared into his eyes and they held each other's gaze. Then he put on his own apron and smiled tenderly at her. The atmosphere felt heavy. *What was he holding back?*

He broke the tension. "Let's get started." He gathered the ingredients for the chocolate mousse and placed them on the worktop. As he started to melt the chocolate over a pan of hot water, Suzy started to chop peppers and onions. It felt surreal to have their virtually naked bodies so close to each other without making contact. Was he planning something? Part of her hoped he was. She couldn't imagine going to these lengths simply to prepare a meal and then get dressed again!

She worked with her back to him and was vaguely aware of him moving around a little. She had finished the vegetables and started to wash the strawberries that would be served with the mousse. She felt his breath on her back and shuddered as he trailed a wooden spoon lightly down her spine. The play was beginning. She felt his tongue follow the spoon, and his hand came round inside the apron to cup her breasts, covering each one in some of the dark melted chocolate. She turned to face him and held a strawberry to his mouth, her face betraying her longing for him. He bit into the fruit as she held it up, and then she moved it into her own mouth and licked her lips provocatively. *Please don't resist me.*

He held his chocolatey hands up to her tongue and she licked, closing her eyes and savouring the taste of the chocolate, and him. She felt him undo her apron and lift it over her head. She reached out and unfastened his and he lowered his head as she freed him from it. He held the bowl of melted chocolate between them, and they each dipped their hands in, smearing it over each other's lips, placing fingers in each other's mouths and painting patterns on each other's bodies. He took her arms and held them. Slowly and laboriously he licked her clean. When he had completed his task he held his own hands out and stood before her so she could do the same to him. She looked up at him as she slowly knelt and took his now erect penis in her hands, gently pulling his foreskin back and forth, and then wrapping her tongue around it, trailing along it and then consuming it with her mouth. As his excitement grew, he pulled her up before lifting her onto him and pushing her against the wall. She gasped at the coldness of the tiles, and then began to invade his mouth with her tongue. Gradually they each reached orgasm and she clung to him, fearing he would vanish if she let go. *What is happening to us?*

"What about the food?" she whispered, barely caring, trying to dismiss the melancholy that hung in the air between them, and not wanting to be parted from him.

"Don't worry, there's some I prepared earlier." He smiled as he carefully withdrew himself from her and scooped her into his arms to carry her upstairs.

She placed her arms around his neck and brushed her cheeks against his chest. He was warm and smelled of chocolate.

They stood in the shower, jets of water shooting at them, and held each other, swaying to Adele's soulful voice singing "One and Only".

The water washed Suzy's tears away.

"Come on, baby." He led her out of the shower and dried her with a tenderness she had come to know and love.

They had twenty minutes to get the rest of the food ready and set the table.

They were done just in time to greet their guests with a glass of chilled Dom Perignon. The tension between the couple was gone now, and the four diners enjoyed each other's company, sharing the making of the fajitas and enjoying the delectable chocolate mousse (number one) with strawberries.

Suzy and Jane began talking about Julia Kershaw and the children.

"We had a lovely time with them on Christmas Day here, with Melanie beating everyone at table tennis. It's so nice to see that girl smile. Julia, Mike and Carolyn do a brilliant job for those kids."

"You know, I'd really like to get to know them a bit more, and maybe help in some way."

"I think it means a lot to them just to show some friendship, and treat them with some respect, especially the older ones. I can't help feeling sorry for Daniel. I think he's got a lot on his plate right now."

"Yes, I know. Lawrence told me about his chat with him. He's going to give him some work, so at least he'll have some money to help with the baby."

"From what Julia says, I think the young girl is from a pretty rough background herself. I believe her parents are already talking about the baby going for adoption, as they are not prepared to support her."

"Oh my gosh. What chance would it have in life?"

Lawrence picked up on this conversation.

"Do you know where they live? The girl's parents?"

"I think it's Macclesfield. Daniel met the girl at school."

Lawrence looked thoughtful, and Suzy wondered what he could be thinking. What more could he do to help?

"Melanie seemed very proud of you painting her nails, Suzy."

Suzy glanced at Lawrence and smiled.

"So, Suzy, Lawrence says you have a new contract with Winstons, for your translating. How is it going?" Steve joined in the conversation.

Suzy laughed. "I've sent over some memos on the latest results against budget, which the UK staff got before Christmas, and also about the group gaining a new distributorship. It was quite basic translation work, really. It's been good for me to start learning a bit about the company and how the two sides of the channel communicate with each other. Would you believe I got an email from the French *gérant* stating they already knew about the new distributorship! I think I need to meet the head of the French team and hopefully get some sort of relationship going with him and his staff. Something tells me I need to show some allegiance to their side!"

"That's the French for you!" exclaimed Lawrence, still not feeling happy about her going to Paris.

"Well, it sounds as though you're enjoying it, Suzy." Steve had not missed Lawrence's anxious look.

Suzy looked over to Lawrence, "Yes, I am."

As the guests were getting ready to leave, Jane invited Suzy and Lawrence over to the vicarage next Wednesday.

"That would be lovely." Suzy glanced at Lawrence, who appeared reluctant to respond.

"I think I have an oil lubricants dinner that evening." His eyes burned into Suzy. *Let her go. Let go of her.* "You go, Suzy."

Steve stared at his friend for a moment, sensing something wasn't quite as it should be.

"Yes, Suzy, you come. It will be a good opportunity for you girls to have a chat without hearing all about motorbikes. Jane, why not get Suzy's mobile number and you two can make arrangements." He turned to Lawrence. "Can I have a word before we go?"

Lawrence tried to think of an excuse not to have a one-to-one conversation with this man, who had helped him so much in the past, but he couldn't. He was definitely not on good form at the moment.

He led Steve into the office.

"What's wrong?" Steve moved over to the bank of TVs and looked at his own reflection in the blank screens.

"Nothing, Steve. Everything's fine," Lawrence lied.

"Are things OK between you two?" Steve had sensed some tension between the couple from the moment he and Jane had arrived at The Sway, but hadn't believed it to be anything acrimonious, more like a shared trouble for them both. But he knew from the look on Bane's face that he was not going to be told anything now. "You know you can talk to me, mate." Steve was very serious.

Lawrence was sitting on the end of his desk, and started to doodle with a pencil on his notepad. "It's OK, don't worry about me, Steve. I'm glad Suzy and Jane seem to be getting on well." He wanted to add *please look after her for me*, but didn't.

Chapter 48

When their friends had gone, Suzy started to clear the dishes from the dining room.

"I just need to do something. Back in a tick." Lawrence went back into his office and closed the door.

It was 10.30 p.m., but he knew Julia Kershaw was not an early-to-bed sort of woman.

"Hi, Julia, it's Lawrence."

"Hey. How are you? Happy New Year."

"Yeah, thanks, you too. Look, I just heard that the young girl may want to get rid of the baby." He paused.

Julia waited, wondering what he was going to say. After a few moments she broke the silence. "I believe she's not interested in it, and is getting no support from her family."

"Get Daniel to stay involved, and don't let them do anything. I…" He trailed off.

"Lawrence, it may be best for Daniel if the baby is adopted."

"Please, let me come over tomorrow. I need to talk to you about it. Tell me when's good for you, and make sure Dan's there."

"Better make it 4 p.m., he'll be back from school by then. Stay for tea."

"OK. That will be good. Thanks. See you then."

"Will Suzy be with you?"

"No, she will be working. See you tomorrow, Julia."

Seeing his office door shut, Suzy walked upstairs and started to get ready for bed. She was tired and emotionally drained. He was acting strangely and she couldn't cast off a feeling of trepidation.

She climbed under the duvet and curled up on her side to wait for him.

Lawrence walked through the bedroom and into his en-suite. Suzy lay in the moonlight as it shone through the balcony doors, and listened to him getting ready for bed, until finally the door closed, and he was wrapping his naked body around hers.

"Are you sleepy?" he asked, his voice emitting solicitude, rather than hopefulness.

I don't think he wants to make love tonight.

"Yes, I am a bit. Is it OK if we just go to sleep?"

"Of course. I'm feeling tired myself. It must be all that chocolate we ate earlier." She sensed he gave a weak smile.

She couldn't feel the hardness of his penis. How strange was the softness at her back. She turned over and faced him. She was about to ask him if everything was alright, knowing his answer would probably not quite be the truth, when he put his arms around her and kissed her tenderly, as though he knew her concerns and was trying to allay them.

His hands moved down her sides, feeling her soft skin, and he continued the tender kiss.

The words he'd said to her earlier echoed through her mind. *I love you, Suzy, and can't imagine having to live without you. I hope you remember our pact that the past is history. Would you wait for me if you had to?* His eyes were burning into her and his face was dark with sincerity.

The intensity of his words frightened her.

"Right now I feel I would wait for you until the end of time, Lawrence. I…" She took his hand and put it up to her lips. "My life would be so empty without you. You have become my world in such a short space of time. Do you have to go away? Can't I come with you?" She was applying her clinical tone, a matter-of-fact approach, as it seemed obvious he would be away for a while.

"I need to sort something out, that's all. I just wanted to know that you still love me."

"Of course I do. Don't be away too long, and make sure you text and ring me. Maybe we'll do telephone sex." She blushed a little as she smiled at him.

"Maybe." He strained to return the smile, knowing it wasn't going to be like that.

"Let's sleep," she said, feeling she couldn't manage any more of this conversation without her tears breaching her bravado. She turned her back to him. They lay curled together, and endured a restless night.

Chapter 49

At breakfast, Suzy suddenly remembered Dominic's invite for her and Lawrence to spend the evening with them. She had forgotten to ask Lawrence.

"Can you make the twelfth?" she asked, looking hopeful, and fearing some feeble excuse. She didn't think she could handle any more indications that he didn't want to be with her.

"OK." He didn't look up from the newspaper. "I need to speak to Richard today, so I'll confirm it."

Is that it? No conditions, no counter-proposal?

"What?" he asked, looking at her, and reading from her expression that he had said something wrong.

"Nothing. I just can't believe you've agreed to it so easily."

Lawrence felt he just couldn't win. He didn't want to fight any more, didn't want to dictate the rules to her. It was his way of starting to let go.

His laugh lightened the mood. "I haven't had a night out in Manchester..." he raised an eyebrow, remembering the dinner with the Underwoods. "Well, not a fun one, in ages." *And we'll enjoy these last few days; we've done enough moping about!* "See if we can go to a club or something, let's go dancing."

Suzy beamed. "Well, I'm not very good, but that sounds great. Should we stay at their apartment?" She remembered his gift and the telephone sex, and she challenged him with her eyes.

"Why not? I hope they've got soundproofing, 'cos after some good music I will not leave you alone." Raised eyebrow, no smile, and no questions – it was a done deal.

Suzy was relieved that he seemed to be back to normal.

Suzy left after breakfast to go to the bookshop. Christine started tidying the kitchen and then told Lawrence she was going to start closing up some of the rooms. She had also arranged for the pool to be drained on Monday. Lawrence just nodded and shut himself in his office. He rang Richard Groves.

"Hi Richard. Happy New Year to you."

"Cheers, Lawrence. I hear you had a good one."

"Mmm." Lawrence wondered what exactly Suzy had said to Dominic. "I believe we have an invite to yours for Saturday. Are you sure about it?"

Richard was aware that Bane was challenging him to commit to the evening, but he had already discussed the situation with Dominic and the two of them wanted to try to get a relationship going with him if Suzy wanted him to be part of her life for the long term. Richard had not been entirely honest with his partner about his concerns surrounding Bane's imminent disappearance, or how long he may be gone for, but he wanted to show him he was willing to try to have a more friendly relationship with Bane, for Suzy's sake.

"Suggest somewhere with good music and the chance of a dance." Lawrence was taking charge here, and Richard knew it.

"Sure. There's a place on Sackville Street where we'll all be comfortable. You guys going to stay over?"

"Yep," Lawrence replied firmly, and then added, "I appreciate it, Richard. Let's not get heavy about stuff, OK?"

"Sure." Richard realised it was getting close to him leaving, and Suzy having a good time was probably foremost in his mind. "I didn't know you were a clubber!"

"I'm not, but I've never been dancing with Suzy. I'm sure it'll be a good night." Lawrence sensed the atmosphere between the two of them was improving. "I just wanted to talk to you about something I've done."

"Yes?" Richard managed to maintain a tone of interest rather than accusation, not sure where this already strange conversation was going.

"I will be transferring one hundred thousand pounds to Suzy next week."

There was silence on the end of the phone. Richard had not been expecting this.

"I just wanted to ask you to give Suzy any advice she may want on where best to keep the money, unless she wants to spend it all, but I doubt she will. I just want to be sure she is OK. Tell her it's a rainy day fund."

"Don't worry. I'll talk to her. Have you spoken to her?" Richard wondered if he was asking too much.

"I think she thinks I'm going away on business. I don't want to lie to her, but that thought may help her to cope better. I would appreciate it if you and Dominic help her too. It will be temporary." *I hope!* "I just don't know how long." He omitted to say Suzy thought she would be able to communicate with him while he was away, but that wouldn't be possible.

Lawrence went upstairs to check that Christine was managing to put the dust sheets over everything in the spare bedrooms. His room and downstairs would be left for as long as possible. Suzy's suspicions must not be roused, and he planned to spend the last night at hers.

Christine worked efficiently and unemotionally. She was accustomed to hiding her emotions in the most extreme situations. She removed the clothes from the Top Shop bag and packed everything into a dark brown holdall. She placed this, together with an old rucksack, at the back of Lawrence's dressing room. Lawrence smiled as he threw her seven pairs of Armani trunks.

"Why don't you pack your dinner suit while you're at it?" she teased, grateful for something to make her smile. It was only the assurance that she would be with Lawrence that was keeping her going through these dark days.

Lawrence's phone rang.

"Hi, Lewis."

"Lawrence. Just picked up that Harry Rawlins is snooping around asking after you in Whitechapel. I guess we got it right on the location and where you're going to live, mate. They haven't got a bloody clue how much things have moved on. Just a pity you're not already there."

Lawrence knew Lewis was still cross that he had delayed everything by a week, and he was probably right to be.

"Look. I'll try and get down there for a couple of hours. Do you fancy a quick trip and a pint in the Black Dog?"

"When were you thinking?"

"Friday. I'll book the train and pick you up, probably about 9.30 a.m., but I'll confirm it. We'll come back about three in the afternoon. Dress down, I guess."

"You bet. See you then."
"Yeah, cheers."

* * *

Later in the afternoon, Lawrence drove over to Fairchance. His business affairs were pretty much in order now, and he had already advised the boards he was associated with that he may not be available to attend the next quarter's meetings. Richard Groves would go in his place, if necessary. He was tempted to ring Winstons to suggest it wasn't really appropriate for Miss Harper to go to Paris, at least not for a few months, but he knew that was not for the best: not for the company, the French team or Suzy. *Let go and trust her.*

"Make some coffee, will you?" Julia greeted Lawrence as soon as he walked into the kitchen. "I just need to file these papers."

Lawrence checked the board to see who was in the building and shouted up the stairs to Dan and Melanie to see if they would like a drink too. Melanie came running down to see him, and he remembered Suzy thinking she had a crush on him.

"Hi, Melanie. What would you like to drink?"

"Apple juice, please."

He noticed she was watching every move he made.

"How's your day been?"

"Good, thanks, Mr Bane. I'm just doing my science homework." With a flash of a smile she took the glass and turned and raced back upstairs.

"Be careful with the drink, honey," he called after her.

She turned back, beaming. "I will."

He smiled warmly after her, noticing she appeared a little more confident than usual. She wore a short-sleeved shirt, which was a good sign that she wasn't currently cutting herself.

Daniel just shouted down that he was OK and didn't need a drink. He obviously didn't want to face Bane right now.

Lawrence was about to go up to him, but thought it better to wait and talk to Julia first.

"OK, I can give you my full attention now." Julia picked up

her coffee and Lawrence followed her into the office, closing the door behind them. "So, Lawrence, just what are you thinking?"

He glanced out of the window and caught sight of the children playing in the garden. It gave him a moment to confirm his resolve about this baby.

"I want to be sure that this baby has the chance of a good start in life." He was looking directly at Julia and she could see he was serious.

"You need to consider the parents too, you know, and their chance for a good start in adulthood."

"I know. They're two young people with their whole lives ahead of them. You may be right that adoption or fostering could be the best thing. I agree. But if you're saying the mother's parents aren't going to help, what's to stop them handing it over to goodness knows who? How would Daniel feel as he grew up and wondered what had become of his own child?"

"Lawrence, the prospective carers would be vetted. And I'm not sure it's good for you to get too involved. I don't think Daniel needs too much pressure putting on him right now. He's hardly talked about anything other than working for you and riding a motorbike since Christmas. I'm not sure he's focused on earning money to pay for a baby, one he's probably hardly ever going to see, if he sees it at all!" Julia had raised her voice slightly, and then spoke more quietly, as she perceived Lawrence's resolve strengthening, despite what she said. "Perhaps it would be a good idea to speak to the girl and her parents and try to ascertain exactly what their intentions are for the baby. Maybe then we could discuss any options and include Daniel and the girl too."

"Julia, if nobody wants this baby then I would like to be in a position to be its guardian."

He was a little taken aback by the shock on his friend's face. *How can she not appreciate that I don't want someone to have the same start as I did?*

He went on. "Look. Get me the girl's name. I'll do some background checks on her and her family. Keep talking to Daniel and try to find out what he really feels; maybe talk to the school." He paused, wondering when – if – he would get his life back after his departure next week. Would there be time to go through any necessary legal processes by the time the baby was born?

"And do as you suggested, speak to the mother's parents. Let's at least know their initial thoughts. Please, will you keep me posted?" He needed to speak to Frazer Meadow, his lawyer, and to Lewis.

"OK. But don't rush into this, Lawrence. We all need to think about it and consider the options very carefully."

"I know. Can I talk to Daniel?"

"I think he's worried you're going to give him a hard time." She smiled as Lawrence raised an eyebrow in an "as if!" sort of way. "Go on up to him. He's probably sitting in his room waiting to hear you knock on his door anyway. Put him out of his misery!"

"Give me a chocolate bar. Maybe I need a peace offering for him." Lawrence headed upstairs armed with a Mars bar.

Lawrence avoided talking directly about the pregnancy to Daniel. He told him about the *Top Gear* show and the fastest cars in the world. Daniel relaxed a bit and admitted he was looking forward to working for Lawrence, and then volunteered that he had been talking to the expectant mother, whom Lawrence now discovered was called Kate, and that he was worried she might want to get the baby adopted. Lawrence got the distinct impression that Daniel was worried there would be no job for him if there was no baby to maintain.

After tea with Julia and the children he drove back to The Sway. He rang Frazer and asked him to send him information about guardianship and adoption, and the rights of an unmarried father. He knew he needed to speak to Suzy at some point too. What would she think of his plan?

Chapter 50

It was Friday. Having spent the night with Lawrence at The Sway, Suzy was going to stay and work on the Winstons' translations. She knew Lawrence had to go to London for a meeting, and she wanted to make the most of being alone to talk to Christine.

Christine had come over to prepare breakfast, and as Lawrence left to catch the train Suzy asked her if she would like some tea.

"I'd love to hear about your holiday." Suzy was already getting cups from the cupboard, to entice Christine to sit and chat for a few minutes.

She was relieved that her plan worked!

"It was wonderful, Suzy. We stayed in a small hotel in Soufrière with a swimming pool looking right out over the ocean. We went on a couple of excursions. One was a sky ride on a gondola, up through the forest canopy. You could see some beautiful flowers, and trees with massive vines hanging right down. I think Lawrence would have loved it. We visited some sulphur pools, where the water was so hot you could've boiled an egg!"

"Oh, it sounds lovely. Was it sunny the whole time?" Suzy remembered some of the torrential rainstorms in Cameroon.

"We had a couple of downpours, but to be honest it was quite refreshing, and it soon dried up. We were planning to go deep-sea fishing, but that was one of the rainy days so we didn't do it in the end."

"Oh. Do you enjoy fishing?"

"It was more for Dave, but I'll go along and have a try. I did catch a barracuda off Barbados one year." Christine smiled, looking proud of herself.

Suzy suddenly realised she had never heard Lawrence speak of travelling or holidays. "Does Lawrence ever holiday overseas?"

Christine looked at her thoughtfully. "No. To be honest, I don't think he likes to be away from here for too long." She paused a moment and sipped her tea.

Please don't close down on me!

"It's almost as though he's afraid of losing The Sway." Suzy perceived that Christine was actually just realising something about her employer and friend, something she hadn't considered before. "Of course, there's no reason to think he would." She got up to sweep some imaginary crumbs from the worktop.

Has Lawrence got money problems? Is that what all this talk of leaving has been about? Does he think I only want to be with him for his money? Suzy's mind was going into overdrive. She still had a small amount of savings from her aunt's inheritance money. He could come and live with her...

"Christine, has he got into financial difficulties?"

"What? No, of course not!" She actually laughed. But she stopped as she saw the look of anxiety and confusion on Suzy's face. "If he doesn't tell you something, it's for a reason. He only wants to protect those around him."

She knows he's not telling me something!

"Protect me from what? Is he trying to protect you, too?" Suzy's voice rose with exasperation.

"Yes," she replied solemnly. "It's what he does. I really have to get on with some work now, Suzy. I'm sure he will tell you what you need to know. Don't worry, honey." She took their cups and put them in the dishwasher.

Suzy sat for a moment, then walked as calmly as her shaking legs would allow into his office. She thought about sitting at his desk, but suddenly felt that she was intruding. In fact, her first thought was to turn his laptop on and look through his emails, but she couldn't bring herself to do it. In fact, she didn't feel comfortable in his office right now. She picked up her own laptop and went into the snug.

She reckoned she had a couple of hours' worth of work for Winstons. Lawrence wasn't expected to be home until five. She needed to speak to someone. She rang Steve Jameson.

"Hi Suzy, nice to hear from you. What can I do for you?"

He had a calming voice, typical of a vicar.

"Steve, you said I could talk to you. I would really appreciate it if I could come over."

He detected the anxiety in her voice. He had almost expected it of a woman choosing to get involved with Lawrence Bane.

"Of course. I'm at the vicarage. Or I could come over to you if that's easier?"

"No no, I'll come over. Is about two this afternoon good for you?"

"Sure. We'll see you then. Take care."

As she put the phone down, Suzy began to feel a little better already, and able to face getting on with her work, knowing she was at least trying to do something about the situation she was in. Surely Steve would know if Lawrence was in any trouble.

Chapter 51

Lawrence and Lewis walked into the Black Dog and ordered two pints of Guinness. The guy behind the bar did a double take.

"Bane! Is that you?"

Lawrence smiled. "Been a long time."

"Like fuck! Where have you been? What ya been up to, mate?"

"Oh, this and that. Still trying to get out of London but never quite managing it. Too many sweet pussies around." He winked, almost disgusting himself. *Thank God I got out of this life.*

"Well, I don't know which part of London you've been staying in, but I know it wasn't here!" The landlord looked around the bar and started laughing.

"He always was a lucky dick with the girls." Lewis joined in.

"You still guarding warehouses, then?"

"Yeah. But it's getting tough to find work, to be honest. How's it going for you?"

The chit-chat continued, and as the two men sat down with their drinks they kept on the lookout for old acquaintances, especially those who would also know Black and Rawlins, and made sure everyone got the message. They were back in these parts.

They couldn't wait to get back on the train to go home!

Lewis checked his phone. There was a message from Dan.

"Suzy's gone to Steve's." Lewis saw Bane's expression darken.

"He doesn't know anything, Lewis, so no fear of her finding anything out. I just wonder what made her go." He looked out at the passing countryside.

By the time he pulled up on the drive, Suzy's Mazda was also back, and he went into the house to find her. She was curled up on the sofa in the snug reading a book, his copy of *Inspired*.

"Hey baby, missed me?"

She looked up. *What's he wearing?* Hoody, jeans, not suitable for a business meeting, and definitely not Lawrence Bane attire!

She smiled and stretched out along the sofa, making space for him to lie next to her.

"Where've you been? You're very dressed down for a meeting!"

"Well, sometimes it's better to be ready for a quick getaway from some of the dodgy places Lewis decides to meet in. It doesn't do to stand out from the crowd."

He lay beside her on the sofa and started to play with her hair.

"You smell lovely." He nibbled at her neck. It was pure Suzy; no perfume. "Let's work out in the gym." This was an order.

He took her hand and led her along the hallway.

Suzy was in a place of inner calm. She had voiced her fears to Steve:

> He's going away.
> Is it me he's escaping from?
> Is it money problems?
> Is it something from his past?
> Is it a secret business deal?
> How long would he be gone?
> Would he come back?
> If he does come back, will he still want me?

Steve had listened patiently, letting her thoughts flow out into words, not commenting until she paused and looked at him expectantly.

He sat back for a moment, remembering that Lawrence was unable to come over with Suzy next week because of some function.

"Look, Suzy. I think you're right. Something is troubling him. Jane and I noticed it on Wednesday, but we are also certain that it is not because of you. I know he has never been close to anyone before, and I think he loves you, Suzy – he's never let anyone into his world the way he has with you. So don't worry on that score. I can see that you are good for him."

Suzy flushed a little, as she was pretty certain Steve knew Lawrence had renounced his celibacy.

"I doubt it's money, he's a very wealthy guy, and I know he's sharp when it comes to protecting that wealth, like all his possessions." Suzy looked at him, thinking back to what Christine had said, and even Lawrence himself. *Wasn't that why he wanted an arrangement in place with me? But why has the arrangement stopped?*

Steve continued, noticing that she was thinking about something, but not wanting her to become despondent.

"I think it must be some business deal, probably confidential and maybe sensitive, like a local development that residents might not like, some shopping mall that puts smaller shops out of business, perhaps. Anything like that won't sit easy with him, but at the end of the day he is an investor and a businessman, and he has obviously been very successful at it."

Steve omitted to say that he, too, was worried about his friend, and he was trying to convince himself that his behaviour could be due to some struggle of conscience with the ethics of some big business deal. Lawrence had not taken Steve up on his offer to talk, and Steve instinctively sensed that it wasn't because Lawrence had been busy with other things.

"I think the best thing we can do is be supportive and help him through what seems to be a difficult time for him. I think, for Lawrence, the best way to help is be normal, don't question him too much; just be patient and supportive where you can. Before we know it, everything will be back to normal and we'll both wonder what all the fuss was about." He smiled warmly and took Suzy's hand in his. "It was good to see you in church on Sunday. Did you enjoy the service?"

"Yes, it was very comforting and inspiring. It was probably just what I need at the moment. Thanks for this chat, Steve, I feel better for talking about it. It somehow doesn't seem so bad."

"Would you like to pray with me?"

Suzy looked hesitant. She had accused God of deserting her when her parents died. Now she came to think of it, she had abandoned Him. Was she entitled to ask Him for help now?

"He is always here for us, Suzy. We may sometimes turn our

back on Him, but He never abandons us. Don't forget Jesus' parable of the lost sheep, and the joy in Heaven for the sinner who repents. I think that is one of Lawrence's favourites."

He knelt with Suzy and asked for comfort and strength for both Suzy and Lawrence.

* * *

As Lawrence led her into the gym, Suzy was again ready to do anything for him.

"Let's shower first, baby, I feel dirty." He remembered some of the things he had said in the Black Dog, and it turned his stomach. He was definitely going to have to harden up, for the next few weeks at least.

As they dried each other, he licked his lips, and his eyes shone. She didn't think she had seen that since he got back from the *Top Gear* show!

"I'll go and get the box." Now Suzy's eyes shone, and she made her way to the door.

Lawrence remembered the holdall at the back of his dressing room. "It's OK. You get comfy on the bench a moment, I'll go."

Suzy was too excited to sit down. She twirled in front of the mirrors, her fingers stroking her heart pendant, and she saw her panther ring reflected in the glass. She did not doubt his love for her.

He strode back in, carrying the box.

"Let me fuck you, Suzy."

"Please!" She smiled lustfully and stood waiting.

He took the handcuffs and approached her. "Remember to say 'red' if you want to." She nodded as he placed the cuffs on her wrists. He momentarily unfastened the connecting chain and pulled her by it over to the lat pull-down machine. He put the pin in the bottom weight. The bar was going nowhere. Now he raised both her hands and put the cuff chain around the bar, securing her hands above her head, leaving her facing the machine, and the mirror.

"Comfy?" he asked softly.

A question! She pulled down slightly, but it was secure. "Yes." She panted, almost breathless with anticipation.

She watched his reflection as he walked back over to the box and returned, cradling the flogger. She gazed at him as he raised his hand and trailed the tails down her back, creating a light tickling sensation. She closed her eyes and pushed her head back for a second, before opening them and seeing him watching her silently, a look of appreciation on his face. He was focused on her desire, and sensed she wanted more. He brushed the flogger from side to side, the tails just wrapping slightly round the side of her waist, and brought the palm of his hand to press on her skin to take away the stinging. He leaned into her throat, licking it, and asked, "OK?"

"Yes," she replied fervently, as her eyes burned through the mirror into his reflection.

He brought the leather tails down onto her skin a little harder this time, and as she winced he rubbed his body onto hers, swaying and swinging his hips, as if dancing with his shackled captive.

He breathed into her ear, "Are your arms OK?" As she nodded, he moved around in front of her, lifting her to sit on his penis and pumping himself into her. As he withdrew, she felt his juice begin to trickle down her thigh. He reached up and released her, and then lay her on the floor. He tenderly mixed his juices with her own and diligently and amorously coaxed her into a slow, exquisite orgasm, which sent the most wonderful sensations through her body, leaving her smiling, breathless and very, very happy. *What could possibly be wrong between them?*

"I need some more." He raised her onto her hands and knees and entered her from behind. It was hard and intense, and he tried to make it last. He didn't want to leave her body, but finally he gasped through gritted teeth as he poured into her once more, at the same time fingering her clitoris until she cried out as she reached orgasm again. Staying inside her, he eased them both onto their sides, and they lay on the wooden floor, wrapped around each other.

Suzy moved her hand down to feel his balls.

"After that workout, I need to go to bed. Take me, Mr Bane."

"With pleasure, Miss Harper."

Chapter 52

Lawrence parked his Jag under Dominic and Richard's apartment block. They were meeting the boys there for a drink before going to the bar on Sackville Street. Suzy was excited, and felt good in her short silk leopard-print dress and tassled stiletto sandals. They made her feel she belonged to her man, and his expression when he picked her up showed he thought so, too! He wasn't too sure about wanting anyone else to see her looking this good but, what the hell, they were going to have a great night out.

Dominic let them in.

"Wow, you look good!" He kissed his cousin. "Rick's in the kitchen getting some drinks; go on through." He had to admit Bane looked good, too, in a distressed black Armani T-shirt featuring the silhouette of a motorcyclist, and slim black trousers. The men shook hands.

"Hey, you OK?" Richard greeted them as he opened a bottle of Moët & Chandon. "Late Christmas celebrations!" He smiled as he handed out the glasses and gave Suzy a kiss, "Here's to us!" He started laughing as he realised he had the same T-shirt on as Lawrence. "I believe this is normally a girl thing! I'll change, or someone might get the wrong impression!"

Lawrence laughed and raised his glass. "Cheers for that. Good taste, all the same."

Lawrence admired the two men for the naturalness of their relationship. Suzy had said they'd been together over five years, and they seemed to be well suited. The apartment was minimalist, spacious and bright. There were two laptops on the island in the kitchen, and it was obviously the hub of the place. He admired the sleek black glass induction hob in the cream worktop.

"So who's the chef?" he asked.

"We both are. I hear you're pretty good, too." Dominic recalled Suzy saying he had been on a course with Christine. "Do you experiment much?"

"Not so much. We haven't done much entertaining." He looked at Suzy. "Yet. I guess we'll make more of an effort as spring gets under way." Suzy immediately picked up on the reference to being together then.

The atmosphere was friendly, relaxed and jovial, especially as Dominic recounted some of their successful and not so successful gourmet experiments.

Lawrence could sense the family bond between the three of them. Could he get on the inside of that? They were certainly making him feel comfortable and accepted. Would it be different if they knew more about him? He wondered for a fleeting second if Suzy may have said anything, but then felt certain she wouldn't. Maybe he should check with her if she felt she needed to talk to anyone. He was quite a lot to take on, and she had done it so brilliantly. He suddenly reached out to take her hand, and he was a little surprised when Richard leaned in and kissed Dominic.

"It's Dominic's birthday." Suzy informed him.

"You could have told me, we should have got a gift and card."

"We did. Sorry, I didn't get the chance to tell you." She pointed to a soft black leather wallet on the worktop.

"Come on, then." Lawrence was feeling more relaxed than he'd dared to hope. "Let's get going and celebrate!"

The four found a relatively quiet table, and Lawrence brought a bottle of champagne and some glasses over. "May as well carry on with the good stuff."

The bar was busy, with both gay and heterosexual couples, and possibly some who weren't too sure which way to go. The music was loud, with a good mix of indie rock, dance and pop.

Lawrence dragged Suzy onto the small dance floor for Coldplay, Lady Gaga, Jessie J, and anything else that took his fancy. The boys joined them too, and by the early hours of the morning, several bottles of champagne later, a shoeless Suzy was hanging onto Lawrence's neck and swaying to "Where is the Love?" They decided that was a good time to call it a night, and hailed a cab back to the apartment.

With Suzy propped on a bar stool the three men accepted the challenge of creating a quick chicken curry.

Lawrence gently laid his girl in bed at 3.30 a.m. He had accepted that there would be no action in this room for the time being. But, hopeful for the morning, he was quick to note that their bedroom was sufficiently far away from the boys' master bedroom!

Chapter 53

Thick-headed and looking slightly worse for wear, they sat round at the kitchen island on Sunday morning, sipping coffee and eating eggs, bacon and toast.

"It was a good night. Thanks for having us over." Lawrence felt so much a part of a couple with Suzy, and a member of this private family. He hadn't expected that. Richard had not referred to his imminent departure, and he was praying more and more that it wouldn't be for long. But come Tuesday he would need to start to confront things. Miranda, Rigsby and, of course, Black.

* * *

The clock struck eleven as Lawrence and Suzy arrived at the church, just in time for the service. Steve was pleased to see the two of them together. Suzy confirmed that she would go over to the vicarage on Wednesday. Lawrence would not be around.

When the hungover couple got back to The Sway, they both went back to bed for a couple of hours. Lawrence had never done that before, but when he awoke at about two o'clock his headache had gone, and he felt refreshed and happy as he reached out to Suzy at his side. "Are you awake, baby?"

"Mmm. Better had be, I suppose. I feel a bit better. I think!" she smiled.

"Let's swim."

"It might be more of a float!" she yawned. "And a Jacuzzi. I'll race you down there." She scrambled to get to the top of the stairs before him. Having succeeded, he picked her up and she giggled, shouting, "Not fair!" as he lifted her off her feet and swung her round. Once he'd got in front of her he jumped down the stairs three at a time and dived into the pool, shouting back to her, "What's keeping you?"

Suzy dive-bombed him, and he caught her under the water, raising her up like a ballerina, and bringing her back down, stroking her body with his own.

"You're distracting me! I'm trying to swim here!" He plunged her back into the water. She grabbed his foot and provocatively lifted it to her mouth, nibbling his toes.

"You know what? I'm starving."

Lawrence, now in predatory mode, dived down, and she could feel him running his hands up her legs. Oh wow! She felt his fingers inside her… *Is this good for the pool water?*

He didn't give a damn about the water; it was being drained tomorrow.

When the pool shenanigans were completed, Lawrence decided they would shower in his room rather than the pool changing rooms, and it was another race upstairs. As he waited at the top for her, Suzy observed his raised eyebrow, accompanied by the gleam in his eyes.

"And just what did you have in mind?" she asked, wondering just how much physical activity she was capable of today.

"Follow me!" He led her into the en-suite. "Put your arms out and spread 'em, baby."

Her eyes followed him as he took a hard bristled brush from the drawer and got down on his knees, methodically body-brushing his girl, awakening her skin with the tingling he created. She closed her eyes and listened to his melodious humming of "Let Me See Beneath Your Beautiful". By the time he had reached her shoulders she thought she would climax any second, and he hadn't even touched her there.

"Your turn," she whispered, almost breathless with desire to touch him. She had studied his movements, and she replicated them over his body, replacing the brush with her tongue as she licked around his balls and along his penis, feeling the pressure from his strong hands on her shoulders as she continued. The brushing ceased for a few minutes until she could taste him in her mouth. She then made him stay still while she completed the task of brushing his body.

"Dear God, Suzy, what are you doing to me?"

"I want to keep you." She repeated his words from Christmas back to him.

Just until tomorrow, baby! His thoughts consumed him.

Chapter 54

After an early night, plenty of sleep, and a cooked breakfast, Lawrence announced they were going to Chester zoo.

He needed to be distracted, with no time to brood over his departure. Everything was on schedule, and he would spend this evening at Suzy's, so Christine and Dave could finish closing up The Sway. The Jag would be collected in the morning and Dave would drop him and Christine off at the station. Dave knew they had some unfinished business to attend to in London. He didn't want to know any more, and had warned his employer in no uncertain terms that he was to take good care of Christine, and that he was hopeful she would finally agree to marry him when they returned home.

No pressure then! Lawrence had thought to himself.

Suzy was on cloud nine. Yesterday had been wonderful, and today she was here with him at one of his favourite places. Her concerns about him leaving had been replaced by confidence, partly because of what Steve had said that it was some business arrangement and he would be back in a week or two. She could handle that. In fact, it would give her time to finalise her website and see if she could drum up more translation work. She was really enjoying working with Winstons, and one more similar assignment, together with her work at the bookshop, would be enough to keep her fully occupied. She also had her trip to Paris to look forward to. It was all booked for Wednesday, the thirtieth of January. Peter Dane had volunteered to accompany her, but Suzy felt her acceptance by the French would be easier if she went alone. She could converse in French the whole time, and also get to know more about the business from the French team, without any possibility of prejudice from the English! Yes, things were looking up, and she felt ready to take on the world.

She had also secretly taken the flogger from the box and was looking forward to an erotic and sexy evening. She pressed her hand against her bag, feeling naughty and excited about the toy that lurked within, and she squeezed Lawrence's hand. Oh, how time had moved on, and Suzy Harper had grown up in the last few weeks.

It was only natural that they visited the jaguar house first. Suzy was not feeling at all hopeful of catching a glimpse of the big cats, but Lawrence had no such pessimism and, hey presto, strolling right along the glass in front of them, they could almost reach out and touch the black panther. Suzy could have sworn it hesitated and stared at Lawrence for a moment. But surely not!

"You see!" he exclaimed like an excited schoolboy. "Oh, ye of little faith! Come on." He wrapped his arm around her and led her back out into the cold.

With orang-utans, cheetahs, lions, tigers and chimpanzees all ticked off the list, Lawrence led them over to the far side of the zoo, in search of the African painted dogs. Previous experience had taught him that these animals were very elusive, far more so than the panthers and jaguars. He also knew that it was very quiet over there, a little off the beaten track, especially on cold January days. After staring through the glass trying to spot one of the dogs, Lawrence led Suzy into an enclosed area and pulled her to him. He enveloped her in his arms and began to kiss her, inserting his tongue tenderly at first, and then increasing its intrusion further and further until she struggled for air as his need intensified. He was suddenly unfastening her jeans and his hands invaded her knickers, his fingers entering her vagina, loosening and moistening her. He withdrew them and licked them hungrily.

She felt conspicuous and nervous. "Not here!" she whispered, sensing he couldn't get enough of her here without risk of being arrested.

"Can I take you back to yours?"

"Please do." She pushed her tongue into his mouth now, alerting him to her own need.

He squeezed her tightly and finally broke their hold. "Come on, let's go."

By the time they got to the top of her staircase they were both naked.

"Wait here." She was in command mode, and disappeared downstairs, returning a second later with her bag. She led him into her bedroom and he stood with his arms folded as he watched her pull a pair of black tights from her drawer.

"Lie on the bed, face-down."

He raised an eyebrow.

"Please." He obeyed, and she straddled his back. She then tied his hands to the metal headboard with her tights. Slowly and rhythmically, she made patterns on his back with her vulva and he raised his head, turning back to see her, and murmured in pleasure.

"Does that feel good? Am I doing it well?" She sought his approval.

"Oh yes, baby, you're doing just fine." He lowered his head and arched his back slightly, intensifying the connection with her.

Then he felt her shift to the side and became aware she was reaching for something. He didn't try to see, but closed his eyes as his cheek lay on the pillow. He moaned in exquisite pleasure as he felt the leather tails brush across his back. He had so wanted this, but had been afraid to ask her. He had assured her he wouldn't ask her to hurt him again after that night at the Hilton. Now he didn't have to ask. And he loved her a little bit more.

She laughed softly as she sensed his excited anticipation, and she leaned forward to his ear. "Remember the safe word is 'red'."

"Go for it, baby." He lay outstretched before her as she brought the flogger down onto his beautiful skin, watching him heave and sigh and hearing his moans of pleasure.

She let the flogger perform its duty, watching as the marks began to appear on his flesh, and it was as if she were a mere observer of her man taking his erotic delight in this masochistic act. He raised his back and forced her to move down to hover over his legs. He lifted himself onto all fours, and she read his instruction, bringing the tails across his buttocks, and he held himself up, wanting more.

Then he flipped himself over and, despite being tied to the bed, he was suddenly in command.

"Mount me." It was an order. She lifted herself onto his hard penis and began to ride and ride. She leaned forward, kissed him and bit at his lip as he strained against the tights to touch her, but his efforts were in vain.

He gasped as he came inside her, and she closed her eyes and revelled in her power over him.

You can't leave me now! She was confident of her hold over him.

"Come and sit on me." He was commanding again. "On my face." He stared at her intently, daring her to disobey. She did not, and she screamed as he hit her favourite spot. Having drained every last sensation out of him, she fell onto the bed at his side.

"Red," he said as she released his hands, and he rolled on top of her, entering her again, taking her roughly and superbly until they climaxed together.

Chapter 55

The next morning after breakfast, Suzy gave him a quick kiss and watched him drive away in his Jag, as she climbed into her own car to go to the bookshop. He said he might call in at the shop, otherwise he would see her later. She remembered he didn't say where.

Lawrence went to his bedroom, which was darkened by the shutters across his balcony. He stripped and sat quietly on the floor. Twenty minutes later, he rose, devoid of the present incarnation of Lawrence Bane. He had returned to the one who had been in London, living alone, sleeping around, trying to forget his life of prostitution while he made his fortune on the stock markets. This was how he would cope, with nothing to remind him of what he had left behind. He put on his Top Shop clothes. He took off his Tag Heuer watch and left it on his bedside table.

The guy from the Jaguar garage arrived and Lawrence gave him the keys. The sale proceeds were being forwarded to Fairchance and the drop-in centre.

By 11.30 a.m. all the windows of The Sway had been shuttered. Dave pulled away in the pickup truck, taking Lawrence and Christine to the station for their train to Euston. Lawrence made his way to the platform, leaving Christine to say her private goodbyes to Dave before she joined him.

He squeezed her hand. "Let's get on with it, shall we?"

They were both quiet on the train. Christine was nervous of how things would go in London, but comforted that she was with the man who had saved her from it all three years ago. Lawrence was desperate to get on with trying to prove that Black had murdered Jimmy, and struggling to come up with something that would save him from being accused of stealing £100,000 from Veronica Rigsby.

On arriving at Euston, he retrieved the keys to their digs and they made their way to Old Montague Street, Whitechapel. For the second time that day, he squeezed Christine's hand as they crossed the threshold into the rented one-bedroom flat in the high-rise apartment block. The dim lighting revealed a dark brown two-seater sofa-bed, an armchair, a heavily scratched drop-leaf dining table with two chairs, a cupboard-sized kitchen with two gas rings on a grubby-looking hob, a microwave oven, toaster and small fridge. There was a single-basin stainless steel sink and a small set of drawers. The bedroom was just big enough to accommodate a single bed and a small chest of drawers – more than big enough to hold all their possessions for their current existence. There was a small cloakroom with a toilet and washbasin. The bathroom was situated down the corridor, and shared with the other tenants.

Lawrence's heart sank as he saw tears trickle down Christine's cheeks. He took her hand

"Come on, let's go and get a drink."

Chapter 56

By four o'clock that afternoon, Suzy was beginning to realise that Lawrence wasn't going to call in at the shop. She had arranged with Alison to go to the gym, and she rang Lawrence and left a message asking if she should come over to The Sway that evening.

On leaving the gym she checked her phone for any response from her boyfriend. Nothing.

She made her way back to her cottage and checked it again. Nothing.

She rang him as she climbed into her bed. Nothing.

She texted him to say goodnight. Nothing.

The morning came. Nothing.

Suddenly, she thought of their earlier conversation. *When are you going?... In about a week.*

Things had been so good between them that she had lost track of time.

The week had gone.

She got in her car and drove to The Sway. The pickup truck was parked at the gatehouse. She hadn't ever seen it there before. Panic rose as she continued along the driveway and saw the shuttered windows of the house.

He doesn't even like having the curtains drawn!

She got out of her car and ran round to the back of the house. More shuttered windows and doors.

There was a man up a stepladder installing what looked like a security camera.

Why?

"Do you know where Mr Bane is?"

"Bane? Sorry love, no. We're doing this for the new owner, John Ryder."

What? Suzy sank onto the patio. She felt numb. The house loomed over her; sad, gloomy, blindfolded from the daylight.

She gazed out at the gardens and over to the wood.

She saw Dave heading towards her along the path leading from the pond. He sat down next to her.

"He's gone, hasn't he?"

"They both have."

The sorrow in his voice made her face him, and she was shocked to see that he too had been crying.

"What do you know?" she asked quietly, now regaining her composure, her clinical tone giving her a trace of bravado.

"Not much. They've gone back to London." He suddenly felt weak next to her apparent strength. He got up to leave. "I'll still be at the gatehouse if you need me."

"Do you know John Ryder?"

"Never heard that name before." He walked away.

Suzy returned to her car and sat for a moment, gripping the steering wheel.

What have you done?

Conversations started to swirl around her mind. *If I did need to go somewhere, I would try to come back to you. As soon as I could.*

When some things need to be done, wrongs to be righted, and we have an ability to do that, then God would want us to try, don't you think so?

What are you trying to do, Lawrence? Deep down, she felt he hadn't deserted her. Not forever.

She drove home and formulated her own plan. She had some work to do for Winstons, and she felt the connection with him.

She was seeing Steve and Jane later, and she felt the connection with him.

And suddenly the name Lewis Deane of Blue Securities came into her head, and she felt the connection with him.

She had two short translations to do for Winstons, and she confirmed her travel arrangements to Paris on Wednesday, the thirtieth of January to Peter Dane. She would come home on Friday, the first of February.

Then she googled Blue Securities and rang the number asking to speak to Lewis Deane.

"I'm sorry," Angela replied. "He's away from the office until Friday. Can anyone else help? I can get Mr Deane to ring you if it's urgent."

Was it urgent? She didn't know yet, and she was determined not to panic.

"It's OK. I'll ring back later."

"Can I take your name and I'll let him know you called?"

"No, it's OK, thanks." Suzy put the phone down.

It was now 3.30 p.m. She had said she would be with Steve and Jane for 5 p.m., but surely they wouldn't mind if she was a bit early.

* * *

"Hi Suzy, come on in. It's lovely to see you." Jane couldn't help noticing the anxiety in the young woman's eyes. "Let's go and find Steve."

"He's gone," Suzy murmured through the lump in her throat as Jane led her into Steve's cluttered but welcoming office. He went straight over to her and put his arm around her as the sobs finally came.

He led her to the sofa and shooed a black-and-white cat off the cushions.

"Let's have some tea, please, Jane." He sat down next to his crying guest. "OK, Suzy, when you're ready, let's talk. Take your time, honey." He held her hand and passed her a box of tissues. He watched her as she played with the panther ring on her finger. He didn't need to guess who that was from. After a couple of minutes the tears subsided and Suzy tried to smile through her now sore eyes.

"Dave says they've gone to London. And I think he may have sold The Sway."

Steve looked down at her hands again as he took on board what she was saying. "What exactly did Lawrence tell you?"

"He hasn't told me anything. Except… about a week ago, he said he may have to go away … and that he would try to come back to me as soon as he could." Her voice was shaky and she tried to block out the image of his green eyes penetrating her soul.

"Right, let's focus on that, Suzy. He won't have lied to you. What makes you think he's sold The Sway?"

"All the windows at the house have been shuttered. There was somebody putting up a security camera, and he said it was for the new owner, John Ryder."

Steve had never heard that name before. His next thought was to ring Lewis. But perhaps he'd do that when Suzy had left. He remained thoughtful, and the silence was broken as Jane brought in the drinks and joined them. Steve filled her in on the events so far. Then he aired his own thoughts.

"I think there is something from his past that has to be dealt with. That can be the only explanation for him taking Christine with him. He has obviously felt unable to discuss it with any of us, and that will be his way of dealing with it, and possibly protecting us." He looked at Suzy and glanced, knowingly, at Jane. "I find it hard to believe he will have sold The Sway. That house is such a big part of him, and I think there would have been rumours going around the village. I'm sure we would have heard. I don't know who John Ryder is, but there must be a good explanation."

Suzy sipped her tea and was glad of Steve and Jane's friendship and support.

Chapter 57

Lawrence read Suzy's goodnight text, then threw the SIM card into the icy water below the bridge.

After a very restless night, Lawrence and Christine were sitting in the Black Dog with Lewis and one of his security men, Ian Pritchard. Ian was going to be working closely with Lawrence in London, while Lewis returned to Manchester.

Lewis updated Lawrence on the latest report from Dan. Lawrence remained silent as he heard that Suzy had gone to The Sway, spoken with Dave and then later that day went to see Steve and Jane. He also knew she had confirmed her trip to Paris. She would be travelling alone, apart from Dan, of course!

Lewis continued. "I've spoken with the unsolved crimes unit, which deals with cold cases, and they've given me a copy of everything they have on Jimmy's disappearance. It's not much." He looked at Lawrence, who was studying his untouched pint of Guinness. "But at least it's a start. It would appear our initial thoughts about the football stadium may be correct. The police believe that's the last place he was seen. I'm waiting for copies of the CCTV footage."

Lawrence looked up. "Let me go through it." He knew his eye for detail and his ability to absorb images and retain large amounts of data were second to none. And he needed something to focus on. "We must make sure people know what we're doing, especially Rawlins. If Black thinks we're on to him, he may well want to make sure he hasn't left any loose ends. We need to be ready." He looked directly at Ian and then Lewis, knowing that most criminals have the urge to return to the scene of their crime.

He was disappointed that he didn't know more about Ian Pritchard. It had slipped off his radar, and he was beginning to feel nervous about what else may have slipped since Suzy had come into his life and bowled him over.

He began to drink his pint, and reached for Christine's hand. She was sitting quietly by his side, trying to focus on what the men were saying, desperate to have some distraction from the memories that were starting to haunt her.

After a couple of hours Lawrence and Christine left the Blue Securities guys and made their way back to their digs. As they sat staring at the discoloured wallpaper, Lawrence rang Lewis.

"Get us a fucking TV and sort the licence out ... please." At least it made Christine smile.

For the next two days, Lawrence hung around the flat waiting for the CCTV footage to arrive. It didn't appear.

Lewis was due back in Manchester on Friday. That morning he went to see the guy in charge of the cold case.

"Lewis, I'm sorry. The tapes appear to have been misplaced."
"What?"
"They're not in the evidence box."

"I don't fucking believe it! We've been discussing this case for the past couple of months. I spoke with the detective on Monday and went through the evidence you had. He said he would get me copies of the tapes."

"Well, now he's discovered they're not here. The case hasn't been looked at for the last four years, Lewis. We are investigating the error. I'm really sorry."

"You will be when Bane finds out!"

"Let me speak with the desk sergeant and see what our records show."

"Call me as soon as you've got anything. I'm going to have to go and break the news. I hope there's a bloody good explanation!"

Lewis made his way to Old Montague Street.

"How's the TV?" he asked, as Christine let him into the flat.

"It works." She smiled. "He can't sit still long enough to watch anything. He's gone for a run, by the way. Are you going to wait? I can make some tea, if you'd like."

"Sure, and tea would be good."

A few minutes later, Lawrence entered the room. His smile on seeing Lewis soon disappeared when he saw his troubled expression.

"Have you got the tapes?"

"They appear to have been mislaid," Lewis replied quietly and took another sip of his tea.

Lawrence grabbed a towel. "I'm going for a shower. Will you wait?"

"Sure. I've warned Angela I won't be back until later tonight. And there's nothing in the office that can't wait. Take your time, mate."

Lewis had taken in his friend's unshaven face, darkened eyes and gaunt appearance. Lewis wanted his friend, client and investor in good shape.

As Lawrence left the room, he looked over at Christine. "He needs to eat more."

"Tell me! I can't force-feed him, you know. He hates it here." She looked around the small room. "We both do. And he's missing Suzy. He's barely glancing at Dan's reports; it's almost as though he'd rather not know what she's doing."

Lewis looked sheepish as he cut in. "She's rung the office. I haven't told him. There was no message, but I'm expecting to hear from her. She seems a bright woman and I think it won't take long for her to associate me with him. And then there'll be questions!"

"Probably best he doesn't know, not until you know something more concrete. He'd probably have her under house arrest if he could! He needs those damn tapes. He needs something to do." Christine was becoming agitated, trying to keep a feeling of hopelessness at bay, and dreading the approach of the twenty-third of January, just five days away, when Josh Black would be released. "I've made some chilli." She laughed, almost hysterically, as she pointed out the limited kitchen facilities. "It's one of his favourites. Join us and I'll dish it out when he comes back."

With perfect timing, Lewis's phone rang and he spoke briefly with the detective.

As the three of them ate lunch, Lewis updated Lawrence with what he had discovered.

The evidence box had been booked out three years ago. The signature looked like it could have been a contact of Harry Rawlins. It would seem the box was returned, minus the tapes.

"It could be that Josh Black's got them." Lewis looked directly at Lawrence. He was amazed when, after considering the situation for a moment, his friend said calmly, "OK, leave it with me. Get back to Manchester and I'll call you."

Lewis shot a questioning look at Christine, who shrugged. Lawrence was up to something, and she hoped it wasn't something stupid.

As Lewis was leaving, Lawrence walked down the stairs with him and went over to the pay phone on the corner of the street. When Lewis had said the police tapes were missing, Lawrence had remembered the conversation he'd had with Lewis and Miranda in the hotel room at Manchester Airport. Their suspicions that Black had murdered Jimmy were based on Black's words to Lawrence the night he attacked Christine: "You'll end up like Jimmy when I get my hands on you, Bane." They all knew the police were doing nothing about the investigation. So it was up to them to find out where Jimmy was now – or, rather, where his body was.

Now Lawrence wondered who had that CCTV footage. Why did Miranda seem so confident that she had what he needed? He started to put two and two together and prayed he was right.

He rang Miranda.

Chapter 58

By Thursday morning, Suzy realised Lawrence's phone had been disconnected, and she had received notification of failed deliveries on the emails she kept sending.

He had disappeared.

She rang Dominic. "Please, Dominic. I know he's somewhere in London, and I have to find him."

Dominic sighed on the other end of the phone. "I'll come over tonight and we'll get an early train in the morning. I'll book a hotel for a couple of nights. We'll talk about this when I get there." As he put the phone down, he thought, I must be mad. And what will I tell Richard?

Chapter 59

It was Saturday morning, and Lawrence finally had a shave. Christine wondered why. He hadn't bothered since they'd arrived in London. Wearing his Top Shop jeans, white T-shirt, dark brown hoody and grey trainers, by 9 a.m. he was ready to go. He spoke earnestly to Christine as he left the flat.

"Don't go out if you can help it. It may be late when I get back, but don't worry. And keep the door locked, OK?" He leaned in and kissed her on the cheek. "I'll see you later."

He pulled his hoody up and set off.

* * *

Lawrence stepped into the lift and pressed the button for the fifth floor. He was alone now, and had approximately one minute until he would reach the apartment. He closed his eyes, trying to clear his mind and find an inner strength before he crossed the threshold and became consumed by memories of his former life.

As the lift doors opened he saw a door with the brass digits 504 directly facing him. He crossed the landing and instinctively turned the door handle, certain that it would be open and that she would be waiting for him. Strange that he was the visitor this time. These rooms had been his home for almost eight years, although it had been more like a prison than a home most of the time.

He stepped over the threshold, closed and locked the door behind him, and slowly walked into the lounge. Miranda Cleveley was sitting on a deep purple velour sofa, flicking through a magazine. She carefully closed it and placed it on the coffee table. As Lawrence watched her, he noticed the worn notebook on the table and his heart sank. She was going to play games with him.

"Hello, Lawrence." Her light grey eyes shone as she took in the man standing before her and her thin, red-painted lips curled into a lascivious smile.

"Hello, Miranda." His voice was impassive. He looked directly at her, and thought she had aged more than he'd expected during the eight years since he left her. He didn't remember noticing that when he saw her at the airport. She was wearing a loose-fitting velour jacket and trousers in a pale lilac. She blended in perfectly with the décor of purples, blues, golds and yellows. Nothing in the room was familiar. He wondered momentarily about the rest of the apartment.

She noticed him taking in the room. "Do you like what we've done with the place?"

He felt a slight relief at the use of the term "we". *At least she isn't alone.*

He forced a slight smile. "Well, it's different, though not quite my taste." The austere black-and-white look she had allowed him to choose flashed through his mind.

Miranda threw her head back and let out a mocking laugh. "Don't worry, dear, not everything has changed." Her look challenged him to question her.

He wasn't quite ready to play her games yet, though he had a feeling it was going to become inevitable if he was to get what he came for. He didn't respond.

"Oh, Lawrence, humour an old friend and don't spoil it for me. Please, go and get out of those dreadful clothes and take a shower." Her tone immediately took him back in time.

"Can I get you anything first, ma'am?" He lowered his head. It had started.

"Lemon tea. You know where everything is." She watched him walk into the kitchen.

Lawrence used all his inner strength to switch to autopilot, not to think, not to analyse, just to survive for as long as it took.

He poured the boiling water into a small china cup, placed a teabag, together with a slice of lemon from the fridge, into the water, and a second slice on the side of the saucer. He then took the cup and saucer into the lounge and placed them on the coffee table in front of Miranda.

"You remembered. Good boy." Her voice rang with derision.

Lawrence swallowed, fighting back a feeling of nausea. This was going to be a long day. His eyes moved to the notebook.

There were eight notches, written as ⲎⲎ III, marked on the left-hand side of the page. Quickly he stood up straight, Miranda's eyes watching him the whole time.

"I'm sure you remember where your old room is." Her eyes were burning into him, waiting to see his reaction. Lawrence restrained himself and did not reveal any hint of the anger building up inside him.

He walked into the hallway and went through the second door on the left. There was a large double bed, covered by numerous pillows, together with a dark oak double wardrobe, a tallboy and a high-backed leather armchair. The curtains were patterned with a dark grey and mushroom chintz. It had all been changed, and he tried to determine whether the new occupant was male or female. He glanced back at the doorway and, seeing that he was alone, opened a wardrobe door. It was empty.

"You shouldn't have looked, Lawrence." He caught sight of Miranda passing the doorway.

He turned back and slowly began to undress. He took his trainers off first and then placed his socks inside them; a schoolboy habit. Next he unfastened his hoody, neatly folding it and placing it on the armchair. He hesitated for a moment. What if she hadn't been telling the truth on the phone? Could she really have the information he needed? He prayed to God that he wasn't doing this for nothing. He sighed. It was inevitable that his fate was in her hands, just as it had been fifteen years ago. He lifted his T-shirt over his head, folded it neatly and placed it on the chair. He unbuttoned his jeans and slipped them off, together with his trunks, and placed them on the chair with the other clothes. He walked across the hallway into the bathroom. Past experience had taught him to check around the room. There were no towels.

* * *

When Miranda had first seen Lawrence Bane in Josh Black's squalid rooms, she had immediately been excited by his handsome features and athletic body. There was something about this boy that made him stand out, even in the torn, dirty clothes he was wearing.

"I'll take him." She had spoken with authority and, within an hour, Lawrence Bane's life was to change forever. He remembered the look on his friend's face as he was led from the room, leaving Jimmy to his fate with the cruel pimp, Josh Black. They both knew the pain he could, and did, inflict on them if they didn't do as he ordered, and an even more painful memory was witnessing the cruel violence he had enacted on the female prostitutes under his influence. Christine had been one such wretched girl.

Lawrence did not immediately comprehend the consequences of leaving that controlling, sadistic, brutal bastard in order to be enslaved by a different kind. Miranda was to teach and discipline him to do exactly as she dictated for the next eight years.

At first he was sure he could escape her. He wasn't going to have any stuck-up bitch telling him what to do or how to live his life. Get some food inside him and some decent clothes and he'd be gone, and she could go to hell.

But he wasn't given any clothes, not for several weeks, until he learned to do as he was told and earn his garments. Even a towel after a shower had to be earned. Likewise with food; misbehaviour was punished with starvation. Quality and quantity of food was carefully controlled, so that his already athletic body was toned and strengthened. He actually began to take pride in his own physique, possibly the one thing he could be grateful for out of this whole sorry episode in his life.

And then there was the training.

"Give yourself an erection," she would order.

"Go fuck yourself!" And he would end up naked, locked in a room for twelve hours. He certainly had plenty of time to practise getting his body to do what he wanted, or needed, it to do. Surprisingly, it seemed he was very good at it – perfect gigolo material.

That was what Miranda wanted. She groomed him in the arts of lovemaking, massaging, styling women's hair, putting their make-up on and telling them exactly what they wanted to hear.

She also taught him how to dress and groom himself. As a very mature seventeen-year-old, he was entertaining old, rich, bored housewives, and by the time he was twenty he was in demand across London and the Home Counties. For him, this was the life! Good food, wine, clothes, and lots and lots of sex; occasionally with a woman too young to be his grandmother. He didn't really care about that. He enjoyed coming at every opportunity, despite it mostly being into a condom, and he took pride in making sure his ladies climaxed beyond all their expectations, and he had a hundred per cent success rate. At least one of his techniques worked for every client.

Miranda had been a good teacher, but her teaching had come at a price. She was an unashamed sadist, and she enjoyed "playing" with Lawrence. His cooperation was rewarded by a comfortable standard of living, a nice apartment, good TV and gaming equipment, and nights in with Jimmy. Lawrence was more appreciative of the comfort and occasional normality he could offer his friend than anything else Miranda attempted to continue to control him with. It would be too late before she realised that giving him his "toys" would finally set him free.

Lawrence turned the shower on and walked into it, letting the hot water pour all over his body. The brand of shower gel hadn't changed. With lather over his head and body, he heard the bathroom door open. Automatically, hardly conscious of what he was doing, he fell to his knees and lowered his head. *She still has control over you, Los!* He heard her footsteps come closer and then go away again. The door closed. After a second, he raised his head and, wiping the soap from his face, he saw a bath towel hanging on the rail. So, he had done something right and earned his reward. Time to leave the shower. He got to his feet, let the lather run from his body and hair, and turned the water off.

He took his time drying himself, as he was in no rush to see Miranda. He needed to get his mind in the right zone, and summon ultimate self-control for the rest of this visit. *Remember, this is just a visit. It is no longer your way of life.*

He looked to see if a bathrobe had been left with the towel. No. Fuck it. He wrapped the towel around his waist and walked into the bedroom. His clothes were gone. He decided not to risk looking in the wardrobe again, and walked into the lounge.

Miranda was writing something down in the notebook. As she placed it on the table Lawrence registered the notches 𝕀𝕀𝕀𝕀 𝕀𝕀𝕀𝕀 I. This time he was also able to decipher the writing on the right-hand side of the book:

```
Eight years' absence
Intrusion - looking in wardrobe
Too long in shower
Wearing towel around waist
```

Lawrence looked at the woman sitting on the sofa. "Miranda, please, can we…"

She leaned forward and added another notch to the book.

Lawrence took a deep breath and removed the towel, placing it beside the woman on the seat. He knelt before her and lowered his head. "I'm sorry, ma'am." He was using all his mental strength to keep his mind blank and just concentrate on doing what she wanted.

Miranda stood up. "That's better. Come on. Let's eat." She went into the kitchen. Lawrence followed, completely naked. He stood tall and straight, a little thinner than she remembered, but his body was still like a sculpture, with his muscles finely chiselled out. He looked calm and confident. Miranda liked that.

"What can I get you?" He was on autopilot. He spoke with authority. He was thirty, rich and successful in his own right, not twenty and under her control any more. She wanted to play? Well, he was ready to play. A little, at least. He opened the cupboards and fridge. He moved around the kitchen as if he owned the place, with confident and graceful moves, and she could see his muscles ripple as he lowered and stretched, lifted and mixed.

Miranda leaned against the worktop, watching him intently, absorbing his movements with relish. She had to admit to herself how much she missed him. Even now that she had control for a very short time, she knew she was wasting it, really. She wanted to hear about his new lifestyle, see him smile and laugh. She remembered how his face used to light up on the rare occasions he was genuinely happy. She had heard about his success in the investment world. He had made it, and could now afford to live comfortably. She knew he did some work with children in care, and the homeless. She was pleased that things had worked out so well for him – her favourite protégé deserved that. Oh yes, her contacts had kept her well informed, but she had no desire to know where he lived or how to contact him. That information could be dangerous for him if she was ever forced to let it fall into the wrong hands, and she had feared the release of Josh Black for that very reason. She never wanted any harm to come to her Lawrence and couldn't live with herself if she thought she could put him in danger. She believed she had saved him. Certainly his fate would have been much worse with Black, but she admitted she was no mother figure. He had made her a lot of money, and also satisfied her sadistic appetite. She had always been perplexed that he had never really fought back, at least not once he accepted her rules, after those early raging months when he was so young and naïve. He had never physically abused her, always restraining himself and walking away from the situation until he had calmed down. She admitted there had been times when she really didn't deserve that respect. She was also proud of the protective, almost paternal, friendship he had with Jimmy. She believed he would have done anything to help him. But after the first couple of years with Black, there wasn't much anyone could do for him. He had been drip-fed goodness knows what concoctions of drugs, exposed to the worst kinds of abuses, and had simply given up and accepted his fate. Spending time at the apartment with Lawrence had got him through his miserable existence – until he disappeared. Miranda wasn't stupid. She knew that was the only reason Lawrence was here now, letting her manipulate and humiliate him for her own satisfaction. If it was just about the accusation against himself he would never have come back, preferring to go to prison rather than put himself through this.

Within fifteen minutes Lawrence had rustled up a cheese and ham omelette with a salad with vinaigrette and crusty bread.

"So, you learned to cook! It looks delicious," Miranda exclaimed, like an expectant schoolgirl on the cusp of a first-date kiss. "Let's eat in the dining room."

Lawrence hesitated for a fraction of a second. *Hold it together, Los.*

The dining room was accessed from a door at the end of the hallway. On the right-hand side of the doorway was a dark mahogany dining table with six high-backed chairs. Two place settings were laid out.

A large cardboard box and brown A4 envelope were also on the table. Lawrence registered these immediately and thanked God.

There was a freestanding lamp poised to shower the dining area with subtle lighting. It almost created a relaxing atmosphere. Almost. On the far wall there was a large sideboard on which stood two brass candlesticks containing tall, tangerine-coloured dinner candles, together with a leaded crystal vase brimming with white lilies. Above it was a landscape painting depicting a couple strolling through a field of lavender. To the right was a large window looking out over the London skyline, framed with heavy gold curtains, tied back in a plaited natural coloured rope.

A chandelier was suspended over the left-hand side of the room. It was unlit, but Lawrence could still make out the chains running down from the two shadowy corners of the ceiling, leading to what looked like a series of pulley systems. A section of the floor was raised by about a foot, and there was a large storage cupboard against the far wall.

Lawrence glanced around the room. Nothing had changed. She had even left black leather trousers and a black mesh vest top on the edge of the raised floor. He showed no sign of having noticed this clothing.

He placed the tray of food on the sideboard. "I'll just get some wine." Without waiting for a response, he returned to the kitchen.

He drank in the air as though he had been starved of it in the dining room. He needed to muster all his composure to get him through the rest of this ordeal. For the first time since getting out of the lift, he allowed himself to picture Suzy and Jimmy. He was doing this for them.

He gulped down a glass of water and then returned to the dining room with a bottle of Sancerre Les Baudrières 2009 and two crystal wine glasses. Miranda was seated, and the food had been put on the place mats. He sat down and poured the wine.

"So, you have a girl in your life now."

How the hell does she know? She can't know! "I don't know what you're talking about. There is no one, never has been. And, before you ask, I'm not coming back to this." He gestured around the room.

Miranda smiled. "Lawrence, don't think I can't tell there is something making your eyes twinkle, and I'm sure it's not me!"

"It must be the light." He really wasn't in the mood for small talk.

The tension between them seemed to have eased slightly. He tasted the omelette but couldn't face more than one mouthful. He was beginning to feel sick. He just wanted it to be over. He slugged some wine. And then some more.

Miranda watched him as she ate and sipped her wine. What she would have given to know his thoughts. Soon he would be free of her. But not just yet.

She could tell he wasn't going to talk much, as he started to shuffle the food around his plate, his eyes dark, masking his emotions. She couldn't feel sorry for him. She wasn't that kind of woman. Why waste energy on such a useless emotion? Rather, she wanted to cherish this last time spent with him. Watching him eat and drink. Hearing his voice. Witnessing him carrying out an everyday task such as whisking up an omelette. Admiring his beautiful body and the grace and elegance with which he carried himself. Studying his handsome face with its perfect features, his deep-set green eyes, animated eyebrows that could as easily convey humour, beguilement and anger, his angular nose, his high cheekbones, his sensual lips – surely any girl would beg to be kissed by them? – and his golden-brown hair, which fell across his face. Oh, she was going to miss him.

As she emptied her wine glass Lawrence poured them both another. Their eyes made contact, and he looked quickly away, feigning great interest in the room and its contents, as if he had never seen them before.

"Oh, come on, Lawrence. You can see I haven't changed anything in here." She threw her head back again, with a soft laugh. "I confess it's not used as frequently. Business hasn't been quite so good since you left. Actually, I'm getting a bit bored with it all. In fact, I have a very good friend of my own now who knows exactly how to keep me happy." She studied his face for a reaction. It wore a look of relief that momentarily replaced the sadness that had begun to consume him over the course of the meal. She had hoped, foolishly, that he would enjoy this last little game of hers, but she realised she should have known better. He had grown up, moved on. He was a good man and didn't need reminding where he had come from. Yet, as she gazed at the top half of his naked body, and remembered the bottom half as he strode around the apartment, she knew she wasn't going to miss out on this last chance to play with him.

"I told you I have everything you need. You will just need to track down a witness."

"A witness?" His eyes shot to the cardboard box on the table. "You have proof?"

Now she had his attention, and he was suddenly animated and determined.

As soon as Lewis had suggested Black could have access to the missing tapes, Lawrence was sure Miranda would have used her own contacts to get them, especially when she calculated what he himself would be willing to do to take possession of them.

He stood up to walk over to the box.

"You must be patient, dear." Miranda marked another notch in the notebook by her side, and smiled salaciously.

Oh, he was angry now. "Don't screw with me, Miranda." She knew she had him. He would do anything for her now for such a valuable reward. He wanted to return to his girl, she was sure.

And, of course, she was right. Lawrence was yearning to see Suzy, to touch her. She was saving him. He was hers and he desperately wanted her to know that, to tell her he loved her and wanted to spend the rest of his life with her.

He lowered his head. His eyes glistened and he prayed for strength to get to the end of this ordeal.

"Sod it, let's go for twenty." Miranda broke his reverie. "Are you ready?" She spoke with a harshness and hunger.

Pay the final price, Los.

Lawrence walked towards the door, closed it and turned the dimmer switch, watching the light glow from the chandelier until it cast an eerie halo, providing just enough light to make out the edges of the room. He lifted the lid from the storage cupboard and removed a pair of black leather handcuffs and a steel spreader bar with two metal cuffs attached. He placed them on the edge of the stage and watched Miranda.

She slipped off her velour jacket, revealing a black lace basque, then removed her trousers to complete the picture with a thong and black lace-top stockings. She had maintained her slim, taut physique. He had to admire her for that. She swaggered over to the cupboard, removed a pair of black stiletto ankle boots and pulled them on. She licked her lips. Lawrence didn't take his eyes off her. She pondered theatrically over the other contents of the cupboard, taking obvious delight in deciding what she wanted to take out.

"I'm in such a good mood, you know. I must make the most of this."

Lawrence wondered why he didn't hate this woman. In truth, he had simply come to accept her for what she was. Warped, misguided, delusionary, sexual, erotic and sadistic.

Lawrence folded an arm across his chest and brought his other hand up to his chin, appearing contemplative. With a sudden wicked smile, he spoke. "Well, then, let's not disappoint you, ma'am." Bang on cue, he felt himself growing. "Do you like it?"

"Oh, you know I do." She stepped meaningfully towards him. Lawrence took hold of her roughly and pulled her into him, pressing his erect penis against her.

"What does madam want to do to me?" He spoke with determination and control, quietly and forcefully, emphasising the word "what", his eyes drilling into her as though reading her mind. She knew he was in game mode again, but wasn't so naïve that she didn't know that this was how he planned to cope. Any hope she held of him enjoying their little reunion had vanished the minute he had walked back into the lounge with the towel around him.

She held his erection and smoothed her hand along it. His face contorted slightly, trying to fight the urge to display any expression of arousal. Such was his control that Miranda was disappointed she hadn't managed to break him into revealing some kind of emotion, even anger.

"Well?" he asked in a tone devoid of feeling, as though the reply would not impact upon him in the slightest way.

Brave show, Miranda thought to herself, but she knew the reality would be a little different for him.

She took his hand and picked up the spreader bar. Leading him, she carried the bar into the centre of the raised floor and positioned it under one of the loops of chain hanging from the ceiling. She stood up and faced him. His expression was impassive, though he continued to look straight into her eyes. She did not allow herself to be swayed by him. With a determined, steady movement she reached up and kissed his cheek and then his lips, and once again caressed him. He did not flinch or take his eyes off her. He felt hard, and she was impressed with his self-control, as she had always been. She lowered herself to her knees and kissed the end of his penis. He did not react, but looked down at her, and instinctively set his feet apart as she held one ankle, positioning it against the spreader bar and cuffing his foot to it. She did the same with the other ankle, leaving about twenty-five centimetres separating his feet. He was now facing the left-hand side of the room with his back to the dining table. He twisted his body to watch her as she walked over to a pulley and lowered the chain above him. He shifted slightly, and felt the cold steel hard against his ankles. She looked into his face, then went to the cupboard and took out the black leather riding crop. She placed it on the floor in front of his feet, then picked up the cuffs he had taken from the cupboard and approached him again.

Lawrence watched as she took his left hand and slowly put one of the cuffs around it, tightening the buckle just enough to fit snugly around his wrist. She repeated the process with his right wrist. She then unfastened the interlinking chain and attached each cuff independently to the chain she had lowered from the ceiling, leaving him with his arms outstretched and the chain hanging across his chest, not quite taut.

Lawrence no longer looked at her, but stood tall, staring straight ahead at the stark blank wall. Miranda had positioned herself behind him, and she ran her red fingernails along each arm, trailing them lightly down from his neck to the base of his spine, then gently caressing each firm buttock. She moved back to the pulley, and slowly and deliberately raised the chain, lifting his arms towards the ceiling, a little higher with each turn on the pulley. Just as he was about to shift to his toes, with his arms not quite straining above his head, she stopped turning. He heard the door open and close again. He breathed deeply and closed his eyes, totally incapacitated and at her mercy. He pulled on the chain and raised his feet, lifting his body momentarily, but the leather cuffs dug into his wrists and he felt the pain of the weight of the bar pulling on the steel cuffs at his ankles. He lowered himself back down and waited. He opened his eyes and searched the wall in front of him for some imperfection in the paintwork, something to focus on as he tried to meditate and, mentally at least, escape this enslavement she had placed him under.

His breathing slowed, and he achieved a state of calm, losing himself for the few minutes before hearing the door open and close again. She was standing in front of him. Their eyes made contact, and they held each other's gaze. He wished he were far away from here. She wished he would stay forever.

She lowered herself to her knees, still looking at him, and picked up the whip. As she raised herself, she trailed it softly up his left leg, towards his inner thigh, upward along his penis, lower abdomen and chest, travelling up his neck and lifting his chin high with the handle. He strained on the cuffs, his dark eyes following her, his body alert to her every move. She lowered her toy and slipped behind him, immediately flicking the whip forcefully across his back, giving him no time to prepare for the lash, and he tensed with the stinging sensation, gasping through clenched teeth. ONE. He held himself rigid and stared at the small mark he had found on the wall in front of him. TWO. THREE. In quick succession she brought the whip diagonally across first his right shoulder and then his left. It skimmed his skin this time, and he remained totally still. FOUR. She used more force, and whipped him down the middle of his back, the leather biting into his flesh. This time his gasp was louder and he involuntarily threw his head back, arching his back. He lowered himself and eased forward. All was still and he realised she was drinking. She must have brought some water from the kitchen earlier. FIVE. SIX. SEVEN. She made rapid strikes across his lower back, from left to right each time. Again he exhaled through gritted teeth. EIGHT. NINE. TEN, this time from right to left, and now the searing pain was burning into him. He opened his eyes and searched for the mark, trying to lose himself. ELEVEN. She whipped him across the buttocks. This time he pushed himself back, towards her, threatening to break free, and involuntarily she shrank back, but he was securely shackled and they both knew he could not escape. TWELVE. THIRTEEN. Again she lashed out at his buttocks, with full force this time. She cried out from the effort of her movement and he cried out as the burning sensation tore through him. FOURTEEN. She brought the whip down the middle of his back. FIFTEEN. Again. He twisted, futilely trying to escape the weapon. SIXTEEN. This time his flesh tore. She exclaimed "Lawrence!" as she saw the blood trickle down, but she was obsessed with her ritual, enraptured by his enslavement. SEVENTEEN. EIGHTEEN. In quick succession and with all her might she brought the riding crop down heavily across his shoulders and the searing pain crashed into the blankness of his mind. He let out another cry and struggled against the chain and cuffs. NINETEEN. She ripped into the skin across his buttocks. He took a sharp intake of breath, struggling to breathe at all. TWENTY. She flicked the whip across the middle of his back.

His strength depleted, he fell forward, his arms stretched out behind him, his legs barely supporting him. He hung on the chain, and Miranda slowly lowered it until he fell to the floor.

She knelt next to him and slowly undid the cuffs around his wrists and ankles. He lay motionless on his stomach, breathing slowly and quietly. She gently caressed his back, which was criss-crossed with painful-looking weals. She poured some sweet-smelling oil onto his skin and very tenderly smoothed it over him. He winced as she carefully traced the cut across the middle of his back, and again as she poured more oil onto the one across his buttocks. After a couple of minutes, he raised himself onto all fours.

"I think that is enough now, Miranda." His head hung down as if he was talking to the floor. She kissed the back of it.

"Yes, my Lawrence." She smoothed his hair with her hands. Her voice was no more than a whisper. "Thank you. You'll find everything you need on the table. Drop the latch when you leave, and good luck, my darling." She grabbed her clothes and left the room. He heard her quickly dress and then the door slammed. He was alone in the apartment.

The pain seared through his body, and each movement was agonising, but it was over. Soon the whole thing would all be over and he could go back to Suzy. Could he be lucky enough that she would have him back? Could she have any idea how much he loved her? Was she hating him now, because he had left her?

At last, above all, he was closer to getting justice for Jimmy. That bastard, Black, would be behind bars for the rest of his life, and other innocent kids would be protected from him.

Very carefully, he stood up and headed for the dining table. He passed the trousers and vest on the edge of the stage. He was done with all that now. He stood at the table and considered going through the contents there and then. But, no, he didn't want to be in this place a moment longer. He put the envelope inside the box and carried it into the bedroom. His neatly folded clothes were back on the chair. Very gingerly, he put on his clothes and shoes, and with his box under his arm he left the apartment, dropping the latch as instructed.

Chapter 60

Back on the street, he stood for a moment taking some deep breaths. He needed a drink. He headed for a busy bar across the road. His shirt and trunks were sticking to the blood and pulling on his skin, and every movement made him wince. He trod warily, and ordered a double whisky at the bar. He felt exhausted and the bar stool looked tempting, but he thought better of it. He downed his drink quickly and was just about to leave when he heard her voice.

"But we can't leave yet. Dave said he used to live around here somewhere, and surely this is the most likely place he would have come back to. We have to keep looking – ask the neighbours. Somebody must have seen them."

He pulled up his hood to hide his face and looked around, frantically trying to see her.

"Come on, Suzy, we're both tired and it's getting late. We can have one more stab at it tomorrow, but then we need to think about going home. I'm sorry, honey but it just seems he doesn't want to be found." Lawrence knew it was Dominic speaking.

He threw his money down on the bar and left, the box under his arm. Walking faster than was comfortable, he pulled out a phone and tapped in a number.

"Lawrence." Lewis's tone implied he was expecting this call.

"Where the fuck is Dan? And how the hell has he let Suzy come to London?"

"He was standing right next to you at the bar a minute ago. And other than kidnapping her, how would you propose we stop a young woman trying to find the man who has mysteriously walked out on her? What are you playing at, Lawrence?"

"Shit!" He hesitated a moment. "Look, I think I've got the missing tapes." He thought he almost heard his friend sigh with relief on the other end of the phone.

"If you have, then that's great news, Lawrence."

"I'll be able to confirm it later. Tell Dan to somehow get Suzy to the Hilton at Tower Bridge at 6 p.m. tomorrow night. Book a room, and let me owe you this one, mate. Tell him to use Mr and Mrs Jones." Lawrence ended the call. He then took the SIM card out and threw it in a waste bin.

Lawrence caught the next available bus back to Whitechapel, and stood all the way. Hell, he was hurting now, and he needed to get out of his clothes. The journey seemed longer than he remembered, and he braced himself for each bend and jolt, trying not to flinch as his garments pulled on his skin and his ankles and wrists throbbed from the bruising and swelling.

He could barely walk up the three flights of stairs to the flat. Christine opened the door to find him grasping the banister on the landing. "Oh, dear God, Lawrence. What happened to you?" she exclaimed, shocked at the agony he was in. She took the box he was carrying, then grasped his arm and helped him into the room. She led him over to the small brown sofa, but he remained standing.

Finally he looked at her and smiled. "I'm OK, but I need to get these clothes off. Is the bathroom free?"

The shared bathroom was down the hallway, and although it was now very late, there was no guarantee one of the other tenants wouldn't be using it. Christine came back saying she was sorry but the door was locked.

"You've been to see her then. Bloody hell, Lawrence, why did you let her do it? She's a heartless, selfish bitch."

He cautiously walked over to the box. "I did it for this. With any luck it won't be long before we can get out of this shithole and go home."

Christine desperately wanted to put her arms around him, protect and comfort him, but knew that that would just increase his pain. Very carefully and efficiently, she unzipped his hoody and took it off him, requiring him to make only the slightest of movements. She heard his breathing quicken. Then she saw the blood that had oozed onto his T-shirt. It was now dry and acted like glue, attaching a thin line of cloth to the deep cut across his back.

"For crying out loud, who's in that fucking bathroom?" She ran back to the door, banging on it, screaming out, "We've got an emergency here, can you please come out and let us use the bath?"

A moment later the lock was pulled back and the door handle turned. A young woman came out wrapped in a towel and carrying a bundle of clothing and toiletries.

"Sorry, love. Help yourself. I have rinsed it." She walked off down the corridor.

Christine walked Lawrence to the bathroom, then ran back and grabbed some towels and secured the flat before returning to him. She also had some Dettol, rubber gloves and two cloths. Lawrence stood, leaning against the wall, smiling to himself as he watched her quickly douse the bath with the disinfectant, rub it all over with one of the cloths and then rinse it thoroughly. She turned the hot tap on, and before too long the room began to get steamy. One good thing about this place, there was plenty of hot water. She knelt on the floor, untied his laces and took his shoes and socks off. She gasped as she saw the swollen red marks around his ankles and the deepening blue of the bruising. She tried to remain calm, and she glanced up at his hands, searching out the cuff marks around his wrists.

"I am alright, Christine. Ha, I can even remember when I actually quite liked it!"

"But she's gone crazy this time. This is brutal. Don't tell me she gets kicks out of this!" Christine watched as his brave face fell away to reveal sorrow and regret. She had never seen him look so desolate in all the years she had known him. In fact, during the joy of the last three years it had become hard to remember some of the difficulties they had both previously been forced to live through. Time certainly had been a healer for them, and she hoped that it would be again, and they would get over all of this.

She reached forward and took hold of the top button of his jeans. He didn't stop her. Swiftly, the buttons came undone and she carefully eased the denim over his hips and down his legs. He stepped out of them, then took her hands and helped her to her feet.

She leaned over to check the running water, turning back just as he was reaching for a towel. She saw the blood soaked into his trunks and tears started to trickle down her cheeks. Quickly she looked away and wiped her face with her hand. Hopefully, it would just look like moisture from the steamy bath.

Lawrence laughed a little. "OK, Mum, I think I can manage now." He raised his eyebrows and looked at the door, but as he went to lift the shirt over his head he cried out in pain.

"I'm not going anywhere until you are out of those blood-stained clothes."

He thought better of trying to argue with her. She helped him to step into the hot water. He eased himself down and let the water soak into the trunks and shirt. His skin stung and smarted as he lay face-up.

"Turn over," Christine ordered. Slowly, he did as he was told, and she very gently eased the fabric from his skin, helping him to remove the trunks and T-shirt. She gasped in horror as she saw the numerous weal marks across his shoulders, back and buttocks. She took the clean cloth and drenched it in the bath, then began to trickle water over his wounds. "I'll get some cream in the morning. This looks awful. I hope it doesn't get infected."

He sighed and turned to face her. "Thanks, Christine. For everything you do for me." He closed his eyes.

"You can turn back over now." Christine gently pulled the door closed behind her, and he was left alone.

When he walked back into the flat with the towel around his waist, he saw that she had made up the sofa, turning it into his bed, and that there was freshly brewed tea and hot toast on the small drop-leaf table.

"I presumed you would want to go through the box before getting into bed."

He smiled. "Dead right. Though I'll do it from my bed." He lay on his front and started to analyse the contents. Despite the awkwardness of his position, he categorised each piece of information and formed three piles, including the CCTV tapes.

"This is a great start!" he exclaimed. Christine went over to him and hugged him as best she could in the circumstances. Then she watched his face turn deathly white as he read the contents of the brown envelope, which he had saved until last.

Chapter 61

In the morning Christine rushed out to the chemist and bought some Savlon spray. She knew that Lawrence had hardly slept. She had left him dozing, which at nine o'clock in the morning was unheard of for him. He opened his eyes when she returned to the flat. He was still lying on his front.

"Keep still, this might be a bit cold." She pulled the sheet back, sickened by the sight of the swollen red marks. She sprayed quickly and accurately, steeling herself against his cries of pain. She checked his ankles and wrists. "You'll live," she said softly, though she had no desire to make light of his injuries.

Lawrence thanked her, and carefully got out of bed. Deciding to go commando, he pulled on jogging bottoms and a loose-fitting sweatshirt.

He looked preoccupied, and Christine couldn't make out whether it was because he was still suffering so much or if it was anything to do with the brown envelope. He had not spoken about it, but merely put the contents back inside.

"Can I get you some breakfast?" With only two rings on the tiny gas stove, choices were limited.

"It's OK, thanks, I'm meeting someone later and I'll probably have a bite to eat then. Oh, and I'll be out tonight, all night. Will you be OK?"

"Of course. Just let me know if anything needs doing, and promise me you will look after yourself." She looked at him intently.

He walked over to her and hugged her close to him. He laughed, saying, "I will. And don't go doing this to me just yet." He squeezed his arms around her again, trying not to flinch. "Keep the door locked. I'll let Ian know you are on your own tonight. He'll be watching out, so don't worry."

Lawrence had gathered some information from Lewis on Ian Pritchard, and was now more comfortable with his abilities, his main one being protecting people. He was a bodyguard. He would keep his eye on the flat tonight.

Lawrence gave Christine very little information, for her own benefit. If Black should find her, at least he wouldn't get anything from her. Lewis hadn't really wanted the two of them to live together, but Lawrence had insisted. There was no way he'd leave her on her own. If Black did get to her, Lawrence wanted to make sure he would be there with her, to protect her. He couldn't live with himself knowing that she could suffer any more than she already had, and certainly not because of him. Now he felt renewed hope that they would soon have the evidence they needed to go to the police.

When it was time to leave, Lawrence managed to ease his feet into his trainers, but he wasn't sure how far he could walk, due to both his swollen ankles and the pain from the whipping marks. He would take the Tube to London Bridge station. He put some clean socks, his toothbrush, the Savlon spray and his wet shaving kit in a supermarket carrier bag.

He then inserted one of many SIM cards into the mobile phone he had given to Christine, and tapped in Suzy's number, sure she would have her phone with her.

I will be there, Mrs Jones. Please be there too. LB

He removed that SIM card and replaced the original one. As far as he knew, no one except Lewis had this number. He rang Lewis and explained that he had the tapes, together with some photographs and transcripts of various conversations. He explained that he would go through everything tomorrow and Tuesday, and be prepared to see Lewis on Wednesday – the day Josh Black would be released. At this stage, he decided not to mention the contents of the brown envelope. He returned the phone to Christine.

As he stood on the Tube, his mind wandered to the brown envelope, and a distant memory:

He'd been stretching after his usual strenuous workout in the apartment: the chains and pulleys could be adapted to give him a challenging fitness regime. As he picked up his sweat towel, he heard the main door unlock. He walked into the hallway and fell to his knees, lowering his head as he became aware of Miranda entering the room. He had learned well in the four years he had been with her. *What does she want? I'm not seeing anyone tonight. She must have taken a late booking, but why not phone me? A new client, perhaps?*

"Make some tea, dear, I need to talk to you." She went past him into the lounge.

He joined her, with a lemon tea in a china cup; a slice of lemon on the side of the saucer, and a Lucozade Sport drink for himself.

She sat on the sofa, and indicated for him to sit on the chair. "Relax, darling. How's your day going?"

He hated it when she tried to make chit-chat. It was much better when she told him what he needed to know and then fucked off. He hoped she wasn't after a "play" session. He really did feel too tired.

"Not bad. I was just going to take a shower. I wasn't expecting to see you today, ma'am."

"Is Jimmy coming over tonight?"

"No, we haven't arranged anything. I think that bastard may have him working." Lawrence had got used to blocking out images of the life Jimmy lived. They both forgot about everything when they got the chance to spend time at the apartment together, playing on the PlayStation and drinking beer. Lawrence never let Jimmy take drugs there, though.

"Good. We have a new client. It's worth a lot of money. I want you to be ready for six o'clock. Dress smart."

"How old is she? Does she like anything kinky? Do I need to get some champagne in?" He was a little surprised, as she usually provided all of this information for a first-timer.

"Don't worry, play this one as you go along. Use your judgement. I know you can do that, darling."

"Has she been with any of your others?" He was intrigued now; she wasn't usually this guarded. Maybe for once he was going to get a sexy young chick!

"No. It's a brand new client, and he has specifically asked for you. You have such a good reputation, Lawrence." She looked directly at him, waiting for his reaction.

He glared at her. "You've got to be kidding me! Did you say

HE? Is this some fucking joke?" He was standing over her, his voice raised in disbelief and anger.

"Sit down, Lawrence. It is not a joke."

"No. No way. I won't do it. Get someone else to give him one." He sat down and pushed his hand through his hair.

Miranda couldn't fail to notice how handsome he looked, casually dressed in a torn T-shirt and sweatpants, his muscles hard and defined, just the right amount of body hair, perfect facial features, with a becoming shadow of stubble around his chin and lower jaw, and ruffled hair to die for. Was he in the mood for a play? Maybe it would be better to leave him alone to prepare for this one tonight.

"He has asked for you, and he is paying a lot of money. You will do this. Tomorrow, I'll arrange for delivery of the PC and internet connection you keep asking for. He will be here at six, and you will do exactly as he asks. Now I suggest you relax for the rest of the day. Don't think too much about it and go with the flow, darling. Who knows, you might even enjoy it." She smiled wickedly at him.

He slammed his fist down on the arm of the chair and didn't move until she had left the apartment. Then he went to the bathroom and stood against the wall of the shower, with cold water spraying him from above.

At quarter to six that evening he dressed in a black shirt, with a black-and-white pindot silk tie and dark grey trousers. He put on a black leather belt and completed the picture with highly polished narrow-toed black shoes. The shirt enhanced his slim build and his biceps were suitably visible through the fabric. He did not wear any cologne. He was tempted to pour himself a double whisky, but thought better of it. He had gone through a hundred scenarios during the day, and the prize of a computer did not seem anywhere near enough to justify any of them. He had tried to think how to get out of the situation, but he was in too deep with Miranda. He had nowhere else to go – at least nowhere he judged to be any better than where he already was. He had to admit, for the most part, he enjoyed his gigolo lifestyle, and some of her games actually turned him on. She never seriously hurt him, and he admired her control and adherence to limits, but this was way off the scale and he had never, ever expected it. Not from her. And he worried it might not be a one-off as she had implied. Shit. Shit. Shit.

The doorbell rang. He slowly opened the door and in walked a brown-haired man, approximately six feet tall, in his late twenties, with a similar build to his own, wearing a black suit, with light grey shirt and a checked grey tie. Lawrence had to admit he was a good-looking bloke!

"Lawrence? I'm Paul Irvine. Pleased to meet you." He walked into the apartment and held out his hand. The handshake was businesslike, both men taking a firm hold, as if they were at a business meeting.

Lawrence suddenly felt very nervous and vulnerable, feelings that had been alien to him for such a long time now. *Keep it together Los, and get through this.*

"Er, can I get you a drink?"

"A beer would be good, thanks. Bud or something like that, if you've got it."

"Take a seat." Lawrence led him into the lounge, glad of the chance to escape to the kitchen. Shit, he was so nervous. He needed to stay alert and watch for any signs. Could he follow through? Would he know what was expected? For fuck's sake, how was he to know what this guy was into? Shit. Shit. Shit.

He took the bottles through. "Do you need a glass, mate?" *Mate? Mate? What are you bloody playing at, you stupid git?*

Paul took a slug from the bottle "This is fine." He sat cross-legged on the armchair, and Lawrence wondered at how confident he looked. He was suddenly filled with dread. Who would be giving who one? He had automatically assumed he just needed to take him from behind: job done. He was beginning to feel sick at the alternative, and fought with all his determination not to let it show. Somehow, this seemed a lot worse than giving an old hag a good seeing to!

"You haven't done this before, have you?" Paul's tone was so matter-of-fact Lawrence nearly spat out the beer he had just slurped from the bottle.

"No." His voice was expressionless, and he studied his beer bottle intently.

"It's been a long time for me. My long-term partner was killed in a car crash three years ago. I have never really had the desire to get involved with anyone else. I'm still not sure whether I want to, or indeed if I can. Hence, I decided to try this. It's almost a hurdle I need to get over before I resign myself to abstinence or agree to get involved with someone else."

Lawrence looked at him. Paul was confident and at ease. It was as if they were just a couple of mates having a beer in one of the more upmarket pubs. He was smartly dressed, and looked as though he worked out. For the first time he could remember, Lawrence felt a slight disgust at his own lifestyle. Charging women for sex was far worse than having a same-sex relationship with someone you loved. He suddenly realised he had very little chance in his current existence of finding anyone to be happy with. This guy apparently had that once, and was now thinking of looking for it again.

"The reason I'm here, Lawrence, is because I have heard about you, and some of it reminded me of my relationship with Roger. We liked to do some of the rougher stuff, and, quite frankly, I miss it. I just want one night – no strings, no questions, just a good time, to give me a buzz. You know what I mean?"

No, not bloody really! "I guess so." Lawrence stood up, not really sure why. He went to the bathroom and just waited for an appropriate number of minutes to pass before flushing the toilet and going back into the lounge, trying to feel more composed.

"Where is your games room?" Paul stood up and placed his empty beer bottle on a coaster on the coffee table.

Lawrence stared at him for a moment. He felt Paul already knew he would have to tell him exactly what he wanted Lawrence to do.

"This way." Lawrence led the way down the hall and opened the door. He turned the dimmer switch to give a soft glow of light over the left-hand side of the room. Paul walked around, studying the pulley system and briefly examining the contents of the storage cupboard, giving the impression there was nothing in there to shock him.

Lawrence stayed near the door, leaning against the wall.

Paul walked over to the dining table in the other half of the room and sat on the chair nearest to the raised floor. "Please take your clothes off."

Fuck! Slowly, Lawrence moved onto the raised floor, breathing deeply and looking straight at Paul as he removed his tie and began to unbutton his shirt. Once he had taken that off, he bent down and removed his shoes and socks. *Make it easy on yourself, Los. Do as you're told. Imagine Miranda is telling you what to do.* He pulled the belt from his trousers, pushed them down and slowly stepped out of them. He left the clothes crumpled at the edge of the stage, not quite steady enough to worry about folding them neatly. He tried to calm himself as he drew down his trunks and placed them on the pile. He tried to urge himself to go hard, sure he would look better and feel a little bit more in control that way. He had never had any issues with his own nakedness before, but now he was as nervous as hell. *Come on, don't fucking let me down now!*

"Put the cuffs on, just wrists, and don't attach them to each other."

Lawrence walked over to the box and picked up a pair of black leather cuffs. He became aware of Paul moving over to the pulley, and lifted his head to watch the chain lower from the ceiling.

"Show me where you are most comfortable." Paul was facing him now, and Lawrence saw his gaze cover his entire body. He summoned the strength not to let his legs give way with the total dread that was coming over him. He knew once he was cuffed he would have no power over this situation and little way to avoid anything he really didn't like. He was used to lashing out with his feet with Miranda, on the odd occasion when she didn't use the spreader bar, but this guy looked strong, and Lawrence knew he would be totally vulnerable. Reluctantly, he spread his arms along the chain, indicating the distance at which he could comfortably hold on to it. Paul attached each cuff to the chain.

"Tell me when the height is right." Paul turned the pulley to lift the chain.

"OK." Lawrence was raised to his full height, and his arms were stretched out above his head. His feet were placed at ease on the floor, with no strain. He moved forward and hung on the chain.

Paul took his jacket off and placed it on the back of the dining chair. He went to the storage box and withdrew a black leather flogger with plain soft tails. He stood on the edge of the stage, and with sweeping strokes, he brought the flogger across Lawrence's back ten times, slowly, each time producing no more than a slight sting, as though satisfying an itch in a pleasurable way. Lawrence leaned back from the chain, relishing the sensation, feeling himself getting harder with excitement, totally shocked at the eroticism he was experiencing. Fuck, this guy knows what he's doing. Miranda had taught Lawrence how to use a flogger to give pleasure to clients, but she had never used it this way on him. It had always been more brutal.

He became aware of Paul returning to the box. A moment later he felt a hard slap and sting across his buttocks, as Paul spanked him with a studded black leather paddle. This time Lawrence gasped out loud and pulled himself forward, raising his legs. The pain was only just bearable. The humiliation was not!

"Stand still," Paul ordered, and he brought the paddle down again another nine times, in exactly the same spot.

"Fuck!" Lawrence cried out, but remained totally still. He then heard something snap, and felt ice on his backside. Where the hell Paul had got that from, he had no idea, but the sensation soothed the burn on his arse. To his surprise, Paul then came round to face him. Lawrence tensed and turned away as he felt his hands on his penis. Paul let go, sensing this was getting too much for his partner for the evening. Quickly he unlocked the cuffs, releasing Lawrence's wrists, but leaving the cuffs attached to the chain.

"My turn." He began to undress in front of Lawrence. The latter could see how well Paul looked after his body. Lawrence found himself feeling respect for this man. His own body felt invigorated after the assault. He had no idea where this evening was going, but as far as he was concerned, it was going, and it had to end at some point.

Paul was now naked, and he held his hands out to Lawrence.

Lawrence glanced at them and looked at Paul.

"Go ahead."

Lawrence began to wonder about the relationship between Paul and Roger. Had they been equals? Was he expecting Lawrence to take Roger's part? Is that what was happening here?

Slowly, he fastened Paul's wrists in the cuffs and went to the pulley. He looked fixedly at the back of the naked man, hanging on the chain. Paul held himself straight, with apparent ease, though Lawrence noted his breathing had become heavier. He was preparing himself for the lash. Lawrence went through the same motions with the flogger and paddle as he would have done with his usual clients, with the exception of using the paddle with more force this time. He thought briefly about his women. Then he thought of Jimmy.

At the end of the ordeal, Lawrence struggled inwardly to touch Paul. But he focused on his earlier sensation of relief from the coldness, and summoned an inner strength to carefully smooth the ice over Paul's buttocks as best he could. In this short space of time, Lawrence had come to respect this man, and he wanted him to have the same sensation that he had been thoughtful enough to give Lawrence. No one had ever really cared about what Lawrence ever wanted, it just wasn't appropriate. After all, Lawrence was working. It was amazing that this experience of being cared for should be provided by another man!

As Lawrence unfastened the cuffs, he started to feel extremely awkward. The games were over: what was going to happen next? They were both naked, and Lawrence struggled to look at Paul.

"Grab a couple of towels," Paul ordered and, glad to be able to leave the room for a moment, Lawrence went into the bathroom. He hesitated a second. Don't think about it too much. Just get through it. He went back into the games room and handed Paul one of the towels. He was relieved, as Paul wrapped it around his waist. Lawrence did likewise.

"Where's the bedroom?" Paul was looking at Lawrence steadily, gauging his expression, but giving nothing away.

Lawrence looked at him and didn't move for a moment. Paul continued, "I want you to fuck me hard now. Can you do that?"

How in hell can he be so matter-of-fact about this? He must know I'm not gay. Shit, Miranda, you bitch. Sod it.

"It's this way." Lawrence turned away and headed for the bedroom, standing aside to let Paul enter first. He tried to control the tone of his voice and not give any indication of the hell his mind was going through. *How the fuck do you do it, Jimmy?* Suddenly the penny dropped. *How would he hope a guy would take Jimmy? Not brutally. Fuck! Fuck! Fuck!*

He watched as Paul looked around the room. The latter placed a small bottle of lubricant on the bedside table and picked up a book: *The Art of Expressing the Human Body* by Bruce Lee. He flicked through some of the pages and looked back at Lawrence. Lawrence continued to watch him, and Paul wondered momentarily if Lawrence had relaxed slightly. "Do you study any martial arts?"

Lawrence actually laughed. "My lifestyle doesn't really lend itself to me studying anything! I think I would quite like to, though, if I had the chance, particularly the aspects of control and meditation."

Paul sat on the edge of the bed. They were both still wearing towels. "I've read some of this. I meditate as part of my daily routine. It helps with work, among other things." Their eyes made contact again.

Lawrence walked over to the window and muttered, half under his breath, "I'll put a condom on." He realised a matter-of-fact tone helped ease the atmosphere, as he reached into the bedside drawer and took out a foil packet.

Paul stood up and let his towel drop. He opened the lubricant and smoothed it over and inside himself before moving to stand at the bottom of the bed, facing the pine headboard. Then he handed the bottle to Lawrence. Lawrence held it a moment in his hand as he removed his own towel and gently massaged himself until he was hard. He didn't look at Paul, but he knew Paul was watching him, and Lawrence became conscious of the fact that he wanted him to see him, naked, erect and calm. He pictured Jimmy. He wouldn't want him to be afraid. He struggled to wipe out his own fear and distaste. With deliberate movements, he slowly pulled the condom on, and began to sense Paul's arousal. He walked round to stand behind him and put his hands on Paul's shoulders, gently rubbing them, massaging away any tension. He wanted to be gentle with "Jimmy". Paul arched his back, wallowing in the pleasure of Lawrence's strong warm hands and, as he leaned forward, Lawrence rubbed his back in sweeping movements. Paul moaned appreciatively, and then moved forward onto the bed, on all fours, slightly separating his legs. Lawrence breathed deeply and climbed up behind, taking hold of Paul's lower back and carefully inserting his penis. Paul pushed back onto him, and Lawrence knew he wanted to feel him push harder and harder. Paul's groaning became more intense and sensual, and Lawrence knew he was giving him pleasure. Then he came. He was shocked, not sure if he had intended to actually ejaculate. But it was done, and Paul knew it. Lawrence steadied himself and became aware of Paul holding himself, pushing his penis through his own hand as he reached his climax, semen splashing onto the sheets. The two men remained joined for a few moments as their breathing returned to normal. As Lawrence carefully withdrew, Paul continued to lie there. Lawrence lay on the floor. His mind was blank, and he had no idea what would happen next. He closed his eyes and heard Paul go into the bathroom. When he opened them, Paul was sitting beside him on the carpet.

"You won't understand this, but that has made me feel great. It's been a long time since I felt anyone, and I think I am ready to go looking for a relationship again. Life without sex sucks, actually, but I need some love in mine too, so don't worry, I shan't ask to see you again. But thanks." He stood up and headed for the dining room, Lawrence assumed to retrieve his clothes.

Lawrence went into the bathroom and looked at himself in the mirror. He still looked the same, slightly fucked-up hair, but still bloody good-looking, as well he knew! He flushed the condom down the toilet and grabbed his bathrobe.

Paul was dressed, perusing the storage cupboard with a smile on his face. He turned to look at Lawrence as he entered the room. Paul stood looking at this incredibly fit and handsome straight guy. "In another life, maybe." Paul turned to leave. He handed Lawrence his business card. "Just in case you ever need any legal advice." He smiled, and with that he left the apartment, and Lawrence was alone to remember.

Now, on the Tube, Lawrence was alone to remember again. Who would have thought his one and only gay encounter from the past would save him? The brown envelope was from Paul Irvine, lawyer for Veronica Rigsby. It contained her will and a letter, written by her, declaring that she had loaned Lawrence Bane £100,000 and that it had been repaid in full, together with an overpayment. There was a repayment due to Mr Bane of £100,000, and this was being held in her estate until the said Mr Bane could be located. He wondered if Charles Rigsby knew about the will, and the debt on her estate!

He got off at London Bridge and headed for the hotel. What would he tell Suzy?

Chapter 62

When Suzy finally left the bar that night, she felt exhausted. She was so sure they would find some sign of Lawrence in the area he used to live. Isn't that what he had gone back to? They had been in London for three days now, and she knew Dominic needed to get back to work. She also knew she needed some sanity back in her life. She hadn't slept properly since he had left her, and she needed to speak to Alison about her own job. She had told her something had happened and she had to go away for a few days. Suzy was now drained of the confidence she had when they first arrived here. As each hour passed, with no information to go on, she was sinking deeper into hopelessness.

But this morning she had found a note in her coat pocket:

"Miss Harper – go to the Hilton London Tower Bridge Hotel, at 6 p.m. Room booked for Mr and Mrs Jones."

She had no idea what it meant or how it got there, but it had her name on it, and she felt it had to be him. Who else would use Mr and Mrs Jones? Her heart was pounding. Should she tell Dominic? They were due to get on the train at 6.30 tonight to go home. She would leave it for now, and see how she felt as it got nearer the time.

Dominic suggested they had breakfast in one of the cafés on the main road. They could sit and people-watch for a while. They had as much chance of seeing Lawrence Bane stroll past as they had of finding him by any other method they'd tried! Suzy still had the feeling that he was in trouble. They had been through so much together in such a short space of time, she simply couldn't believe he would just up and leave. And why take Christine away from Dave? It had to be something to do with his past. Oh, how she wished she knew more about him.

After breakfast Suzy decided to suggest they do a bit of shopping. She felt this would distract her for a while from puzzling over the note, and also give Dominic the impression that she was preparing herself to leave and accept the fact Lawrence was gone. That would certainly ease his conscience about dragging her back home.

Dominic suggested they browse around Covent Garden. He hoped she might be able to enjoy being a tourist. After all, this was her first time in London, though it was far from being the fun trip one would normally expect!

With her mind on the Hilton London Tower Bridge Hotel, Suzy smuggled clean knickers, toothpaste, toothbrush and make-up into her shoulder bag, just in case!

On the way to the Tube, Suzy got the text message. She felt a thrill run through her body. *Oh my heart, it is him.* She knew this wasn't his mobile. She had tried calling that enough times before registering it had been disconnected. She wasn't going to reply. She put her phone in her pocket and squeezed her hand over it, as though it was her connection to him. She could almost feel him. She was definitely going to the hotel now. How should she explain to Dominic? Mentally she went through the timeframe – she needed to be at the Tower Bridge hotel by 6 p.m. Their luggage was in the lobby of their hotel in Blackfriars. How long would it take on the Tube to Tower Bridge? Was there even a station at Tower Bridge? She glanced at the Tube map in front of her. They were currently travelling on the Northern Line, and she could see no mention of Tower Bridge or even Covent Garden, for that matter. She would have to come clean with Dominic and get him to help her. He needed to know she wasn't going back with him tonight anyway.

"I found this in my coat pocket this morning." She looked at him, trying not to sound too nervous. "I'm certain it's Lawrence, and he just sent me this text." She took her phone out and handed it to Dominic.

He stared at the paper and the phone for a moment. "What the hell is going on, Suzy?" He spoke in a hushed voice but his tone was definitely one of anger and frustration. "You have me come down here to try to find a guy like a needle in a haystack. You hardly know him. And don't interrupt." He added, as Suzy opened her mouth to protest. She had never seen him this angry before. "And now he appears to be playing some sort of game with you. I don't know what the hell he is into but it doesn't sound good, and I really don't want you getting involved, Suzy."

"But I am involved." She glanced around to see if any of the passengers were looking, but it seemed that everyone was invisible to each other on the London Underground. "I love him, Dominic. I must see him, even if it's just to find out why he left me. I deserve that, at least."

"He should have damn well rung if he didn't have the guts to tell you face to face." Dominic shook his head. "There's something not right. To walk out on you is one thing, but to leave his home and all his possessions? And what about that woman, Christine? I'd like to fucking meet him in the hotel with you and find out what's really going on." He glanced out of the window, staring into the blackness of the tunnel. He had not been totally honest with Richard about this trip. He had told him he was taking Suzy to London for a few days to take her mind off Bane! Now he was regretting not being open with him and listening to what his partner would advise him to do. He looked at his cousin sitting quietly beside him and his voice became calmer. "Look, I know you think you love him. I saw you two together, and it was obvious he was totally besotted with you. I suspect he has a shady past which has caught up with him, and maybe he is trying to protect you from it. If that's the case, then I would rather you didn't go anywhere near him." He looked at her, pleading with her to agree with him, but as he saw her face, he knew she needed to see Lawrence. He also knew she needed his help. He took his phone and started browsing the net. The connection was poor, but he found what he needed in his history and texted the hotel to book one more night.

Suzy squeezed his hand. "Thank you," she whispered.

"I just hope I'm doing the right thing, and I'll fucking kill him if he hurts you."

"Dominic," she reprimanded. "You know he's not like that. Let me see him, and then I'll ring you to come and get me, OK?"

"Mmm." He stared out of the window again.

At half past five, Dominic stood in the Hilton London Tower Bridge Hotel with Suzy, as she checked in under the name of Mrs

Jones. She was told everything was ready and given directions to room 208. No, Mr Jones had not arrived yet. The attendant gave Dominic a mystified glance. He raised his eyebrows and looked away.

"Text me when he gets here and let me know if everything is alright. I'm not leaving the lobby till I hear from you, got it?"

Suzy nodded. He continued, "Then let me know when I can come and get you. I doubt he is just going to say let's all go back to Manchester!" His voice was thick with bitter sarcasm. He turned to go and get himself a drink, then he looked back at Suzy and added softly, "Good luck, Suzy, and let me know if we can help at all, hey?"

Suzy walked into room 208 and placed her bag on the luggage rack. The room was brightly lit, with a large double bed and a modern easy chair at one side. There was a flat-screen TV, drinks facilities and a large shower room. She remembered their eventful night at the Hilton in Manchester, when he had bought her Coco Mademoiselle.

To busy herself, she put her toothbrush and make-up bag in the bathroom and decided to brush her teeth. Her heart ached a little at the recent memories of their time together. Why had it all gone so wrong? Hopefully she was about to find out. She shuddered at the thought that he might tell her it was all over, and that he never wanted to see her again, but she was rational enough to know that didn't fit with what she had come to know about this man or the events surrounding his departure. She thought of Christine, and found herself picturing the ugly scar on the woman's arm.

She went back into the bedroom and sat on the chair.

The clock on the TV showed 6.01. There was a knock at the door.

With her heart pounding, she went over and pulled it open. There he was.

Oh my heart!

As he stood in the middle of the doorway, his eyes drilled into her, and relief flashed across his face. Then she flew at him, pounding his chest with her fists, tears gushing down her cheeks, unable to speak. He took hold of her wrists and gently eased her back into the room, closing the door with his foot and grimacing with pain as he did so.

"It's OK, Suzy," he whispered into her ear and, letting go of her hands, he cupped her face, tilting it up towards him. He silenced her sobs as he kissed her passionately, as though his very breath depended on her. He fed on her with his tongue, hard and hungry, and his grip tightened as though he would never let her go. All memories of yesterday's pain and humiliation were gone for a moment.

She responded to his demands, giving her mouth to him, breathing her life and joy at seeing him again into his very soul.

As she put her arms around him to hug him to her, he winced and stepped back, letting go of her, but looking at her with sparkling eyes and smiling through his pain. "Be gentle with me!" He took her hand and led her to the bed, sitting her down as he carefully knelt before her.

She looked at him and took in his unshaven face. She had never known him not to shave every morning. His hair appeared more ruffled than usual and he looked thinner. His clothes were cheap. Her face filled with worry and torment.

"Lawrence! Are you OK? What has happened? Where have you been?" Her voice trembled through her weeping, and her questions were only just beginning to flood out.

He put his finger to her lips. "Yes, I will be now I have seen you."

He placed his hands on her knees and she stroked his hair, as she had longed to do so many times over the last few days.

"I know I have a lot of explaining to do, but give me a little time. Please." His eyes implored her to be patient. A few moments passed.

"I … I need to text Dominic. I said I would let him know…" She hesitated.

He looked at her with an expression of regret. "That you are safe with me?"

Suzy nodded, and he looked down.

"I can't blame him for wondering what kind of sick bastard I might be."

"It's not like that, Lawrence. He knows you would never hurt me. He thinks you've been protecting me. From something in your past, maybe." She paused to see if he would say anything.

He stood up and carefully paced around the room. "It's OK. Someone is talking to him right now in the bar. I guessed he would be here with you, and he needs an explanation too." Lawrence had instructed Dan to go and tell Dominic only the information that Lawrence wanted him to know. Then he looked at her, still sitting on the bed watching him, and his voice lowered. "Suzy, were you afraid I would hurt you?"

"You have already hurt me, Lawrence." She paused and suddenly felt exhausted. "After all I have been through with you." They both thought about Elizabeth Underwood. "You just left me. You didn't trust me."

He knelt down beside her again and took hold of her hands. "It wasn't a question of trust. I am just trying to protect you from my past. As I always have."

"Has it ever occurred to you I don't need protecting?"

"No, it hasn't," he said quietly, wondering how angry she would feel if she knew about Dan. "You don't know what I am trying to deal with here."

"Well, try telling me." It was her turn to stand up now. She walked over to the window. The curtains had been drawn. She opened them and looked over towards him. "No one can see us here," she smiled.

He returned the smile. "Come and help me shower. Then we'll talk." He struggled to stand again, the pain from his wounds beginning to become unbearable.

"Lawrence, what's wrong?" Her voice was fearful, almost as though she dreaded his answer, and she followed him into the shower room.

"I'm wrong, Suzy. I have been about so many things in my life. Now I have a chance to put things right. But I have had to pay a price. Try not to be shocked. I am OK, just a bit sore." He held her hands, strumming his thumbs gently along the back of them, and smiling to reassure her and prepare her for what she was about to see.

He positioned her in front of the mirror and then stood in front of her, so as he removed his top he would see her face.

"Please understand – it is not as bad as it looks, and I wanted this to happen for so many good reasons, one of which is that I can be with you again. For the rest of my life, if you'll have me."

He no longer smiled, and his eyes were sadder than Suzy had ever seen before. He blew a kiss to the mirror, to her reflection. Then, his face contorting slightly with pain, he removed his sweater. He studied her face intently through the mirror.

Suzy stared in disbelief, her eyes widening and her colour draining. "Oh, dear God in heaven, Lawrence, who did this to you?" The tears started to stream down her pale cheeks. She surveyed all the weals on his back and shoulders and felt sickened at the sight of the broken skin. They were shadowed with a yellow mist. Someone had tried to soothe him, and she thought of Christine.

He likes to be hurt … he likes to be hurt … but surely, not like this.

"Please tell me you didn't ask for this? You didn't want this? You didn't enjoy this?"

Lawrence lowered his upper body, grabbing hold of the washbasin for support as he felt sick with fear of her rejection.

"No, I didn't, Suzy." He tried to feign a laugh as he looked at her through the mirror, but the sound was too weak. "It hurt too much. And it wasn't you."

Then, before he realised, she was standing in front of him. She very carefully pulled him towards her and kissed him gently. She caressed his face and stroked his arms. She whispered in his ear. "You are my Lawrence Bane. My questions will wait for now. You can tell me when you are ready."

She felt calmer as she knelt down and unfastened his trainers, removing them and his socks. She ran her fingers lightly around his ankles, tracing the marks and trying desperately to keep her tears at bay as she wondered what could have happened. Her tears would serve no purpose now. She looked up at his wrists, already guessing what she would see.

She eased his jogging pants down, looking up quizzically at him as she discovered he was not wearing any underwear. As he stepped out of the joggers, she looked at his behind.

"For mercy's sake … I-I don't understand," she exclaimed, calmness evading her, and tears flowing once more.

He pulled her up.

"I am so sorry, Suzy. I really didn't want you to see me like this. But I heard your voice in the bar last night and I knew I had to see you. I couldn't wait."

Suzy moved away. She took some deep breaths and tried to remember some of the meditation techniques he had been teaching her. She wanted to remove her emotional being from this scene, but she wanted her physical being to be here, strong and supportive, for her guy, her lover.

Now she moved with determination. She was going to get through this. She turned the shower on and let the water run. She checked through the toiletry bottles and placed two on the tray. She removed her own clothing and, after checking the temperature, she took his hand and they both stepped into the shower. She ran her fingers over his face and chest, then lower, gently caressing his penis.

"Thank goodness this isn't injured!" she smiled, searching his face for him to do the same. He gave a little smile, and his eyes looked less sad.

He was watching her the whole time, loving the strength she was showing, loving her.

She opened a bottle, pouring the lightly fragrant liquid into her palms and then covering his body, turning him around so his back was facing her, and with featherlike touches she ran her fingers along each of the wounds, mentally counting them. He stood still, clenching his teeth and studying a mark on the tiles, letting the water pour down over them both. She eventually covered the whole of his body, cleaning him, caressing and kissing him. He felt a calm tranquillity consume him, a confidence in her love for him, and thanked God for this chance to be with her.

She ordered him to kneel. She washed and rinsed his hair, then gave him the shampoo bottle and turned her back to him so he could wash hers. Then they stood face to face for several minutes, holding on to each other with the water wrapping them together.

When they got out of the shower, he took a towel and dried her as she stood before him. His skin gave in to movement a little more easily now, and for the first time since his ordeal, he began to feel an inner strength. He handed the other towel to Suzy and braced himself as she tenderly patted his skin dry, and rubbed his hair.

"Can you get me the bag I brought, please, baby?"

She quickly brought it into the bathroom and he took out a toothbrush and placed it on the side of the washbasin. Then he withdrew a razor and shaving gel and Suzy stood beside him, watching as he slowly revealed his chiselled, firm jaw to her once more.

"That's better," she said quietly.

Next he handed her the Savlon spray. "Would you mind doing the honours, please?" He turned his back to her.

Suzy felt a lump in her throat and concentrated on forbidding the tears to fall any more this evening as she surveyed his wounds again. She made sure the antiseptic liquid covered his cuts. Then she took a little bottle of massage oil she had in her bag, took his hand and led him back into the bedroom.

"Let's order some room service and then I'll try to make you feel more comfortable."

"That sounds good, Suzy. I could eat some pizza." He grinned at her.

She had never known him eat pizza before, but was so pleased he seemed a little more relaxed now. *Make the most of it.* She had a feeling the conversation was going to get serious.

He walked over to the bedside phone and ordered a large ham and pineapple pizza, garlic bread and two Cokes, looking over to Suzy for her approval.

Then he lay face-down on the bed, head at the bottom, and watched her as she gathered their clothes together, folding them neatly and putting them on the chair.

She took the small bottle of oil. "I want to touch you all over." There was just a hint of lust in her voice. "Tell me if it hurts."

"Don't worry about me." He closed his eyes while she gently applied the oil, softly humming "The First Time Ever I Saw Your Face". Then she lay on her side next to him and traced her fingers along his waist.

After a few minutes there was a knock at the door and,

wrapping her coat around her, she thanked the waiter, took the tray and placed it on the floor at the bottom of the bed. They both lay on their fronts and ate.

Lawrence tried to keep the conversation light, already forming in his mind how he would tell her about everything. "Can I ask how you've been doing?"

"How do you think?" She couldn't help the cutting edge in her tone, and he didn't blame her. "You leave with no goodbye, no explanation, your phone no longer works, and The Sway is closed up. Have you sold it to John Ryder?"

He looked away from her. "I can't tell you anything about that." He did not want her to know about his fake ID.

"Still keeping your secrets," she said sadly. "What about trusting me, and your friends Steve and Jane, not to mention Dave? We are all worried about you and Christine. What has she got to do with any of this?" She looked at his body and then turned away.

"I had no choice. I needed to make sure you were safe, you were all safe!"

"Safe?" she spoke with disbelief. "From you? I love you, Lawrence. How can I ever be safe without you?" She started to trace a pattern on the duvet they were lying on.

He managed to get comfy on his side and laid his hand on hers to keep it still. "Look at me, Suzy. Can't you see? I was the danger. Knowing me can be dangerous. My sordid past has caught up with me, as I knew it would. I always tried to warn you about it." He paused. "In the early days, I thought you would tire of me and leave me. Before I had to leave you."

"I don't understand why you had to. And look what has happened to you! I'm damn sure you didn't do that to yourself!" She tried to look deep into his soul, as he so often did to her.

"I..." He hesitated and gulped his drink before continuing. He spoke very quietly, with little emotion. "Someone will be after me when they get out of jail. That will be on Wednesday. I lived a really bad life when I ran away from the children's home with my friend Jimmy. We were both fifteen. We were taken off the streets in London by a pimp. There was this woman, who came and took charge of me. I was her pet, as she disciplined me to make love and make women feel good. I became a gigolo and she rented me out. For a while, I think I actually enjoyed it. I made her a lot of money, but I had no freedom, no way to escape her. And sometimes I had to satisfy her sadistic needs, and let her do what she wanted to me."

Suzy got up and walked over to the window. She was trying to comprehend her own feelings: relief that he was here; fury because he had left; anger over the fact he still had secrets; compassion as he confessed; love that he was here; love because he came to her; love, love for him.

She went back over to him and sat on the floor near his face to listen intently as he continued, trying not to judge, but to take in what he was revealing.

He carried on in the same dispassionate tone. "You see, I thought I was the lucky one. Jimmy was left with the pimp, used for prostitution on the streets, and kept under control with drugs and violence, along with several young girls, one of whom was Christine."

Suzy wanted to question him about Christine, but decided not to interrupt the flow of his confession, as he seemed set on revealing all to her now. She let him continue.

"Then one day Miranda, my madam, forced me to entertain a different kind of client." His tone altered and he seemed remorseful. He shifted onto his stomach and stared down at the carpet.

Then he grabbed her hand and held it tightly.

"I had to have sex with a man."

He stopped. He didn't look at her, but continued to stare at the carpet. He picked up his Coke and sipped it slowly. Then he let go of her hand and struggled to get off the bed, flinching.

Suzy stayed motionless and watched as he walked over to the minibar, took out a whisky and poured it into a glass. He drained the glass in one go and opened another bottle.

"Lawrence, please don't drink too much," she said softly.

He emptied the second bottle into the glass. Finally he looked at her, his voice uncertain as he asked quietly, "Do you want to ask Dominic to come and get you?"

"No," she said firmly. "History, remember?" Slowly, she took the glass from his hand and placed it on the bedside table. "You don't have to tell me any more, you know." Her eyes held his for a second and she wished she could take away the pain she could see in his face.

But he continued.

"I didn't want to do it. I'm not gay, and I never experimented in that way, before or since."

Suzy sensed he needed to justify himself. She was silent again.

"I didn't sleep well for several months after that night. I told Miranda I would never see a man again and she just laughed at me, saying it wouldn't be good for business."

Suzy was taken aback by the bitterness in his voice. She wanted to reach out and touch him, but didn't dare.

Then, very carefully, he attempted to sit on the edge of the bed.

"Fuck, I can't even sit down." Feebly, he attempted to grin, and Suzy could tell he was trying to lighten the mood.

She looked at him as he clenched himself again and sat on his hands, trying to make as little contact with the bed as possible. She forced herself to smile at him briefly, and his grin grew a little wider.

His tone became slightly more cheerful and animated as he continued with his confession. "But it did me a favour. She rewarded me with a PC and internet connection, and I discovered I had quite a knack with computers. I devoured any information I could lay my hands on. I also realised what a shit life I was living. In a way I envied Paul, the guy … you know…" and he looked at her, his eyes asking for her understanding. "He knew what he wanted and enjoyed, and it didn't seem superficial. I kept thinking about what he had said to me. 'Life without sex sucks, but I need some love in mine too.' I was so fucked up in my own little world I believed I didn't need love. Then, when I thought about it, I had never experienced love. I had no idea what a mum or dad was, and I was damned sure none of my clients gave a fuck about me, with the exception of one, possibly, Veronica Rigsby. You see, I sort of took some money from her and started to invest it. I repaid it all, together with a share of the profit I made. I just didn't bother to tell her about the money that I had taken in the first place." He paused again and watched Suzy's face for a hint of what she was thinking. Usually he had a good idea, as her face was so expressive, but she was giving nothing away this time.

"Well, the guy who is coming out of jail has found out about the money, and the police want to talk to me. I have spent the past month wondering if I might end up in jail because of something stupid I did eight years ago."

Suzy remained silent and expressionless, all the while thinking, *How can I help you? You're the one who needs keeping safe!*

He stood up again and wandered around the room as he continued. "This whipping, so eagerly given to me by Miranda, my former employer" – he glanced over to Suzy, the sadness back in his eyes for a moment – "earned me a copy of a will and a letter from the woman whose money I took." He still wouldn't use the word "stole". He had never meant it to be like that. "Veronica states it was a loan and that it was repaid. In fact, it was overpaid, and her estate now owes me one hundred thousand pounds, would you believe? It was Paul who had the will and the letter. He was Veronica's solicitor. I guess you could say he saved me. Anyway, Miranda also gave me a box of tapes which were previously missing, and some photographs which will help Lewis and I prove that the pimp, Josh Black, murdered Jimmy. We just need to find a witness, and then we can try to make sure he gets put away for good and can't harm anyone else."

Suzy walked over to him and took his hands in hers.

"Will you still take me on, Suzy? Please?"

"Try stopping me," she said softly. "Thank you for being honest with me, Lawrence. I can understand now how painful it is for you, but I think you've talked enough for the moment." She was already analysing what he had said. She wanted to help him sleep now, and formulate a plan of what to do next. She felt certain he wouldn't really want her to do anything, but doing nothing was not on her agenda!

They were both still naked, and she knelt before him. "Can I try to make you feel better? Would you like me to?" She began gently stroking his penis, pulling his foreskin back and forth. She steadily worked to harden him, to excite him, to take him to a better place than he had been lately, a place only she should share with him. She touched him with her tongue and he closed his eyes and softly ran his fingers through her hair, holding her to him, as she worked him with her mouth and hands. Eventually he gasped and released himself into her, and she drank him like an elixir, giving her eternal life, eternal love for him. She lingered, sucking, licking, caressing him with her tongue, until carefully he lifted her up and kissed her tenderly, longingly, passionately. Then he led her to the bed and motioned for her to lie down. He raised her knees and tenderly and masterfully began to lick, nibble, suck and drink his way to her orgasm, until she could take no more, and he was satisfied. For now, at least.

Finally they put their heads on the pillows and lay on their sides as he curled his body around her, each trying to grasp what sleep they could for the next few hours.

Chapter 63

Suzy was awake at 5 a.m. She was fearful of sleeping too deeply, in case he left in the night. She had made a mental list.

> Get him to tell me about the evidence and this witness they need.
> Ask him how I could help him.
> If he is reluctant to discuss it with me, speak to Lewis.
> See how Christine is and find out if she can go home to Dave.
> Don't let him go! Don't lose him again!

"Hey, baby." He opened his eyes, and they shone.
Oh my heart!
She turned to face him and gently kissed his lips. "Good morning! It's not even six o'clock yet!" She managed a smile, though her heart was in turmoil, dreading him saying he was going to leave. "Do you want some coffee?"
"That would be good."
They climbed out from under the duvet. He moved a little awkwardly at first, and after brushing their teeth they got under the shower. Suzy made sure he could feel the water on his back, hoping to alleviate the pain once more.
As they drank their coffee, she asked him about the evidence he had retrieved.
"The police had always believed that the last sighting of Jimmy was at a football match – Arsenal versus Paris Saint Germain. There are some photos of him talking to a guy. It looks like a Paris Saint Germain supporter. I need to go through the CCTV footage and hopefully see where they went. If we could just find an area to concentrate on – find a weapon" – then he looked at her, deadly serious – "and a body." He hesitated and took another sip of his coffee, his eyes not leaving hers. "I can't stop until I have done this, Suzy. You know that, don't you?"
"You have to let me help you, Lawrence." She tried to look equally serious, but somehow she felt a little weaker.

"I will not have you in danger. Black is going to try to prevent us from finding anything, and he will do anything to stop us. I can't live with the risk that he will find out about you. God knows what he would do if he could get to you!" His voice had risen, and he began to pace the small hotel room again.

"Did he cut Christine?"

He looked at her, unable to conceal his surprise. "Yes. How did you know?"

"I saw her scar one day in the kitchen. I'm putting two and two together here, Lawrence, from what bits of information you are choosing to give me." Her own voice was becoming a little more heated. "And sometimes I make it add up to a hundred and bloody one, damn it! How many times do I have to tell you, I want the truth so I don't have to make it up myself!"

"OK, OK. Yes, he cut Christine. He nearly killed her. That's how he ended up in jail. That's why I took her to Cheshire, to get her away from all this. That's why I need to keep her with me now, to protect her from him when he comes looking."

He hung his head, and momentarily wondered whether he was doing the right thing.

Suzy voiced his own thoughts. "Maybe she would be safer with Dave? They could go away for a while, just the two of them. How would he find her?"

"I ... I thought I could protect her best."

"Just think about it, Lawrence. Maybe you could focus on your task better knowing she was somewhere safe with Dave? Who is she with now?"

"One of Lewis's security guys is keeping his eye on her, and Black isn't released for another two days."

"Have you asked Christine what she wants, given her any options? Do you really think you can protect her all the time? How long is this going to take?"

"We discussed it and I believed I knew best. You know me, I don't much care for giving options." He remembered the time she had decided to go home instead of waiting for him at The Sway. He grinned. "People don't always choose the one I want!"

She couldn't help but smile back. But she had made her point.

"Please, consider if it would be better if she and Dave went away somewhere. Surely she would still be safe, and don't you think she would prefer that, deep down?"

Lawrence remained silent for a few minutes. He thought of the disgusting flat they were living in. Maybe Suzy was right. Christine and Dave could go back to St Lucia, for a few weeks, months, as long as it took…

"I'll talk to her," he conceded.

Suzy ticked that point off her list!

"Do you think the guy with Jimmy was French, then, from Paris?"

He glared at her, his expression stern and the words, *Oh no you don't, young lady!* written all over his face.

"Don't even think about it, Suzy. You don't seem to want to let me protect you. Well, I'll be damned if you think I'm going to let you put yourself in any danger. You are NOT to go to Paris." He was shouting, clearly very angry.

Suzy tried to remain calm, hoping it would make him less cross. "I am only trying to help, Lawrence."

"Worrying me that you are going to do something stupid isn't helping me, Suzy." The anger remained in his voice and she decided to bide her time before broaching this subject again, with Lewis Deane if necessary. And she was going to Paris. But she wouldn't raise that just yet, either.

"Do you want some breakfast? I could ring room service."

"I think I need to be heading back to Christine." His voice quietened. "I guess we had better get dressed."

Please don't go yet! She couldn't bear the thought of him leaving without her, especially not with this tension between them.

He picked up her clothes and walked towards her. He ran his hands across her shoulders and down her arms. He touched her breasts and felt her breath on him as she leaned into his chest.

"I don't want you to go, Lawrence. I can't stand to lose you again."

He lifted her face up to look into her eyes. "It will be alright, baby. Everything will be OK. I promise. Come on, let's get dressed and go for a walk."

Suddenly there was a knock at the door.

"Just a moment." Lawrence quickly pulled on his jogging bottoms and motioned for Suzy, still naked, to go into the bathroom. He opened the door.

"Mr Bane."

Lawrence stepped into the hallway, and pulled the door to. "It's OK, Dan, she's still here."

"I just wanted to check you and Miss Harper were OK."

"We're fine. Do me a favour. Check with Ian that Christine is OK, and ask him if he has the video scanning equipment. I need to start going through the tapes. We'll hang around in the foyer. Wait there and I'll meet you in the gents." Lawrence raised his eyebrow, indicating he could think of no other way of keeping out of sight of Suzy.

"Got it, Mr Bane."

Lawrence went back into the room.

"Who was that?" asked Suzy.

"Someone got the wrong room, that's all." He felt bad about lying to her. *She just wants you to trust her, and so far she has done everything to earn that trust, you prick!*

He looked her up and down. She was fully clothed.

"I wanted to dress you!" He suddenly looked unsure of himself. He picked up his sweatshirt, but as he was about to struggle to pull it on Suzy took it from him.

"Kneel down and I'll dress you for a change." She smiled, certain that he would, and he did.

They gathered their things and, holding hands, walked down into the foyer.

Lawrence caught sight of Dan and excused himself to visit the loo.

"Ian has the equipment and can set it up at your flat when you're ready. Christine is fine; still asleep!"

"Mmm. Sorry for the early start. Give me your phone and let me speak to Ian." Lawrence took Dan's mobile.

He arranged for Ian to go to the flat at 10 a.m.

He returned to the foyer. Suzy was sitting on a sofa, staring out of the window. He observed her for a moment, trying to retain the image of her, to keep him going, for how long he didn't know, until he saw her again. He knew her mood would be far from relaxed, and he thought about her trip to Paris. Should he speak to Peter Dane and tell him it must be cancelled? *She will never forgive you.*

"Hey, baby. Penny for your thoughts."

She turned to face him, and he saw that she was straining to hold back tears. He sat beside her and stroked the back of her hand, twisting the panther ring around her finger. He brought it to his lips and kissed it. Then he put his arm around her and hugged her to him for a few minutes. Finally he broke their shared silence.

"Come on. Let's get you back to Dominic."

He was beginning to feel physically more comfortable now, and as he sat next to her on the Tube he tried to reassure her that he would soon be finished here, that he would call her to keep her informed of his progress, and to let her know when he would be returning to Cheshire. He told her to let Steve and Jane know that everything was alright, and to tell them he just needed to finish off some outstanding business.

He also asked her not to go to Paris, not until he came home to her and this whole episode was over.

"Don't you think it better I just carry on as normal? At least it will take my mind off you, and help pass the time!" She couldn't quite keep the bitterness from her voice, and their journey continued in silence.

Chapter 64

Before Suzy realised it, the Crowne Plaza Hotel was in front of them. She looked up at Lawrence.

"How did you know we were staying here?"

He squeezed her hand and led her into the hotel. Of course, once he found out that Suzy was in London, and that Lewis had instructed Dan to omit that information from the reports he sent to Lawrence, Lawrence made sure he knew everything that happened that he didn't know before, including where she had been staying.

"I heard someone mention it in the bar the other night," he lied. Again.

She looked at him quizzically.

"Will you stay and have a quick bite to eat?" She wanted to hold on to him for as long as possible, and they needed to talk. She needed to talk.

He looked at his cheap plastic watch; it read 7.30 a.m. Hell, it had been a long morning so far!

"OK. Do you want to let Dominic know you're back?"

She sent a quick text to say she would come up to the room in half an hour. She didn't want to handle Dominic's questions right now, especially not in front of Lawrence.

As they sat having some juice and cereal, Suzy wriggled a little in her chair, and then sat upright. Lawrence observed her from the corner of his eye and waited for her to start talking. Her voice was low and a little wobbly as she forced back any tears on the brink of escaping her eyes.

"I have taken you on, Lawrence, with all your shit. Goodness knows you've got enough of it. I don't recall ever mentioning this hotel. It wouldn't surprise me to find out you've had someone spying on me!" She didn't look at him, but kept caressing her glass of fresh orange juice.

He stopped eating and looked directly at her.

She continued, "But now you have to let me in. I won't stay on the outside of your life any longer. I always wanted to be part of a team with someone, with you. I won't be kept in the audience while you are the player, Lawrence. Let me at least see if I can help you, help with Jimmy's disappearance, if it means that much to you." She lifted her head and her eyes met his.

He took her hands from the glass. His face was expressionless and his eyes drilled into her.

Why does he do that to me?

"I only ever want you to be safe, Suzy, and you won't be if you are around me at the moment." He was imploring her to give in; to acquiesce to what he thought was best.

But she thought he was wrong.

"You cannot wrap me in cotton wool – I don't want to be cosseted and safe. Damn it, Lawrence, I need to do something. I need to be involved in your life; all of it, including what you feel you have to do here. Let me take Christine's place and help to look after you. I can work with you on trying to find a witness or a weapon or something! You said yourself that there are security guys to help us. You once said I was a bright woman. I can help you. I love you, Lawrence, and I need to be with you. I'm not afraid."

He continued to stare at her in silence. Eventually he stood up.

"Take me to Dominic," he ordered.

Oh, is my Lawrence back?

* * *

With a puzzled expression on his face, Dominic let them into the hotel room.

Dan had met with Dominic in the Hilton last night and explained that Bane was just seeing to some old unfinished business, and it was better that Suzy, and his friends in the North, were not seen to be connected with him. When questioned further by Dominic, Dan explained he was not authorised to say any more!

A visit from Lawrence Bane was, therefore, not expected.

Lawrence carefully sat on one of the twin beds. The pain in his arse was nothing compared to that in his head and heart right now!

"Your cousin wants to stay and help me prove that a pimp murdered my best friend about four years ago. Do you think she should?"

Dominic stared at the man in the cheap clothes standing in front of him. Was this the rich and controlling Lawrence Bane?

Suzy stared at Lawrence and then at Dominic. She wasn't about to let the two men in her life gang up on her. "I help or I'm leaving. Both of you! Talk about it if you like. I'm going down to the bar." With that, she stormed out.

Lawrence held his head in his hands and stared at the carpet. "I never meant for this to happen."

Dominic went to the minibar and took out two cans of Coke. "I bet you didn't." He passed one to Lawrence.

"No," he replied. "I think we had better go down to her. She may as well hear what I have to say. Richard is going to be pretty pissed off with me." Lawrence got to his feet and glanced at the other man.

"If it's any consolation, he'll be mad at me too. He thinks I've brought her on a sight-seeing trip." Dominic shot Lawrence a sly schoolboy grin. "But he can be damned good when he's angry, so it may not be all bad."

Too much information, but Lawrence appreciated the humour.

Lawrence shook his head when he saw Suzy at the bar with a half-empty glass of white wine in her hand, already taking another gulp. The bartender looked apologetically at the two men.

"She insisted..." he began, and Lawrence just nodded.

"Double Jack Daniels." Lawrence looked at Dominic. "Er, can this go on your room tab? I don't have money for this right at the moment."

"No problem. I'll have the same."

"Let's sit over here." Lawrence took Suzy's arm and led her to a seat by the window. He waited until Dominic joined them, and then said that they would all go to Christine's and see what a dump he was living in. If Dominic agreed, Christine would return to Cheshire with him, on the proviso that she and Dave went away for a few weeks. Richard would sort out any finances, including the cost of a wedding – if that was what they wanted.

Suzy shot him a quick glance as she tucked into the nuts the bartender had brought over, to try to soak up some of the wine she was now regretting drinking!

"Although we hope they will wait till we are all together again, and can celebrate with them, of course," he added.

Suzy could stay if she wanted to, but she had to agree to do what Lawrence or Lewis told her, no arguments. Lawrence would take on board all the comments she had made earlier.

In the meantime, he was thinking about how she could be with him, and help him, and stay safe.

Suzy thought that she had successfully ticked everything off her list.

Chapter 65

Christine opened the door to the flat and stared at Lawrence, Suzy and the handsome dark-haired guy standing with them.

"Lawrence?" She looked at him enquiringly.

His look told her not to ask.

Lawrence had already seen the shocked, sombre expressions on Suzy and Dominic's faces as he led them to Whitechapel and the high-rise flats on Old Montague Street. Part of him hoped that the wretchedness of their abode would make Suzy see sense and return home with Dominic. But, for the most part, he clung to the possibility that they might just make this big change of plan work. Since leaving the hotel, he had mulled over Suzy's words. "Let me take Christine's place … You once said I was a bright woman. I can help you…" He was determined to try to make it work, if she decided to stay.

The flat was full. Ian was going through the VCR equipment, ready to view the tapes. Dominic and Suzy perched on the two-seater sofa, Christine had given up trying to offer a drink to everyone, as they only had three cups, and Lawrence was perched on the arm of the armchair, studying Suzy's expression, trying to gauge whether she was really ready for this task she was so desperate to help him with, and all that it entailed.

He explained to Christine that it might be better if she returned to Manchester with Dominic and went away for a while with Dave.

She looked upset at the suggestion at first, and protested she wanted to be with Lawrence and didn't want to go back without him. She realised, as he had used the term "with Dominic", that Suzy was intending to stay with him. She looked at the younger woman.

"Suzy, you don't deserve to have to stay here."

"Neither do you, Christine. I don't know what happened in your past…"

Christine looked embarrassed, and Suzy regretted her last words. She simply added, "I need to be with him."

Lawrence walked over to Christine and put his arm around her shoulders.

"And I think you need to be with Dave now. I can't thank you enough for all you do for me, Christine, and before too long we can all be together again. But right now, I think you should go with Dominic and we'll arrange for you guys to get away for a while."

* * *

By one o'clock that afternoon, Lawrence and Suzy were alone in the flat. Christine had taken her on a very quick spending spree, to buy two pairs of jeans, two sweatshirts, a few more pairs of knickers and socks, a bra and a pair of trainers, all from one of the bargain bazaars in Whitechapel, with money borrowed from Dominic.

"Keep a tab and I'll pay you back." Lawrence had told him.

Lawrence did wonder about the hundred grand that should be sitting in Suzy's bank account. *Does she even know about it?* He made a mental note to check just how she managed her finances.

Dominic and Christine said their goodbyes in the flat and left to take the train to Manchester. Dominic was to arrange for Dave to meet Christine at the boys' apartment, from where they would book a flight and accommodation in St Lucia and spend another month in the sunshine. Lawrence would contact Christine one way or another to let her know when she could expect to be home at The Sway gatehouse, once Josh Black was safely back behind bars.

Ian went through the video equipment with Lawrence, before leaving to telephone Lewis with the change of plan. Dan was on his way back to Manchester, seated not too far from Christine and Dominic on the train, and still trying to work out whether it was better to be the one to see Lewis once he'd time to digest the latest news from Ian, rather than the one to have to break the news to him over the phone. He shifted uncomfortably in his seat.

In the meantime, Lawrence went through his rules with Suzy.

She was not to go out of the flat without Lawrence or Ian.

She was not to make any protest if Lawrence was to go out alone – Ian was there to protect her first and foremost.

Her main task would be to keep them fed. After all, she wanted to take Christine's place.

She could choose to comfort her boyfriend and help take his mind off things, when it was safe and appropriate so to do. (This part had never been one of Christine's tasks!)

Suzy wasn't sure about No. 2, but she liked the idea of No. 4, and was willing to give it a go.

"How about now?" she asked playfully, trying desperately not to dwell on this small, unwelcoming space that was to be home for, she hoped, a short while.

Lawrence finally smiled at her.

"Not yet, baby. I am going to go through these tapes, and let's see if we can find ourselves a witness to start looking for!" He leaned over and kissed her. He was starting to realise how good it was to have her here with him.

Chapter 66

Lawrence had already taken in the information contained in the transcripts of conversations and photographs. He wasn't sure who the photographer was or why they had taken shots of Jimmy, but, as he went through them, he was beginning to think he knew what had been going on. There was a picture of Jimmy entering the Arsenal Emirates football ground alone. Then there was one of him with another man, wearing a Paris St Germain scarf. Another showed the two of them leaving together, via Clock End Bridge, which was the away supporters' end. Why was Jimmy there, with this guy?

He quickly glanced through a few of the other pictures and then decided to concentrate on the video footage. Ian had set the equipment up in the bedroom.

Suzy had been sitting quietly at the little table, compiling a shopping list for food they could manage to cook on the two rings available: omelettes, soup, chilli...

She realised that she had presented Lawrence with quite a predicament when she threatened to leave him if he didn't let her help him. Now she wanted to make sure that her contribution would be valuable, and she did not intend to get in his way or distract him, well, not too much anyway, from his mission. She observed him looking at some photographs and then going into the bedroom. He didn't close the door, so she decided to follow him in there.

"Would you like some coffee?"

"OK," he replied, looking at her face. "I am glad you're here, you know. But you can leave at any time. I'll get someone to take you home and make sure you are..."

She knew he was going to say safe, but he hesitated. He knew she didn't want to hear that.

"I'm staying right here." She ran her hand down his arm. "Are you comfy? Do you need any cream on?" She pictured the lines and cuts across his back.

"It's getting better." His face was serious and he didn't move away from her touch.

"Why did you choose to live here, in this town, in this flat?" She glanced around.

"Lewis chose it. I think he was teaching me a lesson for being such a pain in the arse to him a lot of the time. Goodness knows what he'll do when he finds out I've brought you here!" He smiled for a moment. "I just hope he doesn't smash my bike up!"

"You've given him your bike?" Suzy couldn't believe he would have parted with either of his bikes. And what about his car? She remembered how cagey he had been about The Sway and John Ryder. There was still a lot for her to understand.

"It's just on loan – until I can get my life back. Come and look over here."

He took her hand and went back into the living room. He led her over to the window.

"From here, you can see that three-storey house over there."

Suzy looked out to where he was pointing.

"That's Josh Black's place. As far as we know, he will be coming back to it the day after tomorrow. The plan is to keep tabs on him, and no doubt he will be doing the same with me." He squeezed her hand as if to reassure her it would be OK. "We're hoping he will make some slip-up and lead us to where Jimmy was killed. That's why we're here in this dump. Now, coffee would be good, and do you want to see some video footage? I must warn you, though, I don't know what's on there or how long it's going to take."

"Yes." She brought his hand up and brushed her cheek against it. "I'm glad you let me stay."

He raised his eyebrow. "You didn't give me a choice. I cannot have you leave me, Suzy Harper." He planted a soft kiss on her lips. "I'll get the tape ready."

* * *

Three hours and two cups of coffee later, Lawrence suggested they go for a walk to get some fresh air. They made their way to a small park, and sat quietly on a bench watching the passers-by. Progress on the video had been very slow. Lawrence was hopeful they were getting somewhere when he detected Jimmy going through one of the turnstiles at the football ground. The photographs had revealed he was wearing a bright blue anorak, which stood out so that even Suzy had been able to pick him out in the crowd. But there were no further sightings in that part of the stadium. After their walk, Lawrence intended to concentrate on the coverage of the away supporters' end, to see if they could find any trace of him with the Paris St Germain supporter in the photograph.

On the way back to the flat they called in at the supermarket for some provisions, and had just finished a supper of soup and crusty bread when Ian knocked on the door. It was now 8 p.m.

"Lewis will be here in the morning." He looked at Lawrence, and Suzy sensed he had more to say and was reluctant to say it in front of her.

"It's OK." Lawrence obviously thought the same. "You can say anything to both of us from now on. Looks like we're a team." He took Suzy's hand.

Oh my heart! A team.

"Dan said he's not in a good mood! And he wants to know what is happening about Charles Rigsby."

"Well." Lawrence almost sighed with relief. "I can give him some good news on that front at least." He went into the bedroom and retrieved the brown envelope, passing it to Ian so he could read through the contents of the letter.

"So you get a hundred grand out of it to boot? You lucky git!"

Not if you knew what I had to go through to end up with that letter. He thought of both Paul and Miranda.

* * *

Ian was staying in more comfortable accommodation just down the road, with an even better view of Black's property.

"How are you getting on with the tapes?" he asked Lawrence.

"We're just about to go through some more footage. Progress is slow, but we've picked him up entering the ground. Have a look through those photos and let me know what you think."

Ian studied one photo in particular. It showed Jimmy in his bright blue coat, standing with another man, and it looked as if the other man was getting something out of his coat pocket.

"If I had to guess what that was, I'd say it was a passport."

"That's what I thought." Lawrence studied the photo again. He was puzzled about this other man, and still more about the fact that Jimmy had never spoken to him about it.

* * *

When Lawrence first left Miranda he had rented a small flat, much like the one he was in now, except it had its own shower room. He had set it up with computer equipment as he started to invest in the stock markets and watched his money grow. It was at this time that he first made contact with Richard Groves, who assisted him in his dealings. He slept around with a few women, and saw Jimmy as often as he could, but mostly he kept himself to himself and wondered what to do with the rest of his life. He had not said anything to Jimmy, but he intended to get him away from Josh Black and set him up with a place and possibly a job, if Jimmy could handle it. If he could get him off the drugs. But then his friend had disappeared. The police weren't interested in a missing lowlife junkie rent boy. Their view was that, at twenty-six, he was old enough to look after himself, and there was nothing to suggest that anything bad had happened to him. Lawrence thought at first he had gone off on a bender, and expected him to appear back at Black's any moment. He had given up hoping that Jimmy would have the guts, let alone the means, to leave him.

But when Black attacked Christine, and threatened Lawrence, saying he could end up like Jimmy, Lawrence became certain that Black had killed his friend. He discussed the situation with Lewis, and they formed the plan to wait until Black was released and see if he could be lured into revealing some piece of evidence to prove that he had killed Jimmy.

Suzy asked Ian if he wanted a drink, but he said he would get going.

"I'll be over later in the morning, after you've had a chance to talk to Lewis." He raised his eyebrows at Lawrence, grateful that he didn't need to be there to explain to Lewis Lawrence's change of plan with regard to Christine and Suzy.

Chapter 67

By 11 p.m. Lawrence had been through another tape, and found nothing. Suzy had been unable to keep up with his study of the small screen, and had already made the bed up in the living room. The TV was on but she wasn't really paying much attention to it. It had been a very long day for her: tears, early-morning wine, and the fear that he was going to send her home had all taken their toll on her, but now she lay naked in bed and waited patiently until she could feel his body next to hers. Finally, he climbed in beside her.

It was a squeeze compared to their bed at The Sway, and even her own bed at her cottage back in Nantwich, but that just made it cosier. She sat up and told him to lie on his front.

"Let me put some more cream on your back. It's looking better already." She looked at the marks, which appeared marginally less angry, and realised just how much pain he had been in, and still was, to some extent.

"That feels good," he said appreciatively. "Not quite home here, is it? You've renewed my energy being here with me."

"Sing to me," she asked as she massaged the cream onto his back, and in his mellow voice, he quietly and beautifully sang, "You Make Me Feel Brand New".

"How come you have such a good voice? Have you ever sung in a band or anything?"

He laughed, glad of the distraction from the day's task. "We messed about a bit at school. We couldn't really afford any instruments, so singing was the cheapest option. I remember a music teacher telling me I had soul and should join the choir, but it wasn't cool and nobody expected anyone like me to join. I didn't conform, really. Jimmy could play the drums pretty well. We were a couple of idiots, now that I look back."

"You've come through it, though, Lawrence, and you should be proud of what you've achieved, what you have done for the children and the drop-in centre. It's helped to make you who you are today."

"You are the best thing in my life, Suzy, and I'm so grateful you can put up with me and my shit." He raised one eyebrow, and she thought of what she had said to him back at the hotel only that morning.

He smiled. "Come on. Let's get some sleep, I'm gonna need a good night's rest to be ready to face Lewis tomorrow."

They both slept more peacefully than they had done since he left her.

They were awake at seven and Suzy enquired about taking a shower.

"It's not quite that easy. There are six flats sharing the bathroom, and the queue starts about 5.30! Let's do it our own way." He grinned mischievously.

She stood naked before him, and stepped onto the towel he had placed on the floor in front of the sink, which he had filled with hot water. He then took a flannel, poured a little shower gel onto it and began to cover her body with soft sweeping motions, refreshing the water and the soap until he had cleansed his girl, then wrapped her in a towel that had been warming in front of the heater.

"Thank you," she whispered, as his lips came to hers and he kissed her delicately, as though she would break if he put too much pressure on her. *This is a bit different!*

She wondered why he seemed to be holding back from her. "Is everything OK?" she asked a little anxiously.

"Sure, baby. I'm just sorry it has to be like this. I only want the best for you, you know."

"You are the best for me, Lawrence, and I wouldn't want to be anywhere else."

They dressed and, after a quick breakfast, Lawrence started going through the third tape.

Suzy realised there was very little she could do at the moment. Lawrence studied the tapes far too quickly for her to follow, and she felt it was best to leave him alone to concentrate. The flat was clean, but she thought she could wash the little dirty laundry they had, and also the bed linen.

"Where is the washing machine?" she called to him.

"In the launderette down the road." He smiled to himself,

knowing she had probably never been to one before. "I think there's one on Aldersgate Street, about a ten-minute walk away. I'll come with you later."

"Can I go now? Just give me directions."

He stood in the doorway. "No. I'll get Ian to take you when Lewis gets here. Rule number one, remember!"

"OK," she conceded. She wondered what Lewis would say about her being there. All she wanted to do was help, but taking dirty washing to a launderette wasn't what she had in mind!

Lawrence had gone back into the bedroom, and he returned with a folder full of papers.

"Here." He indicated for her to sit at the small table. "You can go through these papers if you like. They appear to be transcripts of phone calls between various people. I've taken on board the information, but haven't had a chance to analyse it yet. You could try to put them into chronological order and see how they might piece together. Make a note if you come across anything interesting. Only if you want to." His eyes fixed on hers, as if he needed some assurance he wasn't asking too much of her.

"I'd like to." She smiled, glad of something to occupy her mind and stop her dwelling on the home comforts they were missing.

She quickly became engrossed in sorting the pages by the dates printed at the bottom of each sheet, before beginning to read what people had been talking about four years ago. She found references to drug deals, quantities of cocaine to be received on certain dates, names of sellers and consumers, information on goods stolen from warehouses, mobile phones, DVD players, with dates and destinations referred to as lock-ups and garages. One page recorded car registration numbers – were these stolen too?

Then on a page from November 2008 she came across a reference to "that fucking rent boy" who was going to "dish the dirt". There was an instruction to watch him.

She took the sheet into the bedroom. Lawrence was staring at the screen. It was fixed on a shot and he was trying to zoom in and refocus the image.

"Can I disturb you?" Suzy asked tentatively.

He looked up at her and smiled. "Any time, you know that."

Oh my heart! "Look at this." She passed him the transcript.

Lawrence scanned it and noted the date. He scribbled on a pad he had at his side, and sat back on the dining chair.

"Well done, baby, and I think there is something here." He showed her the screen. "Look at the guy's hand. I'm sure it's a ticket. I think this French guy was giving Jimmy a passport and a ticket. He was going to leave, Suzy." Lawrence ran his hand through his already ruffled hair, not for the first time that day. "I just can't understand why he didn't tell me."

"Maybe he was trying to protect you from Black. What do you think Black would have tried to do if he'd known you knew about it? Maybe you weren't the only one who felt the need to protect those around you." She knelt beside him and began to stroke his legs. Before she realised what she was doing she moved her hands up towards his crotch and began to feel for his penis through his jeans. He leaned back and closed his eyes, and she could feel him getting harder. She unfastened him and released him and hungrily took him in her mouth. He moaned and before long he released himself into her.

"I needed that." She looked up at him.

He pulled her to him and hugged her tightly. "I need you."

She went into the kitchen and brushed her teeth. He followed her and stood at her side.

"I will make this up to you," he was trying to reassure her. She silenced him as she put her finger to his lips.

"Stop worrying," she insisted. "I am here because I want to be. I need to be."

There was a knock at the door. Lawrence let Lewis in.

"Hey, it's good to see you. How's the bike?"

Lewis smiled at Lawrence, and the features on his face softened in acknowledgement of the true friendship between these two men. Suzy wondered how much Lewis knew about Lawrence's past. Including Paul…

"I've brought you both a gift." Lewis took off his coat and passed a gift bag to Suzy. She glanced at Lawrence, who raised one eyebrow.

"Thank you," said Suzy, surprised at this man whom she hardly knew. "Can I get you some tea or coffee?"

"Coffee would be good – strong, with a bit of milk, no sugar thanks."

Suzy then opened the gift bag and withdrew a bottle of Bollinger and two crystal champagne flutes.

"It's not a housewarming gift!" Lewis laughed at Lawrence. "Just a reminder of home and the need to get on with this job so you can come back, mate." He added quickly, "Not that I'm in any rush to give you your bike back just yet. It goes like the clappers and rides like a dream."

"Just don't tell me, and thanks." Lawrence was about to show him what he and Suzy had discovered this morning, but decided to wait a minute. "Can you get Ian to come round and take Suzy to the launderette?"

"Sure." Lewis rang Ian.

Chapter 68

The two men were alone.

"Well, start talking then. I'm eager to know about this change of plan." Lewis made himself comfy on the sofa.

Lawrence sipped his coffee and eyed his friend with a "what did you expect me to do" kind of look.

"She made it pretty hard for me to try to send her home..."

"I bet she did!" Lewis cut in.

"Look, she's bright, and eager to help us all get back home. She's been going through those transcripts I told you about, and some things are beginning to make sense. I think the key could be the French guy Jimmy appears to have been with at the Emirates."

"Did you know about this?"

Lawrence shook his head and looked away for a moment. "No. That's what bothers me, really. I thought Jimmy told me everything. I think he might have been trying to get away. It looked like he was being given a passport."

"Suzy speaks fluent French, right?"

"Yes." Lawrence was hesitant. "She has a trip planned, for Winstons, flying out to Paris next Wednesday. I didn't want her to go. Maybe now if someone goes with her, it would be a good place to start looking for this guy. Maybe now the fucking police will take more of an interest."

"We can handle this, Los." Lewis hadn't used Lawrence's nickname in a very long time. "But we may get some help from the French police. Show me the information you've got. I'll go with her. Dan will be in the shadows anyway. His ticket's already booked. Does she know about him?"

"No" At last Lawrence smiled. "And my life will be easier if we keep it that way. She's suspicious enough as it is about a couple of things." He wasn't comfortable keeping things from Suzy, but he felt sometimes it was better, for both of them! As well as making his life easier, it kept Suzy safe.

"OK, come on, let's have a look."

The two men went into the bedroom and Lawrence went through the transcript from November 2008, the photographs and the video footage. He also told him about the possible drug trafficking and thefts.

Lewis looked directly at him, his face expressionless, and asked in a serious tone, "Where did you get all this from? You realise Black will be after it."

"I know. I haven't told anyone else. It was Miranda."

"I hate to think what it cost you."

"Don't ask." Lawrence raised his eyebrow and his behind started itching where the cuts were healing. "Take a look at this." He gave Lewis the brown envelope.

Lewis studied the contents in detail, taking his time to review the information and assess its authenticity. "Well, whatever this cost, you're still standing, and my guess is it was worth it."

Lawrence drained the dregs from his coffee cup. "I guess so. Do you need to take it to your friend at the station, or do we go direct to Rawlins or even Rigsby with it?"

"Rigsby will need to know. Do you think he's pulling a fast one with the will? Does he know about the hundred grand, I wonder? I'll let my contact know anyway, and the police won't come hunting you down!"

By the end of the day, Lawrence had gone through the third tape. He had analysed all the scenes with footage of Jimmy.

> Arrives at the Emirates stadium
> In the away team's end with the French supporter
> An exchange of documents and confirmation that the two men stayed together throughout the match. Was this a gay friend of Jimmy's? Was Jimmy gay?
> Leaves the stadium via the Clock End Bridge, with the French guy

Lawrence observed the two men standing at the Drayton Park railway station. Then he noticed a third person loitering between them and the bridge. What was he doing? It looked like the camera angle wouldn't pick up any more activity, until the two men moved off after about ten minutes. Then the third man followed in their direction. It looked like they were heading somewhere directly opposite the station. He needed to know where they had been going.

He asked Suzy for her phone and switched her SIM card for one of his. Then he looked on Google Earth. It was a block of allotments.

Lewis was staying the night with Ian, and would be making an appearance tomorrow morning. Ian would be surveying Black's place, expecting him to return at some point that day. Radio communications had been set up using Blue Securities' equipment – transceivers which provided encrypted communications for the team. Dan was also due to join them.

Lawrence would discuss this latest turn with Lewis in the morning. He was also going to discuss the trip to Paris with Suzy.

Chapter 69

Lawrence woke at six the next day. Suzy was still asleep. He quietly slipped out of bed, pulled on a sweatshirt and jogging bottoms and went into the bedroom.

He closed the door so as not to wake Suzy, and started to print off the stills he had selected last night from the CCTV footage of Jimmy with the French guy. The clearest shot revealed a tall, thin man with brown hair, aged about twenty-five. A Paris Saint Germain supporter, wearing their scarf, black jeans and a dark blue Nike jacket. He was also wearing a baseball cap as he left the stadium. Lawrence struggled to enlarge the still frame, while retaining the focus; the cap appeared to have a logo on the front – was it a corporate logo, possibly somewhere the guy worked?

He turned to the box and picked up a fourth tape. This was not labelled with the police identification numbers, and he wasn't sure where this had come from. He inserted it into the machine and sat back to view its contents. He suddenly sat upright and looked more closely at the screen as he realised it was footage of the allotments. He slowed the speed down as the camera picked up two men climbing over the fence into the allotment block. It was Jimmy and his companion. He then speeded the action up slightly, as he realised they were going to have sex. Lawrence felt dismayed that he had never considered his friend choosing a homosexual relationship. It was an unspoken subject between them, and Lawrence had assumed that Jimmy was so damaged from the abuse he had suffered for so long that he didn't actually have any kind of sexual activity – by choice.

With his guilt tormenting him, his mind was dragged back to the video footage. The third man from the previous tape was suddenly in the frame. Jimmy and his companion were adjusting their clothes. They saw the other man heading towards them. There was a scramble, and the French guy moved away, taking something from his pocket. Lawrence watched as Jimmy was knocked to the ground, and the third man brought a knife from his coat. His back obscured the camera, and it was impossible for Lawrence to see what was happening. The man then walked away. Jimmy didn't move. The French guy had vanished. The third man went out of shot, and then nothing happened for the next thirty minutes of footage.

Lawrence paused the tape and made himself a strong coffee. Suzy opened her eyes.

"You want one?" he asked quietly.

"Yes please."

"Don't get up yet. It's a bit chilly. Let the place warm up before you come out from under the duvet, baby."

"Do you want to come and join me?" She looked at him, hopefully.

"Not just yet – keep it warm for me and I'll come back. I just need to check something out."

Suzy could tell he had something on his mind. She watched him go back into the bedroom and close the door. Had he made a breakthrough? She decided she would leave him to focus on the task in hand and wait for him to come back to her. She pulled the duvet around her and flicked the TV on, sipping her coffee as she half-heartedly watched the news.

Lawrence started the tape again, and watched as the third man returned to the allotment, armed with a shovel! Lawrence sat, horrified, as the man dug a shallow grave, and placed the body in it. He looked up to check he hadn't been observed. The camera captured a clear shot of Josh Black's face, before he turned and walked away, clearly satisfied that no one would look twice at just another freshly dug allotment.

Lawrence called over to Suzy and she gripped his hand as she sat beside him in front of the screen.

"Oh, Lawrence!" she exclaimed.

He remained silent by her side, his mind racing. The phone transcripts, the references to drug dealing, Jimmy murdered, the French guy. *Where is he? Surely this was enough to go to the police with. Who knows about this tape? This wasn't from the police evidence box. Miranda!*

Lawrence looked at his cheap watch. It was just after 8.30 a.m. There was a knock at the door, and he opened it to Lewis.

"You'd better come in and look at this."

Lewis's face darkened. He glanced at Lawrence and then turned to Suzy.

"Could you make some coffee, please? Strong."

"Sure." Suzy left the bedroom and closed the door behind her. The two men needed to talk.

"We need to contact the police and get over to Miranda's. Black was seen leaving the prison at eight this morning, apparently trying to disguise himself. He hasn't come back to his place yet, and his last conversation with Rawlins ended their relationship. I think he's found out about the tapes and is looking for Miranda. Does he know where she lives now?"

"I don't know." Lawrence thought for a second. "You call the police and then stay here with Suzy. I'll go to Miranda's."

"Wait for Dan, he'll be here in five minutes." Lewis was communicating with Ian and Dan on his transceiver. Lawrence agreed it was the right thing to do.

It was a long five minutes, and Suzy listened to Lewis's conversation with the police. She gathered someone was being sent to Miranda's apartment.

Lawrence became nervous, wondering if Black could possibly know where his former madam currently lived. He paced the room thinking of Jimmy, Christine and Suzy and some of the things he had been wrong about recently. *Now is not the time to be doubting yourself. Where the hell is Dan?*

Dan finally knocked at the door with Ian at his side. Lawrence grabbed his jacket and headed to the Tube station with Dan. Ian stayed with Lewis and Suzy, and they continued to observe Black's house.

Chapter 70

Miranda had known something wasn't right about the disappearance of Jimmy Havers.

Although she had never liked Josh Black, and how he treated his whores and rent boys, she had never felt the need to do anything about it. He took whatever he could get from vulnerable, desperate young people, and made a pittance out of their miserable lives. She took the cherries, the ones who would command a higher price. They were usually girls, but on one occasion she had made an exception and taken that beautiful boy. She was satisfied, and her dependants seemed to quite like what they got out of it – comfortable living standards, the odd treat, and eventually, in most cases, release and a chance to start afresh somewhere.

But she remembered that fateful night when Black had brutally attacked Christine, fully aware that he would no doubt have killed her if it hadn't been for Lawrence. So, could he have killed Jimmy? Was it because he was threatening to leave and dish the dirt on Black and his cronies? She had one of her men keep a watch on Black, and also Harry Rawlins, as he appeared to be in Black's pocket. She was interested to know why they had gone to such efforts to get hold of the evidence box the police had on Jimmy's last known destination – the Arsenal football match. She had lots of favours to call in from all sorts of acquaintances, and so had no difficulty in stealing the stolen tapes from Rawlins, and he didn't have a clue!

She collated her own box of evidence, with photographs, transcripts of telephone conversations between Black, Rawlins, and various other dodgy associates. She was quite pleased with herself.

She always knew they would come in handy. It was even better knowing that Lawrence would want them. Her price wouldn't be too high; just a bit of fun with him.

She hadn't expected Veronica Rigsby's name to come up, and she was positively ecstatic after she had spoken to Paul Irvine about Lawrence's little problem of being accused of stealing £100,000, which, of course, she was quick to find out about. Suddenly her price had gone up, and she couldn't wait to see her favourite protégé.

Of course, after Veronica's death, Paul knew he had a duty to find Lawrence and inform him about the letter, the will and the £100,000 owing to him, but Paul believed Bane would prefer not to have his past come back to hit him. It may be hard to avoid publicity, and Paul knew Lawrence didn't need the money. He had reluctantly passed everything to Miranda when she advised him that Lawrence may have need of some proof about the money he had initially "acquired" from Veronica.

Miranda hadn't been disappointed, except that she knew she would never see her young gigolo again. Being well aware of the danger of possessing that fourth tape from the allotments, she and her new man made plans to leave and start a new life together. Lawrence could take care of it and finally get the justice for his friend he so desperately sought.

* * *

By the time Lawrence and Dan had raced up to the penthouse flat on the top floor of the exclusive apartment block in the middle of the city, two policemen were in the hallway, the paramedics were in the penthouse, and a cloth covered Miranda's dead body.

Dan had heard from Lewis on the radio that Black had been arrested for the murder of Miranda Cleveley. Due to Lawrence and Lewis's prompt action they had caught him at the scene. Unfortunately, it had been too late to save her.

The police had found packed suitcases in the hallway and two tickets to Antigua on the telephone table. They were later to discover that Miranda and the new man in her life were to have flown out to Antigua the day before Black was due to be released, to begin a new life. However, her boyfriend's business commitments had caused a delay of two days, and neither of them foresaw the consequences that this delay led to.

* * *

Two days before Josh Black was due to be released on licence, he was informed that Lawrence Bane had paid a visit to his old digs, his former gigolo pad owned by Miranda. She was seen leaving the apartment with a smile on her face. Black was not the brightest spark in the box and it took him two days to discover that the incriminating tapes, including his "trophy" tape of Jimmy Havers' murder, had gone missing. He was owed a favour from a crooked prison warden for some free pussy Black had been making available to him, and he finally discovered Miranda Cleveley's most recent address.

Black didn't need Rawlins any more. The pimp now had all the information he required. He would go directly to Cleveley's and sort that bitch out once and for all; he was done with her interfering with his whores and rent boys and now she'd got it coming to her. Then he would sort out Bane; at least Rawlins had been useful for something, and Black knew exactly where that bastard was holed up in Whitechapel; cheeky fucker, staying right across the road from Black's own digs!

Black lay in his prison cell for the last time, knowing the prison warden was busy shagging one of his most accomplished whores – a price worth paying for a forged entry on Josh Black's release papers. Departing at 8 a.m. would give him just enough time to kill two people before his recorded release time of 10 a.m. He would have the perfect alibi – how could he commit murder if he were still a guest of Her Majesty's prison service?

But Black was never the brightest spark in the box.

He was also charged with the murder of Jimmy Havers, following Lewis's discussion with the detectives, assuring them he had all the evidence they would need, and a location for the body.

Chapter 71

Suzy and Lawrence gathered their few belongings from the flat and locked the door as they left. They had some matters to discuss, like the £100,000 sitting in her bank account that she still hadn't noticed! And the question of the possible guardianship of a baby! But the future was looking bright.

"We can go home now."

Chapter 72

Three months later, the inquests had been completed. Black was back behind bars – for good this time.

On a cold sunny day, while Suzy was working with the French team from Winstons in Paris, Lawrence Bane was pictured standing alone beside the grave of the woman who had changed his life. She believed she had saved him. He hadn't been able to save her. Silently, he apologised, and thanked her. He realised she had understood he needed to know what had happened to his oldest friend, and to seek justice for him. It had cost her her life.

Two days later, under a grey sky, with the trees swaying in a light breeze, Suzy stood beside Lawrence, listening to the vicar's words as Jimmy's body was finally laid to rest.

Lawrence wiped away his tears and prayed that his friend was now at peace. He squeezed Suzy's hand.

Chapter 73

Christine called to say she would see them in the morning, as she closed the door to The Sway behind her, leaving Lawrence and Suzy to enjoy their candlelit meal in the dining room, with James Morrison singing "I Won't Let You Go" on the iPod.

As soon as he heard the door shut, Lawrence raised one eyebrow.

"Shall we?" He stood up and walked around to pull her chair back, as she got to her feet. Slowly he lifted the dress over her head, quickly released her breasts from her bra and leaned down to suck at her nipples. He eased her pants down as he lowered himself to lightly trail his tongue along her abdomen, brushing over her pubic hair, then running his hands down her slender legs.

As he did this she pulled his Karl Lagerfeld T-shirt over his head. He raised himself up and she unfastened his Armani jeans, and lowered them, together with his Armani trunks, before removing them entirely. This was her designer label Lawrence. As they became naked, he took her right hand in his left, placed his right arm around her waist and they twirled around the room to the soft music, kissing, before slowly lowering themselves to the floor and making love on the carpet. With the super-king-sized bed upstairs, and the box on the bedside table, all was as it should be.

THE END

About the Author

I am happily married and live in Cheshire with my husband and our eight-year-old son.

Having studied English, French and German 'A' levels, I'm not sure how I ended up going down the accountancy training route – but I did!

Working full time and studying at home alone was not the best way to achieve a professional qualification, but I did it. I guess it brought out my "I work alone" ethic, and made me believe that I could achieve anything, reaching my target of being a finance director at the age of thirty-four.

Having been part of a very successful team in a privately owned UK company with subsidiaries in France and South Africa, I was considering changing my X-Type Jaguar for a Porsche Boxster at the age of forty-one when I got pregnant.

My husband (well, eventually he became my husband!) and I had been together twelve years and didn't think we could have children, so it was a huge shock for both of us. It was also a big shock for my boss and colleagues at work. At the age of forty-two, I left to start my maternity leave amid assurances that I would be contactable by email, I would call in at the office and I would be back in time for year-end. Any change of car was put on hold!

My baby was ten days late and I remember taking a phone call in the hospital to take part in a board meeting to complete an acquisition of an industrial site in France we had been working on. At three months old, my baby started his own career in a nursery, 7.30 a.m. till 6 p.m., five days a week. His father was busy working in his own practice and I needed to be running at full speed with group year-end. And, for the first time in my life, I didn't want to be there.

I remember, just before I was due back at work full time, I had arranged to see the bank manager. He waited patiently upstairs while I finished breastfeeding my baby in my office downstairs. Oh, how things had changed.

My life was radically different. I realised I did not want to be at work any more – I wanted to be home, holding and feeding my baby, taking him for walks in his pushchair, hugging him and being there for him. I had changed. Maybe it was because I was forty-two and thought we would never have children, or maybe it was the fact that my job was very demanding; I knew I would have to travel to France and South Africa and that working part-time was not an option, but I decided I needed to leave. Of course, financially that wasn't a viable option, and I *had* just treated myself to an E-Class Mercedes!

But an opportunity arose and for the next two years I worked my butt off and left with a shed-load of money when my son was three and a half.

I loved being a mum, but I kept some professional contacts doing pension trustee work. I enjoyed the school run and got involved with my son's primary school very early on, wanting to give something back to the community as I felt I had been so lucky in my life.

However, by the time my son was seven, and I had quit volunteering on the school's board of governors, deciding that it wasn't for me, I wondered what to do with the rest of my life.

First I started piano lessons. Second, I had always wanted to write a book and had ideas for a series of children's stories. Then I read *Fifty Shades of Grey*. Twice. I treated it as a reference book and decided I wanted to write a book like this! I read more erotica.

I sat down to write in June 2012 and thought, "This is actually quite hard!" But I persevered and, when Sam went back to school in the September, I began in earnest to put the story in my head onto paper. I was soon going to be fifty; I wasn't ready for that, but the fun I've had writing erotic romance has made me happy and excited about the next phase in my life – not to mention my husband too! We got married in 2010, by the way.

I love what I do and I hope people will enjoy reading my stories. I hope they will make them smile, feel good about themselves, and have fun!

Mollie Blake

Dear Reader,

In my story I have referred to some brutal, illegal events including prostitution, abuse and physical violence. My stories are all fictional, based on characters and events entirely drawn from my imagination. But, as we all know, situations can arise in real life that no one should have to endure. If you have ever been the victim of abuse, please remember there are people who can help.

Please visit my website at mollieblake.co.uk/help for more information.

Please never feel that you are alone or unimportant.

Mollie x

Coming next from Mollie Blake ...

The Secret at Arnford Hall

September 2014

Here's a teaser ...

Chapter 1

Gabriel Black sat on the black leather and chrome chair in front of the beech desk. It was Monday, the twenty-eighth of August, 2017, and the sunshine was streaming through the windows of the fourth-floor offices of Abacus and Cornworthy Solicitors in Manchester. The sunlight formed a vivid bright triangle on the corner of the desk next to Gabriel's coffee cup, and he was mindlessly creating the image of a sword in its sheath with the shadow of his pen; a slight distraction from the document in front of him. His dark expression matched his Hugo Boss black suit, dark blue shirt and deep grey silk tie. He had not taken his jacket off, despite the heat of the day. He took a sip of his coffee and frowned.

One of the family solicitors, Andrew Cornworthy, was sitting back in his chair observing his client through his rimless spectacles. Andrew was fifty-eight and had represented the Black family for the last thirty years. Over eight years ago, he had been instrumental in preparing the document now under review, and was mildly amused at his client's growing frustration with it. Of course, no one had actually expected something to happen to necessitate this document to come into effect … but it had.

Andrew leaned forward and spoke quietly to the man who was still staring at the shadow of his pen.

'It accurately reflects your and Eliza's wishes at the time of John's birth. Of course, its, let's say, unique character could make it unenforceable.'

Gabriel looked up at Andrew and his frown deepened.

Andrew refused to be unnerved by his formidable glare. He knew his client well and continued, 'But we both know that wouldn't be in the spirit in which it was written, and wouldn't follow Eliza's wishes. When you're ready, perhaps you could let me know how you wish to proceed.'

He sat back again and, placing his elbows on his waist, formed an apex with his fingers and thumbs, and contemplated nothing in particular. If it were not for the tragic circumstances which were responsible for the necessary appointment, he would have almost enjoyed it.

'Don't patronise me, Andrew. I know what I agreed to. But I should consider what's in the best interests of the child.'

'I think Eliza already did that, in getting you to agree to the conditions in the first place.'

Gabriel stood up and walked to the window, his highly polished black shoes glistening in the sunlight. He had his back to his solicitor and couldn't see the faint smile on Andrew's lips.

Looking out across the skyline at the new skyscraper under construction, large billboards on the building site prominently promoting Black Construction, Gabriel wondered if it was still on schedule, and made a mental note to check with his managing director. He was very conscious that, since hearing about Eliza's death, certain changes needed to be made in the way he worked. This included lines of communication between the subsidiary companies and Black Holdings Ltd, of which Gabriel was Chief Executive Officer.

He turned to face his solicitor.

'Have you ever even heard of Arnford Primary School?'

'No, but I'm sure it's a perfectly acceptable institution for the education of small children. I'd imagine it won't differ significantly from John's current school: the curriculum, targets, parents' activities...' At this point, Andrew couldn't fail to notice the raised eyebrows of the man still standing at the window, and his smile became more evident as he continued, '...will be very similar.'

'You're enjoying this, aren't you?' Gabriel returned to his seat and sat down, sliding the chair back slightly and resting his right ankle on his left knee.

Andrew thought he was finally beginning to relax, but was careful not to dismiss the huge change that recent events would bring to Gabriel Black's life. He remained silent while the other man continued.

'How well educated will the teachers be? How good is the curriculum? And I don't just mean reading, writing and maths. And what sort of children will he be mixing with?' His voice was filled with a superior scorn. 'I should have made her see sense and got the boy a decent education, to prepare him for Eton! They were the best years of my life. What chance will he have in the ineffective state system?'

'I think you're exaggerating, Gabriel. Check the EdBest reports, go and see the head teacher, and form your own view on the competency of the school. There are other state schools and academies too, you know. What about the other conditions in the document?'

Gabriel Black sighed, resigning himself to acquiescing to the demands of his son's dead mother.

'Tell Carol I will adhere to the conditions. She has my word. When can I see John?'

Andrew pressed his intercom.

'Andrea, can you please get me Eliza Redfern's sister, Carol, on the phone.'

A moment later his telephone rang.

'Hello, Mrs Beardly. I have just had a meeting with Mr Black and he has agreed to reconfirm the terms of the agreement he made with your late sister. May I take this opportunity to say how very sorry we are for your loss.'

There was a pause, as Andrew listened to the woman's response.

'Yes, I understand, and I will, of course, be acting as intermediary, as had always been agreed with Eliza. I'll forward a copy of the signed agreement for your information. Mr Black will arrange to collect John in the morning.' At this point Andrew glanced over to Gabriel for confirmation that this was in order, and his client nodded. 'I presume that will be from your home in Mobberley, Mrs Beardly. Would 10 a.m. be convenient?'

There was a moment's pause.

'Good. I'll inform Mr Black and he can confirm this with you. Can you please ensure that all John's personal belongings are ready too? Thank you, Mrs Beardly, and please don't hesitate to contact me at any time in the future. I think you have my details.' Pause. 'Good. Goodbye.' Andrew put the phone down.

Gabriel scribbled his signature on the document and slid it over the desk to his solicitor.

'This had better satisfy her, and she can damn well stay out of our lives.'

'Don't alienate this woman, Gabriel.' Andrew spoke disapprovingly now. 'She is the closest relative John has now, after you. And, let's face it, he doesn't know you yet. You'll need to give him time and support to adjust to his new life, not to mention the fact that he has just lost his mother. Have you sourced a counsellor yet?'

'Roger is onto it. I thought I would try to spend a few days with my son; just the two of us.' Gabriel was on the back foot now, sheepishly aware that Andrew was right about Carol. She and her three children were going to be part of his life from now on, starting tomorrow, when he would drive over to meet John for the first time.

'Ring and get my car out front, please.' Not waiting for any response, Gabriel walked over to the door and headed for the lift.

Andrew let this abrupt ending to the meeting go. He realised Gabriel Black had a lot of thinking to do.